DUKKHA

Dukkha: a Pali term that corresponds to such English words as pain, discontent, unhappiness, sorrow, affliction, anxiety, discomfort, anguish, stress, misery, and frustration.

LOREN W. CHRISTENSEN

DUKKHA

the suffering

AN EYE FOR AN EYE

*A SAM REEVES
MARTIAL ARTS THRILLER*

YMAA Publication Center, Inc.
Wolfeboro NH USA

LOREN W. CHRISTENSEN

YMAA Publication Center, Inc.
Main Office
PO Box 480
Wolfeboro, NH 03894
800-669-8892 • www.ymaa.com • info@ymaa.com

Paperback edition	Ebook edition
978-1-59439-226-9	978-1-59439-246-7

Editor: Leslie Takao
Cover Design: Axie Breen

10 9 8 7 6 5 4 3 2 1

Printed in Canada

Publisher's Cataloging in Publication

Christensen, Loren W.

Dukkha, the suffering : an eye for an eye / Loren W. Christensen. -- Wolfeboro, NH : YMAA Publication Center, c2012.

p. ; cm.

ISBN: 978-1-59439-226-9 (pbk.) ; 978-1-59439-246-7 (ebk.)

"A Sam Reeves martial arts thriller."
Summary: Detective Sam Reeves is a martial arts instructor and a solid police officer with the Portland P.D. When he is forced to take a life in the line of duty, he struggles to recuperate psychologically and spiritually. Then, it happens again. With a series of interlocked events of violence, Sam's life spirals into a dreadful new direction.--Publisher.

1. Reeves, Sam (Fictitious character)--Fiction. 2. Police shootings--Oregon--Portland--Psychological aspects--Fiction. 3. Police--Job stress--Oregon--Portland--Fiction. 4. Police psychology--Fiction. 5. Martial arts schools--Oregon--Portland--Fiction. 6. Martial arts fiction. 7. Mystery fiction. I. Title.

PS3603.H73 D85 2012   2012951860
813/.6--dc23   1212

PROLOGUE

Old Gravedigger Quang had never seen anything quite so extraordinary in all his seventy-five years living in Saigon, now Hồ Chí Minh City, and he had seen some strange occurrences working in the graveyard for the past forty years, unworldly sights that made his body shiver and his heart pound. He would never tell anyone about those things and he certainly would never tell anyone about what he saw this afternoon, especially his drinking buddies, the other old soldiers at the noodle stand where they drank themselves to oblivion each night. No, they would just laugh and say that his war memories had finally driven him *điên cái đầu*.

Yes, the war did make him a little crazy; no one could experience those years of horror and not be. In the gravedigger's mind, a little crazy was a good thing. It gave him courage to face the *Việt cộng* every night in his dreams and defy the ghosts that visited him in the graveyard. Yes, his head might not be right but he knows that what he saw today was real, and it nearly stopped his old heart.

Over the years, Old Gravedigger Quang had watched the Chinese master, Shen Lang Rui, a white-goateed man in his late seventies, whenever he came to teach his student, the one named Le.

The gravedigger had his doubts that that was really the man's name, one so common to his people. There were villagers who thought he might be Vietnamese with Caucasian features, or perhaps half Vietnamese, half French. He looked American

1

to the gravedigger who fought alongside them so many years ago. Still, the man's mannerisms and his demeanor were Vietnamese, and his mastery of the language was flawless.

The gravedigger guessed that Shen Lang Rui and Le had been master and student for at least twenty years, which is how long they had been training their kung fu in his graveyard, over at the north end where there is cool shade beneath the fruit trees. He never tired of watching the two, their fluidity, their power, and especially their unbelievable speed.

As a boy, Old Gravedigger Quang had trained in the martial art style of *Vovinam* with a master whose prowess was renowned. As skilled as his teacher was, it paled in comparison to Shen Lang Rui and the man named Le.

The two did not mind that he watched; they would often smile at him and wave a greeting. The master moved slowly when he demonstrated movements to Le, but the few times the old man did move fast, the gravedigger could hardly catch his breath. Le's skill was amazing, too, and though it was not yet at the level of the master, it was clear that it would be soon.

As often as the two men had dazzled the old gravedigger, what he saw today was beyond his comprehension. It sent him straight to the roadside noodle stand earlier than usual to buy his first of many cups of rice wine.

His nightly routine was to drink until the decades-old sounds of the bombs and the screams of men muffled in his skull. Then he would struggle to his feet and stagger home. Not tonight, though. Tonight he would drink until he became unconscious and fell off his stool. Tomorrow? He might not go to the graveyard to dig tomorrow, or the next day, either.

The incredible thing he witnessed happened late this afternoon. If he did tell anyone, they would argue that shadows and the late sun streaking through the trees played tricks on his eyes. They would be wrong. There was no question about what he saw, a sight more soul shaking than those incoming Communist rockets so many years ago. He could explain the rockets; what he saw today, he could not.

Shen Lang Rui and Le had been meeting under the trees all week. This afternoon, it appeared that the master, in accented Vietnamese, was pushing Le to move faster and faster. To Old Gravedigger Quang, Le was moving extraordinarily fast already. His quick hands would snap out and back like the crack of a whip; still the old master looked dissatisfied.

From fifteen meters away, the gravedigger could only hear bits and pieces of their conversation, words like, "too slow," "engage your thoughts," and something about "the fourth level," whatever that meant.

Then Shen Lang Rui walked over to an old urn, a black and crudely ornate piece of no religious significance that sat beside what was left of a broken down cinderblock wall that used to border this part of the graveyard. A communist rocket destroyed a big section of it early in the war and, because the adjacent property had been purchased to accommodate the growing number of war dead, it was left to crumble into the ground with the passing years. About a year ago, Old Gravedigger Quang and two other much larger men chipped the decaying mortar away from under the urn's base and nearly broke their backs lowering the thing to the ground.

Weathered and coated with three decades of grime, the urn stood about one-meter high, the bowl about a meter across and deep enough to hold ten liters of rainwater, or so. It was full today because it had rained for the last several nights.

Shen Lang Rui positioned himself slightly behind the urn, close enough to touch the water. At first, Old Gravedigger Quang thought the master was going to plunge his fist into it, an exercise he himself had done as a boy during his *Vovinam* lessons. He and the other students would punch to the bottom of a barrel and then retract their fist as fast as they could. The smaller the splatter, the better the technique. Given what he had seen of the Chinese master's great speed and purity of movement, the gravedigger guessed that the water disturbance would be minimal.

Shen Lang Rui stood motionless over the urn, his palms pressed together under his chin as if in prayer to the Buddha. There was something odd about how he stood so very still. It was as if the old man were a photograph. Yes, that was it: as if the master and everything in his immediate aura were a photograph.

Le stood two strides off to the side, his hands clasped in front of him, his expression one of deep respect for his teacher. The way he stood motionless was not the same as Shen Lang Rui. Le's hair moved in the afternoon breeze, as did his loose, white shirt, the tree leaves above him, and the long weeds at his feet.

Just as the gravedigger was thinking that all of this was more than strange, just as he was wondering how the master would thrust his fists into the bowl given his odd position, the water exploded upward out of the urn like a geyser. His first startled thought was that someone had thrown something into it, such as one of the many broken bricks that lay scattered about. No, he had been watching; there was no brick.

The splash shot up nearly as high as the master's face, not once, but twice. The second time it erupted, which followed the first in about the time it would take to blink three times,

4

the heavy urn cracked loud enough that Old Gravedigger Quang heard it from way over where he had just dropped his shovel. Then it shattered, all of it, spraying pieces of pottery and rainwater over the ground.

Old Gravedigger Quang's heart nearly stopped right then. From where he had watched, it looked as if, and this is hard to fathom, that the force that broke the urn came from... inside of it. How could this be? But, as frightening and confusing as that was to ponder, there was something even more startling. What nearly stopped his heart was not what he saw the master do, but rather what the master did *not* do.

As God is his witness and as Buddha surely saw with his holy eyes, and what is driving the gravedigger to drink earlier than usual, is this: When that rainwater exploded upward out of the urn, not once, but twice, and the vessel shattered into pieces, Master Shen Lang Rui remained as still as a photograph, his palms ever pressed together.

CHAPTER ONE

I lunge diagonally away from Alan's roundhouse kick and manage to shield my upper body with both forearms a hair of a second before his padded shin slams into them hard enough to jar loose my bone marrow. Before he can retract, I give him some low pain with a snap kick to the shin of his support leg and then split his attention with a brain-jarring palm against his forehead. I drive his head back and down until he plops onto his back. He jerks away from my attempted elbow lock, rolls up onto his knees, and launches a barrage of punches at my legs, two of which land hard enough to send biting shock waves into my thigh muscles.

I teach my students that training in the martial arts is a metaphor for life, with ups and downs, wins and losses, and pain and pleasure. Alan's T-shirt reads: "Get knocked down ten times, get up eleven." That's a good one, too. Actually, sparring with one of my most skilled and inventive advanced students is a metaphor for the way my life has been going for the past few weeks. Just when I think I know what's coming next, he throws something unexpected that jars my brain and forces me to regroup.

About a week ago, I was watching a reporter on the news interview a woman about to turn one hundred and seven years old. When the old gal was asked what it was like to have another birthday, she said, "Life is a gift. Everyday is an opportunity." That was almost an epiphany to me. It's definitely more positive than "life sucks," which is where my head has been for the last sixty days and nights.

I step back to lure Alan into thinking that it's safe to get up. My quickly formed strategy is to let him plant his weight on one leg, and then seize the opportunity to lunge in and unleash a category five all over his unbalanced body. Okay, there's the foot plant and—

He springs off his foot, tucking his head into a fast somersault that for an instant I think is going to bowl right through my slow-to-react body. At the last instant, his legs shoot out from the ball and scissor one of mine. So much for that opportunity metaphor. I wonder if that old woman ever sparred a third-degree black belt. He traps my ankle with one foot and hooks behind my knee with his other, sending me to the mat face-first. I slap out, roll up on my side, and shield my chest against another hard roundhouse kick. Those are getting old, fast.

His shin stays on target a hair of a second longer than it should—a gift, perhaps—allowing me to trap his ankle with my hands and snake my leg over his knee. He tries to sit up to punch, but he's a tad tardy because I've already seized the opportunity to put a crank on his ankle and a hyperextension on his knee. He winces and taps out.

How about that? Maybe the old woman's metaphor is just fine after all.

I'm up first and help Alan to his feet. I lightly punch his shoulder. "You got one nasty roundhouse. Where'd you come up with that somersault? You Tube?"

He places his weight carefully on his foot. "Thanks," he chuckles. "And double thanks for not breaking my ankle and knee." He studies me for a moment. "When was the last time we sparred? Five weeks ago?"

I nod, knowing what he's thinking. Five weeks ago, when apathy ruled my days, only his respect for me as his teacher kept him from handing my butt to me in a basket. Thankfully, the indifference has been dissolving progressively as my old, charming self reemerges. I'm not all the way there yet, but I will be. "About that. Thanks to you and the others, I'm getting better."

He nods with a faint smile. "Good," he says, testing his weight on the ankle. "I think."

"Is it okay?" I ask with concern. Hitting each other hard is one thing but you have to go easy on the parts that keep you moving. That might be another metaphor but I'm too tired for any more philosophy.

"It'll be fine. Just trying to make you feel bad."

I snort a laugh before turning to watch the others spar for a moment.

They call themselves "Sam's Bloody Dozen," ten males and two females, all wearing black pants, sopped T-shirts, and salt-stained black belts. The "newest" has been with me for ten years, the oldest for eighteen. Each one knows that to be at this level in my school, they have to push their muscles and minds past fatigue, past exhaustion, far beyond that place where other supposedly advanced martial artist whine, "This is bullshit, I quit."

I slap my hands together. "Okay, people. Fall in." The couples stop immediately, bow to one another, and form into two rows.

They see me as a stern father, one with a twinkle in his eyes. Unlike my newer students in the white and colored belt classes who stutter and blush when I look at them, these veterans know, like kids in a loving family know, that their "father's" sternness is at once bluff and genuine. I reprimand them and I give them positive strokes; I encourage them to do more when their enthusiasm wanes and I rein them in when its overabundance risks their health; I push them to find their individuality in the fighting arts and I give them subtle hints when they lose their way.

They know that I care about them in and out of the school. I've been there for them when they've lost loved ones, lost their jobs, bled through divorces, and suffered a host of other miseries. Tillie, my twenty-nine-year-old second-degree, used her skills a couple of years ago on a jerk who apparently failed to notice her muscular neck and calloused knuckles before he tried to date rape her. She did such a job on him, that while he might have fantasies of doing it to someone else, his equipment was no longer up for the task. Or as she put it, "The little guy is permanently down for the count." His Oregon State Prison cellmate was either happy or sad to find that out.

Tillie was all bravado when she first told me how she thumped the guy inside his car and out on the sidewalk, but only her mouth was smiling as she kept shifting her weight from foot to foot and tugging on her belt ends. Being the victim of a sex crime can leave a major gouge on a person's psyche, even when the victim is able to defend against it. But when you train at this level together, you learn when to step in and when to step out. So I went along with her play and I stepped out.

A week later, after Tillie and I had wrapped a children's session that we co-teach, Tillie stepped in. As we cleaned up the studio I asked how things were going. The forced smile she'd been wearing all week disappeared, and she began to weep and twist her belt ends again. Not a shoulder shaking cry, but the kind where the tears creep slowly down the face, gathering pain with every inch of travel, and turning me into mush in their wake.

She didn't answer and I didn't push for one. We sat quietly, stretching a little, and just being together. After about ten minutes, she sucked in some air, and whispered, "He grabbed my breasts... and between my legs." Her jaw was trembling as she talked and, after a few seconds, I was struggling to control mine. "He grabbed me so quickly and so out of the blue that it caught me completely off guard. It was our second date. I've known him for about a year at work, a quiet guy, attractive. I didn't expect this and when he did it, it took a couple of seconds for it to sink into my head what was going on." She started to say something else, but instead thinned her lips and swiped the back of her hand across her teary eyes.

Again, we sat quietly. When she hadn't said anything after several minutes, I cleared my throat, and said that there was no way that I could relate to what happened to her and to what she was feeling. I did know that she should not blame herself for this man's actions. He was the lowest form of vermin, a sick creep and a bully. I said that she was a wonderful young woman and I considered her a blessing in my school. I told her that she had acted as a true warrior by fighting back fiercely, conquering her assailant, and holding him for the police.

It haunted her that she hadn't acted faster, that the guy had grabbed her before she was able to respond, that she hadn't suspected. I tried to assure her that that was perfectly normal and that's why it was called a "surprise attack." But I knew that the words weren't helping, and when she asked if we could work on a defense against the way her date had grabbed her, I was ready. I knew she was perfectly capable of defending against what he did. What I think she really wanted was to recapture some sense of control that was lost when the guy took her by surprise. What she wanted and needed was to stop the offense on its way in.

So I let her beat on me. I grabbed at her repeatedly, each time a little harder and faster than the last. She blocked my attacks easily and followed with fierce counters that landed all over my body. After half an hour, I was bleeding from my nose and the corner of my mouth, I had a bump on my head the size of a walnut, and my jammed left index finger was swelling. Tillie was feeling great and that was good enough for me.

The next day I connected her with a counselor who works with the PD and within two months she was her old self again, although my finger took about four months to heal.

My senior black belt, my oldest at forty-two and a Multnomah County sheriff deputy, went into a Seven-Eleven one night when he was off duty to buy a quart of milk. When Fred came out, he found his pregnant wife fighting desperately with a teenage street creep trying to carjack their Subaru with her still in it and his six-year-old daughter screaming in the back. Fred yanked the thief out and commenced to go rat-a-tat-tat all over his body, breaking the man's jaw and thighbone, and inflicting a dozen knots and abrasions. Turned out that the carjacker's old man had bucks and the mayor's ear. Within a week, Fred was standing before the district attorney who claimed his actions were too rough on the street thug who, after all, didn't really steal his car or his family. Fred hired a good attorney and managed to come out of the mess without a record and without losing his job, although he was ten thousand dollars poorer.

I talked with him a couple days after the incident to get his take on what happened. I was a little concerned because Fred has a temper, and although it has mellowed over the years he's been training with me, I wanted to be sure that all the damage he inflicted on the guy was needed. I'm all about dishing out necessary force but I'm not in the business of teaching people to be assailants.

I was satisfied after talking with him that he had acted responsibly. In fact, I praised him for his restraint considering that his wife had been injured, a detail the police-hating *Oregonian* newspaper had omitted.

These guys have been there to help me, too. They were there for me when I got divorced in my early twenties, when my mother died in a traffic accident, when Tiff and I ended it a couple of months ago and, just recently when I was placed on administrative leave, they've filled in for me when I felt like lawn fudge and couldn't bring myself to leave my house. They know that in the weeks since I fired a nine-millimeter round into that tweaker's acne-splattered face, that some days I'm up and some days I'm down.

"Fighting positions!" I center myself in front of them, stagger my feet, and raise my fists. "Okay people, let's get fast. We're going to punch out as hard and fast as we can, but only half way. Half reps only. Got it?"

"Yes, sir!" they chorus.

"Don't think fast. Think explode and fast will happen."

"Yes, sir!"

"It was a tough class tonight but pay no attention to how your body feels; it's all about right now, this moment, and creating energy within your mind. It's within you and it's dynamite, and it's about to explode all over that big, fat, ugly imaginary assailant in front of you. Feel your energy starting to boil over, Fred? Dave, you feel it? Cathy, you see that ugly predatory beast in front of you? Good."

"The fuse is lit folks! It's burning down, shorter and shorter and shorter… Readyyyy… Explode one!"

Whump! Twelve punches slam forward in unison toward mine.

"On-guard. Half punch… readyyyy… two!"

Whump!

I pace along the front of them again. "You're not exploding. You're punching hard, but you must explode. This drill is about fooling your brain."

Twelve voices: "Yes, sir!"

I move back to center and assume my stance. "To fool it, you must explode."

"Yes, sir!"

"Feel it, feel it, feel it. Explode! Three!"

WHUMP!

"Excellent! Four!"

After training with both back-to-back ninety-minute classes and sparring hard with Alan, my energy is still good, still focused. My black belts watch me closely, rep after rep, as if I were a conductor of a symphony orchestra, an orchestra of controlled violence.

"Ten!"

WHUMP!

"Switch sides. Readyyyyy. One!"

An orchestra of controlled violence. Hey, that's pretty good. Reminds me of something an old *hung gar* teacher once told me. "Fighting is chaos," he said. "And as a trained martial artist, your job is to bring order to the chaos." I've always remembered that. Now as a teacher, I'm trying to orchestrate my black belts into a masterpiece.

"David, stay focused," I say to myself as much as to David. "Three! Don't think about work or that cutie you saw at the mall today. Four! Your whole world right now is a half punch.

Five! Not your fatigue, not your aching shoulder. Six! Not the sweat in your eyes. Seven! Just the punch. Eight! The punch. Nine!"

My training, especially the extra training I've been doing for a few weeks, is helping to bring order to the chaos that's been my life these last couple of months. It's been more helpful than the sessions with the police shrink. Neither is working as fast as I'd like, but I'm better now than I was.

Okay, practice what you preach, Sam: focus.

"Ten!"

WHUMP!

I'm pacing in front of them. A student once said that I pace like a panther at the zoo. Maybe I walk like one, but I don't feel captive here. I have at home recently and I was starting to on the job. But here in my school? Here I feel free. Here is where I can be me.

"Full-rep punches! You just put all you had in those half reps and they were fast. Now let's bring that same speed to your fully extended ones. It took a quarter of a millisecond to punch out half way. Now let's punch *all* the way out in that same quarter of a millisecond. *Think* half punch, but extend all the way. You can do it!

"Yes, sir!"

I again center myself on them. "Nothing else exists right now. Not the half reps you're still panting from or all the other drills we did tonight. Your drive home doesn't exist, nor does that welcoming shower. There's only the punch that you're doing right now. Got it?

"Yes, sir!"

"Reeeeady... Explode! One!"

WHUMP!

Two minutes later, we collectively ram out the last punch with a sharp exhalation and then come to attention. They're exhausted but they know that if they were to sag their posture or blow out a gush of fatigue, I'd give them more. Since they were white belts, I've drilled in them the old saying "Hide your broken arms in your sleeves." Never show that you're hurt or tired.

"Very good, everyone. Thank you for teaching me."

"Thank *you* for teaching *us!*"

"Fred, would you please close up?"

"Yes, sir," he says, though my asking and his response is merely a formality since I've been asking him to see everyone off for several weeks.

"Ready!" We simultaneous slap the sides or our legs. "Salute!" In unison, we cover our right fists with our open left hands and extend them forward.

"Thank you, everyone." We applaud.

As the group moves toward the dressing room, chatting affably and teasing one another like the old friends that they are, I head quickly toward the small room next to my office. In the twenty-some years that I've owned this school, it's a first not to always be available to my students or be able to teach all my classes. I'm missing fewer than I was a month ago and I'm guessing—make that, I'm hoping—that I won't be missing any by the end of the month. I'm feeling better, a lot better than last month, and a heck of a lot better than in those awful days right after the shooting went down.

I step into the room, close the door behind me, and stand motionless for a moment to collect myself and enjoy the feeling of being in my private space. I like the sparseness and simplicity in here. A hundred-pound heavy bag hangs from a low beam in the center of the room and a large mirror covers most of the opposite wall from the door. That's it. I might not have a simple life outside my school right now but I still have it in here, and I savor it.

Within a minute or two of coming in and locking the door behind me, I get a small bump in my pulse rate and begin sweating. The only time I've experienced that outside of class was two weeks ago when I drove through that intersection for the first time since the shooting. The power of the mind never ceases to amaze me.

Being in here is all about my head. When I attack the bag, I do so with all the frustration, rage, fear, and pain that I can bring up from the depths of my being—"the bowels of hell"—as my friend Mark calls it. Five minutes into the sessions, I feel an explosion of emotions coming from somewhere deep, fueling my punches and kicks with high-octane energy. Ten minutes in, I'm a machine, one with arms and legs slamming my bulk into the leather with blows that, in this empty room, sound like bursts from a sixty-caliber machinegun. When I can't punch or kick any longer, I clinch the bag and slam it with my forehead, elbows and knees, and I keep going until I collapse to the floor or power vomit into the toilet. When I'm fresh, it takes an hour before I slump into a heap. Times like tonight, when I've trained hard along with two classes, I'll crash after about thirty minutes.

After the first couple of these insane sessions, I realized they weren't for my body; they were just too harsh to be of any physical benefit. Head-wise, they were helping me to… what? Cope? Yeah, that's it, and to not dream the dream so much. To not see the man's exploding face every damn night.

I strip off my sweat-sopped T-shirt and drop it to the floor. Seeing my reflection reminds me of a line I heard Bill Cosby say once on one of his TV programs. He looked into his bathroom mirror, nodded smugly, and said to himself, "Not bad. Not bad at all." Well, these extra bag sessions have been etching in a nice six-pack on my two-hundred pound frame. Actually, I've lost some in the past weeks, so I'm probably more like one ninety. Yup, not bad at all for a dude pushing thirty-five years old.

The face, well, that's a different story: skin tight, dark circles under the eyes, a couple days growth, and a head in need of a haircut. On the positive side, it's an improvement.

What does the other guy look like? Not so good. He's covered with six feet of dirt.

I step over to the big bag, give it a little push and commence to go totally ape shit all over it.

*

"If you're a burglar," Tiff calls from the kitchen as I come in the front door, "please don't hurt me. I'm not wearing a bra." If she hadn't parked her Honda in the driveway I would have probably jumped a foot. I forgot she was coming over tonight. She steps around the corner, wiping her hands on a red hand towel, wearing blue sweat pants, a brown tank top and, yup, no bra.

"Have you no decency," I ask, shooting her a mock evil smile.

She bobs her eyebrows. "Nope."

"That works for me," I say, following her back into the kitchen. Two months ago we would have done the hug and kiss greeting. Not doing it feels awkward. Doing it would feel even more so.

"How were your classes tonight, Sam?"

She doesn't give a rip about my classes. She used to be a little interested; at least I think she was, unless that was just more role-playing. I was role-playing, too. Looking back now, I'm amazed at how easy it was to slip into pretending, to be both the performer and the audience. My shrink said that a couple pretending does not make for a meaningful relationship. Got that right.

I drape my jacket over a kitchen chair, move over to the sink, and begin washing my hands. "Classes were good."

"You stay after to beat the bag?"

"Yes. Sorry I'm late." I hope my tone hides the fact that I completely zoned about her coming over. We made plans for it on the phone just this morning, but when I got to my school, it escaped my mind, *ffft*, like that. It's not that I have a bad memory, it's just that my brain has been bouncing around like a ball on a spinning roulette wheel these last few weeks, and when it stops—sometimes it doesn't—it lands on whatever my head is going through at the moment. It skips over other things, even critically important ones, like a booty call.

She shrugs. "It's not a problem. I just got here, anyway." She looks at me for a moment, somehow managing to get curiosity and disapproval on her face at the same time. Thing is, I don't care about the disapproval part. I used to, at least until it became abundantly clear to both of us that we were the mismatch of the century. Still, we went on pretending for about three more months. Maybe maintaining the status quo was easier than facing a breakup. Married couples do that all the time. For me, I liked the idea of someone wondering where I was when I didn't get off work on time, even if that person was just pretending. That seems nutso now but that's where my head was at the time. Why we were attracted to each other is one of those mysteries of the universe. The physical attraction was a biggee and we both enjoyed the same kind of humor. We were an attractive and professional couple in our thirties so it seemed like a logical pairing. Of course, logic doesn't always make things right.

Tiff works part time as a legal advisor with Children's Services Division and part time with the Public Defender's office, the latter being part of our conflict. The other part is because I'm a cop. Now, I like to think that I might—*might*—have eventually learned to tolerate her defending the kinds of people I arrest, but I know that she would never learn to tolerate that my job was to "oppress the already oppressed," as she put it about twenty times. A lot of old hippies and young granola eaters say that stuff, wave their signs at protests, and call law enforcement the "Gestapo." Some actually believe it while the majority just want to protest something and raise a little hell. Tiff is one of the believers, a hardcore one.

Tiff took the first step to end our "relationship." One night, when neither of us had much to say to each other and the quiet was not a comfortable one, she came right out and said that we needed to stop this, that it wasn't healthy for either of us. I knew she was right, but since I was still in my Lawrence Olivier mode, I protested, though not all that hard. There was no more pretending for Tiff, though, not even to soften it for me. The more she spoke, the more bitter she became. She didn't shout or call me names, but spoke quietly using words that burned into me.

"I can't deal with what you do," she said. "I understand it on an intellectual level, I get that we need police, but it scares me. Not that you might get hurt—"

Gee thanks.

"—but I'm scared of what it will do to your psyche. It frightens me to think what being exposed to so much violence will do to you. I'm worried that you will become bitter and angry and a racist. I hate that cops have to put on that swagger and macho bullshit air just to survive their job. I think it's only a matter of time before you're that way."

I started to tell her how weak and ridiculous her argument was, how she was charging me with a crime I had yet to commit, and how she was worried about my swagger all the while she was turning into the Thought Police. Also how—

"Sam?" Tiff says, waving the hand towel in my face and bringing me back to the moment.

"Huh?"

"I said I'm still painting my place."

I'd already determined that since she's got gray paint smears on her fingers and tank top.

She tosses the towel to me, a move that launches her unencumbered breasts into glorious motion.

Her breasts! The sex. It was the kind that's so frighteningly intense that you're convinced that it's okay to die after because life couldn't possibly offer you anything better. It's also why we've been seeing each other for booty calls. "Friends with benefits" one of my students called it when telling me about his setup with an old girlfriend. Good name. Good deal, too. So far.

About three weeks after we'd stopped seeing each other she called to see how I was doing. I couldn't tell if she really wanted to know or if she was just feeling me out for a conjugal visit. When it comes to sex she thinks like a man, which I've always thought to be a real solid attribute. Whatever her reason, I was glad she called.

"Got the den to do and that's it," Tiff says, as I lean against the sink drying my hands. I have to think for a second what we were talking about. Oh yeah, painting her place. When we were both in the glow of the first few weeks of our relationship, we talked about her moving in with me. Dumb, I know, but we were both enamored and blind. The idea was for her to spruce up her condo to sell. Apparently, she's still painting. My friend, Mark, would argue that she hasn't given up on us cohabitating, but that's not it. She knows and I know that there's just no way. I think she just wants different colored walls.

Tiff walks over to me and places a hand on my chest. "You look better tonight than you did last week. I'm thinking the sessions with Kari are helping."

"So are the sessions on my heavy bag. Maybe even more than the shrink." I touch the back of her hand and smirk. "And the sessions with you, too."

She smacks my chest. "You're impossible. No matter how down you feel you're always up for that."

"Cute pun. And you're not?"

She moves toward the refrigerator. "When do you see Kari next?"

"Tomorrow at noon. Gotta do it; she's got the power to release me."

Tiff pulls out a plastic bowl, pries off the lid and sniffs the chicken I made up last night. She looks at me questioningly. "There wasn't much enthusiasm in that. Thinking twice about not going back?"

Is that hope I hear in her voice?

"No, I want to go to work." I think I do, anyway. "It's been two months and I'm feeling better about the idea. It's just that… you know…" I turn around and fill a glass of water. "… my head."

"Kari said it takes time. Are you still having the dreams? Last time I came over you were shouting in your sleep. Scared me half to death."

"It was pretty intense on my end, too." I pick up a chicken leg, look at it for a moment and drop it back into the bowl. Sometimes it's hard to get food down, which is why I've lost weight. "The dream always starts out the same… first it's his face, then it changes to mine. To *my* face. I'm shooting… my friggin' face. Can you believe that?"

Tiff shakes her head without comment. I can't tell if the gesture is out of empathy or disgust. The couple of times I've brought up the shooting during her sleepovers, she's never said anything, which is more annoying than if she'd shout her disapproval that I killed someone.

I turn back to the sink and begin washing my hands again. "I'll get through it."

"You will, Sam," she says, stepping up along side me and frowning as she watches me rinse off the soap. "I know you and I know you will." Her attempt at being supportive is almost funny; I give her props for faking it. Actually, we're both continuing to fake it. Oh man, I don't want to get back doing that again.

I pick up the towel and rub at my hands. "Thank you," I mumble. "You hearing anything new at the defender's office?"

Tiff shrugs. "My friends always ask me how you're doing."

Suuuure they do.

"I heard some cops in the courthouse a couple of days ago talking about you. They said it was a 'clean shoot.'"

Clean shoot. Man, she had to struggle to utter those words. If the cops had said "righteous shoot" she would have probably needed the Heimlich maneuver.

"That's nice," I grunt. I turn back to the sink and twist on the faucet.

"Your hands are clean!" Tiff snaps, reaching around me to turn off the spigot. She tugs my arm to turn me toward her. "They—Are—Clean."

I look at her for a long moment. Where did that come from? Why does she care? Or is she just irritated?

Her face relaxes, looking like it was a struggle to do so. "You know, I'm tough enough to kick your butt all the way to Fifth Avenue."

I widen my eyes in mock fear, happy that she brought us back to the task at hand.

"So you want any chicken or not?"

"How about I take a quick shower first then I'll have a couple of pieces?"

Thirty minutes later, Tiff's in the bathroom and I'm sitting on the edge of the bed freshly cleaned, wearing black boxers and a red T-shirt. I'm looking at a page in my checkbook, though I'm not seeing the numbers. Can't concentrate. If I could just get a good night's sleep, I'd feel like a million bucks. Well, maybe a hundred bucks. I do feel a little better after the scalding shower, a fresh shave, and some chicken.

As good as Tiff looked in her tank top a while ago, I'm not sure if I'm in the mood. We've done this booty call thing about three times over the past month or so and while it's been a nice distraction during my so-called recovery, the irony of it isn't lost on me. Tiff hates what I represent and what I did that day. In turn, it angers me that she can't see that the tweaker decided his fate. She argued early in our dating about the police and their use of deadly force. She believed, absurdly so, that officers should never use it. She said that shooting someone is always a choice and that too many cops choose to shoot. I argued that perps put officers into grave situations that compel them to respond with deadly force. She wouldn't buy it. After a while, we agreed to disagree and the elephant in the room grew larger and larger until it began knocking things down.

A few days after we ended whatever we had, I got into the shooting. Two days later, she called. She said she'd been out of town, and then she asked if it was necessary to shoot the man. I started to snap the lid shut on my phone but her fast apology stopped me. "That was out of line, Sam," she said. "I'm so sorry." She sounded legit but who knows. "I just wanted to make sure that you were okay." That was about it. It could have been worse, I guess.

Three weeks later she called again, to see how I was doing. After I lied that I was doing fine and she pretended to believe me, we had an animosity-free talk about how each of us was feeling about our failed relationship. When it looked as if we had exhausted the subject, she said quietly, as if feeling me out, "The sex was good. In fact, it was great." I affected an official tone and concurred with her assessment, which made us both laugh. We talked another half hour about sex until I couldn't stand it any longer and asked her how long it would take her to come over. She said ten minutes if she didn't stop for traffic signals.

Three weeks earlier, I sent a guy to hell and three weeks later I had sex that nearly blew my head off. I even had to take an Excedrin after. "Where did that come from?" Tiff asked breathlessly, looking at me as if I were from outer space. I decided it was best not to mention that I had been thinking about the shooting the whole time.

So here we are again. I have no idea if this is good for me, or us, but for now my inner caveman says to go with the flow and I'm guessing Tiff's inner cavewoman is thinking the same thing.

I listen to her doing whatever women do in the bathroom. I liked those sounds when we were together and she would stay over on weekends. Then it gave me a sense of togetherness and stability. Now the sounds make me feel uncomfortable and unsure about what the hell I'm doing.

Tiff walks into the room, my pale blue terrycloth robe cinched tight around her waist. Even in an oversized, bulky robe, there is no hiding those dangerous curves, scrumptious peaks, and ultra-hot valleys. That's what I'm talking about.

"What are you lookin' at?" she says with a grin, moving over to where I'm sitting. She stops by my knee, looking down at me.

"You *know* what I'm lookin' at."

"Yeah? You just a looker or are you a doer?"

The phone rings.

"It's Kari," she says, looking down at the ID screen.

"Nine at night?" I pick up the receiver. "Hi Kari."

"Sam. You doing okay?" Kari is the shrink I've been seeing since the shooting. A tough woman who never wastes words.

"Doing pretty good."

"Got a conflict at noon tomorrow. Let's meet at one-thirty instead."

"Yes, sure."

"One-thirty it is. See you."

"Good bye," I say, wasting my breath since she's already hung up. I turn toward Tiff. "Kari's got a conflict and we're changing the appointment to…"

She's rummaging through her overnight bag on the end of the bed. The bathrobe has fallen open a little revealing all kinds of good things. I have no choice but to lunge for her like a shoot wrestler diving at an opening. No choice at all.

"Help! Police!" Tiff calls out, as she falls back onto the bed laughing.

"You're in luck." I say, pulling the robe from her shoulders. "I am the police."

"In that case, "Heeeeeelp! I thought you were exhausted."

"I'm going to feel better in a minute."

"It's going to last a whole minute? Oh lucky me."

CHAPTER TWO

"How you been, Sam?"

"Peachy keen."

"You going to start out with the shitty attitude again?"

"Nice shrink-talk, doc."

Dr. Kari Stephens crosses her legs, sips from her coffee mug, on which there is an image of John Wayne and the words *A man's gotta have a creed to live by,* and lifts her eyebrows. She's a plain looking fifty-year-old Chinese woman, fit, gun-silver hair that's cut a tad longer than a Marine's, and wearing an expensive and impeccably tailored navy-blue suit. Her eyes watch me as if I were a field mouse and she a bird of prey. I'm dreading the big question she's going to ask and that I have to answer.

I look out the window for a moment, not really seeing the Portland skyline, and exhale some of my resignation. I don't like being here, plain and simple. I hate talking about my feelings and about the loony tunes that's going on inside my skull. It helps a little that the mad doctor is tougher than a gunny sergeant; if she were all hugs and touchy feely this wouldn't work at all.

"Sorry doc."

"For acting like a prick?"

I sputter a short laugh. "Yeah, I guess."

"It's your word, Sam. You referred to yourself as one during your first visit. If it's true, well, maybe you can't help it." Her eyes penetrate, though a small twinkle gives her away.

I snort again. She's got a rep for not tolerating fools and big tough cops who act like spoiled children. "Okay, okay. Man, I can't believe the PD hired a leatherneck to be our psychologist."

She rotates her wedding band a couple of times, then smiles, but only faintly, a rarity from her. I'm thinking she's married to an Ellen. Or, god forbid, a Rosie.

"You want Mother Teresa?"

I laugh. "Well, maybe a little."

She peers at me over her glasses as she swigs from her cup. "Uh-huh," she says, though the tone is more like, "Buuuull shit."

I chuckle, nodding. I liked her from my first appointment, though I hated the department mandate that forces all officers involved in shootings to see her. Few cops go without grumbling, though most admit later that the visit, sometimes multiple visits, helped get their heads back on straight. Taking a life, no matter how deserving the departed, shakes most to their core. Some cops lose a few nights sleep before they're back resuming their normal lives. Others need about a month to feel right, and still others take several months, even years to find peace with what they've done. I've known three who never recovered.

"I'm still having the dreams except now it's *my* face I'm… shooting."

"It's common to reverse the roles. That too shall pass. Remember, Sam, and you've heard me say this twenty damn times, everything you're experiencing is a normal reaction to an abnormal event."

I nod and look out the window. I know that, but knowing it doesn't help much at night when I'm soaking my sheets in sweat.

"It will in time," she says, as if reading my mind. "You just have to keep telling yourself that each time you have a dream or any other negative experience. Or even a positive one that seems out of the norm for you."

I grunt a yes. She tilts her head and does that eyebrow lift again, her way of telling me to keep talking. "I do understand, doc. On the surface, anyway. I just got to understand it deeper so it's there for me in the witching hour."

"In time," she repeats.

I nod and look at her for a moment. *In time.* Fortunately, training in the martial arts has made me a patient guy. I get the *in time* thing but I still want this behind me.

My mind flashes to Tiff. Not Tiff the person. Her body. I look back out the window irrationally embarrassed that the doc is reading my mind.

"What?"

I look back and instantly wilt under that raptor gaze. "'What' what?"

"There's something else on your mind."

"You ought to be a detective," I say shaking my head. At least she didn't read my lurid thoughts.

"I am. Tell me."

Actually, I have been wondering about something but there's no way I'm going to ask it. No way at all. Her eyes bore; her eyebrows lift.. Damn her. I sit up higher like a kid in the principal's office. "It's my, uh, relations with my ex… with Tiff."

"You get back together or cut it off completely? Or are you still doing the carnal visits?"

Tiff left around midnight last night. We began the evening with self-conscious chitchat, moved to lust, and then laid there after without a whole lot to say to each other. A half hour later, I walked her out to her car where there was an awkward moment of internal debate whether to give her a goodbye peck. Finally, she leaned forward, did an air kiss off to the side of my face, and mumbled, "See yuh, good lookin'." I nodded and snapped a military salute as she slid behind the wheel. I saluted, for crying out loud.

"We're not getting back together."

"But you're still meeting occasionally?"

"Yeah."

"For sex?"

"Yeah. We barely talk at all after. She just goes home."

"So what's your question? Mr. Happy isn't so happy or is he happier than he's ever been."

I snort a laugh. "Well..."

"Whichever it is, it's still a normal reaction to an abnormal event."

"It's the last one. I mean, I can't get enough of her. Then afterwards I don't like her anymore. I mean, I like her, it's just that... Damn, I don't know what I mean. We're that cliché of two different people from two different worlds." Could I sound anymore like a seventeen-year-old.

"So while you're having all this confusion you're still okay jumping her bones?"

"Yeah. That make me bad?"

"No, just male." She leans forward, resting her elbows on her knees. "Listen Sam," she says in a softer voice, recognizing that this isn't an easy conversation for me. "Some people lose their appetite for food in response to stress, while others have an enhanced craving to eat. In the same way, some individuals can lose their sex drive in response to great stress, while others experience a tremendous sex drive, especially after a combat situation in which they were triumphant. Faced with death, destruction, and horror all around, there can be a powerful life-affirming drive toward sexuality."

I exhale slowly. "I thought I was some kind of a pervert. I... kill... and it makes me want sex."

The doctor does that faint smile again, and sits back. "You're not a perv, but you aren't too far off on the rest of your analysis. Some psychologists believe that the enhanced need for sex by some just might be the drive of a male, having defeated another male in a mating battle, if you will, to claim his prize—the woman."

I look at the doctor for a long moment as I mill that over. It makes sense, I think. I can feel a slow smile spreading across my tired face. "So, it's sort of a perk of the job?"

"One they can't tax."

I laugh hard and reach for my coffee I've yet to sip. It's cold but I don't care.

"You ready to go back to work, Sam?"

Finally, *the* question, part of it, anyway. I can't appear too anxious. "What do you think?"

She looks at her computer screen, scrolls down, and reads some more. "You're sleeping better now."

"I am," I lie.

She scrolls again. "Still having nightmares, though they've changed of late."

"Not as many. Maybe twice a week. And there's that change of roles thing that started last weekend."

"All normal," Kari says, still reading the screen. "I'm so glad you don't drink. How is your martial arts training going?"

"Great. I lost a few kids when the press attacked me. Concerned parents. But in the last couple of weeks I've gotten new ones to take their place. I've been doing extra training on the heavy bag. It seems to help. It… whatever *it* is… just pours out of me and into the bag."

She turns to face me. "I wish all my patients chose exercise over intoxicants. So, are you ready to go back?"

I nod, though somewhere deep inside I feel a pang of reluctance. Fear of getting back on the horse she called it during our last visit. That, plus there's something else that's been bothering me.

"I'm ready. Yes." That sounded squirrely.

"Okay," she says. She leans toward me. "One more question."

Part two of *the* question.

"You're out on the street and things turn to shit again. You got no choice but to blow some son-of-a-bitch to hell. Can you do it?"

I lean back in my chair and close my eyes. Once again, the faces—the elderly Jewish man and the tweaker—emerge out of the darkness:

The old man's eyes are large with fear, his body writhing on the floor, his face bleeding from where the hold-up man struck him with his pistol. The tweaker's eyes are glassy, crazed, his teeth and facial skin rotten from meth. He glares at me with stupidity and defiance, his long-barreled revolver jutting obscenely toward the whimpering old man.

"Shoot me, you fuck," he spews through blackened and broken teeth, his dead eyes struggling to focus on the big hole at the end of my semi-auto.

"Listen, pal," I say in a surprisingly calm voice. "Put your weapon down and let's talk. You don't have to—"

"Shoot me and I'll shoot this old Jew as I die." His gun hand trembles so hard that he will likely shoot the man before he intends to, anyway. "Come on, shoot me and—"

I fire.

The 9mm round punches a neat hole just below the shitbird's nose, smack into his medulla oblongata. The bullet kills his sad brain and stops his heart instantly, dropping him like the bag of bones that he is, his muscles unable to fulfill his promise to shoot the old man.

I hold my Glock on him until the just-arrived uniform officers move in and handcuff him. "What a shot!" one of them says, as I holster. I ignore him, walk calmly out of the secondhand store, and sag helplessly to my knees. The shaking begins in my arms and spreads rapidly to my entire body. I struggle to my feet only to slump against the shop window, my body covering the "Get" on the sign Get More Bang For Your Buck.

I look up at Kari who is again giving me another of her field mouse-hunter looks. She knows where I've just been. I once partnered with an older guy for several weeks before he commented that he had spent eighteen months in Vietnam. When I asked when he was there, meaning what year, he looked at his hands for about a half minute. Finally, he said, just above a whisper, "Last night."

"Sam?"

"Like we've talked about, Doc, it was never about pulling the trigger. All my martial arts training kicked in and I was amazingly calm. The aftermath, though, that was the hard part. The nausea, sleeplessness, agitation. The guilt. And feeling different from the other cops."

"All normal."

"Yeah."

"Not pleasant, not fun, just normal." She drinks the last of her coffee and sets the cup down. "The press is no longer attacking, eh?"

"I'm not complaining. Bastards." The first newspaper head-line after the shooting read in large print: Police Detective Shoots Teen. Then for the next two weeks, there were articles demanding a thorough investigation, and several additional stories about the "boy's" hard life and how he had been turning it around. Two stories included photos of the nineteen-year-old as a toddler sitting by the family Christmas tree. Then when the media found out that I was a high-ranking martial artist and a past champion of full-contact fighting, they asked in their editorials why I hadn't I kicked the gun out of the boy's hand. Why, when I had options other than shooting, did I *choose* to shoot?

Same thing Tiff asked.

"Do you want to give me your answer now, Sam? You don't have to. You can wait another week. You know I can't release you to go back to work unless you can tell me that, should a situation call for it, you could use deadly force again."

"What are the odds?" I ask rhetorically. I know there's no answer, but that doesn't keep me from asking myself that twenty times a day, and every night at two AM and at three. And four.

"You know the answer, Sam. The chance of it happening again is no greater than of it happening the first time. But the department doesn't—"

"—want an officer," I say it with her, "on the street who would hesitate and risk his life, or the life of another officer or citizen."

"Exactly," she says.

"Yes, I can do it. I just don't want to go through all the shit again."

"That's part of… 'the game,' to use your words from a cou-ple of weeks ago. Right?"

I nod and look out the window again.

"Tiff okay with you going back?"

"She's not a consideration in this."

"Okay. You're good to go then. I'll forward my recommendations to your bosses."

Good. Well, I think it's a good thing. Actually, I'm not sure.

CHAPTER THREE

"Glad to see you back on board," Mark booms, pumping my hand and nodding toward a chair. My boss is handsome, fifty-eight years old, trim, with dark hair sprinkled gray. He's been my lieutenant for the three years I've worked in detectives, but we've been friends much longer. He's twenty-three years my senior so sometimes our friendship is a tad father/son, and I'm okay with that. As a boss, I consider him one of the good guys, a leader unaffected by his rank, one who loves his people, and who has never used anyone as a stepping stone to get ahead. That's rare in the police biz.

"Thanks, Mark," I say, plopping into the chair at the front of the desk. "Sort of glad to be back."

Laughter erupts outside the glass-enclosed office where the night shift dicks are slipping on their jackets and exchanging barbs with the day shift crew as they remove theirs. I've missed the camaraderie.

"So," Mark says in a between-you-and-me tone as he moves around behind his desk. He doesn't sit. "You're ready to do it?"

"I am. I think."

"Tiff okay with it?"

Tiff and I enjoyed a few dinners with Mark and his squeeze, David. Mark's gay, no biggee to me, though I'm guessing it is with some of the guys in the squad. I've seen the occasional smirks and eyebrow bobbing, but I've never heard anyone trash talk him, probably because he's one of the best lieutenants around.

"We had our weekly last night. That part was fine, but it's pretty clear it's not happening."

"Too bad." He said once that we make a beautiful couple and that Tiff could turn a gay man straight. Asking me about her is his way of asking how we're doing. He doesn't say it, but I know he thinks we're just having a bump in the road, that we'll work through it. He knows a lot about our relationship, but he doesn't know everything.

"Not really." I sigh. I'm tired of thinking about Tiff. "So what do you got me doing?"

Two months earlier, I was working the Burglary Unit and returning to the office after interviewing a witness, when radio sounded the hot-call warning beeps, followed by dispatch announcing an armed robbery in progress at a second-hand store at the intersection of Southeast Fifteenth and Taylor. As fate would have it, the address was right outside my car window where I was waiting at a stop light. Half a minute later, the hold-up man was taking a non-stop to Hell, and the old man and I were enjoying breathing.

Mark moves around to the front of his desk and sits on its edge. He looks down at me. "The doc ask you the question?"

"Can I drop the hammer again? She did and I said, yes."

"Let's just pray that you never have to. But no one will work with someone who can't."

I nod at my friend. "I know the drill, Mark."

"I know you do and you know I got to ask it. Okay, enough of this shit. You got your gun back from the Evidence Property Room, right?"

I pull my jacket flap back and reveal my Glock. "A couple weeks after the Shooting Board gave me their stamp of approval."

"You're back in the Burglary Unit and I've teamed you up with Tommy for a few days. He's on his second day off and will be back tomorrow. Why don't you set up your desk or something, and then take off early. But come back *mañana* raring to roll."

"Can I work these short hours everyday?"

"No."

By noon I've cleaned everyone's lunch remnants off my desk, made sure my computer was working, talked with several of the dicks, and had coffee with a uniform friend. Now I'm taking a stroll along Water Front Park which parallels the Willamette River to soak up a little spring sun and watch the first sailboats of the season skim over the water. I think it's still too chilly for sailing but in rainy Portland any brief sun break brings out the shorts and water toys.

It feels good to be back at work, better than I imagined considering that I'd been having second thoughts about police work even before the shooting. I joined the PD for the classic reasons, security, and to help others, but I quickly found out that most of the time crime fighting is tantamount to trying to lower the ocean by removing one glass of water at a time. Liberal judges release dangerous predators out onto the street, the media criticizes the PD's every move, new laws and restrictions make it ever more difficult to protect and serve and, with the exception of Mark, too many in command positions use the backs of those under them for knife plunging practice.

I knew about these things before I took the long battery of tests to join fifteen years ago but, in my naiveté, I was convinced I could handle the challenge. Now I'm starting to question if I want to. Do I want to do this for the rest of my working life? Is it satisfying enough? Do I want to spend the next fifteen years dealing with all the politics and the monstrous negativity? If I'm growing weary at the half way point in my career, at a time when I can resign and move somewhat easily into another job, how weary will I be ten years from now when I'll no longer be as marketable to employers? I don't know the answer.

Then there's the shooting.

The uniform officer I had coffee with summed up his shooting this way. "I went to work, met a man, and I killed him." That's it stripped of all its fat. Problem is, it's the fat that rips and chews the soul. I've been dealing with it, though, with hard training, a half dozen visits with Kari and my love shack meetings with Tiff. I might be feeling better, but the bottom line is that I didn't sign on to kill people. SWAT guys have a saying: "The man deserved killin'." That was the case with the tweaker, but that's not why I want to work in law enforcement. Damn, I'm thinking in circles. I've been doing that a lot lately. Monkey brain.

There is one place I can clear my mind: my *dojo*. A few hundred punches will organize my thinking. Besides, I got a new private coming in this afternoon at four.

I wait for a blue Toyota Corolla to pass and jog over to my car.

*

Although I've thrown hundreds of punches and kicks in my private training room for the last forty-five minutes, and I worked the heavy bag last night until I nearly collapsed, my jab and cross punch still rip through the air with authority.

I lash out five more, then spread my feet and bend forward until my chest nearly reaches between my thighs. I hold the stretch for a few seconds, feeling the tightness dissolve in my legs, lower back and in my over-worked shoulders. After a minute, I straighten and begin pulling off my T-shirt as I walk out the door and head to my office to get a dry one. Before I get there, the street door opens at the far end of the room, bringing inside a blare of traffic noise, light, and a slightly silhouetted figure. It belongs to a big man, twenty-something, longish blond hair, neck like a Grecian column and, obvious even from thirty feet away and with harsh backlight, a palpable attitude. He hip bumps the door shut behind him and looks around the room with disdain. His eyes stop on me. He doesn't smile; he just looks.

"You must be, Torres," I greet with a smile.

"Yeah, must be."

In only three words and a silhouetted demeanor, the guy manages to tell me that he's defiant, arrogant, and a basic asshole. Why would a new student come in with an attitude like that when the private lesson is costing him seventy-five bucks an hour?

Relax, Sam. Maybe he's just nervous.

"Let me put on a dry T-shirt, Torres," I call out in my best customer relations voice as I back into my office. "I'll be out in twenty seconds."

"Whatever floats your boat, man," he says, which sounds more like *I-don't-care-if-you-eat-shit-and-die.* My fight or flight juices begin to percolate. I take a deep breath and exhale slowly. Why am I letting this bozo get to me so fast? Why have I let other people get to me this week? Get control of yourself, homeboy and give him the benefit of the doubt. I tuck in a dry, black T-shirt and tie my belt around my waist.

"Sorry about that, Torres," I say, moving across the floor. "Just had a little training session myself." I extend my hand.

"You said on the phone that you've done some martial arts before?" I casually quick-scan the way his thick chest and arm muscles strain his white T-shirt, and how his ham hock forearms look as if they're stuffed with steel cables.

There are three indicators that hint at how well a guy might do in a fight: his neck, forearms, and his ass. A strong neck means he pays attention to details in his fitness regimen and that maybe he can absorb a punch; muscular forearms means he has strong hands for grabbing, pulling, and punching; and a strong butt means he might be a kicker, a powerlifter, or a wrestler.

Torres is wearing baggy jeans so I can't tell about his ass, but he's got the neck and forearms working for him. He stands over six feet, weighs maybe two-ten, two-fifteen.

"Yeah, I've trained," he says, his handshake like a dead fish. For a second I thought he wasn't going to take my hand. His eyes size me up but he doesn't check out my ass. *Pfft.* Novice. "Cop, huh?"

"Yes, I am," I say, noting the disdain-thick tone. "Did you bring your gear?" It's a rhetorical question since he's empty-handed.

"Nope. I train in whatever I'm wearing. Aren't you supposed to teach a street style?" He reaches toward my belt. "What's up with the belt and karate pants?"

I turn my hip a couple inches so that Torres's fingers flip the air. I smile, as if my casual evasion were a coincidence. Was he really going to flip the end of my belt?

"Oh, you know. Old habits are hard to break. The belt's part of my roots." The guy's starting to crank me off and I'm not sure what my tone was just now. "Listen, Torres," I say, kicking up my friendliness shtick a notch. "This is your time.

What would you like to work on? I can show you our basic punching style, a couple of kicks, maybe a—"

"I want to see you block some of my attacks to see if I'm wasting my money."

Okay, I get it. I haven't been around assholes for a couple of months so I'm a little slow on the uptake. Only two men have come into my school to challenge me. The first one ended up being a student and the second one went to the PD to file a complaint after I smacked him around a little. Okay, I smacked him around a lot. I might have gotten in hot water over that one but luckily he had warrants and the desk officer arrested him before he could file his complaint.

There are always those who see a martial arts school as a threat. These are the same bozos who pick a fight with the biggest man in the bar. They have nothing to lose and everything to gain, at least in their little brains. Then there are the trained fighters—people who never learn the discipline and self-control aspects of the arts—those who see every other martial artist as a personal challenge.

Whatever the psychology is with Ol' Torres here, I'm not in the mood for it today. Kari might have released me to return to work, but I still feel like a coiled spring.

"Look, Torres. How about I give you the first class free and you can decide if you want to continue on a paying basis?"

The big man looks around the school for a moment, eyeing the hanging bags at the far end, the stack of hand-held pads against the wall, the belt display over the dressing room door, the wall-to-wall mirrors. He looks back at me. "Sure," he says, somehow making it sound like a challenge.

"Okay, great." I smile, pouring it on. "Why don't you loosen up and—"

"You don't *loosen up* in the street," he says, mocking my choice of words. "You just bang."

'True," I say, again with my fake smile. "But we're training and—"

"I'm ready."

"Okay. Go ahead and remove your shoes and—"

"You don't *remove your shoes* in the street," he says, in that same mocking tone.

Okay, I've just about had it with this prick. "You're right, Torres. So where have you trained?"

"Here and there." He steps out into the training area. "A little in the joint."

There it is. An ex-con. Cop hater.

"Show me your blocks," Torres says, setting himself into a stance, feet staggered, hands at his side.

I start to say that there's seldom time to assume a stylized stance in the street, but I decide not to antagonize him. "I'll try," I say.

He launches a fast chest-high roundhouse kick. I turn a little, allowing the big foot to streak past. "Nice kick, Torres. Surprisingly fast for a big man. But try not to lean your upper body so far forward. Leaning back a little will open up your groin area, and give you greater stretch and distance."

Torres's face reddens but he doesn't say anything. Again, he assumes a staggered stance, hands down at his sides.

"Good stance," I say. "Looks like taekwondo. For the street you might want to keep your hands up near your head."

Clearly angered by the instruction, Torres kicks again, same leg, but higher and harder." I slap the leg by with an open palm.

"Much better. See, you didn't cramp yourself that time and your kick looked more effortless. Good flexibility, too. You should move out of range when your kick is evaded or checked. If you stay in range, you need to follow up with something. If you don't, your opponent can easily—"

Torres snaps a lead-leg front kick at my groin. I twist a little so that my hip catches most of the impact, though the tip of his Nike just barely nicks my ever-so-more sensitive target. It's obvious he isn't trying to control his blows. I keep my face neutral, although I feel a surge of hot adrenaline surge through my muscles.

I swat his jab aside. He jabs again, this one hitting a strand of wet hair hanging down my forehead. "I'll take that as a hit," he says, chuckling. "Good thing I don't have to pay for this *lesson*."

I nod, as more adrenaline charges my muscles. "Good thing."

I've been told many times that when I get angry or when I'm completely absorbed in hard training, my eyes assume a sort of luminescence. Either Torres doesn't see it or he's too stupid to recognize a bad thing when it's standing right in front him. He pops out a backfist. I turn my head just enough to avoid his big knuckles. Had it landed, I would have been visited by Tweety Bird. "Good one," I say flatly. The young man is clearly getting frustrated. He can't hit me, intimidate me, or get any emotion out of me. Actually, he's provoked my adrenaline, but I've done a marvelous job hiding it, if I say so myself.

Okay, I'm tired of this dickstick. I have too many other things on my mind to have to deal with an upstart gunslinger.

"Would you like to see a counterattack, Torres?"

He chuckles. "*You* want to try to counter *me*? I've gotten a piece of you two times. Let me see you *try*."

"I'll show you what we call 'Lesson Thirteen.'"

"Lesson Thirteen? Why do you call it that?"

"Just makes it easy to remember. I'll control myself, so there's nothing to worry about."

"Worry?" he says, sneering like a bad guy in a Hong Kong chop-socky movie. He throws a punch.

I smack my palm against his arm hard enough to spin him around. He's mine now and I commence to do a little saturation bombing with kicks, punches, elbows, and knees, hitting him just hard enough against the back of his legs, spine, kidneys, and ribs to let him know he's been tagged. I slap my palms down onto his shoulders, sending a shock-shimmy through his big body, and spin him around to face me.

The look on his mug nearly makes me laugh before I flick my fingers against his eyebrows, lightly smack his throat with my other hand, and snap a kick just short of his groin. The fingers into the eyes would have temporarily blinded him, the fist could have sent him into a choking spasm, and the kick could have crumbled his cookies for a couple weeks.

"That's twelve," I say, calmly, my breathing normal. "The last and thirteenth move—hence the name—Lesson Thirteen, could be—oh—how about this." I slap my left palm against the right side of his shocked face and hook my right index finger just barely inside his right nostril opening. I grin at him. "Here's how this works, Torres. If I ram my finger deeper into your nose and then rip it toward me as I push your head away, you'll experience a lot of hurt. It's a good technique, as you say, for the street."

The big man's eyes couldn't be larger as his head vibrates on the verge of exploding.

I step back. "That's Lesson Thirteen. Controlled of course, unlike the blows you were throwing at me. I controlled them because I'm a martial artist. I have nothing to prove by hurting you. You, however, are a thug and a very stupid one."

Torres rubs the back of his hand over his eyebrows where my fingers had touched. "I just—"

"There is nothing for you to say and it's time for you to go."

Looking like a deflated tire, the big man nods and turns toward the door.

"Think about what just happened. And should you want to come back sometime, you're going to have to take off your shoes."

He nods and leaves.

I shake my head and move toward the dressing room. That's all I needed with all the other stressors in my life. I sit on a bench and roll my shoulders a few times to rid some of the tension there. What's going on with me? For a moment, I wanted Torres to push it so I could grind him into hamburger. What's that about? That's not like me at all. I have a rep on the PD for being the last one to engage in a fight. I've never administered street justice as some coppers do, though I've definitely gotten into my share of brawls. I'm known for BSing violent people into compliance and for using force as a last resort. So why would I want to trash Torres when it would serve no purpose?

In a grocery store a couple of days ago, I thought about how good it would feel to break a rude clerk's kneecap. Last week, I imagined pulling an idiot tailgater out of his truck and beating him into a gutter drain. I guess the good news is that I didn't act out on any of these things. The bad news is that I'm fantasizing about it.

Kari would probably say that I'm psychologically beating up myself because I feel guilty. Tiff would probably high-five her.

Of course, that's ridiculous… Or is it?

I pick up a bucket of cleaning supplies, step into the shower and spray cleanser on the walls. The butterflies in my stomach have a riot every time I think about going to work tomorrow. Funny how a shooting and two months away from the street can make me feel all twitchy, as if it were my first day out of the academy. Not funny ha-ha, but funny weird. Funny unpleasant.

Kari said it was a common worry among officers who have used deadly force; it haunts them that they might get into another shooting. I get that. Most cops never fire their weapon outside of the firing range. They train for it and talk about it all the time, but most believe deeply inside that it will never happen. Then when they do have to drop the hammer, the ugly reality of it shocks some to their core. The it's-never-going-to-happen-to-me barrier comes down with a bang, and it stays down. The officer becomes hyper-vigilant and the thought that he'll have to kill again makes his insides feel as if he had chugged a bottle of Drano.

Kari said there is no greater chance of it happening a second time than there was the first. Easy enough to grasp intellectually, but emotionally…

I inhale deeply and blow it out. Okay, a little more cleaning before tonight's first class. Tomorrow will come soon enough.

CHAPTER FOUR

We're at the Kick Start coffee shop on Weidler Avenue getting exactly that, a morning kick start, and doing the buddy-bonding thing before jumping on our first case. I drain the last of my Americano, eyeing Tommy as he sits perched on the edge of his chair carefully wrapping the Earl Grey tea bag string around his spoon. I've always thought he looked a little like Niles Crane, Frazier's woosie brother on the old *Frazier* sit-com. His impeccably tailored suit and slacks are too spendy for police work, he has a demeanor that's a little on the prissy side, and with his fair skin and blond hair, it's hard to imagine him ever getting dirty. My mother would say that, "He could fall into a toilet and come up smelling like roses." The big difference between Tommy and the actor is that my partner has a physique like a football linebacker, which he was in college, and he can bench four fifty.

I've never worked with him, but word has it he's a good investigator with a gift for gab. I've heard that during inter-rogations, he often turns hardened criminals into slobbering infants wanting their mothers. Supposedly, the captain has a foot-thick folder of commendations from people who wrote that his compassion and gentle words were comforting during their frightening ordeal. A separate folder contains a dozen let-ters from the joint written by crooks he's put away, all thanking him for being respectful during *their* frightening ordeal, their arrest and interrogation.

Tommy and I have chatted in the office break room and the police gym a few times, mostly about lifting weights. One time we got all touchy-feely, talking about how citizens and other coppers see us. We're both long-time iron pumpers, though he's probably tipping the scale at two thirty and I'm bouncing between one ninety and two hundred. He told me that people see him and instantly think that he's all about his muscles and that he's as dumb as a rhododendron. I told him that I've always been seen as a muscle head, too, and because I train in the martial arts some people think that I'm just itching to go all Jet Lee on someone.

The truth is that Tommy has a master's degree in European history, which he jokes has hardly helped him at all on the job, and he teaches a course in Ukrainian folklore two nights a week at Portland State University. He definitely lifts hard and eats healthfully, to the point of being a fanatic, but he always dresses to play down his physique at work.

I have a bachelor's in social science from PSU, and I always, *always*, use my fighting skill as a last resort. In fact, I've never had a hint of an excessive force complaint, not even from the guy who spent eight days in Kaiser after our *mano y mano* in a skid-row armpit of a bar.

I'm partnering with Tommy until I get my groove back, probably for a week or so, then I'll be handling my cases all by my lonesome. He's a good guy and I enjoy chatting with him, but I prefer working alone, always have. I liked working a one-man car when I was in uniform and I like working alone as a detective. I'd rather just focus on a case and not have to think about what my partner is or isn't doing.

Since we sat down, we've been talking about ways to increase poundage on our bench press. He wants to add a little more chest size because he's thinking about entering the Mr. Northwest Physique Championships in six months, and I want to increase my poundage to add a little more zip to my punching power and speed.

"I suppose we ought to do some detective work," I say during a pause. "What's on the agenda?"

He dabs his mouth with a napkin. "Got a burglary of an Asian boutique. Uniform took the report and found some good prints. The owner left a message on my phone this morning that she had some photos of the missing items, real unique stuff. We just have to retrieve the pics and do a little PR with her."

"Sounds good. Let's do it."

Ten minutes later, Tommy is guiding our brown, unmarked sedan through the core area of downtown Portland. It feels good to be in a police car again but also a little strange. It's at once new, familiar, comfortable, and off-putting. What would Kari say about that? Probably that I'm like that soldier who returns home and thinks everything is different, when in reality only he has changed.

Tommy stops for a light. I watch a bag lady push a loaded-down-with-crap grocery cart across the crosswalk. She shoots us a toothless smile, not fooled by the unmarked police car. I start to ask Tommy if she might be carrying his baby when it dawns on me where we are. Forty feet from the driver's side window is the now infamous second-hand store. I squirm a little and drum my fingers on my knees. I've got to deal with it. It's a main intersection and I'll be driving through it for the next twenty years.

"Sorry, Sam," he says, looking over at the store and then at me. "I wasn't thinking. I should have gone another way."

"That's okay." My voice is tight. I know why I'm reacting to it but knowing doesn't keep me from feeling like girly man.

"How long were you off, anyway?"

"Two months."

"Why?"

I look over at him. "Why what?"

"Why did you take so much time off? It was a good shoot."

I tighten my lips and take a deep breath. I look at a cluster of people waiting at a bus stop. Tommy might be the first but he won't be the last to show his ignorance. I tell myself to calm down, stop over-reacting to innocent questions.

"I needed the time. It's one thing shooting at paper targets and bullshitting about blowing somebody up, but it's a whole other thing to do it and then watch the life drain out of the person's eyes."

He frowns. "The guy deserved to be—"

"True," I interrupt. "But it's still hard. Maybe it's my Catholic upbringing, but it's hard to have killing etched on my soul."

"Understood," he says softly. He drives another block, then, "Please don't think I'm being insensitive. I'm just interested in this new program the bureau has for cops who've used deadly force. I minored in psych."

"No offense taken," I say, meaning it, and happy I didn't give voice to my initial conclusion jumping.

"Speaking of religion," he says, "I don't know if it helps, but what I understand of the Bible is that the commandment is supposed to be 'thou shalt not murder,' but it was changed in translation to 'thou shalt not kill.' You didn't murder the guy. The decisions the suspect made created a situation where you had to make a choice: Stand there and allow the perp to kill an innocent man, or shoot the perp to save a life. You did what you'd been trained to do: Protect the people. You did the right thing, Sam."

I nod. "I've thought about it a lot. In fact, I thought about it for two months, ad nauseam. Sometimes thinking about it as 'the right thing to do' helps and sometimes it doesn't help at all. What does help is to hear someone else say it, especially a copper."

Tommy grins. "Good, you can buy lunch."

"Soy burger with tofu and sprouts?"

"Ten four, spaghetti arms. Hey, what's dispatch saying?" He turns up the radio.

"... *Tenth and Yamhill. All uniform cars are tied up on a fatal.*"

I retrieve the mic. "Four-Forty, we're at Twelfth and Yamhill. Say again."

"*Thank you Four-Forty. All district cars are tied up on a fatal crash on Four-oh-Five. Need someone to see a white male transient at Tenth and Yamhill. He's thirty to thirty-five, medium build... appears to be drunk, shadowboxing and swinging at passersby. Complainant is anonymous.*"

"Let's do it," Tommy says.

"We'll take it," I tell radio. I replace the mic feeling myself smile. It feels pretty good to be back in the saddle. I might have some doubts about remaining in police work, but I can't deny the adrenaline rush I still get from it, even on a no-big-deal call like this one.

A couple minutes later we're at the corner and, sure enough, there's a raggedy-looking guy in front of Oscar's Jewelry dancing around and snapping out air jabs like a white Muhammad Ali. A huge backpack leans against the store's wall, complete with bedroll, an attached canteen, and dangling eating utensils. An uncapped bottle of wine lay on its side by the pack. Curious faces peer out the jewelry store window and a group of noon-time office-types look on from the sidewalk.

Tommy activates the flashing grill lights and anchors it about twenty feet away from the guy. We get out and excuse our way through the rubberneckers.

"Sir," Tommy calls out, moving to the guy's front, stopping about ten feet away. I move around behind him and stay back a couple of strides, an old trick that splits and confuses the subject's attention. Tommy casually raises his palms. The man stops bobbing and weaving, and blinks dumbly several times at him.

"Good morning, sir," I say, to make him turn around, which he does with a stumble and a couple of sways that nearly sends him to the sidewalk.

"Who the fu...?" he mumbles, struggling to focus on me.

"Sir, look back this way," Tommy says. "Right here, at me."

"Godz-damn-its," the man slurs, working his way back around.

"How can we help you?" Tommy asks kindly.

"Joo a big one. But I canz still take joo." He stumble-turns and gives me another struggled look. "Joo looks like a punk," he slurs, blinking slowly. "I can take joo, too." He thinks about that for a moment. "Jootoo. Jootoo," he sings, then laughs, which evolves into a wet, hacking cough.

"Sir, Tommy calls. "Look back at me. Good, thank you. Listen, we're the police. Understand? We're detectives. We don't want to fight you. We want to help joo, er, you. How can we do that?"

I stay quiet letting Tommy do his thing.

The man jabs toward Tommy, though they're ten feet apart. "I canz takes joo," he slurs again. "Don't need nose goddamn help. I just want to kicks schome ass. Fought pro for twee years in the... eighties, I think it was." He jabs again. He might be drunk but the jab looks good, trained.

"Listen," Tommy says, resting his foot on a fire hydrant. He fakes a good casual but I can tell he's ready should the man move into his space. "May I ask your name, sir?"

My first year on the job, I worked just one day with an antagonistic hate-filled uniform cop named Stan. We got a call almost identical to this one, except the wino had wandered into a Victoria's Secret store at Lloyd Center Mall and plopped himself smack in the middle of a discount bin of frilly panties. The guy clearly hadn't showered or changed his clothes forever and, judging by the horrific smell that greeted us as we approached him, he'd just released a whole lot of wine-diarrhea into his greasy trousers.

First thing old Stan asked was, "What's your name, pal? The name your whore mama gave you on that dreary day she gave birth to the shitbird sitting and shitting here in this pile of thongs and French cut skivvies?"

Asshole Stan was a master of clever insults. The drunk must have had some pride left because he launched himself out of that bin with both arms flailing like a windmill, and the fight was on.

After the shift ended, I asked the sarge never to work with Stan again.

"My name's Tommy, sir. That's Sam behind you. What's yours?"

The guy snapped out another jab. "Jace 'The Ace' Widmer." He's jabbing faster now. "Fifteen… fifteen sometin'… oh yeah, twelve wins by KO, one lossh. Got disqualified for thumbin' Ricky 'Too Tall' Place's fuckin' eyeball."

Tommy moves a stride away from the hydrant but not enough to be a threat. His arms are still up and bent, his palms toward the guy. "Listen Ace, I bet you were one hell of a fighter. I can see that you got the moves."

"Oh, I gotch duh moves." He jabs a couple of times. "I canz kick the asshole of any cop in front of me." He shuffles two steps toward Tommy and throws a jab-cross combo. They look good.

"Hold on, Ace," Tommy says without reacting to the man's advance. "Here's how I see it. No doubt you can kick my ass. I'm big but I'm slow. But if you kick my ass, you're going to have to kick Sam's ass."

The man shuffles around, bobbing and weaving in place. He looks at me, registering slow surprise, as if he's forgotten about me. "Oh I canz kicks his asshole, too. You damn betcha."

I shrug and nod. No need to antagonize. A couple of people in the gathering crowd chuckle.

"Ace, look at me."

The Ace laboriously shuffles back around to face Tommy.

"So after you kick Sam's ass, there's going to be another police officer show up. Then you're going to have to kick a new guy's ass. By the way, Sam and I are the smallest cops working today."

The Ace stops shuffling but he keeps his guard up. "I canz do thats," he says, but with a tad less confidence than a moment ago.

"You beat him up, and another police car will come and that one is a two-man unit, real short-tempered guys. Red heads. We got twelve two-man cars working this morning. East Precinct has sixty-eight guys working, and North Precinct has one hundred and six working the day shift. You're going to have to kick all those guys' asses, too. Let's say you indeed do kick 'em all, and that's what… a hundred fifty asses? The chief will call in the night shift or maybe the fire department. That's nine hundred more asses. Then you got the city street sweepers, the road maintenance guys, and maybe even the mayor will get in line. I know he's in shape because he swims at the Y."

The Ace laughs at that and so does the crowd. "The mayor schwims?" he asks, lowering his guard a little. "How's thats going to help his asshole?"

Tommy nods. "I hear what you're saying, Ace. I do hear what you're saying, and it's a good point. But remember, you got to go through a thousand some asses first before you got to deal with the mayor's skinny one. By then you're going to be so tired and bruised that His Honor will easily smack you with his soggy swim trunks."

Someone applauds in the crowd and Ace laughs again, though his merriment quickly fades and his expression changes to uncertainty. He unclenches his hands and lowers them.

"How about this instead?" Tommy says conversationally, stepping toward him a little, still showing his palms. "We give you a lift to the Drop in Center where you can hit the shower, get lunch in an hour and maybe some clean clothes. Doesn't that sound better than fighting a boatload of cops just to prove something we already know? That you're one hell of a fighter? Wouldn't you rather be a cleaned-up lover?"

The Ace points at Tommy and giggles. "You got that right, Tommy my man. I'm one hell of a lover, too. Aaaaand…" He lifts his pointing finger to the sky in a Statue of Liberty pose, and slowly turns toward the crowd, searching, searching… He points at an attractive lady in a business suit standing with a group of others, "I want *that* one."

"Ace," Tommy says to distract him as the frightened woman scurries away on clicking heels. "Come on. Hop in our ride. My pard will grab your gear and put it in the trunk; I think we can make it in time for lunch. You like turkey and mashed potatoes?"

The Ace nods as he saunters toward our car. I grab his backpack and follow them, feeling like a third wheel. Tommy buzzes open the trunk and opens the back door of our car. "Have a seat, Jace 'The Ace' Widmer. We really appreciate your cooperation. A fighter should also be a gentleman and you are one for sure."

"Don'ts forget I'm a lovers, too," The Ace slurs.

Tommy slaps him on the shoulder, guy style. "Ha. I bet you are, Acey. For sure. But first you got to get a shower."

"And cakes. I get some goddamn cakes at the Center, toos, right?" the man asks, plopping onto the seat.

"Pull your feet in there, sir. That's it. Yes, yes, and cake. Two pieces, damn-it. You get two." Tommy shuts the door and winks at me as I close the trunk.

The small crowd begins to disperse but not before half a dozen of them applaud.

Tommy wraps one arm across his waist and bows deeply. "Thank you ladies and germs. We'll be right back after a little break. And don't jaywalk."

The crowd laughs again and disperses with a story to tell back at the office.

I smile at Tommy over the top of the car as we open our doors. "You're good," I say. "Everything I heard about you is true. You're definitely good."

We lodge Jace "The Ace" Widmer into the Drop in Center without incident. He even shakes our hands and wishes us a safe day. We wish him the same.

Back in the car, I tell Tommy again that I think he did a good job talking the guy down. We both know we could have ended up on the cold, hard sidewalk thrashing around with him, all of us getting scuffed and Tommy and me ruining our sports coats. Tommy's threads must have set him back a stack of hundreds. Mine, not even one bill.

"You know," Tommy says, as he steers the car out into traffic, "there have been a couple three incidents during my time when guys like him, street guys, winos, guys who we deal with every day, have stepped out of a crowd and saved some cop's bacon.

"About six months ago, a gangbanger had the drop on a uniform guy out in North Precinct, Tim Storlie, I think it was, and a guy like Ace bashed the banger in the back of the skull with a wine bottle. Probably saved Storlie from eating a round or two. Point is, every time someone asks the street person why they helped, the guy said that some cop treated him with respect once, and he wanted to return the favor. Sort of a pay it forward, I guess. So I always think about that when I deal with people. Plus it's just the right thing to do."

I agree with him one hundred percent, but I can't resist. I put my hand gently on his shoulder and stroke it a couple times. "I am sooo turned on right now."

"Okay, okay," Tommy laughs. "Let's go get those photos at the Asian store."

The rest of the day is routine. We chat with the shop owner, get the photos, and suggest ways to better secure the business. In the afternoon, we get statements from two witnesses of a church burglary and then finish the day picking up a still-in-the-box surround-sound system that an honest homeowner had found in his shrubs. Apparently, the thief had gotten spooked carrying it down the street and stashed it with the intention of retrieving it later.

All in all it's a good day, a nice transition into the job after two months off. I didn't realize I'd missed it so until after we had lodged Ace. I like the feeling of treating a guy right, of making one little corner of the city safe for passersby, and about being part of a bigger picture. For the last several weeks, it's been all about me and my effort to come to terms with taking a life. Today was all about problem solving and making other people feel a little bit better. Corny, but that's what I'm feeling.

I get off work on time, which is always a good thing since it rarely happens, and I grab a burger at Wendy's on the way to my school. I have just one class to teach, a group of twenty-five beginners. They've been training about a month, so they know enough now that I can work out with them a little.

I worked up a nice sweat with the students and after the class I don't feel a need—mental, spiritual, or whatever—to beat the heavy bag to a pulp. Maybe this getting back on the horse idea really does work.

So I head home, shower, watch CSI, and hit the rack at eleven.

I'm almost asleep when the phone jolts me awake. It's eleven ten.

"Reeves."

"Hey, did I wake you?"

"Uh, yeah."

"I wanted to ask about your day and how you're feeling."

Tiff doesn't like what I do but she wants to know how my day went? I don't' think so. Damn, she's hard to figure out and I'm tired of trying. To be nice, I tell her about Tommy and how he handled The Ace. She laughs hard and says that that was really good police work. I'm not sure if she's implying that shooting someone isn't really good police work, but I'll give her the benefit of the doubt.

She asks how I'm feeling. I know she's referring to how I feel after going back to work, but her tone, a sexy one, sounds more like she's asking what I'm wearing. I tell her that I'm feeling good, better than I have in a while.

"I'm so happy to hear that, Sam, I really am." I picture her hair fanned out on the empty pillow next to me.

"Thanks," I don't know what else to say.

"So what are you wearing, good lookin'?"

I grin. "A smile."

"Mmm, and you have such a beautiful, uh, smile. So tell me..."

"Yes?" I whisper.

"Is that beautiful smile getting bigger?"

CHAPTER FIVE

We're at the Kick Start again and I'm watching Tommy squeeze the last and the bitterest drops of Earl Grey out of his three bags. He gulps it down. Gross. Don't know how anyone can drink that.

"What's on the agenda this beautiful morning?" I ask, just as the cutie waitress, who's flirted with us both days, lays the bill on the table and smiles, first at me and then at Tommy.

"If there's anything else I can do for you boys…" She turns and wiggles her way back toward the cash register. "Just ask," she says over her shoulder.

"You're doing it now," Tommy calls to her. She giggles but doesn't look back.

"Earth to Tommy?"

"What? Oh, I got seventeen new business break-ins down in lower southeast. Could be the same guy. What do you got?"

I open a manila folder. "Three old cases I was working before I went off. Small jobs. One guy likes to steal silverware and women's under things."

"So there's two of us who steal undies?"

"Yeah, but this guy swipes women's."

Tommy laughs, tosses a five-dollar bill on the table and scoots his chair back. "My treat. Ready to roll?"

Five minutes later, I'm driving and Tommy is slumped low reading a police report. A nice violin concerto wafts softly from the speakers.

"How are you sleeping after your shooting?" Tommy asks, flipping through reports.

"Much better now, thanks" I answer, impressed with the genuine interest in his tone. "It was rough for a while there but I'm coming to terms with it. I've been talking with a shrink and training extra hard. I actually slept last night."

Tommy nods. "Glad you're slipping back into the groove. I've worked with a couple other guys after they'd dropped the hammer. Both came out of it fairly quickly. But I remember an old timer at Central Precinct when I first came on the job. Jack Watkins, I think it was. He capped a teenager who had just shot his own mother. Kid shoots her and then sits down on the sofa and starts playing a video game, while mom lay bleeding out on the carpet ten feet away.

"Neighbor calls about hearing a gunshot. Jack responds, walks in the open front door and sees the kid playing *Donkey Kong*. You believe that? *Donkey Kong!* The kid picks up the gun from the coffee table—gun in one hand, game controller in his other—and points both at Jack. Jack was in his fifties and fat, but he drew fast and drills him in the five ring, sending the little prick to answer to his mom in the afterlife. Righteous shoot, but Jack never got over it. Resigned six months later, just two years from retirement."

"Pretty sad," I say. "Department was in the dark ages in those days, wouldn't even give you a day off after a shooting. Thankfully, they know more about how to handle it now. Still, it's no cake walk."

"I bet," Tommy says, reaching for the mic. "Wanna take a family fight on Yamhill? Beat car is tied up on an alarm."

I didn't hear the dispatch. I guess my brain's still at home lying on the sofa watching *Jerry Springer*. "Sure," I say. "Still like the uniform calls, huh?"

"Four-Forty's close."

"Thanks Four-Forty."

"I might be wearing a pretty suit now," Tommy says, replacing the mic, "but I still got the blue on underneath. Cool thing I like about working dicks is that you can pick and choose what calls you want to take."

"And you like family fights?"

"We're close, that all. Let's see, sixteen seventy-two… there, that big house with the paint chipping off it. Look at that, you can't even tell what color it used to be." He clicks the mic: "Four-Forty's arrived."

"Four-Forty's there."

"Yup, this is it," I say, acknowledging the obvious since we can hear fierce yelling coming from the place even with our windows up. "And you volunteered us for this."

"That there's the house," an elderly white-haired woman calls out from the porch next door as we get out. She jabs her cane at the front door. "Just follow the screamin' up the steps, that's all you got to do. You cops, right?"

"We're on it ma'am, thanks," I say.

"It's awful. Drunk as a skunk they are. Mutha fuckers been screaming all night. I haven't slept a wink. I need my rest. I'm eighty god-damn seven next week." She jabs her finger toward our car. "You got night sticks in your trunk? Might need 'em. They're nasty mother fuckers in that there house, for sure. Get your nightsticks and beat their hides like they're Rodney King."

"Beat 'em like ol' Rodney. Ten-four, Ma'am," Tommy says. "We're on it."

The voices inside, loud and slurred drown out the old woman as we move up onto the big front porch.

"… shoulda never married your drunk ass…"

"… yabba yabba. You ever stop?"

"… least my first ex husband had all his teeth."

"Yeah? Well, least my third wife had an ass smaller than a Hummer.

"This reminds me," I say to Tommy. "Your wife wants you to call her first chance you get."

Tommy rolls his eyes and pounds the warped door with the bottom of his fist.

"If I'd had a licka sense I would have stayed single," shouts the man's voice.

"Well, there you go. You ain't got a lick of no sense, let alone nothin' to go on."

"'Nothin' to… That don't even make no sense."

"See," the old lady on the other porch shouts, surprisingly loud for as old and frail as she is. "Drunker than two sailors on shore leave. Where's your nightsticks? You never got your god-damn nightsticks!"

Tommy turns the handle and the door opens. "Police," he says through the crack. "Portland Police. May we come in?"

The door jerks open all the way. "Who the hell called the cops," a pajama-wearing, vomit-covered, fifty-year-old balding man sputters. "That old beater next door? Yeah, it was her. Always bitchin' 'bout something." He leans around the door facing. "You call the cops, Annie? You old witch bitch. Witch bitch, witch bitch."

'I hope they beat you like Rodney," the old woman shouts back.

"Hey you!" coos an equally vomit-covered middle-aged woman, slipping under the man's arm and heading straight toward me, her well-fed body rolling like thunder under her short, pink transparent nightie. "You're one fine-looking man. Look like that one on the TV, what the hell's his name? That good lookin' guy on… what the fuck is the name of that show? Except you're thirty years younger. And you're a white man." She reaches for my arm. "I'm Hildie, what's yours?"

I sidestep her and follow Tommy into the living room, or at least what used to be one before a Category Five hit it. There is a five-foot high pile of chairs and end tables against the fireplace. Broken flowerpots, dirt, and ripped-up houseplants cover the hardwood floor, torn curtains dangle from the windows, and at least three lamps lie broken next to a screen-shattered television. Part way up a staircase, a tattered orange sofa rests on its side and a few steps up from that a yellow and chrome upside down dinette table.

"Your housekeeper Typhoon Mary?" Tommy asks, scrunching his face at the old timer's splattered blue pajamas.

The woman, whose see-through pink nightie leaves nothing of her two-hundred quivering pounds to the imagination, slurs, "Housekeeper? Shit, don't need no damn housekeeper." The puke starts in her hair, covers most of the nightie, with splatters here and there on her cellulite-covered legs and the tops of her bare feet.

I've seen homes trashed like this before in family fights, but I've never seen two people covered in throw-up. How did they even accomplish that? How did the woman puke in her own hair? Some of it is fresh and some of it's dried from… last night? I'm this close to losing the peanut butter-covered English muffin I had for breakfast.

Hildie, advances on me again, her bloodshot eyes drunk and lusting. "God, you're handsome," she breathes on me. Stay down muffin, stay down. She places both palms on my chest and whispers something, but I sidestep away quickly, not hearing it.

"I'm thinking," Tommy says over his shoulder as he sheepdogs the man next to the pile of furniture by the fireplace, "that you and Hildie could team up with me and that waitress at the Kick Start for a double date."

"Are you two married," I ask Hildie, ignoring Tommy.

"Hey, copper," Tommy's man shouts louder than necessary. "My wife fancies you. Take her. She's pretty good; better when she's cleaned up, I ought'a say."

"So you two are married?" I ask again, brushing her hands off me. I so don't want to touch her. Her stench makes my eyes water.

She nods. "But it's okay. Bruce doesn't care."

"What are you arguing about? Has he hit you?"

"No one has hit anyone," the man calls over to me. "We're just arguing. Lover's quarrel."

"He's right," she says, crotch gazing me. "You're built good. You got a good package, too?"

The man cackles at that. "Yup-a-roonie, Hildie loves a good package."

"How long you been married?" I ask, feeling my face heat up.

"You like these?" she lifts her ponderous breasts that have been swaying about under her pukey nightie. She could knock someone out with those.

"Since Wednesday," the man calls over, giggling at his wife. "Those are some big-ass hangers, ain't they, officer?"

Tommy has stopped trying to talk to Bruce, apparently deciding that it's more fun to watch my predicament.

"We got married Thursday, you dumb shit turd," the woman snaps, letting her breasts drop. Seems like that would've hurt.

"Wednesday!"

"Thursday!"

"You guys talking about last week?" I ask. "You got married *last* week?"

"Five days ago," the man says.

"Four, you damn ass turd!" Then cooingly to me, "You like a big ass?" She turns around and pulls up her nightie a little. Amazingly, she has puke on the back of her legs and her bottom. "More cushion to the pushin'," she says over her shoulder.

I look at the ceiling for a moment to cleanse my eyes. Reluctantly, I look back at her. "How long have you been fighting?"

"All night," she says, eyeing my package again. I'm starting to feel violated.

"That's about right," the man offers. He thinks about it for a moment. "Yup, 'bout right."

The woman reaches for me again, but I step around her and move to the center of the debris. Time to take charge. "Okay, here's how it's going to go. No one has hit anyone, right?'

"No, we don't do that," Bruce says.

"Big ass and big tits, all yours," Hildie reminds me, sashaying my way.

Tommy isn't even trying to keep his laughter in.

I thrust my palm toward her. "Hildie, Stop!" Incredibly she does, but with hurt in her eyes. "Okay, thank you. You been married a few days and—"

Hildie nods. "Three. Four, I mean."

"—aaaaand you are supposedly on your honeymoon."

"Yeah, we're on our honeymoon," she says, looking over at her husband.

"Then you know what you're supposed to be doing, right?"

They both look at me, then at each other, then back to me again.

"Right?"

She nods first, then he does, both solemn.

"Where's your bedroom?"

The man smiles and points upstairs.

"*You* wanna go up there?" Hildie asks me, with a look of anticipation and a nod of her head toward the stairs.

"Hildie, stop talking!"

She makes a zipper motion across her mouth and snaps to attention, which sets her mammoth breasts rolling about.

"Now, listen up you two. I'm going to give you an official police order. Do you understand what I'm saying here?"

They both look at me, their faces serious. They nod. I lift my right hand as if I'm going to administer an oath, which I am.

"By the power vested… lift your right hands, both of you." They do, both sober as two judges, puke-covered ones. "By the power vested in me, an official of the Portland Police Bureau and an official of this city, I'm ordering you to go upstairs and do what you're supposed to be doing on your friggin' honeymoon."

Tommy looks at me incredulously.

"Partner?" I prompt, nodding my head toward the couple.

"What? Oh, uh, yes." He turns to Bruce. "He's right," Tommy says. "It's official now."

"But maybe you and I could—"

"Hildie, stop," I say, putting my index finger to my lips. "I have just given you and Bruce an official—*official*—police order to go upstairs and go to bed. Now go!"

"Okay, okay," Bruce giggles. He looks at Tommy, who gestures that he's free to go. The groom walks over to his bride.

"Take his hand, Hildie," I say. She does. "Now go upstairs. And don't trip over that dinette on the steps. By the way, how did the dinette get... never mind. Just go upstairs."

"Yes, sir," Bruce says seriously.

"Yes, sir," Hildie says, slipping her arm around her husband's waist. They kiss, and for the third time in ten minutes, my breakfast muffin creeps up the back of my throat. They manage to maneuver around the dinette before stopping to look down at us.

"Go on, you're doing fine," I say with a wave of my hand. "We'll just let ourselves out." They smile and Hildie gives me a little wave. They stumble about, interlace their arms and head up the stairs.

"Ready?" I say to Tommy, heading toward the door.

"Incredible," he says, following me. "You ordered them to—"

"You beat them mother fuckers?" the white-haired woman calls out from her porch.

"Within an inch of their life, ma'am," Tommy says with a salute.

Three minutes later, I skid to a stop at a Shell service station restroom. Tommy bails out before I can and dashes into the restroom to wash every inch of exposed skin. I go in when he returns, though I'd prefer to take a complete shower or, better yet, go to a furniture stripping place and let them hose me down with scalding steam. I spent four years in college so I can communicate with puke-covered newlyweds?

Tommy is talking into the mic as I get back behind the wheel. "Don't tell me we got a call back to the lovers' house?" I ask.

He's scrawling an address down in his notebook. "No, it's an intruder call, about ten blocks over in that new Argay Park area. Twenty-three seventy-five on Oak."

"Cars responding. Complainant's hysterical. We think she's saying that her son is still inside the house. Intruder kicked through a backdoor, struck the complainant… Okay, we just got this in: Another caller can hear a man yelling on the second floor. Units responding to twenty-three seventy-five southeast Oak, give me your numbers again."

"Six-Forty, we're stuck behind a disabled truck on the Hawthorne Bridge."

"Six-Fifty, I'm at least eight minutes away."

"Six-Five-Five I'm there now."

"Let's do it," I say, guiding our car back out onto the street.

"Four-Forty is close," Tommy says into the mic.

"We ought to just put on uniforms and start taking calls," I say over the roar of the accelerating engine.

"This is Six-Five-Five. I've got the complainant. A blind woman. Really out of it. What I'm getting is that the suspect, her sense is that he's white and tall, smashed through her backdoor, kicked her in the stomach and charged up the stairs. Says her seven-year-old son is up there. Don't know if the man is armed. Don't know if he's got the boy. How close is my cover?"

"Betcha it's another family fight," Tommy says. "If so, it's yours. I bow to the master."

Yup, that's me. The guy who settles other people's relationship problems all the while mine is nutso. "There's Six-Five-Five.

Flashing lights up there, mid block," I say, pressing the throttle even harder. "And that must be the complainant standing by the marked unit."

"Four-Forty's arrived," Tommy tells dispatch. "Looks like it's just you and me, Sam, and Six-Five-Five. Wow, look at these houses. I haven't been here since they've finished the area. At least a million five smackers each."

"Where's the officer, ma'am?" I ask, climbing out of the car.

She turns part way toward me, hugging herself, her eyes looking slightly off to the side, not focused.

"Ma'am, I'm Detective Reeves. Where's the police officer?"

"House," she sobs. "The man… he screamed. The officer… said he couldn't wait.. Please, get my baby. He's upstairs."

"Is the man your husband," Tommy asks.

"What? No no no. My husband is in California… on business. He—"

A horrific scream rips from a second-story open window, human, but beast-like. It's like the scream of a bobcat my grandfather and I once found in the woods, its leg caught in a steel-toothed trap. Grandfather shot it to put it out of its misery. I was thirteen.

"That's not… Jimmy," the mother wheezes.

I take off at a sprint toward the house. "Come on, Tommy," I call over my shoulder. "Dispatch," I say into my portable radio. "Six-Five-Five is in the house and my partner and I are going in. Have the next unit secure the back and another secure the front." We stop on the porch, each of us taking a side of the door.

"Be advised that the last we heard from Six-Five-Five was that he was standing on the stairs waiting for backup."

"Copy that," I whisper into the radio; I shut it off. "You got your radio off, Tommy?"

"Yup. Look, the door's ajar. Probably from when mom came out or maybe when Six-Five-Five went in."

I nudge it open another three or four inches and quick-peek around the frame: expanse of burgundy rug, edge of a black leather sofa, lit lamp. My heart is thumping hard but I'm in control. I thought I'd be a little rusty after two months away but I feel good. I'm on it.

I'll go right, you go left," I whisper, removing my nine from under my sports coat. Tommy already has his out.

"Now," I whisper, gripping my weapon with both hands and angling it toward the floor. I push the door the rest of the way open and step quickly to the right. Tommy steps in behind me, moving left.

It's a beautiful living room filled with rich leathers, marble, and expensive-looking art pieces. There's an archway at the far side, through which I can see the bottom steps of a spiral stairway. As we move closer, I see black shoes and blue pant legs farther up the stairs. I nod toward them.

Tommy whispers, "Uniform pants, I think. Let me move over for a better see… Yes, it's Six-Five-Five."

We inch slowly across the plush carpet toward the archway, each step exposing more and more of the officer. Not until we're all the way through the arch can we see all of him near the top of the carpeted stairs, his overweight body leaning for support against a richly varnished banister, his .45 semi-auto gripped in both hands. Name's Mitchell Heiberg, mid forties. He looks down at us, the relief obvious in his face. He gestures with his head toward the hallway at the top of the stairs.

"One man," he whispers out of the corner of his mouth. "First room, right there. Mom says it's the boy's room. Kid's seven years old."

"We heard a yell," I whisper, moving up the curved stairs and bracing myself on the banister across from Mitchell. I look down at Tommy standing at the side of the archway; he's holstered his Glock, probably because we're between him and the threat.

I look toward the door in question and the hall that extends about twenty feet to the right. There are doors on each side, all closed except for one at the end of the hall, from which a rectangle of light falls across the carpet. Bathroom, probably.

"Don't know what that yell was about," the veteran officer says, breathing raggedly but more than ready to pounce. "It scared the shit out of me, though. Heard the boy's voice after, whimpering. Haven't heard anything for a few minutes."

"How do you want to do it?" I ask, acknowledging that he was first on the scene and therefore calling the shots.

Mitchell looks down at Tommy under the archway. "Check with radio to see if SWAT and a hostage negotiator are on the way." To me: "I think we should hold our positions and—"

A window-rattling bellow from the boy's bedroom.

"Jesus!" Tommy gasps from below, as Mitchell and I crouch reflexively, thrusting our weapons toward the door. "What in holy hell was that?"

A nasally voice from the room. "I'm going to kill the little shiiiiit. Nowwww. Just you wait and seeeee." Taunting voice, syrupy. Was he talking to us? He had to have heard us.

"We got to move *now*," Mitchell says between clenched teeth.

My stomach churns a huge bubble of acid. Please don't let this be a repeat of two months ago.

Tommy moves up behind us.

"Okay," Mitchell says. "I'll move to the other side of the door and you guys take up on this side. We'll listen from there."

We move up the last few steps and then quiet-walk over to the door. Mitchell places his ear against the wall and listens for a moment. He looks at me and pretends to rub an eye.

I nod that I understand. The child is crying and that means he's still alive.

My heart thumps so hard that I wonder if the other guys can hear it. I don't want to shoot again. I don't want to shoot again. I don't want... Damn. Kari said there was no greater chance of it happening again. She promised me. It can't be my turn again.

Mitchell pantomimes that he'll go right and that Tommy and I should go left. I nod and position my trembling hand just above the doorknob. Mitchell holds up three fingers, closes his fist, extends two fingers, closes his fist, extends one.

I twist the knob hard and push it forcefully. Mitchell slides around the door facing, moving to the right. I step in an instant later, moving to the left, my gun pointing into the room; Tommy's on my heels.

"I'm going to killllll the little shit. Wanna watch?"

I hear and understand the words before my mind fully comprehends the image before me.

A man, skinny, mid twenties, head shaved, and naked, sits spread-legged on the corner of the bed. Between his legs, a blond-haired little boy, also naked, struggling weakly against the forearm that pins him within a tight embrace. The man looks in my direction, but his eyes—gray, opaque—seem to look trance-like into another world.

"Let us help you, my friend," Tommy says. "I'm coming over to sit next to you so I can hear you better. I—"

"I'm going to killllll the little shiiiit," the man repeats in that same slimy voice. The boy stops struggling and looks at the uniformed officer, his eyes impossibly large. The man's vacant stare seems transfixed on me; I don't think he's blinked once. "They want the little shiiiit in the bowels of hell, you seeeeee. I've been sent by the legion to bring—"

"Show your other hand," Mitchell says, stepping toward the man, his gun angled to the side. "Show me your muther fuckin' hand. Do it *now*!"

"Mommy," the boy utters softly. Then screams, "Mommy!"

"This one?" the man says, bringing his arm out from behind the boy's back, a large kitchen knife white-knuckled in his grip. He places the cutting side against the child's thin neck, casually, as if he were going to cut a melon for lunch.

"Jimmeeee!" the blind mother screams desperately from outside.

"Mommeee!" the piercing return.

"Drop the blade!" I command, my voice vibrating. His unblinking, lifeless eyes look at me as if I'm the only one in the room. Almost imperceptibly, his mouth begins to smile—knowingly? What... What does he know? What the hell does he know?

Then, like a gut punch, it hits me. There is no way out of this. He's in charge and there is no way in hell he's giving up. It amuses him that we're all locked into this moment... a moment that will be forever in our minds. He wants us to shoot him. His eyes smile into mine, communicating. To me. Not to *us*. Me. He wants *me* to shoot him.

Oh please, please, this can't be happening again. This can't be happening again. Thiscannotbehappeningagain.

"Drop the blade, asshole!" my voice is high-pitched, like a girl's. "Drop the blade!" Then I hear myself begging. "Don't make me do this again. Please, *please* drop the blade." I don't want to be here. *Idon'twanttobehere.*

"I'm going to cut the little shit on onnnnnne," the voice oozes as slowly as tree sap, his fish eyes locked on mine. "Tennnnnn, ninnnnnne, eeeeeeight…"

Mitchell's gun and mine point at the man's face. There is just enough clearance above the boy's head for a shot. A dangerous one but it's all we—

Tommy brushes past me toward the bed, holding up his empty palms as he did with the street boxer yesterday.

"Tommy, no!" I urge hoarsely. "He can't be talked out of—"

"Let me help you, sir," my partner says, as if talking to a confused elderly person who has walked away from his care facility. "First give me the knife."

The man's eyes are empty, like a dumb animal's. "… sevvvvvven, siiiiiix…"

Tommy stops three feet in front of the man's knees. "Just give me the knife."

I sidestep to see around him. "Tommy, back away. Damn-it, Tommy…"

The naked man turns his head slowly, mechanically like a robot. His eyes widen and he grins ugly. "Heeeere's my knife, Tommy boyeeeeee." His knife hand quick-flicks out and back, a soundless streak of silver.

Tommy yelps, jerking his hand upward past his head, a fan of red droplets in its wake.

What the hell?

He spins toward me, his hand in front of his face, his eyes staring in disbelief at three cleanly severed fingers dangling by thin flaps of skin. Blood arcs from the raw meat.

The smiling man returns the knife to the boy's small neck and then rotates his head toward me, staccato like, until his eyes meet mine. Jimmy has moved to the side just enough that I can see the man's—shit!—erect penis.

I aim at the freak's nose, just as I did at the tweaker two months earlier. Got to stop his brain so he doesn't cut as he dies.

The man's mouth turns up into a malevolent smile. He resumes counting, but faster. "Fivefourthreetwo—" The blade begins to slice.

Mitchell's gun explodes.

I'm squeezing my trigger—

Movement off to my side. Tommy's hand. Waving in the air. Something splatters across my nose and mouth. Wet.

I fire.

I'm seeing everything in ultra detail, in living color, in high definition, in 3-D. The man remains upright, his smiling face now blood-spotted. Red oozes from a hole in his shoulder. The butcher knife has stopped cutting but remains against the boy's neck. I fire at the man's left eyeball but I can't hear my shots. I hear Mitchell's but not mine. He fires three rounds in succession. Or am I firing?

Holes appear in the man's face: one over his left eyebrow, one in the center of his forehead, one at the corner of his mouth.

The knife drops to the rug and, clutching the boy tightly against his chest, the man falls back onto the bed, his dick still hard. I want to shoot it. Shoot it off. Empty all my remaining rounds into his crotch.

"Cease fire, Mitch! Cease fire!" My voice, I think.

From cacophony, to a vacuum of silence. The silence is worse.

Acrid smell of gun smoke. Eyes watering.

Mitchell and I shuffle-step toward the edge of the bed, our guns thrust forward. My face is on fire and it's hard to breathe.

Blood rivers from the man's neck, down onto the boy's face still nestled under the unshaven chin, and down onto the lad's small chest. More blood pours from holes in the man's forehead and left eye.

Those must be my rounds.

From behind me, Tommy's pained voice: "Damndamn-damndamn!"

From in front, the boy whimpers.

"Come on, son," I say softly, prying the dead arms away from him. "It's over. You're safe now." I quick-glance at Tommy; he's leaning against the door frame looking at his hand. "Tell radio to get us an ambulance for the boy. Neck cut. And one for yourself. Ask for a shooting team. Tell them the suspect's fatal."

I glance at Tommy's severed fingers; I can taste his blood and feel it on my face.

"The boy okay?" Mitchell asks, his voice suspicious, desperate. I lift the boy into my arms. "That blood on him… it's the perp's, right?"

"Yes," I snap. "Of course it's the perp's." I pull my head back so I can see the boy clearly. "He's just in shock. The cut looks superficial…"

A cold chill shivers my body.

"What?" Mitchell asks, stepping toward me. "Oh… my… God!"

Blood trickles from a hole a couple inches below the hollow of the boy's neck. It mingles with the other blood that was streaming down onto him seconds ago.

"Ohshitohshitohshit!" My voice sounding like there's a pillow over my face. My legs begin to buckle, but I fight it and move toward the door, still cradling the boy in my arms. Tommy moves out of my way. "He's been hit!" I scream. "He's been hit!"

I bolt across the hall, down the stairs, across the burgundy carpet and out the front door, nearly slamming into two uniform officers on the porch.

"He's been hit! No time to wait for an ambulance. Let's get him to Emmanuel."

"Over here," the larger of the two officers says, pointing toward their marked car.

"What's happening?" the boy's mother calls out, as another woman guides her hurriedly across the lawn. "Is Jimmy okay?" The friend says something to her and the mother stumbles, dropping to one knee. "My boy? Oh my God! My Jimmy! Is he all right?"

I can't tear my eyes from the mother. There's a windstorm in my head, a hurricane. No a twister. Is there that much difference, sound wise? The survivors on the news always describe the destructive wind as sounding like a freight train. They're right. It does.

"Take Sam and the boy to Emmanuel, Ed," the big officer says, his hand reaching for my shoulder. "Sam, you don't look so good. Let Ed take the boy."

"No!" I say. Maybe I screamed it.

The officer jerks his hand back as if burned. "Okay, okay. Follow Ed, then. I'll call for another car to take the mother."

He turns and walks quickly toward the two women as I drop into the passenger seat. "Ma'am, he's going to be fine," I hear the big officer say calmly. "We'll have a car here in a moment to take you to the hospital."

I maneuver Jimmy so that his back is against my chest, his mop of brown hair below my chin, just as the naked man had positioned him minutes earlier. The boy's hair smells of blood and shampoo. His mother probably insisted that he take a bath this morning. If he's like I was at seven, he probably tried to negotiate his way out of it. My mom always won, just as Jimmy's must have. What is it with boys and baths? Why do kids always—

The side of my head whacks the passenger window, snapping me back to the boy's limp weight against my chest and the car's acceleration that's pressing me back into the seat. My head fills with the awful sounds of squealing tires, the incoherence of the police radio, and the hysterical wail of the siren. I'm not crying but my eyes are tearing so heavily that I can't see anything clearly.

The driver shouts something into the mic. "Shot boy," is all I can make out. The words bounce in my skull like a ping-pong ball: *Shot boy. Shot boy, shot boy, shotboyshotboyboyboy...*

Did the driver just call my name?

I look over at him.

He points at the boy's chest.

I peer around Jimmy's head. My forearm, which had been pressing against the bleeding bullet hole, has slipped down a few inches. His blood has filled the space between my arm and his body, and it's cascading over my wrist and down onto his bare legs. I snatch a pocket notebook off the dash and press it against his chest wound.

"It's going to be fine, son," I say into his ear. "You're okay. Just hold on…"

The boy suddenly becomes heavier. I twist about to better see his face.

"Oh shit shit shit. I think he's stopped breathing."

We slide around a corner and the officer literally stomps the throttle, pressing me back into my seat so hard that I have to struggle against the invisible force to turn the boy around far enough so I can see his face. Slack mouth. Partially shut eyes. Chest not moving.

I tilt his head back and breathe into his mouth. I pull away. Nothing. "Come on, son." I breathe into him again. And again.

Impossibly, the siren screams louder, more desperate. We careen around a corner.

"I think I saw his chest rise," the officer shouts, fighting the steering wheel as he corners again barely slowing.

"Come on," I whisper, searching for a pulse on the boy's wrist. "Comeoncomeoncomeon." I feel my chest tightening. Hard to breathe. I gasp for a moment… got to get some air… got to give it to the boy. I'm breathing raggedly. Can't… get… enough… oxygen.

"Half a block, Sam," the uniform officer yells. He touches my upper arm. "You okay? Hey Sam! Stay with me. Keep working on the kid. Come on; stay focused. One more turn. Okay, we're here. There's ER people out front."

*

"What were you thinking, Tommy?" I shout at the big detective, as I lean over the front of his desk, my hands gripping the edge to keep them from attacking him. He stares wide-eyed at my blood-soaked shirt and slacks as he scrunches himself deep into his chair, holding his heavily bandaged hand and trembling like a fall leaf. It's all I can do to restrain myself from leaping on him and unleashing my rage. "Gun holstered, stepping in front of Mitch and me like that? What the hell were you doing?"

Tommy's eyes dart to the other detectives who sit motionless behind their desks. "I… I thought I could talk to the man." To me, his voice like a child's, "I'm a good… talker. I…"

"You-fucked-up-my-shot," I whisper. "You got in the way and you flung blood in my face." I bellow: "You screwed up my clear shot!" I charge around to the side of his desk, my hands formed into claws.

"Sam!" Mark's voice. "Sam, get in my office. Now!"

I spin around and see my friend standing outside his office door. "Did the hospital call?" I shout. Every detective turns toward the lieutenant. It's been four hours since the shooting.

"No. Not yet. Now, get in here." Mark looks at the others. "Everyone get back to work. I'll let you know when I hear something."

I feel every set of eyes on me as I walk toward the boss's office. Are they waiting for me to go totally nuts? Roll around on the floor, maybe? Wail? Thump the dog shit out of Tommy? Where the hell is Mitchell? They still interviewing him?

I'm teetering on the brink. Don't know if I want to cry or leap out the thirteenth floor window. I left a message with Tiff at the Public Defender's office but she hasn't called back. Why did I call her, anyway? I wish I hadn't.

I keep seeing the little boy's ghostly-pale face. The streaming blood. His partially closed, unseeing eyes. His unmoving chest.

My arms felt so empty when an ER nurse reached into the car and took him from me and laid him carefully on a gurney. How small he looked lying there, so fragile. So sad. A moment later, I was half running behind the gurney as the white coats slammed through the double doors into the ER. One of the nurses, a woman, called out "We got a pulse" followed with "But not much of one to brag about."

But not much of one to brag about?

Just as I thought that those were an unprofessional choice of words to use and that "but not much of one" is better than none at all, which is what I got when I checked his pulse in the police car, my knees buckled. An orderly and a uniformed officer prevented me from curling down to the floor.

They guided my stumbling self to a couch in a small room just off ER; it might have been a little chapel. My memory is fuzzy now, but I vaguely recall hearing the mother screaming out in the hall and an assortment of voices trying to calm her. I started to go out there, but the officer stopped me with a gentle hand on my arm, saying kindly that it wasn't a good idea. He held onto me until I sat. He was a good cop but I don't remember his name, or his face.

I was still sitting there when all the brass arrived. First, I told Mark what happened, then the Deputy Chief, the police chaplain, and I think a couple of others. When I said that I was going to remain at the hospital, Mark and the DC shook their heads, and Mark ordered me back to Detective's to make a statement. A hospital spokeswoman said she would call with updates. We have yet to hear a word from her and it's been four, almost four and a half hours.

I know deep in my gut that my bullet hit Jimmy and the thought of that has doubled me over with intestinal cramps a couple times. Yes, Mitchell fired, but I know—I *know*—it was my bullet. I had a perfect shot, just as I had two months earlier with the tweaker. I aimed my first one at the man's medulla oblongata, just below his nose so that the bullet would stop the scum fuck dead in his tracks, stop him from reflexively cutting the boy. Then Tommy bumped my arm.

It had to be my shot that did it. It had. To be. My shot. Not Mitchell's. Mine.

"Sit down, Sam." Mark says, his voice addressing me as a friend, not a subordinate. "You were about to unleash your Bruce Lee on Tommy?"

I sit heavily, arms crossed, like an angry, defiant teen. I look through the blinds out into the work area at the detectives mingling about in groups of twos and threes. Mitchell, still in uniform, comes in and sits at one of the empty desks. The others look at him but quickly turn away when he looks back. I wonder how his interview went. Is he writhing in guilt, too? Or is he blaming me? Yeah, that's probably it. He knows I shot the boy. He knows—

"Sam?"

I jerk my head toward my friend, surprised that I'm sitting in his office. My brain quickly plays catch up.

"You got to keep it together, Sam. A lot of shit's coming down in the next few days and weeks. The press is going to eat us like free hors d'oeuvres. The other coppers look up to you. Do it for you and do it for them, too."

I look at him, fighting unsuccessfully to hold back tears. After a moment, I nod. "I understand, Mark... but a child... it's... it's too much to bear. Too much..."

He nods compassionately, his eyes glistening. "Your interview went well. I know it's hard when Homicide grills you and you've gotten it twice in two months. That's why I sat in this time. There will be more, you know the procedure. They'll grill the hell out of you so there are no surprises for the press to salivate over. There will be a grand jury, too. Maybe a public inquest. It won't be cut and dry like last time. They're going to come at you hard. Count on it. And count on the media stirring the citizens into a feeding frenzy."

I'm trying to listen to Mark but it's hard to focus with all the images, sounds, and smells ripping through my skull. When he said "grand jury," I heard the gunshots in that bedroom. When he said "the media will," I felt the little boy's limp body against my chest.

"Tiff's here."

That I hear clearly. Mark is looking behind me and making a come-in gesture with his fingers.

I stand, spin around, and nearly collapse into Tiff's arms. "Tiff…" I'm sobbing like a toddler and trembling within her embrace. I lean my head on her shoulder.

She pats my back, no doubt confused. "Sam? I'm sorry I didn't get your message sooner." When she leans back to better see me, I burrow my face into her neck. "What's…? I was in a meeting and…" I feel her head turn. "My God, Mark, I can't believe what has happened. I just heard on the radio about a police shooting. I don't understand… what's going on with the police department?"

I feel my face tense. From over her shoulder, I see a few of the guys glance over at us, no doubt uncertain as to how to take her question. Oblivious, Tiff leans her head back. "Sam? What on earth?" Then, without compassion, "Why are you crying?" She looks back at Mark, and says, as if I'm not in the room, "I'm not understanding. Sam left a message that he needed me to come down. Does this have anything to do with that little boy who was killed?"

I jolt as if electrocuted and push back from her.

"Killed!" Mitchell shouts from across the room. "What did you say?"

Confused, Tiff looks at my face, toward the guys out in the work area, and back at me. Her eyes drop to my bloody clothes. "Sam! What in the hell…"

"What did you hear," I whisper.

Her eyes stare at my shirt and pants. "Why are you covered—"

I enunciate each word. "What. Did. You. Hear?"

She takes a step back from me "They said on my car radio that a boy had been taken hostage and that he had just died in the hospital. An anonymous source said the police…" Her eyes travel up my body to meet mine. "… killed him."

"What the fuck!" I hear Mitchell bellow. Out of the corner of my eye, I see him through the window spring to his feet and hurl something across the room. "What the fuck!" he shouts again.

I pinch my eyes closed and cover my face with my hands. Other voices are shouting. There's pounding, like a fist on a desk. I'm dizzy. I lower my hands in case I fall but I don't open my eyes. I don't want to open them. I don't want to see anything. So dizzy.

Why are Tiff and I dancing? Why is she leading me…

"Sam?" Tiff's voice. I open my eyes.

"Wha…" I'm slumped against her, my face pressed into her chest as she struggles to hold me up.

From behind me, Mark is shouting. Into the telephone?

"Nonononono!" Pederson's voice, I think, from out in the work area. "We have to hear it from a citizen who hears it on a car *radio*?"

"Sam?" Tiff's voice. "Sam, what is it? Mark? Help me. Damn-it! Would someone please talk to me?"

Hands on me. Mark's and Tiff's guiding me to a chair.

"Trash can," I manage.

Mark grabs his wastepaper basket and thrusts it under my chin just in time for me to dry heave into it.

In my peripheral, I see Tiff step back from me. "I don't understand…" She sounds like she's a mile away. "Was Sam…?"

I feel Mark's hand on my shoulder. "Sam, Tommy and Mitchell, that uniform officer out there, were at the scene of a hostage situation. Sam and Mitchell fired. The perp was killed and the boy was hit. We've been waiting for a call from the hospital on his condition. We hadn't heard anything until now, until you told us."

I look up at Tiff. Her face is pale and twisted ugly as if she just smelled something awful. "Sam… was there." A statement. She takes another step back and clasps her hands against her chest. Is she going to wipe them off on her blouse?

From behind me: "Excuse me, lieutenant."

"What?" Mark snaps.

I twist around. It's the Public Information Officer, a ridiculously handsome man with a spray-on tan, neatly trimmed gray hair, and wearing his usual gray Giorgio Armani.

"What do you need, Adams?" Mark barks.

"The press is on my ass," he says around a wad of gum. "Can you give me enough for a press release? I need a few details to do what I can to sugarcoat the bad shoot."

Bad shoot.

I spring out of my chair, slamming both my palms against Adam's chest, and push him through the doorway and onto the closest desk, scattering papers, files, and a stack of mug shots.

Mark's voice: "Sam!"

Tiff's voice: "Sam, what are you…?"

I push myself off Adams and spin toward Tommy, who stands quickly and begins walking hurriedly in the opposite direction.

"Sam!" It's Mark from somewhere outside of my head. "Get back in here."

I do a fast zigzag around the desks to cut off the big detective. "You fucked up my shot," I hear someone say, menacingly. "You fucked up my shot!" It's my voice.

Mark from somewhere: "Sam, stop! Harrison, Pederson, get Tommy out of here!"

Several detectives scramble to block me, tentatively, like men having to corner a dangerous animal. I stop. Tommy is hustled across the room, out into the hall and probably toward the elevator.

As quickly as my rage erupted, it ebbs. Within half a dozen seconds, I'm back in the moment. My arms relax and my fists unclench. I stare unseeingly at the floor.

The remaining detectives form a loose circle around me, every face fearful. Some of these guys are very old friends and I've just forced them to have to corral me like a berserk stallion.

"I'm sorry," I say, so softly to the floor that they probably don't hear me.

"Take him home," Mark says, as he and Tiff move up on each side of me. Apparently, now I'm something that has to be dealt with, a wild and out-of-control *thing*. "I'll call you later, Tiff. He'll have to come in for more interviews, but take him home and make him sleep. No coffee, no stimulants. Milk and rest only."

"I'm sorry, Mark," I mumble. I look over at the PIO who is standing now and shakily straightening his suit. "Adams, sorry to you, too."

"Go home, Sam," Mark says. "I'll call you later."

"Yes. Thank you."

*

The kitchen phone is ringing as we come through the living room door; seems louder than usual. Tiff goes into the kitchen and grabs it.

"It's Mark." She extends the receiver toward me, avoiding my eyes, then turns and heads toward the bedroom.

Tiff's been quiet all the way home. At one point, I started to tell her what had happened, but she interrupted me and said it might be best for me to just sit calmly and not talk about it. Good concept, but it was how she said it: acerbic with an almost imperceptible wrinkle of her nose. *Almost* imperceptible.

"Mark."

"Sorry to call so soon, buddy."

"But?"

"Is Tiff there? Will she be staying home with you?"

"I don't think so."

Long pause, then, "The deputy chief just called."

"Yeah?"

Silence.

"Come on, Mark."

"There were nine millimeter hits in both the suspect... and the boy."

I claw at my face, as if doing so might stop my flesh from burning. My phone hand is shaking so hard that the receiver is tapping a Morse Code message against the side of my head: *Y-o-u d-i-d i-t.*

"Mitchell carries a Forty-Five," Mark's voice says from the bottom of a fifty-gallon barrel of oil. "There were six Forty-Five rounds in the perp, and two Nines. There was only one round in the kid... I'm sorry. It was your weapon. That's unofficial but—"

I smash the receiver against the refrigerator, sending hundreds of pieces of plastic raining down on the tile.

*

I'm in my garage, slamming my fists over and over into the hanging heavy bag, each hit landing on the brown leather harder and faster than the last, my bare upper body dripping sweat, my shoulders, elbows, and wrists aching. I ignore my bleeding knuckles and I ignore Tiff when she steps out the kitchen door and leans her shoulders against the wall.

"I just talked to Mark," she says flatly, her arms hugging her middle as if she were cold. "I called him back when you wouldn't tell me what he said."

I change to triple blows - jab, cross, hook; jab, cross, hook. Blood from the torn flesh across my knuckles splatters the leather, my chest, the cement floor, and the scattered dumbbells lying about.

"My God, Sam..."

I clinch the bag with one arm to keep from collapsing and look at my other hand, blinking dumbly at the bloody mess. My lips curl back as the pain from the raw flesh finally penetrates my dull brain. I take a couple of deep breaths to will it away. I look at Tiff and start to tell her that my hands hurt, but

I have no energy to speak. Instead, I rest the side of my face against the side of the bloody bag.

"That boy is dead," she whispers, shaking her head.

I jerk my head back as if she'd slapped me. Never have her eyes looked at me as they are now... as if I were loathsome, something... vile, like dog shit on the floor.

Her beautiful face twists ugly. "I don't understand, Sam. Talk to me. What hap—"

"Shut up," I hear myself whisper, without thinking it first. I look away for a moment. Then I feel that extraordinary heat in my face again, growing ever hotter. I look back at Tiff and feel my eyes narrow, burning like embers. Then just short of yelling, I say it again. "Shut up!"

If my intensity frightens her, she doesn't let on. Instead, she drops her arms and looks at me, dazed. "Talk to me, Sam." When I don't respond, she says, "I can't even begin to fathom—"

"Shut up!" I scream. "Shut up!" I slap the bag, leaving a bloody palm print on its side. Tears stream down my cheeks. "Why are you looking at me like that? I..."

I want her to hold me.

I want her the hell away from me.

"Just... get out! *Get* out!"

"My God, Sam. What's happened to you?." She turns and rushes back into the house.

I step toward the door, then stop, my body rigid, chest heaving as if I had been running sprints. I turn back toward the bag, my arms hanging limply at my side, my eyes unfocused, unseeing. My heart thumps a hundred miles-per-hour, each beat clarifying the image of the naked man drawing the knife across the boy's neck.

The boy. The boy. The feel of his body... limp.

I'm unraveling. My life. My mind.

I slam a front kick into the hundred-pound bag, sending it nearly to the ceiling before it comes rushing back toward me. I angle step and meet it with a hard roundhouse kick, smashing it with my shin and sending it into a spasm of bucks and jerks.

Inside the house, the phone rings and rings and rings, just as it's been doing nonstop ever since we got home at seven o'clock. Tiff was answering it—the one in the living room, since I'd trashed the kitchen phone—telling people that I'm not available. Now it just rings and rings and...

Clicking footsteps out in the driveway.

"Tiff?" I poke the red button by the kitchen door, which sets the big garage door into upward motion. When it's high enough, I see her shoes, part of a suitcase, and the bottom of her open white car door.

"Tiff. Wait." By the time the garage door rolls all the way up, she's behind the wheel and pulling her door shut. A few weeks ago, I would have run to the driver's window and begged her to stay. That was a few weeks ago.

She starts the engine and turns on her headlights, laser beams that pierce into my eye sockets, which I try to shield with a bloody hand. When the Honda begins backing down the driveway, I step backwards, stumbling over one of my dumbbells. My arms flail madly as I sway like a drunk, but somehow I stay upright. Tiff backs out into the street, stops, and accelerates away.

*

It's three a.m., I'm in bed, and I just realized that I can never leave my house—ever.

After Tiff drove off a few hours ago, I slumped to the garage cement and laid there for an hour, maybe three or four, I don't know. I didn't weep and I didn't get angry; I just closed my eyes and breathed in the raw night air that drifted in through the open garage door. After a while, I opened them and stared hard at the bare light bulbs hanging from my ceiling, enjoying the punishing throb in my head. I eventually fell asleep, a cold, wet, slipping-in-and-out-of-consciousness slumber.

Sometime after midnight, maybe one o'clock, a white cat strayed through the open garage door and poked its wet nose into my ear, startling the hell out of me, and getting me to my feet faster than I could have on my own volition. After I caught my breath and shooed it away, I went to poke the button to close the big door, but something gave me pause: a feeling that someone was watching me.

I peered out into the dark but didn't see anything. I walked part way out onto the driveway and looked back at the porch, around the yard, into the deep night shadows made by the giant fir tree near the sidewalk, and up and down the street. Nada. Just my paranoia running Code Three, I guess. So I shut the big door, went through the kitchen, down the hall, and into my bedroom where I crashed onto the top of the covers.

That's where I am now, a couple hours later and still awake.

I like to think I'm good at compartmentalizing; that I can focus on whatever I'm thinking about and nothing else. But this time—I killed a child. It's just so overwhelming. How can I ever put the shooting into its own terrible box so I can think about anything else?

I roll onto my side and draw up my knees. I can smell Tiff on my sheets. Damn, that was an ugly scene. Ugly, but not a surprise. Was I wrong?

A few months ago, several weeks before the first shooting, I joked with her that if we were ever confronted by an angry outlaw biker clutching a kitchen knife, she would try to understand his sad childhood, give him a big, warm hug, send a fruit basket to his family, and offer him free legal representation. Then the guy would stab her.

Tiff argued that without hesitation, I would shoot the armed guy dead with all the rounds in my weapon before learning that he was simply an upset, leather jacket- and black boots-wearing gourmet chef, who had just cut into his prize-winning soufflé to discover that it's raw.

It was our fun inside joke until I capped the tweaker.

"Did you have to kill him?" she said to me on the phone. That was a gut punch. I would expect such a question from a blockheaded citizen, but not from my girlfriend.

Hey, look at me. I'm doing it. I'm compartmentalizing.

Tiff and I were no longer an item when the shooting happened but she was somewhat supportive in the weeks that followed, mostly with an occasional phone call or email. There was always a theatrical flavor to it, though, as if she were playing the role of a sympathetic friend, ex partner or whatever the hell we were. Are. One time when she called, she quizzed me for more details than what little I had initially told her and what had been on the news. Actually, it had been more like an interrogation. I somehow managed not to react to her accusatory, left-wing attorney questioning style. Instead, I just answered her straightforward in hopes that she might see the light and understand that sometimes there are dangerous predator types who need killing so that others can live. But people like her will never let reality get in the way of what they deem to be the truth.

I couldn't see her face on the phone but I swear I could hear it scrunch up when I told her about deliberately aiming at the tweaker's medulla oblongata. I said that had I shot him anywhere else he would have still been able to shoot the old man. I told her killing the medulla oblongata instantly kills the trigger finger. By then I could tell that she was no longer listening. I was hurt and angry by Tiff's reaction and she was upset by what I had told her. I decided not to continue. Of course, not talking about it made things just as tense as talking about it. So we both resumed our acting roles, me pretending that everything was okay and Tiff continuing her phony supportive role.

The booty calls were pretty darn awesome, though.

Now I've killed two more people. One—God, I can hardly even think it—a child. Why couldn't Tiff have at least faked a little support for a day or two instead of being instantly revolted by me? Frightened by me. Why couldn't she have… oh forget it. Water under the bridge.

Okay, I'm done thinking about this. I'm closing the Tiff compartment.

I sit up, scoot over to the edge of the bed and gaze at the backs of my raw hands under the nightstand light. My big knuckles show some abrasions, but they aren't as bad as all the blood around the garage would indicate. Man-oh-man, do they ever ache, though. All the way to my elbows.

I walk over to the bedroom window and peer out into the night, but it's my reflection that dominates the view. My face is a carnival exhibit.

"Right here folks," I say aloud, sounding like a midway barker. "The face of a real-life killer in captivity. Throw him a peanut… .wait, wait, throw him a bullet and he'll kill again for you. It's what he does."

I back away from the window, breathing hard. "I can't go outside," I say aloud. "If I do, I'll kill again. '*It's what he does.*'"

Twenty-eight years of martial arts training, six black belts, two national championships and I've never hurt anyone in anger. I've used my training on the job hundreds of times, and one time off duty when I rescued a woman being attacked in a movie theater parking lot. I've avoided many more fights by being aware of what's going on around me, knowing how to read dangerous situations, and knowing how to talk the biggest and meanest suspects into the backseat of my police car without having to resort to force, something I've always been proud of.

So how did I go from that, to killing three people?

I look beyond my reflection, at the street and sidewalk bathed in the puke-yellow streetlight. Maybe I'm being forced to do it. Yeah, that's it.

No, that's stupid. What kind of force would it be?

Don't know, but it's obviously out there and it's obviously making me kill. The evidence is in the morgue, they're stacking up in there.

So if it's out there somewhere, it's probably waiting for me. *Come on out Sam boy. And don't forget to bring your gun. You got more killin' to do.*

Bite me. I'm not going out.

There, that was simple. Like my approach to the martial arts. Keepin' it simple. I'm staying in because when I'm in, it, that big, evil *it* out there can't make me shoot anyone.

I turn around and lean against the windowsill. "Okay, this is ridiculous," I say to my reflection in my closet-door mirror across the room. "I'm not even going to think about how little sense that makes."

Still, it's true. Don't leave the house, don't leave the house, *don't leave the house.*

I turn back to the window. As if to taunt the beast outside, I lean my forehead against the cold glass, fogging it with my breath. As the fog dissipates, the only beast I see is that same white cat out on the sidewalk, walking slowly, sensuously, ever ready to pounce or to flee. It alerts on a blue car that passes slowly under the streetlight, a Toyota, I think.

I turn and flop down onto the bed, face first. Ahh, sweet blackness.

CHAPTER SIX

It's noon. I can't believe I've slept a full nine hours and I'm doubly amazed that I'm still so exhausted. The two big knuckles on both my hands feel like they've been skinned because, well, they have been, and my shoulders and legs have barely recuperated from last night's assault on the heavy bag.

What triple amazes me, as I sit here on the edge of my bed scratching myself, is that now I want to leave the house. My middle-of-the-night thoughts convinced me that I would never go outside again, but the four walls are suddenly making me feel like a caged panther. Talk about your extreme convictions. Is this another one of those "normal reactions to an abnormal event" that Kari talks about? Is going crazy a normal reaction?

I stumble into the bathroom, do my thing and then walk down the hall to the kitchen. I pull the coffee pot out from under the shelf, hesitate, and push it back. If I don't get out of here, I'll go nuts. Okay, I've already gone nuts. Maybe I'll just cap a round in my own medulla oblongata. I sputter-laugh at that and then stop abruptly. I'm definitely going nutso. I'm getting out of here and I'm going to walk the three blocks to the Coffee Bump.

Two minutes later, I'm dressed in jeans and a sweatshirt and heading toward the living room door.

I'm greeted by a warm morning sun, a soft breeze, and a newspaper lying on the porch, its headline blaring: **Cop Slays Child.**

The bold font lands three hard punches into my heart: Cop. Slays. Child. The earth tilts and I stumble back.

"Son-of-a-bitch!"

A crow answers my curse from high atop a tree.

"Damn them!" I shout, kicking the paper off the porch and into a holly bush. The damn media.

Wait…

I don't subscribe to the newspaper.

My cop instinct kicks in. I quick-scan my yard, the sidewalk, and the street beyond. Nothing. So who would have put it here? Only my friends and a couple of old partners know my address, I have an unlisted phone number and my Dodge pickup is registered to the precinct.

Mark? He knows I'm not coming in today so maybe he left it so I'd know what to expect. Tiff? Maybe she left it as a dig? Could she be that mean? No, I refuse to believe that. Maybe it was a neighbor. A couple of them have never been friendly.

Damn. A simple newspaper lying on my porch is charging my fight-or-flight juices, and I'm leaning toward flight—back into the house. Not because I'm afraid, but because I don't want to hurt anyone again.

No no no. I can't go back inside. I got to face it… *it*.

I scan the yard and street once more—a school bus passes, a couple of cars—and I pull the door shut behind me. I stand on the porch for a long moment, as if I were on the ledge of a thirty-story high-rise deciding whether to jump across the yawning space to the ledge of another roof.

I inhale, counting slowly to four, hold it in for a count of four, exhale for a count of four and hold empty for a count of four. Combat breathing. It's a technique I've taught for years to cops and my martial arts students as a fast way to get calm and collected.

By the time I finish three cycles, my boiling juices drop to a simmer. I'm almost calm. Now I got to step off the porch before the feeling passes. Come on. Come on.

I step.

My heart thumps against my chest with frightening intensity. I force myself to take another step, and another. I make it to the sidewalk where I pause under the big Douglas fir to take a couple more combat breaths. Then I begin to walk, actually walk, heading west toward the strip mall three blocks away.

A couple of painless minutes later I'm at the end of the block. One down, two more to go. I'm feeling better. My anxiety seems to be lessening, the spring air is clean and cool, and the lawns and trees smell invigorating. Maybe I'll get a breakfast roll with my big Americano.

Two blocks down now. One more to go.

I'm there.

The tables on the sidewalk outside the Coffee Bump are filled, and a line of folks wanting a noontime, four-dollar cup of caffeine stretches outside the doors. I hesitate for a moment, not sure if I want to wait. Okay, I'll wait; it can't take longer than fifteen minutes.

I step to the rear of the line behind a woman in a dark blue suit reading a paperback. She turns slightly, looking at me over black rimmed glasses. "Need a jolt, huh?" she asks with a teasing smile.

I nod. I'm not in the mood for chit chat no matter how attractive this woman.

"Me, too. Been one of those days. Know what I mean?"

I nod again. Indeed, I do, lady. Indeed I do.

She turns back to her novel, frowns, then looks back at me. "Excuse me, but are you… you look like… aren't you that police officer in the paper today who—"

"No," I say quickly. Got to get out of here. It was a big mistake leaving the house. I turn to leave, but a heavyset man in a blue flannel shirt blocks my way. Judging by the look of contempt on his face, he's not here for a caramel frap.

"Why you lyin' to the lady, Dee-tective Reeves?" the guy says in a voice like a deep blast from a tuba. "We all saw it on the news," he spits, "read it in the paper, and saw *your* picture."

"It *was* you," the woman declares, looking at me with the same face Tiff did last night. "Oh my—"

"No it wasn't," I say quickly, but lamely. I sidestep around Tuba Man but he steps with me so that I'm between him and a seated man typing on a laptop. Conversations at the outdoor tables stop. My intestines churn as if trying to digest an old baseball mitt. I can't be trapped here; I don't want to hurt him. Please don't let me hurt anyone again.

"I'm leaving," I say. "Just get out of my way."

"What's the big hurry, Dee-tective?" Tuba Man sneers. "Afraid? Ha! It's a hell of a lot different when you're facing a grown man, huh?"

"I'm leaving," I say. Did that come out as whiny as I think it did?

Tuba Man widens his stance, his face turning from red to purple. Who is this guy? A relative? A cop hater? He tilts his head a little and narrows his eyes to mere slits.

"Look, pal," I say, my voice shaky. "Don't write a check your ass can't cash."

The big man smiles. "Now that's some serious false bravado, twitchy boy. Scared 'cause you ain't got your gun?" He juts his jaw, giving me a slow up-and-down.

I move to step around him but again he blocks my way. The guy on the laptop grabs his computer and scurries away.

"You aren't going anywhere, Dee-tective," Tuba Guy says. "Time to man up."

If he isn't going to let me by, then I'm going through him. I'll—

A giant fist...

The world wobbles, tilts; Tuba Man drops below my field of vision, replaced by the underside of a green table umbrella and a roof overhang. My shoulders strike something, and that thing gives way and I'm falling again, but only for an instant before my back hits cement. A thought zips through my brain that if this were two days ago, I would tuck my chin to save my skull. Of course, two days ago, I wouldn't have been punched.

My head hits. A flash of white, a flood of red. Blackness...

Struggling through the black, through the silence... trying to move, trying to see.

A moment passes, a second, a minute. I don't know. I can hear something now. Sounds filtered through thick soup. What the sounds are I don't know, I can't...

Clarity now, and in surround sound. Chairs scraping on concrete. Voices. Shouting. A woman's scream.

"He's the son-of-a-bitch who killed the little boy." I think that was the woman with the paperback. Not flirting anymore, I guess.

"That cop who..."

"Fucking cops!"

The darkness turns to gray then to fog. I can see shapes… now clarity, in living HD. Gray concrete under me, table legs next to my head, and over there, several pairs of feet. *Anyone want to lend me a hand?* Above me a table umbrella. Noise to my left. I turn toward it and see, just inches away from me, heavy legs in blue jeans, brown boots. Doc Martens, I think. One of them rockets toward me. A hair-of-a-second later, I feel a jarring pain in my hip.

I'm still open to getting a helping hand here, folks.

From overhead, Tuba Man's voice shouts a barrage of curses, sprinkled with "Jimmy." I see the flash of brown boot and feel another shot of pain in my hip. Better there than in the ribs, I always say. Actually, it's better not to be kicked at all. Maybe he's trying for my ribs but he's a bad shot.

I have to get up… have to get up, have to…

A brown boot stomps my chest.

All goes red, but then a moment later, at least I think it's a moment, I can see again. That hurt. Hard to breathe.

The impact twisted me around a little, because now I see a different table, this one lying on its side; five or six people stand behind it, one of them the guy with the open laptop. He looks mad. Must have been his table.

Gosh, people, I hope my little boot party isn't disrupting your latte and biscotti.

The big legs in blue jeans come toward me again. I try to move, try to shield my head, but the command from my brain isn't getting to my muscles.

I flash to a kickboxing match about fifteen years ago, another time when I lost my brain/body connection for a moment. It wasn't a good thing then—it was one of my two losses—and it's not a good thing now. I close my eyes and try to roll into a ball, but again my muscles ignore me.

A woman screams. Chairs slide on cement again. I open my eyes, though wary of catching a boot toe in a socket. The big legs in blue jeans are still there but the boots are pointing away from me.

I move my head a little to see another set of feet in front of the boots, these wearing red converse. Tuba Man is saying something, but my ears are ringing too loudly for me to hear. I get just a hint of another voice, a gentle one, accented.

Ignoring the mad *taiko* drummer going ape bananas in my skull, I look up, squinting my eyes for clarity. I can see the bottom half of the fat man in blue jeans, his legs spread, arms at his sides, hands fisted. I can't see the other person, other than the motionless, red converse shoes between the big boots. If it were not for the dark pant legs, I'd swear the red shoes had been neatly arranged there, serenely side-by-side, as if no one were inside them. In contrast, the large, brown Doc martens are scooting, twisting and shuffling.

I want to warn Red Converse Man to look out for Tuba Man's sucker punch, but my neck muscles give out and the side of my head drops back onto the sidewalk. All I can see now are the motionless red shoes and the restless boots. Then they stop moving. The right boot rolls up on the toe. Is Tuba Man launching another sucker punch?

The red shoes disappear and an instant later, they reappear a couple of feet over. What the hell? One of the shoes disappears and at the same time, I hear a loud grunt, then another and another, like three short, single notes through a tuba. A second later, a fat face thumps onto the cement just inches from mine, its eyes closed.

For a fleeting weird instant, I have a disconnected thought that the white cat that nose-poked my ear last night when I was lying on my garage floor might stop by to nudge the fat man awake. I have to get out of here before it does.

Gotta get out of here... gotta get...

*

Hear birds. Feel warmth. Smell grass.

It's a peaceful place, wherever I am, and I want to stay here, to bask in the darkness and to avoid the light. Oh man! Gigantic pain in my forehead. Then like the voiceover in an infomercial, *"But wait! There's more. You also get a humongous throb at the back of your head and, if you call right now, we'll throw in a crushing pain to your chest, ab-so-lutely free."*

The three-for-one price deal opens my eyes, but a searing brightness slams them shut. I examine the red behind my eyelids and mentally check out the pain in my body. It hurts like hell, but it's manageable. I've received worse when I fought full contact... well, not quite worse, but I can handle this. I turn my throbbing head to the side and open my eyes again, just a slit this time. Green. I open them a little more—more green—and then all the way open. Lots of green.

Grass all around, trees, a light-cool breeze, a dog sniffing a bush a few yards away. I look down and see wooden slats. A park bench? I'm lying on a park bench?

"How is the head?"

I snap open my eyes and start to get up. "Uuugh!" I close them again.

"Beaucoup pain, I bet. The back of your head, too, where it bounced off the cement. That had to have hurt." The voice is coming from above me.

Clenching my teeth, I force my eyes open and struggle to sit up. I twist my body toward the voice and cop-scan the man sitting at the end of the bench: white, early sixties, longish gray-ing hair, wearing a white overshirt, and black slacks. I'm sur-prised to see that he's not Asian. He sounded Asian.

"Who are you?"

"Just a guy in the park," he says in a kindly voice. "Thought maybe you needed company while you meditated in the hori-zontal position about how you failed to block that punch.

Is this old guy busting my chops? And what's with the accent? He sounds like Johnny Tran, my Vietnamese brown belt.

"You know, it is said that we must embrace pain and burn it as fuel for our journey. Well, you got lots of fuel today, I think. As Yoda would say, 'Filled up your tank, you did.'"

What the hell is this guy saying? I touch the back of my head. "How'd I get here?" I can vaguely remember a big guy sucker punching me. After that, just images: red tennis shoes, chair legs, a fat face.

"Maybe the real question is: why? Why are you here? Why does your head hurt?"

I turn my face up toward the sun and close my eyes. It feels good and it eases the pain in my forehead a little, but not the pain in the back of my skull.

"I got sucker punched." I say, looking back at him.

The older man shakes his head as if the thought amuses him. "Maybe you should learn self-defense if you are going to go around picking fights."

"I was in line for coffee, pal. I hardly go around picking fights. I teach martial arts."

The man giggles, child-like. "'Your powers are weak, old man.' That is from *Star Wars*." He shakes his head again and looks up at the leaves flittering in the soft breeze. "What are you going to tell your students when they see that big knot on your forehead?"

Now I'm pissed. "*Star Wars!*" I shout. "Who-the-hell are you? Why are you—" I start to stand but a thunderclap of pain simultaneously hits the front and back of my head, forcing me back down onto the bench.

"You should sit for a while," the man says, ignoring my shout. "It would be wise to get checked by a doctor. Personally, I do not think it is necessary. Of course, you are going to be sore. Why not just enjoy the park, the sun, and good air, and in an hour you will be good to go home. If you wish, I would be glad to go back across the street to the coffee shop to get you a cup. If *you* went you would just get into another fight."

I start to react to that but my head hurts too much. I slump, lowering my head, and clasping my hands in my lap.

"That is better," the man says. "You need your rest."

"Yes," I hear myself mumble. "I just need… a moment to…"

I'm holding Jimmy's limp body against my chest but we're not in the police car speeding to the hospital. We're in some dark place, a room, maybe. I can't tell because there isn't anything around me but this park bench I'm sitting on, and Jimmy's dying body nestled in my arms. He slowly turns his head toward me and looks into my face. I nearly scream when I see his lifeless, glassy eyes looking at me, looking into me.

There's fresh blood on his purplish lips, and they're moving.

"Not much of a shot, are you?" he says, matter-of-factly, and in a clear, healthy voice that belies the gaping hole my bullet punched through his small chest.

I open my mouth to scream—

"Heeeere's Johnny!"

I jerk my head up, blinking several times.

"Jack Nicholson from *The Shining.* They shot the exteriors for that film right here in Oregon, up on your Mt. Hood." He's walking toward me carrying two paper cups. "I think you slept for a while. You either feel a lot worse or a heck of a lot worse."

"You're back," I say without enthusiasm, sitting up straighter. The dream fades from my brain but I can still feel the unspent scream lodged in my chest.

"You never got your coffee earlier. Thought maybe it might help diminish the pain from the thrashing you took."

He sits on the bench next to me again and extends a sixteen-ounce cup, the same size I was going to order. "You do not look like a frou-frou coffee drinker so I got you an Americano, double shot with a little cream. Green tea for me."

I take it and nod thanks. The guy's a pain but I need the jolt. "Why are you doing this?" I ask, removing the white plastic lid and blowing across the steaming surface.

The man crosses a leg and shrugs. "Got a soft spot for the down trodden, I guess."

I can't tell if these zingers are his way of being funny or if he's trying to provoke me. If it's the latter, it's working. "Listen, pal, if you..."

Red converse! He's wearing red converse shoes.

I feel my jaw drop. "It was you I saw when I was lying on the concrete? It was *you* who knocked that big guy to the ground. With a kick?"

"Guilty. One kick and two punches," he says with that childish giggle before he sips his tea. "Hard to be humble."

I lean toward him. "Why? I mean, thanks, but why?" I remembered how those red shoes seemed to disappear and reappear in a different spot—like magic. "Are you a martial artist? How old are you?"

"Because. You're welcome. Just lucky. And what was the other question? Oh, I'm old enough, thank you very much."

I look at him over the rim of my coffee. Eccentric dude with his red tennis shoes, long hair, the strange accent and flippant demeanor. The face shows his years, maybe even more than his birthday, but his stature and bearing is that of a Marine Corp officer. A Grandpa's face on a warrior's body. You don't see that very often. Not only did he not back away like all the other people, he stood up to the big guy, knocked him down, and then stuck around to look after me.

"How is it going?" the man asks, then sips. "What is the verdict?"

"What?"

"Your conclusion?"

"What are you talking about?"

"You are analyzing me. Trying to get a read on the handsome stranger. Interesting, am I not?"

That's it. He's gay. Tiff would love this. She always teases me about gay guys checking me out. "It's the muscles," she always said. "They think you're hard all over." Tiff. I feel a tug in my chest.

The man twists toward me, his eyes looking into mine. Oh man, here comes the hustle.

"You have a lot of *dukha* going on right now," he says gently. Compassionately?

A slight chill runs up my spine. He said 'right now.' What does he know about me? "*Dukha?*" I ask with a shrug.

His eyes penetrate mine for an unsettling moment. I don't know why his gaze is unsettling, but it is. He nods. "It means suffering. It is grasping for things that cannot be obtained. You got it up the kazoo. You will not be healed until you come to terms with it." He looks at me again for probably no more than three or four seconds, but it seems longer.

He stands, gulps his tea and drops his cup in a trash can behind the bench. "As Hannibal Lecter says, 'I do wish we could chat longer, but I am having an old friend for dinner.'" He makes with that giggle again. "I like that one. Get it? 'Old friend *for* dinner?' Anyway, I will be here tomorrow around noon." He nods at me, turns and heads out across the grass. "And," he says over his shoulder without stopping. "I am happily heterosexual. So do not get your hopes up."

"What! How did…"

He turns his head back toward the direction he's walking and giggles again. He lifts his hand and waves without looking back again.

I watch him walk toward the far parking lot. What the hell was all that about? I touch my tender forehead and then lightly rub my index finger on the back of my head. Man it hurts. My hip, too. I've been kicked harder there but that fact doesn't make it feel any better.

Peering through an opening in the park's trees, all looks normal over at the Coffee Bump, as if my assault never happened. There is no line of customers waiting outside and there are only a scattering of people sitting at the now orderly outside tables. What happened to Tuba Man? Did anyone call the police? How did Converse Man get me over here to this bench? I must out-weigh him by forty pounds. I look toward the parking lot.

The strange man looks back toward me for a moment, waves with both hands, and climbs into a blue Toyota.

*

"You rang the doorbell?"

"Can I come in?" Tiff asks.

"Of course," I say flatly, pushing the door open wider and stepping aside. "You have to ask?" I'm surprised to see her so soon after last night. With all that's been going on this morning, I'd shoved our relationship, the end of it, into a Tiff compartment and planned to think about it when my head wasn't throbbing.

"My God, what happened to your head?"

I move over to the couch and sit down carefully, holding my sore chest. "Bumped it. You look like hell."

"Thank you. Right back at you."

"It was a rough morning. My celebrity caught up with me up at the Coffee Bump. Took a cross to the forehead."

"You?"

I shrug a what-are-you-going-to-do.

"Couldn't sleep a wink last night," she says, folding her arms as if she doesn't know what else to do with them. She looks down at the carpet. It's new. Beige. Plush. She helped pick it out.

"I'm sorry—"

"Just let me say this, Sam," she interrupts, lifting her chin to look at me. She takes a deep breath for courage. "I loved you. Love, I mean. I think, anyway." But I don't love *who* you are. And I certainly don't love what you do." She looks away for a moment and drops her hands into her jean pockets, Calvin Klines. I was with her when she bought them. Tight. Look great on her.

I don't want to do this right now. Last night was painful but quick, like chopping off a dog's tail. Now she wants to talk about it. Why do women always want to talk about it?

She removes her hands and grips her trembling right one with her trembling left. "Our politics are different. We've talked about it a lot. Joked about it. You see the world as a violent place, or at least that's the part you choose to live in. I abhor that. The very thought of it makes me ill."

Okay, I'm not going to let her make me feel bad about my life. "Look, Tiff, you don't like who I am or what I do, but who I am *is* who I am. And what I do *is* what I do, and it's also who I damn well am. Okay, that sounds dumb, I know."

"It makes a lot of sense, Sam," she says, shaking her head. "And it's that very thing that is the problem. It's the ugliness of what you do."

"Life would be a lot uglier if men and women like me weren't out there trying to keep a lid on it. I don't think you get that or maybe you simply choose not to accept it."

"Then you should have let other men and women do it, Sam. Not you." She shakes her head and sits down on the edge of the recliner's cushion, as if sitting any farther back would make it hard for her to get away quickly. "I'm sorry. That's not right for me to say that. It's selfish and I don't want to be that way. It's just that sometimes I think we could have made it work. But then logic enters and it's so perfectly obvious that there was never a way."

Reminds me of something I read on one of those funny cards you give to people. It said: I love you, you're perfect. Now change.

Tiff stands quickly, moves over to the window and lifts one of the mini blinds, then releases it without looking out. She looks down at her feet.

I take a long, deep calming breath. We're two different people, plain and simple, both of us rigid in our beliefs. Tiff's right on some points and, I'm convinced, wrong on others. I suppose I am, too. I look at her as she toes the carpet. Maybe she's thinking the same thing. A minute passes, the only sound a far off jet.

"A child! Sam… I just… can't. I can't." She turns quickly and in two strides she's turning the doorknob.

"Thanks, Tiff!" I say to her sarcastically to her back. "Thanks a whole hell of a lot." She opens the door three or four inches and then stops. She doesn't turn around but just stands there, holding the doorknob. I shake my head and look away. "I need to think about all this. I need to put the shooting, the *shootings*, into some kind of perspective."

She turns part way around but doesn't look at me. "I don't see how you can."

"Damn-it, Tiff!" I blurt. "Are you so rigid in your… Damn!" I'm squeezing the arm of the sofa so hard that I'm about to rip the leather off. "You have no idea how awful—You don't even want to know how awful. You live in a la la land. A nice, tidy, and violence-free la la land. Well, life isn't that way, goddamn-it."

A few seconds pass and I forget that she's in the room. "My head wants to explode right now," I say, or maybe I just think it. "Last night I… My mind…" I shake my head again.

She moves and I snap my head up, startled. She's turned part way toward me but she's still looking at the floor. "I…" It's her turn to shake her head, then she turns away and opens the door far enough for her to pass through it. "I *did* love you." She leaves without looking back.

I don't get up from the sofa; I just stare at the closed door for a while. "Well, that sucked," I say aloud. At least today's ending was more civil than last night's. Still, I could do without having to talk about it anymore. I'm not cold hearted; I just don't see the point. We both know we're over. Let's don't rub salt in our wounds.

I scoot down into the sofa more comfortably, fold my hands in my lap and release a long breath of stress. What I wouldn't give for a normal day where I'm chasing a burglar through a briar patch or settling a family fight between two vomiting newlyweds. Police work is a lot of boredom punctuated with moments of high stress. My police job of late has been heavy on the tsunami adrenaline dumps.

I read an article once that said the top stressors that tear people down are separation from a spouse, serious health issues, and expensive problems with one's home. The piece didn't mention anything about killing people, especially children, but I can attest that it's number one. My relationship just went down the toilet, everyone in town hates me, a lawsuit is a matter of course, and I just got my ass kicked in front of a bunch of latte drinkers. I'm guessing that I'll be diagnosed with gangrene next followed by my house burning to the ground.

Oh man, I need some ice cream and cake with my pity party.

I jump at the shrill ring of the phone. Still looking at the closed door, I fumble for the receiver on the end table. "Sam here."

"It's me. Sup?"

"Mark," I say, more like a sigh than a greeting.

"You hanging in there, my friend?"

"Yeah."

"You want the good news or bad news first?"

"Shit."

"Sam, you sound awful. You need anything? You want me to come by?"

"I'm... fine. Just tired."

"Okay. Well, the good news is that you can take off as much time as you want before coming back to work. The boss wants you to see the shrink again. It's mandatory. You know all that.

"Yeah," I say softly. What was that word the man in the park used? Some word that meant suffering. I'm starting to understand what he meant.

"Now for the bad news. The shit is going to hit the fan. Koenig, that asshole in the DA's office, wants to get some headlines and make a name for himself. He's going after you, Sam. He wants to hang you for this shooting."

Dukkha, that was the word. *Dukkha*. Suffering.

"Sam, you there?"

"Yes, Mark," I say sleepily, suddenly more tired than I've ever been. "I'll be okay. I just need to rest. Thanks for the time off and your kind words."

"Sam, listen—"

"I want to go now, Mark," I say, almost begging. "You're a good friend. I'll keep in touch." I clicked off the phone and placed it on the table. I stretch out on the couch and push the side of my face into a pillow. Tiff picked these out. Burgundy. Very nice... very soft... like her...

I'm back in Jimmy's bedroom standing before the naked man and the naked boy. They're sitting side-by-side on the bed this time, their shoulders touching intimately, their nakedness like lovers on a Sunday morning.

They're both pointing guns at me. The boy looks at me through those same black holes for eyes, his blood-red lips curled into a snarl. He says, gravelly, "Our turn to shoot, Mr. Policeman."

The man laughs but without smiling, the sound like a machine gun; "Eh-eh-eh-eh-eh." The guns explode and—

I awaken with a gasp.

My head, front and back, throbs and my lower back muscles feel like a huge overstretched guitar string about to snap with a *twang*! I struggle to my feet and begin to circle my arms, slowly at first, then faster. It hurts my chest but I keep doing it anyway. I put my hands on my hips and begin to rotate them in small circles, then larger ones. When I had a kids' class we called this lower back warm-up "The Hula."

The sensation of fresh blood bathing my stiff back muscles and hips feels good, relaxing some of the tension in my face. I spread my legs and lower my forehead to my left knee, and then over to touch my right one. Stiff-legged, I slide my feet out farther and farther until I can touch my forearms to the floor, hold there for a moment, and then slide the rest of the way into the splits. With my palms on the floor in front of me, I slowly lower my torso until my chest and forehead touch the carpet.

I hold the stretch for a few minutes, letting my awareness ride on my breathing, in—out—in—out. The drunken Mariachi group playing at full volume in my skull subsides some, my back muscles loosen, as do my legs and shoulders. I place my palms on the floor, rock forward, and easily push myself up onto my feet. I shuffle about a little before I snap out a fast front kick. Hello, skull! That hurt, front and back, but not as bad as a while ago. I kick again. Okay, I can handle it. I begin popping out kick after kick.

Of all the things I've been through in my life—a failed marriage when I was twenty and foolish, a couple of failed love affairs, my mom getting killed in a traffic accident, my first shooting, and now this one—my martial arts have always been there. It's helped me get over depression, lose weight, blow off steam, and it's saved my bacon a bunch of times on the job.

A throb in my head reminds me of the failed block at the coffee shop. Okay, my martial arts didn't save my bacon there, but I didn't even try to block it. The guy definitely sucker punched me, but I take comfort in knowing that it wouldn't have happened if my head had been on straight.

Maybe I didn't want to block it. Maybe I wanted pain, punishing pain.

That's too weird to even consider right now. I'll ask Kari about it.

I'm feeling pretty good after loosening up. My kicks feel sharp and strong, but I know it's just adrenaline and endorphins momentarily cloaking the inevitable, the unavoidable return to feeling dead and… apathetic.

All the other times I've been down, I've always come back feeling stronger and eager to get back into the game. This time it's just too much. Maybe I'm not worthy of coming out of it. Maybe I'm not worthy of… anything.

I just can't think about this right now. I'll add it to the "maybe-I-wanted-pain" compartment and deal with it later.

I hear people talking outside. I walk over to the window and peek through a mini blind. Whoa. When did they get here? Normally, the tree-lined street is quiet with only the occasional neighbor walking or driving by. Now there are television news vans out front, with a half dozen reporters talking in a group.

I've never cared for the cop-hating press but right now I just don't care. If they knock on my door, I'll invite them in for coffee. Or maybe I'll break their knees. Either is fine with me.

I chuckle at that. There's freedom thinking this way. Hmm, apathy, not a bad concept.

I walk into the kitchen and retrieve a container of cottage cheese from the refrigerator. I dip two fingers in like a Samoan scooping for poi. Don't need no stinkin' spoon. I smile at that and shove it into my mouth.

My mind zips from the taste of the cottage cheese to Jeffrey Lawson, a cop I worked with my first two years on the job. Cruising the graveyard shift, we had talked about everything: our growing up years, the job, the future, women. Although he had only two more years on the PD than me, he was a perfect role model as to how to talk to victims and suspects, how to approach dangerous people, and how to read people. He had talked about taking the sergeant's test and I had encouraged him because I thought he would be a good one, exactly the kind of leader we need.

Then he called in sick three days in a row. I was about to call him to see what kind of bug he got when my phone rang. It was Greg Starkey, the old timer who worked the adjoining beat. "Hey Sam," he said, in that lazy emotionless tone he always used. "Your pard ate his gun tonight. Thought you'd like to know."

That's how he said it: *Your pard ate his gun tonight. Thought you'd like to know.* I must have been quiet for a few seconds because he asked if I was still there. When I mumbled something, he went on in that annoying droll. "Jeff's wife found him sittin' in the family SUV in their driveway, his brains splattered all over the driver's window, his service piece on his lap."

I hung up on the insensitive asshole and called the duty sergeant who gave me the same story but with sympathy to me and for Jeff. He said that I should come in because the precinct commander wanted to talk to me to see if I knew what might have been behind the suicide. I did, but I had nothing of value to tell the CO. Jeff had been perfectly fine the last time we had worked together.

His death at his own hands had shocked and confused the PD; no one understood why a guy in his prime, good at everything he did and with an obvious future on the job, would smoke his gun barrel.

After a couple of days, anger and disgust replace the confusion. Everyone wondered how he could have done it to himself, his wife, and his little boy. How cowardly! How inconsiderate of his immediate family and his police family.

Six months later, another officer committed suicide, but not before killing his wife first. Their three kids were in another room watching a movie, the volume so loud they didn't hear the shots. A while later, a hungry six-year-old went looking for his mother and found them. Some of the guys knew he and his wife were having problems, but to handle it like this? With his children there?

I get a carrot from the vegetable bin and chomp into it. Well, I don't have a family. No kids, my ex-wife's long gone, and Tiff is no longer in the picture. Mark's a good friend, but... but what?

He would understand.

How painful could it be to pick up my Glock Nine and...

"My God," I breathe. I shake my head violently and spew the chewed carrot into my palm. What the hell am I thinking? I step over to the sink and rinse my face under the tap. "My God."

I run my finger down the list of phone numbers taped to the wall where my shattered phone used to be, until I find Kari

Stephen's. I retrieve my cell off the counter. A recording comes on after the third ring. *"Doctor Stephens will be out of the office until Thursday, the nineteenth. She will be checking her messages periodically. Please leave a message after the beep. Thank you."*

I click off the phone. What am I doing? If I tell Kari what's on my mind, I'll never see duty again. Then again, maybe I shouldn't go back. All I do is kill people. Maybe Tiff was right. No no no. I can't think that way.

The hell with the department. To hell with everything. To hell with me.

I front kick a cabinet door, splintering the wood from top to bottom. "Shit!" I blare, looking at the ruined door. "Now I'm killing kitchen cabinets." I look at the counter. "Maybe I'll kick the blender. Shatter it to pieces so that it'll never make another smoothie."

That makes me laugh. I choke it off, but I start again, this time laughing harder. After a moment, I collapse against the refrigerator in hysterics, tears running down my flushed hot face. I try to stifle it, which only makes me laugh more. Eventually, I wind it down to a sputter, and convulse to a stop.

I shuffle back into the living room and sprawl on the couch. Once again, I welcome the dark.

CHAPTER SEVEN

Fifteen hours later, I awaken feeling like warmed-over yak crap. I stagger into the bathroom, whiz, and assess that the little finger on my right hand, and the hair in my ears are the only things that don't hurt. I pop four Excedrin, make a pot of coffee, and lather a couple pieces of bread with a half inch of peanut butter. I down the food with minimum chewing and gulp the scalding hot coffee as if it were iced tea.

The self-destructive thoughts I had before my marathon sleep are gone but I still feel awful: my body and my brain. For a moment, I think about going back to bed, but I shake that out of my head and stumble into my bedroom to get dressed.

The phone rings but I ignore it as I step into my jeans and sweatshirt. Don't want to talk to anyone, least of all from the PD or the DA's office. Maybe a light workout at my school will help, though even the thought of doing anything that jars my head makes it throb more.

I peak through the blinds. No media. Excellent. I'm out the front door and heading toward my pickup.

"Sam?"

"Shit." Did I say that aloud? I'm not sure. "How you doing, Bill?"

Bill, a sixty-something retired grocery manager and the neighborhood's busybody, gives me a half-hearted wave as he walks tentatively toward me, the same way my friends in Detectives encircled me when I went after Tommy.

"Been following the story on the TV," he says.

"Okay."

"Bad stuff. Sad about that little boy."

"Yes it is, Bill." I turn and open my truck door.

"Sam…"

I turn and look at him, enjoying his nervousness. I know what he's going to say.

He looks out at the street, then back at me, and coughs self-consciously. "The misses, uh, the misses is sort of upset about the TV vans and such parked out on the street yesterday and last night.

"I see,"

"Yeah," he says watching me get into my truck.

"Is there something else, Bill?" I ask, through my closed window after watching him squirm for a moment. I know I'm being rude but Bill is about as annoying as they get.

"I was… I mean," he says, haltingly, raising his voice a little so I can hear him through the closed window. "Gloria was wondering if they will be back today. I mean, it kind of disrupts the neighborhood."

"Well, Bill. I don't know." I start the truck.

"I thought maybe you'd know," he says even more loudly over the truck engine, "since they're here on account of… what *you* did, I mean."

"No, I don't know. What do you mean, Bill?" Fucker.

"You know. I mean, killing that child and all. Are you going to get into trouble for doing that? I mean, what happened? Why did you do that?"

The stupid words don't just touch a nerve, they make me want to gouge out his eyes and piss into the sockets. I have to get away from this moron before I do exactly that. "Have a good day," I say through clenched teeth, dropping the shift to reverse.

"I mean, can you do something about the TV folks not parking in front of our houses and all? I mean…"

I back out of the driveway into the street, leaving Bill standing there by my big grease spot, going "I mean" like a broken robot. Half way down the block, a busty little jailbait named Tammy Dee waves for me to stop. She comes over sometimes when I'm washing my truck or mowing the lawn, making it perfectly clear by her body language and words that she's ripe and ready. Tammy says she wants to be a cop some day and has asked a hundred questions about my gun, handcuffs, and how many people I've arrested. Then always the same breathless tease, "How do you know I'm not packing something illegal? Wanna search me?"

I've never encouraged any of it, but she never fails to work herself into a state of chest-heaving arousal.

"Hi Sam," she sings, as my passenger window slides down. She rests her arms on the window sill and presses herself against the door, her cleavage spilling over a white tank top that reads: WHAT ARE YOU LOOKIN' AT? "I heard about what happened. That must have been awful. Are you okay?" Her eyes feed on me as if I were a sumptuous meal. "I'll be glad to come over later if you want to talk or anything." Her lips part a little, which looks practiced, and then she drops her eyes to my lap, holding them there longer than necessary. Her baby blues slowly devour everything on the way back up to my face.

Incredible. The little tart is turned on by what happened.

"I got to go, Tammy. Watch out you don't get pinched."

Disappointed, she steps back as the window moves upward. She plunges her hands into the back pockets of her sprayed-on jeans, which juts her breasts against her tank top. She drops her chin and purses her lips into a fake pout, then smiles little girl like, calling loudly enough for me to hear through the window, "Any time, Sam. *Any* time."

I smile, wave, and drive off chuckling. So it takes a sixteen-year-old girl's come-on to make me smile for the first time in two days.

I take the freeway onramp, drive five miles, and then take the next exit ramp, dropping me within a block of my school: Reeves's Bushido Academy. I pull into a Seven-Eleven first, manage to go in and get a big cup of coffee without anyone assaulting me, then drive the rest of the way to my school. I recognize Sandra's black Mazda out front.

"Hey, Sam," she greets as I come through the door. She gets up from the desk and gives me a motherly hug. "How you doin', honey?" she asks, leaning away to look at my face. Sandra has been working for me for seven years, coming in once a week to do my bookkeeping. She's in her late fifties, heavyset, with white hair, and rimless glasses. I've told her a hundred times that she could pass for Mrs. Santa Clause until she opens her mouth.

"You look like you've been eaten by a coyote and shit over a cliff, honey."

"Uh, thanks?" I smile for the second time in thirty minutes.

She frowns at the knot on my forehead. "One of the Dirty Dozen get you with a lucky punch?"

"A white belt."

She chuckles as she moves back around behind her desk. She's used to seeing me with knots and bruises. "Some bad news, hon. I got here about nine o'clock and so far six mothers have come in to say they're pulling their kids out because of what happened. I've answered three calls, two were parents and one was Karen Thompson from your brown belt class. They all said they're dropping out. Oh, and you got twenty-two messages on the answering machine. I'm guessing that they're all… sorry, honey."

My school enrollment fluctuates between two hundred thirty, and two hundred and fifty students. I need one twenty to break even. If I keep losing people at this rate, I'll be in the red by week's end.

I look through the office window out into the empty training area. Fifteen years I've been running this school. Fourteen classes a week of beginners, colored belts, black belts, and the Bloody Dozen. I touch my chest, as if the sinking feeling there is something I can feel with my fingers.

"You okay?"

"I don't know, Sandra," I say in a whisper, barely able to hear myself. "Everything is… changing. Everything is crashing—crashing in on me."

She comes over to me again. We've liked each other from the first day she began working for me, a sort of mother/son relationship. She grips my upper arms and looks at me. "You lost a few students after the first shooting, but then you got more new ones. More than you had before, seventeen more if I remember right."

I look back out into the school. "It's different this time. Real different. I feel different, like everything I do… like everything I am is… about to change. Or something. I don't know."

I feel her hand on the back of my shoulder. She doesn't say anything.

"Feeling sorry for myself, huh?" I mumble.

"What would you tell a student who was having all these feelings?"

I smile a little as I turn toward her. "Suck it up and get on with it."

"What's that thing I've heard you tell people when you're pushing them real hard? Something about... eat?"

"Eat the pain."

"Damn right. Eat the pain."

When I don't say anything she punches my shoulder. "So?"

"Okay, I get it, I get it. It's just..."

The front street door opens and two women enter, mothers of two kids in my Mighty Kickers class. I don't want to talk to them.

"Let me go out the back, Sandra. If you would handle them, I'd really appreciate it. I'll call you later to see how the rest of the morning went."

"Go," she says. "I got your back."

"Thanks, sweetie. You and Mark are the only ones." I slip out the back door, walk down the short alley, and come around to where I'd parked.

Inside and scrunched low, I can just barely see over my dash to the front entrance of my school a half dozen parking slots away. No doubt, people will be coming in like this all day, especially parents wanting to cancel their kids' membership. Those are just the ones who call in or come by. Some will just stop coming.

No one wants to learn from a guy who kills kids.

Losing the school would hurt financially, but far worse is losing something that is a part of me. To not teach... I can't even fathom not doing it. It's the biggest part of who I am. It's the other part, the cop, that's destroying me.

I have always been proud that I've never used my fighting skills outside of the police job, except for that time protecting a woman in parking lot. I don't frequent bars, I avoid people on the street who look like assholes, and I keep my radar going all day long. Those times off the job when I have run into tight situations, I've gotten out of them using my mouth.

Of course, the police gig is all about going to where the trouble is, where some people aren't impressed with my b.s. ability. They fight because they don't want to go to jail or because they don't like that I'm a cop. Since there are billions of them out there, I've gotten into lots of scuffles and all-out fights. I'm actually grateful for the skinned knees, bloody knuckles, and wrenched shoulders because I've learned from them. They've helped me be a better martial artist. So I consider every one of these dickheads a teacher. Sensei Dickheads.

The two mothers exit out the front door of my school. I start to scoot even lower but they turn right and head the other way, both with angry gaits.

Yup, things just keep getting better and better. Converse Man called it *dukkha*. He said it means suffering.

I look at my dash clock. Noon. He said he would be in the park today at noon.

I back out of the parking space and head that way. Why? I haven't a clue, other than I feel compelled to go, which isn't like me at all. I'm always so anal, Tiff says. I never do anything without a plan or a clear reason.

That was a few days ago, though. The last forty-eight hours have been all about destroying my way of doing things. Still, my instincts are intact and right now they're telling me to go see this strange man.

I've had several amazing martial arts teachers over the years, masters who could kick some serious butt, then dish gentle and pragmatic wisdom about life. All had an aura about them, a quietness, a sense of... a sense that they knew something. Yes, that's it. It was as if they had learned something or become something by virtue of their personal journey. Something special.

The guy in the park had that same aura about him. He wasn't muscular or tattooed. In fact, he was slight of build, probably in his sixties, though there was nothing elderly about his mannerisms. It wasn't anything tangible, but still there was something there, a feeling, a sense that he could be dangerous. But how? All I saw was his feet move when he was probably evading the big guy's punch. Actually, it was more like they were gone one moment and then reappeared a few feet away a fraction of a second later.

That's crazy. Taking a hit to the front and back of your skull can make you see all kinds of loony things.

He was an oddball, for sure, with all his movie quotes and spiritual bumper stickers. What was with his stilted speech pattern? I've been around a lot of Asians during my years in the martial arts and the three years I patrolled Chinatown, so I have a pretty good ear for accents. This guy's sounded Vietnamese. How could that be? Given how weird he is, maybe he was faking it.

I pull into a parking slot at the edge of a park and notice the blue Toyota a couple of spaces over, the same one the man got into yesterday. A small square green sticker on the rear license plate means it's an Oregon rental. I scan the park and spot him sitting on the same bench, still wearing a white overshirt, black pants, and those red shoes. He seems so small sitting there, legs together, hands in his lap. Did this guy really save my bacon?

I make my way across the expanse of green noting as I get closer that he looks to be meditating or praying. He's sitting still, one hand cupped over the other, thumb tips touching, eyes partially closed. He's motionless but there's something about it that's... I'm not sure. It's like he's more than motion-less. Okay, that doesn't make sense.

He's angled away from me about a quarter turn. My gut tells me that he knows I'm approaching, though I'm sure I'm outside of his peripheral vision. I don't know why I think he knows, I just—

"Good afternoon, Sam," he says when I'm about fifteen feet away. He says it softly, without turning toward me, without lifting his head or in any way moving. "Glad you came."

A thousand goose bumps skitter up my spine.

Not until I stop about a stride away does he turn and smile. He places his palms together as if praying, dips his head slightly in an abbreviated bow, and says, "Please," nodding toward the bench next to him.

I don't sit; I'm not sure yet if I want to. I look at him, at his face. It's so... what? Sedate? He again gestures toward the bench.

I sit, but with reluctance and without taking my eyes off him.

"Yes?" he asks, looking out across the lawn.

"I'm sorry. I don't mean to stare."

A flicker of a smile passes across his profile. "'Be afraid. Be very afraid.' That's from *The Fly* with Jeff Goldbloom, one of my favorite actors. You see it?"

"Uh, yeah. The one made back in the eighties, I think."

"Yes!" he says with enthusiasm turning toward me. "Nine-teen eighty-six to be exact. With Geena Davis. She was a babe back then. Not so much now. You like movies, Sam?"

I try not to frown, but I do. "Yeah. I guess." I don't want to talk about movies.

"I watch a lot of them. I mean A-lot. I learn from them, about life, about people.

You see *Karate Kid*?" He swishes his open palms back and forth in the air. "'Wax-on, wax off.' The martial arts in that one was not too good. But the moral of the story was."

"May I ask your name," I ask, trying to get a read on him. "And how do you know mine? The newspaper?"

He smiles. "My name is Samuel."

"What?"

"'Let's keep our last names out of this, darling.' That is from something but I cannot remember the title. Probably a forties film. How are your head and chest?"

"Are you kidding me? Your name is Samuel?"

"Yes. The same as you but you use the short version."

I feel myself flush angry. "Look, whatever your name is," I say, standing up. "Maybe I shouldn't have come here. In fact, I don't know why I came. I…"

He shakes his head and waves his hand like he's disgusted with himself. "I'm too much, sometimes. My wife tells me that often enough. Maybe I should take the man's advice: 'Do not speak unless it improves the silence.'"

"What man?" I snap. "That from a movie?"

"Not quite." Samuel gestures to the bench. "Please. Sit."

I want to turn and walk away from this nutjob, but here I am sitting back down. "Look, I just came here today to say thanks for yesterday. I'm ashamed I needed help and I'm ashamed to admit that." I look out at the lawn and exhale. "I've been ashamed a lot lately."

"We are what we think. All that we are arises with our thoughts. With our thoughts we make our world."

I turn toward him. "What are you a fortune cookie?"

"Yes."

"What?" I'm shaking my head again. "'Yes,' what?"

"I am a fortune cookie."

"Oookay." I stand again. "I'm out of here, pal. You got my thanks for yesterday. Have a nice day."

"Wait! Please."

I stop. Why, I don't know. Cop instinct, curiosity, the urgency in his voice.

"Thank you," he says quietly, studying my face. "I am sorry. I am not good at this."

"I don't understand. Good at what?"

"The timing. I pride myself on good timing but this is not good."

"If you're talking about yesterday, your timing was perfect. I was off my game. Any other time that guy wouldn't have touched me."

"Please sit back down, Sam. We need to talk."

I take a step away and raise my hand. "Look, I don't think we have anything more to—"

"My presence there yesterday," he says quickly, "was not a coincidence."

I stop and look down at him, not sure what he means and not sure if I want to ask him to clarify. I'm not totally convinced that he's not a mental, but I can't deny that there's something about him... something that's keeping me from leaving.

"You weren't there for coffee?" I ask, not knowing what else to say.

He looks at me, his face, his eyes, struggling with something. Maybe he's a religious whack job. There are lots of them in this park on weekends, preaching to the air and badgering sinners. Maybe he thinks he was sent to the coffee shop by divine providence to save my sorry ass. Why would God send this aging, gentle, annoying man to save me after all that I've done? Why would He want—

"I am your father."

I look at him and snort. Okay, he's a whack job. I should have known. "*Star Wars*, right? 'Luke, I'm your father.' Very amusing. Have a good one." I turn to leave.

"Sam," the man says softly to my back. "I *am* your father. I'm sorry to be so abrupt but I don't know how else to…"

I stop for a second. Why do I keep stopping? "Bullshit." I say without looking back. Why don't I turn back to look at him?

"You were born in the summer, probably June, probably here in Portland. You were told that I was killed in Vietnam on July second, nineteen seventy-one. Grossly exaggerated, I might add. Your mother died in a traffic accident. I'm sorry. She was a good woman and she raised a fine son. She—"

I spin about and lunge across the three paces, my arms extended to grab his shirt—

But he's not there.

"What the hell?" I blurt, banging my shin into the edge of the park bench seat. "Damn!"

"Here. Behind you."

I turn, startled. "How did—"

"Sit down," he commands. His arms hang loosely at his sides, his posture straight, his eyes alert. There is nothing threatening about him, but I obey. I step, trance-like, over to the bench, squat part way and stop. "B… but," I stutter, shaking my head, "how did you move so… What were you saying to me?"

He gestures with an open palm toward the bench "Please," he says softly. "Sit all the way down. We need to talk."

*

133

My heart feels as if it were about to do an *Alien* through my shirt. My head throbs, not just where it got thumped yesterday but every other place, too. I try to focus on the man's face but tears cloud my vision.

No damn way! My father was killed in Vietnam before I was born. He was captured by the North and died a month later in captivity. My mother told me about it many times when I was a boy. In high school, I wrote a paper on North Vietnam and K-Forty-Nine, the prison American military captives called "Mountain Camp." According to the Army documents that my mother had, that's where my father died.

There was a box of things in the attic but it had always been off limits when I was growing up, which made it even more of a mystery to me. Once, when I was about nine or ten, I snuck up there to check it out, but my mother caught me just as I was about to open it. She whipped me so long and hard that I never went near it again. In time, I forgot about it until I came across it going through her stuff a few weeks after she died.

To my disappointment, the box contained only a set of military fatigues, a Green Beret cap, medals sent to her posthumously, and two badly faded pictures. So what was the big deal? Why hadn't she shared it with me? The only thing I could think of was that maybe these simple items had some deep emotional significance to her that she wanted all for herself. Her lost love, and all that. It was simple psych 101, but it's all I could figure. Still, I wish she would have told me more.

Unlike some kids who have a ton of issues around their deceased fathers and mothers, my growing up years were normal and happy. My mother's father lived a couple houses away and served as a loving surrogate father to me until he died two days before my twentieth birthday. I took his death hard.

Grandpa Dave had been there through all my growing angst, guiding me with a loving hand that doctored my scrapes and walloped me when I deserved it.

He had taken me to my first martial arts lesson and nodded proudly when he saw that I was a natural. He held the heavy bag for me in the workout area we built in the basement and encouraged me when my progress slowed. We had conspired not to tell my mother when I trained with knives at the dojo and when I got knocked out one time sparring.

Grandpa Dave was my father. Grandpa Dave had been there. Grandpa Dave.

"Please. Sit."

I look into the man's face for a long moment, then slowly lower myself.

This guy has gone from annoying to quirky to mental to—my father? I look at him with that thought in mind: same hairline, same face contours, same broad shoulders, although he's slender and I've been pumping weights for years.

"See the resemblance?" he asks. "I am sorry you did not get my good looks, but the rest is a close match."

I feel my temper flare again. I want to strangle the bastard but apparently I can't touch him.

"Look," I say through tight lips. "I don't know who you are and why you're…" Something about the way he's tilting his head. It's a nuance really, but it's the same way that I… No no no. No damn way.

He smiles faintly. "You're starting to believe me. Sorry to be so abrupt about it. Coming to America was a little complicated. I could not contact you in advance to, you know, soften the blow. Besides, I am sure you would not have believed a letter or an email."

I hold up my palm and shake my head. "This is nuts." I stand up. "Quite frankly I don't know if I want a father, especially one who plays dead for all these years and then suddenly shows up and wants to take me to a ballgame. Now for the last time, what is your name."

"I do not like baseball or football. Too violent. I like watching the *Food Channel*." The man chuckles at that for a moment "It *is* Samuel," he says quickly when I take a step away. "Same as you, except I have always gone by Samuel, not Sam. My real last name is Thacker, but after I got out of prison in Vietnam, I assumed the last name Le. It's a common Vietnamese name and it sounds like the American potato chips. I took that name because I thought it would draw less attention to myself, especially during those years after the war. But that is another story for another time," he says with a wave of his hand. He looks at me for a moment, his eyes remembering something. "Your mother must have named you Samuel after me."

My chest tightens; I'm not getting enough air. I stare at him as I fall onto the bench. Thacker. I remember seeing that name on the fatigue shirts in the box of stuff in the attic. "What's my mother's name?"

"You sure get up and down a lot. It is Cathy, with a C, like in cutie."

I heard mom say that a hundred times to people.

"She was born in nineteen forty-six in Seattle. Moved to Portland when she was sixteen and went to Grant High School. I met her our senior year there. We dated for a couple of years before I got drafted into the Army. I went to boot camp, to Advanced Infantry Training and then all kinds of additional schools to become a Green Berets. I got orders for Vietnam right after I finished." He looks me up and down. "It must have been during my last two-week leave that she got pregnant. Is your birthday June?"

I nod.

"My leave was the previous October. I do not know when she learned she was pregnant because none of her letters said anything about it. At least prior to March. I was captured on March seventh, and never received another letter from her or anybody. In short, I did not know you existed until a couple of months ago."

I can't move, can't blink, can't shut my mouth.

"A bit much to take, is it not? I am sorry. We were kids but very much in love."

I finally blink. "I... I don't know if I should believe... how do I know this isn't all bullshit, and that—"

"When you are in doubt, be still, and wait; when doubt no longer exists for you, then go forward with courage."

I frown, irritated. "What's that? What are these bumper stickers? Is that Buddhist or something"

"American Indian. Got it out of a Louis L'Amour western book. I love his stuff."

I shake my head like a wet dog shaking off water.

"It does not matter where it came from, Sam. What I am telling you is true. And you know it is."

A tinny version of the *Star Wars* sounds from inside my pant's pocket.

"I love that theme," he says enthusiastically as I retrieve my phone and look at the screen.

It's Mark, my lieutenant. I'll call him later. I slip it back into my pants.

"So, how'd you find me? How'd you know about me?" I'm not believing this one hundred percent yet, but I'm getting there.

"Internet. I surf the web all the time. I try to keep up on what is happening in America. In Portland, too. I read the *Oregonian* online about once a week, or so. I actually saw your name mentioned a few times in crime stories but I never thought anything about it other than to think that our first names were the same and that your last name was Reeves, same as Cathy's. Call me dumb, but it did not compute in my head. Plus, I assumed a long time ago that your mother had gotten married and probably moved away. I just never connected it. Then I ran across the story of the traffic accident and there was her name: 'Cathy Reeves.' It said that she was survived by one son, Sam Reeves. I about shit a camel."

I lean back against the park bench, my hands in my lap, my eyes fixed on a far tree. I *believe* this man.

"So I started Googling you. You are all over the place online. You have made quite a name for yourself in the ring. But still you get beat up by a fat guy." Samuel shakes his head as if disappointed and then continues before I can say anything. "Then there were all your crime fighting stories. You have made some good arrests. Very impressive. *You* are very impressive."

I turn toward him. The man claiming to be my father looks into my eyes for a moment and then turns away, clasps his hands in his lap and looks up at the treetops. "It is all a bit much for me, too."

My mind keeps asking: *This man is my father?*

He turns toward me, his eyes wet. "Yes, I am, Sam. You believe me?"

I look at him for a long moment, my eyes tearing, too. I nod. *This guy is my father.*

"The fruit drops when it is ripe," Samuel says softly, smiling.

"That Apache?" I ask, just to say something and to keep from sobbing. "From L'Amour?"

"Japanese. From Zen."

I start to smile but hold it in. My internal cop is telling me to go slowly. Thirty minutes ago, the man was a weird guy in the park. Now he's my long-dead father. Must proceed slowly, must proceed slowly. "Tell me more," I say. "Let's do twenty questions."

Samuel nods and smiles. "Sure, shoot with your questions."

"Okay. What's with the accent?"

"I did not know I have one. If I do, it's from living in Southeast Asia for nearly forty years. This is only my second visit to the states since the war."

"You never tried to contact my mother?"

"We were kids when I left. The letters stopped when I went to prison. After a year or so, I forced her out of mind. Or the prison forced her out of my mind. She was a wonderful girl but the war—I changed—I thought—she thought I was dead. I hoped she had gone on with her life. I didn't want to disrupt it with my resurrection."

"You just said you have only visited one other time since the war. I don't understand."

"I was captured and sent to prison for four years. When they freed me, I stayed. That is a story that might best be told later."

My cell phone rings. Damn. I start to ignore it but something tells me to check the ID. I pull it from my pant's pocket. It's Mark again. Probably wants to tell me about the Grand Jury, or how the press is gathering to lynch me. I'll call him later.

I look at the man sitting next to me, how he seems so centered, so calm. Several years ago, I met a kung fu master visiting from Beijing named Lao Zhang, a man in his seventies. He, too, possessed this strange sense of quiet, one that you didn't want to disturb. Everyone spoke softly around him, as if in a library.

"Trying to figure me out?" Samuel asks, not looking at me but at two children rolling by on Roller Blades.

I frown. "That's the second or third time you thought you were reading my mind."

"Was I right each time?" He turns toward me.

I look away, but I'm sure he saw me smiling.

"Can you still call it twenty questions when you ask only three?"

I look back at him. "You did a job on that guy yesterday. Today you avoided my lunge. Avoided? Hell! You weren't even there. Do you train?"

"I take a lot of vitamins.

"Come on."

"Okay. Yes. I've had many great teachers in Vietnam. Many Vietnamese masters, as well as two from Thailand and one from China. My Chinese teacher I consider my primary sifu.

"Kung fu? Muay Thai?

"Yes, and other fighting arts, too.

"I've trained for over twenty-eight years and I've never seen anyone move like that."

"I told you: vitamins.

"Damn, you're infuriating."

Samuel looks at me soberly. "The frog rises to the surface by the strength of its non-attachment."

I frown. "What the hell does that mean?"

Samuel chuckles as if he had just pulled a fast one. "No clue. Sounds good, though, eh?"

I exhale frustration. "Look," I say, standing. "This is a little too much for me right now. *You're* a little too much."

"Okay," Samuel says, apologetically, waving his open hands in the air as if erasing his tease. "Sometimes I go too far."

"Gee, yuh think?"

"Ask me another question."

I turn away from him for a moment, then back. "What do you want from me?"

"In short, to meet you and let you meet me. After I learned a little about you on Google, I decided to look you up. I was planning to come to see my daughter graduate this week from Portland State University, so I planned to do it then. Then when I was scanning the *Oregonian* one day, I saw the story where you had shot someone. Well, as you say over here, 'been there, done that.' So I decided to come sooner. But the Ho Chi Minh government moves very slowly and I could not get my papers changed to leave sooner. So I waited to come this week as planned, the week my daughter graduates."

"Okay," I sit. "Give me a minute. You read about my first shooting and—"

"Taking a life can be a tough thing to live with. It did not help that the newspaper account was confusing. It made the person you shot seem like a model citizen, but it also said that he was threatening to kill someone. I am guessing that your papers are written by people who do not understand. To me, your shooting looked justifiable. I think that is the right word. I have heard it on *Law and Order* and *CSI*. I love those shows. We get others, too. *American Idol* and *The Tyra Banks Show*." He pauses, his eyes never leaving mine, though they seem to be looking far away. "I know shooting someone can be rough."

"Yes."

"It eats you, does it not? It burns into your karma."

"You said you've been there."

"Fourteen times. In the war."

"Holy shit."

"I have always thought that expression was strange."

"Fourteen?"

"I was a Green Beret. They did not give us desk jobs. Fourteen confirmed. I shot many more but they had been carried off by the time we moved in."

My cell rings again. "Mutha…" I retrieve it. "It's my boss. He's called three times and that's out of character." I poke a button. "Mark?"

"Sam, where are you?"

"I'm sitting in Dunbar Park."

"Then you probably haven't heard."

"Heard what? What's going on?"

"It's Mitchell," he says the name softly. "He's been killed—murdered—in his home."

*

The cell slips from my hand.

I'm barely aware of Samuel snatching it out of the air before it hits the sidewalk. When he tries to hand it back to me, I shake my head, unable to speak. Confused, he puts the phone to his ear.

"May I ask who is calling, please? Me? I am Sam's father. That is correct. Yes, he did not know he had one either."

"Let me have my phone," I wheeze, reaching for it. I blurt at Mark, "When? What's his address? You there now? Okay, I'll be there in ten."

I sprint off across the lawn toward my truck, my mind racing to grasp the enormity of Mark's words. I'm running so fast that I don't slow in time and I have to use my forearms against the door to stop me.

"What is it?" Samuel asks, moving around from behind me and into my vision. I jump, startled because I'd forgotten about him. How did he keep up with me? Why isn't he winded?

My key has snagged on some loose threads in my jeans pocket and I struggle to get it out. "One of the officers with me at the shooting was found shot in his condo." The key breaks free but then I drop it. I pick it up only to drop it again. "Shit!"

"We will take my car," Samuel says, pulling my sleeve toward his Toyota. "You are in no condition to drive."

I start to protest but realize he's right. My head is vibrating at mach ten and is about to burst like a raw egg in a microwave. I nod and hurry toward his rental.

Did Mitchell know the killer? Somebody from a case he'd worked? Did he let him into his place? I don't even know if Mitchell's married. A domestic beef? A love triangle? Was it because of the shooting?

Samuel drives like a Taliban suicide driver. He tailgates, taps the horn continuously, turns on two wheels, stomps it on the straight shots, and nearly rolls us on a ninety-degree turn.

"Turn right at that light," I say. "It should be about mid block on my side."

A dozen police vehicles, angled every which way, jam the otherwise pleasant residential street. It's a mostly sunny day, but the overhead emergency strobes are intense enough to cast flashes onto trees, parked cars, and sides of houses. Gawkers press against the yellow police tape that stretches across the street, along the sidewalk, and up onto the stoop of what must be Mitchell's place.

A cluster of reporters rush toward me.

"Detective Reeves! Is this related to your shooting two days ago?"

"Detective Reeves. What is your sense…"

I ignore them.

"Sam, over here" Mark calls from inside the tape near the porch. His face is drawn, tired and—frightened?

I hurry over to him.

"Mitchell was…" Mark whispers, then stops to look over my shoulder. "Who's this?"

I turn toward Samuel. "Oh, this is Samuel. We're, uh, together."

"He can't go in the condo. You don't want to go in either. It's bad. Fuckers shot him twice in the back of the head."

"Damn," I mutter. "Who… who would have…"

"Step over here, Sam," Mark says, lifting the tape for me to duck under. "Stay put, would you Samuel? Thanks." He takes my arm and walks me a few feet away from the crowd. Then, confidentially, "Is that the guy I spoke with on the phone? He's your father?"

I pick up on his suspicion. Mark knows my family history. "It's a long story, but he says he's my father." I detect the cop face as he checks out Samuel. "He's cool. I… I think I believe him. I think, anyway. But he has nothing to do with this. It's, uh, a family thing. What went down here?"

Mark looks over at the condo and the cluster of officers standing by the door. He turns back to me, his face pale. "Mitchell was executed."

I suck in air.

"It was sloppy. Kicked in the back door. There was a struggle. Mitchell's a big guy, so I'm guessing there had to have been more than one perp."

"Ass-HOLES!" I say loudly. Several people look toward us, including Samuel.

"Detective Reeves!" a reporter calls, apparently taking my outburst as a willingness to talk to the press. "Can you give us a statement about what happened here?"

Mark takes my arm again and guides me a few more paces away from nosey ears. "It gets worse."

I feel my fight juices kick in. Mitchell and I weren't close but he was a cop, one I'd just shared an awful experience with. I would have gotten to know him more during the grand jury, the public inquest, the Internal Affairs investigation, and all the other hoops I knew we would have to go through over the next few weeks. I look at Mark. "Worse? How so?"

"A neighbor heard the shots and called nine-one-one. I was on the road going to a meeting when I heard uniform get the call. It came out as an unknown police officer's condo. We found Mitchell still alive when we got here, lying in the kitchen."

"Two head shots and still alive?"

"Barely. He'd lost a ton of blood. He whispered in my ear, 'Jimmy's...' but he didn't finish it. 'Jimmy's' what I don't know. Then, 'Tell Sam and Tommy.'"

I feel the blood leave my face. "Jimmy's friends? Relatives?"

"Don't know. Maybe he was just trying to say something about the boy. Maybe he wanted to warn us about the kid's relatives. But just in case, I got extra patrol for your house and Tommy's place, too. Things are going to get ugly, Sam. The boy's family has money. Last name's Clarkson. The boy's father, Adam Clarkson, has two brothers, Kane and Barry. Kane, the youngest, is an ex-con, very dangerous. They were all devastated after the shooting, but then their moods turned to rage, accusations, threats, the whole enchilada. We got our intel guys doing backgrounds and, based on Mitchell's statement, we've sent cars out to talk to them. You're going to have to watch your back. And I want you to take home a shotgun and radio."

I take a deep breath. Talking with my *father* for the past hour had taken my mind off the shooting for the first time in two days, but now it's back like an avalanche of poorly stacked shit.

"I'll think about the take-home stuff."

He raises his eyebrows like a parent about to reprimand a child, again. In this case, it's about my issue with guns. A couple times since I've been working Detectives—maybe more like a half a dozen times—I've forgotten to carry my sidearm when I've left the office on a case. Off duty, I never carry one. I'm not afraid of them, hung up on them or anything else. Unlike most cops, I'm not interested in them, never have been. I carry one because they make me. The irony is that I've killed with a gun three times now. I tell Mark that I'll do it and he lowers his eyebrows.

"Any witnesses?"

"Just the elderly woman who heard the shots. Didn't see anything." Mark looks at my forehead.

"A guy sucker punched me yesterday at a coffee joint by my place. Said something about Jimmy, then whacked me. Samuel was there and delivered some payback on him."

"The old guy?" Mark asks, looking over where he's standing serenely behind the police tape, his hands clasped behind him. I look at "the old guy," too, again amazed at how he emanates that strange quiet, as if he were in a hermetically sealed dome. Anyone without a trained eye might think, if they noticed him at all, that he was oblivious to all the officers moving about, the pulsating overhead police lights, the chattering crowd, and the TV reporters talking into cameras. Judging by my brief contact with him, I'm betting that he's aware of every minute thing.

"Believe me, he's not your average old guy."

Mark touches my arm. "Let's get that punch on the record." He waves a female uniform officer over. "O'Brien, take a report from Sam about a run-in he had yesterday. Sam, give her the best description you can. This could be related."

When O'Brien and I finish, the three of us head over to where Samuel is standing.

"Mark, this is Samuel Le," I say, lifting the yellow tape so Samuel can enter the police zone with us. "And Samuel, this is my boss, Lieutenant Mark Dickerson and Officer O'Brien." They shake hands, Samuel with a slight bow to each.

Mark nods, eyeing him. "Let's move a few feet over there," he says, "to get away from the damn press. Okay, this is good." He studies Samuel for another second or two, before asking, "Samuel, I wonder if you'd give this officer a description of the man you encountered yesterday at the coffee shop?"

"I can do that," Samuel says, without making a dig about the guy punching me.

Officer O'Brien clicks her pen and looks at him.

"Big," he says. "I think maybe he used to have a lot of muscles, like my boy here, but now he's eating too much. Maybe six feet three. Two hundred fifty pounds."

"What happened" O'Brien asks, frowning as she scans Samuel for bruises.

"Lieutenant?" Mark and I both turn toward the mini porch where The Fat Dicks are waving us over.

"Come with me, Sam," Mark says. "Samuel, stay here and give your report to the officer."

Partners for over twelve years, the pair began referring to themselves early on as "The Fat Dicks," since both are named Richard, both are detectives, and both weigh over three hundred pounds, Daniels maybe three fifty. They're also the same age, thirty-seven, and they sometimes look like brothers under certain lighting conditions, though Richard Cary has thinning red hair combed forward to hide a bald spot and Richard Daniels has a full head of brown hair, combed straight back.

"Damn shame," Richard Daniels says in a low voice as Mark and I move over to the porch. "An excellent man. He got family?"

"Married twice, no kids, thank God," Mark says. "The job was pretty much his life. Find anything?"

"Not much," Cary says, his eyes glistening. "Asshole or assholes forced open the back kitchen door, and probably immediately confronted Mitch, considering the noise they must have made coming in. There was a struggle. Lots of kitchen stuff on the floor. Looks like Mitch took a few hits to the face, probably fists; the ME can tell us for sure. Then at some point, he took what looks like two rounds to the back of the head, big holes, no exits. Perp took the shell casings. Don't see any other blood except for the pool around his... the body. Hard to say if the perps got hurt. Mitch's gun is in its holster on his dresser."

Samuel moves up beside me. When Cary frowns at him, I mouth that it's okay.

"Oh," Daniels remembers. "A copy of yesterday's newspaper, the one with the big story on your shooting, is lying next to Mitch."

Your shooting. Damn I hate that.

"Funny thing is, today's paper is on the kitchen table and there's another copy of yesterday's paper lying on a stack to be recycled. We're thinking the shooter brought it with him."

"Shit!" I hiss. "Someone put a newspaper on my porch a couple days ago. I don't subscribe."

"Did you see anyone?" Mark asks.

I shake my head.

"I did," Samuel says quietly.

I jerk my head toward him. "*You* saw someone?"

"Yes."

"But how do you know where I live?"

"What did you see?" Mark asks, his expression suspicious again.

"I saw a man stop his old car in front of the next house. He got out carrying a newspaper, and cut across the neighbor's lawn and stopped at the corner of my boy's house. He tossed the paper on the porch and walked back to his car real fast. Then he took off."

"'My boy?'" Daniels repeats. "Sam's your son?"

"Yes," Samuel beams.

Daniels looks at me. I shrug.

"Then what happened?" Mark asks.

"I saw Sam come out onto the porch and pick up the paper. He looked around, got angry, and kicked it into the shrubs. That seemed strange to me so I followed the man to see where he was going."

"*That's* how you came to be at the coffee shop," I mumble mostly to myself. "So, the guy who I had the run in with was the same guy who left the paper?"

Samuel shakes his head. "No, I lost that one."

"Then how did you come to the coffee shop?" I ask, confused and a little suspicious.

"I was passing by the shop heading back to your house to visit you, when I saw you walk up to the line to get coffee.

I parked, got out, and decided that I would make my introduction there."

"Introduce yourself?" Cary says, confused. "I thought you said you were Sam's—"

"Long story," Samuel and I say simultaneously.

"So it was by accident that you were there when that guy got in my face?"

"Karma," Samuel says. "You must have good karma for me to be there."

"Who was the guy in the old car?" Cary asks, his face still puzzled.

Samuel shrugs. "Beats me."

"Maybe he's related to Mitch's perp…" Daniel's voice trails off.

"Samuel," Mark says. "I want you to give a description of the man to Detective Daniels. The one who left the paper."

"So who was the dude I had a run in with?" I ask no one in particular.

"To me," Samuel says, as Daniels retrieves his pocket notebook, "he just looked like a guy who wanted some coffee. Maybe he recognized you from the paper." He looked at Mark and the two detectives. "That is my take on it."

I shake my head. "But he said something about me getting the newspaper."

"I'm getting confused," Mark says, frowning. His cell rings. "Excuse me," he says, flipping it open as he walks a few feet away.

"Where did the one who hit me go after our confrontation?"

Samuel shrugs. "When I looked back at the coffee shop after helping you over to the park, he was gone. Someone must have helped him leave. I was surprised no one called the police. Or maybe they did but they did not know where I took you."

"So there were two guys," Cary states, as if to clarify it to himself. "The guy who left the paper and the one who assaulted Sam."

Samuel nods.

"Sam," Mark calls from where he's been talking on the phone.

"Yes?" I say.

"Yes?" Samuel says.

"Sam junior," Mark says, pointing at me. "Come here a moment. Samuel, please stay right there. Thanks."

I hear one of the Fat Dicks ask Samuel something as I walk over to Mark, who looks even whiter than he did a few moments ago. "What's wrong now? Please, no more bad news. This week has been one of the worse."

"Walk with me for a minute, Sam," he says, taking me by my arm. We move across the lawn to the far corner where the yellow crime tape loops around a holly bush to square off the Police Only zone.

"Do I even want to know?"

"The odds," Mark says, his tone even, deliberately controlled, "the odds of what I'm going to tell you happening is remote, extremely remote, but we can't ignore it. I don't want you to—"

"Say it, Mark. You're scaring the crap out of me."

"The hostage taker had AIDs."

"What?"

"The bad guy had AIDs. I asked the doc at the hospital to ask the medical examiner to check for it since you got blood on your face and in your mouth. But before his tests even came through, the suspect's parents told the ME that he's had it for two years. The ME just called me."

"Wait wait wait, Mark," I say, waving him off, though my heart rate just quadrupled. "Tommy whipped his cut hand around and it was *his* blood that flew onto me. That's what threw my round off."

Mark nodded. "Maybe, and let's hope that's it. But did you read Mitch's report?"

I shake my head.

"Mitch fired first."

"I know."

"It's possible that Tommy's motion distracted you from the suspect for a split second."

"What are you getting at?"

"Mitch says that when he fired, the suspect made what looked like a reflexive jerk of his arm."

"But..."

"The photos show him with blood all the way down to the fingertips of his left hand. It's possible that when Mitchell fired and the perp jerked up his arm, there was blood on it and it splattered on you and into your mouth."

"But he couldn't have bled that much that fast."

'It might have been blow-back."

"I was too far away for blow-back. I just don't see how..."

"Listen Sam, the suspect, Tommy, and even the boy are all B negative. There's no way to know for sure whose blood went into your face."

My mouth is probably hanging open, but I haven't any words.

"Sorry to spring this on you, but I couldn't sit on it, not when there's a serious concern, a risk of exposure."

"AIDs? No no no."

Mark is saying something, but his voice suddenly becomes unintelligible white noise.

My mind and my eyes trail over to Mitchell's condo. The Fat Dicks must have gone back inside. The curtains are closed but I can see flashes around the edges of the windows, which would be the Crimalistics Division photographing the crime scene.

Samuel has moved back over near the police tape, and looking this way. He looks so unassuming from here, his arms behind his back, his posture seemingly relaxed, though I'm guessing that he's taking in everything, missing nothing. Up close his eyes seem... what? Like they know something that others don't, like they've seen things. Is he telling the truth about being captured in Vietnam, about living in that country for all these years? His accent would certainly make it seem so, and his rather formal way of speaking. Is he faking it or has he been gone from here so long that he's forgotten how to say don't and can't? And there's the incredible way he moves.

"Sam, are you listening to me?"

I look back at Mark, almost surprised that he's standing next to me. I haven't a clue what he's been saying.

"I asked you if you know Kent Hegrenes out at North Precinct? Works nights, I think."

"Kent? Yeah I know him. Why?"

"He's got a brother who's a doctor at Good Samaritan, in the ER. He told the ME to have you come and see him. He's the doctor I asked to talk with the medical examiner about running a check on the suspect's blood. Apparently the ME called Hegrenes with the news just now, then the ME called me."

"I don't get the rush."

"My understanding is that you need to begin on medications within forty-eight hours of exposure."

I must have twitched or made a face because Mark reaches out and grips my arm. "I'm glad you understand. Let me go make sure the team has everything they need and then we'll go."

I nod dumbly. What else can I do but nod? Tell me to go there, I'll go there. Tell me to go way over there, I'll go way over there. My life is no longer under my control.

"Your car here?"

"No. Samuel drove me. I was too shook after your call."

"I'll drive you up to Good Sam. I'm parked over there. Let me go talk to the Fat Dicks for a moment and I'll meet you at my car."

Mark heads toward the condo, leaving me standing in the middle of the yard, my mind bouncing all over the place like the silver ball in a pinball machine. Yes, that's it, and I'm playing a game called "My *Dukkha,*" and every post the ball strikes and every gate it passes through is just fun fun fun. I tilt the table to the left and the ball bumps and sticks on a gate called "AIDs." Now *there's* some fun I didn't plan on having. That ought to be worth a bunch of points.

I tilt the table to the right and it bumps a post called "Jimmy," and a rusty dagger plunges into my chest.

The ball rolls on—*ding ding ding*—pausing for a moment on a "Mitchell" post. Oh, man. I'm so, so sorry, Mitch. An image of him streaks across my mind, crumpled in a lake of red. I've been around lots of homicides during my years on the PD but never anyone I knew. Until now.

The *dukkha* ball dings on, stopping at a gate marked "Watch Your Ass."

I definitely got to watch it now. Tiff does, too. I punch in her number and get her voice mail. "Tiff, it's me. Call me as soon as you get this." Wait, if I tell her that, she may or may not call. Or she might think I just want to talk about us, which I don't want to do. "Listen, Tiff. Mitch, the uniform with Tommy and me at the... at the shooting, was killed today. Murdered. There's reason to believe it's related to the shooting. Call me as soon as you get this."

The silver ball passes through that gate and stops at "Samuel."

I walk over to where he's standing so quietly, so motionless. He smiles faintly as I approach. "How are you doing?" I ask.

"I am doing well. I am very sorry for your loss. Was he a good friend?"

"I knew him and worked around him. We weren't close friends but he's a cop. We're all family."

He nods and something passes over his eyes, a memory? "Understood," he says softly.

"I have to go somewhere with my boss. But I'd like to continue our conversation."

"Yes, we must."

"It's two o'clock now. How about we meet at, say, three-thirty somewhere."

"I know where your house is."

That's right, he's been there. "Let's make it at my place then. Three-thirty?"

"Yes," he says with a short nod. He extends his hand. "See you then." We shake. I feel a tugging sensation in my chest as he turns and heads for his car. What's that about?

Then, and it could only happen in my *dukkha* game, the pinball moves backwards up the slope, once again bumping into and sticking on that ugly post called "AIDs."

*

Fifteen minutes later Mark and I are cruising up Burnside on the way to the hospital. "Okay, here's where we are," he says, guiding the gray unmarked around a double-parked delivery truck. "Intel is doing a background on the hostage taker and on the boy's family. The suspect had a California ID in his pants pocket, which we found under the boy's bed. Don't know why he put it there, probably never will. He's got no activity in Oregon but lots of mental holds in Los Angeles and a couple of assaults in San Francisco. His parents live in LA. The mother is the one who told the ME about the AIDs."

"He was something else, Mark," I say, noticing how my right hand is trembling. "like an alien or a beast out of Hell."

"I'm more worried about the boy's family." He hangs a right on Twenty-First Avenue. "I hate to tell you this, Sam, but it's better that you hear it from me first."

"Now what? I'm not sure how much more I can take."

He takes a breath and says it in a rush. "The boy had just beaten cancer, or at least it had been in remission for a few months.

My fist slams into the dash. No pre-think, just hit. Then I hit it again, harder. The glove box door drops spilling papers and envelopes down onto my feet.

"Sam! Jesus, Sam. You've cracked the dash."

"Cancer," I whisper. "Jimmy Clarkson had *just beaten* cancer?"

"I'm sorry, Sam. The press was just informed about it. I thought it was better you hear it from me. There's more."

"There *can't* be more," I say, so tired I can barely speak. At least I think I said it aloud. I'm not sure.

"The mother, Sybil Clarkson, as you know is blind or mostly blind, a result of some kind of head trauma a few years ago."

"It's Clark-son?" I ask. "I thought you said Clark before."

"Yes, Clarkson."

I used to know a Kane Clarkson a long time ago.

"The mother lost her sight, I think in a traffic accident. She's enraged about what happened. Inconsolable. Her husband owns Crown Trucking here in the city. Got more money than the Pope. Of the husband's two brothers, Kane and Barry, Kane is the black sheep of the family."

My left hand is uncontrollable. I grasp it with my right but that doesn't help. I watch them as if they're something separate from the rest of me.

"Done time in the joint twice: dope and assault one. He's a…"

Mark's voice fades in and out as I begin to cry.

"… real bad actor. The other…"

Not just a couple of tears, but shoulder-shaking sobs.

"… the other, Barry, is straight, works for Northwest Power. The whole family's real tight."

Kari says that crying is a good thing because it lets out the stress, tension, pain. *Cosmo* says it's okay for men to cry, and so did a woosie-looking shrink on *Oprah*. So I ignore the fact that I'm a big-ass martial arts teacher, a bodybuilder, a cop, and that my boss is sitting next to me, and I let it rip.

Ten minutes pass, give or take, before I stop. I blow my nose on a tissue that Mark must have placed on my leg, and look around. We've stopped, parked in a police zone in front of the hospital.

"How long have we been here?" I ask.

"A few minutes. How you doing?"

I look over at my friend and smile. "I actually feel quite a lot better, thanks. Can this just be between you and me?"

"Hell no," Mark says. "I'm going to write it up and put it in the police paper. Maybe on my Facebook, too."

I smile. But not much.

"Dr. Hegrenes is expecting us. Ready to go in?"

When I turn to look out the window without answering, Mark says, "Come on buddy. Let's get this done. There's a lot of crud coming your way this week."

"*Dukkha.*"

"What was that?"

"Samuel calls it *Dukkha*. It means suffering. He said I had a lot of it. And he said that yesterday, before I got all the new *dukkha* today."

"*Dukkha*, schmooka," Mark says, pushing open his door. "You got to tell me more about him, but right now let's go see the doc."

Doctor Hegrenes looks to be about forty, full-dark beard, his well-fed bulk straining the seams of his green hospital scrubs. He's overflowing on one of those little chrome stools with wheels, Mark is occupying a chair in the corner, and I'm up on the examination table. Mark fills him in on Mitchell's report and I explain my take on the blood transfer.

"Sam, you know my brother Kent is a cop, right?"

"I do. A good one, too."

"Thanks, we're very close. So I know a little about the cop psyche, and I'm guessing you want me to cut to the chase."

I nod, more in resignation than agreement.

"As I see it, there are two views as to how that blood got into your mouth, both of which were perceived under intense, adverse conditions. So you got to ask yourself if you can afford to be wrong here." When I start to say something, he waves me off. "I'll answer for you: no."

I hate doctors and doctors' offices, hospitals, nurses, and even the hospital custodial staff. I don't want to be here.

"I'm picking up vibes that you'd rather be chasing a bank robber than sitting here, right?"

"Yes."

"Isn't going to happen. You're on my turf and you have to listen. What's more important is that you have to do what I say."

My mind flashes to Kari, my shrink. Are all the doctors in this town trained by the Marines?

Mark snickers. "Maybe you should have been a cop, doc."

Hegrenes keeps looking at me as he answers Mark. "Thought about it, but I like green, long hours without sleep. Listen, Sam. The chance of catching AIDS under the situation you described is quite minuscule, like one in two hundred. But as far as we know, this same thing just happened to a hundred and ninety-nine other people and they didn't get it."

My thumping heart is trying it's best to escape out of my chest. Is my shirt moving?

"I want to start HIV medications today, a procedure called post-exposure prophylaxis, PEP for short."

I shake my head. "There's no way—"

Doctor Hegrenes lifts his palm to stop me. "Sam, I understand you're some kind of a hot shot karate guy, but listen. One of my nurses, name's Betty, yes, Nurse Betty, weighs two fifty easily and I've seen her manhandle some of the toughest, meanest patients we've had. And she always wins. Shake your head one more time at me and I'm calling her in here."

I roll my eyes in resignation and shoot Mark a glare when he giggles.

"Good," the doc says, typing quickly on a small laptop perched on his lap. "This stuff will make you nauseous but the good news is that it's likely you'll only have to take it for about a month. I've been on it twice, as have many on my staff. We get pricked by infected needles and scalpels ever so often. It's not a pleasant month but I've had worse. And the drug won't harm you if it turns out you weren't exposed."

Doctor Hegrenes looks up at me. His expression softens and he touches my shoulder. "The wise choice is to take it, Sam, for yourself, for your family, and for your friends."

I throw up my hands. "Hey, why not add nausea to an otherwise pretty crappy week."

"If you're married or got a significant other, you'll have to use protection."

For some reason that makes me laugh. I sputter to a stop, and say, "Understood."

"Good," the doctor says, eyeing me for a moment before he returns to his keyboard. "Let me send this in. I've got another patient so I'll have Nurse Betty come in to explain the process and a little more about what to expect. She'll also get some blood from you for a baseline."

"It's the right decision, Sam," Mark says.

"Like returning to work, two days ago?" I ask, rhetorically.

Mark stands. "I'll wait for you out in the waiting area. Don't mess with Nurse Betty."

Doctor Hegrenes snorts without looking up from his typing. "Don't make Nurse Betty angry. You won't like it when she's angry."

Forty-five minutes later Mark is driving me back to my car. I'm slumped low in the seat with a couple white sacks of prescription tablets on my lap and a frown on my face that feels permanent. Maybe it's my imagination, but I'm already feeling a little nauseous. Nurse Betty, who turned out to be a petite, cute blond in her late twenties, had me take the first dose, a little white pill, before I left the room. I have to take a second one before I go to bed. Two a day until they tell me to stop. She said I might experience, let's see, headache, nausea, vomiting, fatigue, weakness, cold symptoms, shortness of breath, and a couple other things that I can't remember. Probably projectile diarrhea.

Oh, she also said my blood pressure was high. Imagine that.

"What are you going to do now, Sam?" Mark asks as we near the park.

"You need me at the office for anything?"

"No. I know you want to be involved but you're officially off duty until the grand jury. I'll keep you posted and I'll call you if I do need anything. I asked the commander of Southeast Precinct to have your neighborhood beat car cruise by your house several times a shift. You might even call them and invite the officers to stop by for coffee. We want a strong uniform presence on your street."

"Thanks, Mark.'

"Okay, so what's up with this guy claiming to be your father? No offense, but he's sort of odd. Reminds me of Kwai Chang Caine in that old *Kung Fu* TV show."

"Agreed," I say. "My gut tells me that he *is* my father. I'm going to meet him in a while to talk further. That's my truck down at the end of the lot. The way it's been going, someone's probably broken into it."

*

It's three forty-five by the time I get home and find the Toyota rental parked in my driveway, along with three news vans perched at the curb, and a cluster of reporters poking microphones at Samuel in the middle of my yard as if he were Paris

Hilton. There's no other way to get in. There's no alley behind my house and my garage is jammed with my home-training equipment. If Samuel wasn't here I'd keep on going, but he is, so I pull onto my driveway and get out.

The reporters burst toward me as if simultaneously launched off starter blocks, their microphones extended, cameramen trailing with their shoulder mounts. I'm not in the friggin' mood.

"Stop right there," I say.

"Detective Reeves, what happened at Officer's Mitchell's house today?"

"Detective, can you comment on the shooting of the little boy?"

"What do you have to say to the parents of—"

"I said *stop*!" I thrust my palm at them, my facial expression probably denoting my desire to cram the cameras up their body cavities. They stop this time, bumping into each other. It's almost comical. "Let me explain the Trespass law to you. As the owner of this property, I'm telling you right now to get off of it. That's the first warning. Now, this is how the law works: If any of you continue to remain on my property, now that I've told you to leave it, I can and *I will* arrest you for Trespass. Is there any part of that law that is unclear to you? Is there any part of *get the hell* off my property that is vague to you?" I would threaten to cram the cameras but the damn things are filming.

They back toward the sidewalk but continue to call out questions. I ignore them and gesture for Samuel to follow me to the front door.

"That was pretty cool," he says, smiling faintly as we step into the living room.

"What were you talking to them about?"

"They just asked me what I knew about the shooting and if I was a friend. I did not tell them who I am, just that I knew you. I said that you were a good man and a very good policeman. I have never been on TV before."

I lead him into the kitchen, stopping to pick up a piece of the broken phone I'd missed earlier, and drop it on the counter with the rest of the debris. "Do me a favor and don't talk to them again, please. They can't misconstrue anything if they don't know anything." I think about that for a second. "Well, that's not true. But just humor me and don't talk to them anymore."

"Done. What happened to your phone and your cupboard door?"

"Long story. You want coffee? Tea?" A wave of nausea hits me hard. I open the fridge and retrieve a bottle of Pepto-Bismol. I have a feeling this is going to be my drink of choice for a while. I take a snort of it out of Samuel's sight behind the door.

"Tea, please."

My head is so full of all that has happened and all that is still happening, that I don't know how to even begin talking with this man. For now, I got to compartmentalize Mitchell, Jimmy, and the AIDs thing so I can function with Samuel with some degree of coherence, with some degree of being in control of my life.

I fill a Japanese pot from the tap, place it into the microwave and put two small teacups on the table.

"Excuse me," I say. "Got to hit the john."

When I return, Samuel is sitting at the kitchen table, his hands folded on its top. He smiles at me, shyly, I think. I retrieve the teapot and drop in four teabags.

"I'm interested in your martial arts," I say, sitting down across from him. I figure that's an easy place to start.

"We share that passion, do we not? Must be something in the blood." He smiles. "I got interested in the Army, during my Green Berets training. I trained at all my duty stations prior to going over to Vietnam, studying whatever was available: taekwondo, muay Thai, karate, jujitsu, and a thing called dirty boxing. When I got to the war, several of the Vietnamese Special Forces guys were high ranked in vovinam, Vietnam's own martial art. So I studied with them every free minute I had."

"That's very impressive," I say. I sit across from him thinking about what he did to my attacker and the way he avoided me when I lost my temper. "But that was a lot of years ago. You must still train."

Samuel rotates his cup two or three times without lifting it from the table. He looks at me for a moment, pensively, as if deciding what to say. Finally, "Yes, I do," which sounded like, *And that's all I'm saying about that.* What's that about?

"What do you do in Vietnam?" I ask, thinking that I'll come back to the mysterious training question.

"Family business. 'And a little of this and a little of that.' That is from *Blank Check*, a pretty good kids' movie."

My adrenaline surges. "Look Samuel, I've had a pretty hard week, to understate it, right in the middle of which you drop out of the sky and tell me that I'm your son. I think I'm believing you, so I invite you to my house so we can talk and find out a little about each other. My life is going lights and siren right now and I'm just trying to maintain what little sanity I have left. I don't have the time or the patience for all your quotes. Stop jerking me around or I'll just have to ask you to leave and I'll get on with life as if you were never in the picture."

Samuel smiles almost imperceptibly and nods his head once, Asian style. "You are right and I am sorry. Okay, ask away. I will tell you the truth."

I pause, watching him. "Congratulations. You didn't say, 'You can't handle the truth.'"

He smiles and shakes his head. "Oh, I wanted to—very badly. I really did."

I laugh and a couple seconds later, he does too. His laugh sounds like mine. I fill our cups.

He sips his tea and eyes me over the rim. There's still a little laugher in those eyes but it doesn't take much imagination to know how they'd look if they were dead serious, how they could send a chill through your bones.

"I guess I am uncomfortable with all this. So I get silly." He takes another sip of tea, like a booze drinker taking a snort for courage. "What do you want to know?"

"Let's start with something safe. Your current training."

He seems to struggle for a moment with whether he wants to proceed. What is he hiding? He looks toward the kitchen door, then back at his tea. Sips. Then, "Since my release from Mountain Camp in 1976, that was a North Vietnamese prison, I have been honored to study with a Chinese master named Shen Lang Rui. His style, his family's style, translates to Temple of Ten Thousand Fists. Two years ago, my master bestowed me with the honor of "Head Son," sifu, of the system, but under him."

"You have a Chinese teacher in Vietnam. How's that?"

When China fell to the Communists, many Chinese businessmen and women were trapped in Vietnam and could not return to their home. So they started new lives and families there. Shen Lang Rui was about ten years old when his family was forced to remain in Vietnam. He speaks Vietnamese and of course Chinese. He speaks a little English but rarely uses it. His father and mother taught him Temple of Ten Thousand Fists style. He says his mother was a very good fighter. Faster than him, but I do not think so."

For the first time since I've met him, I notice that the big knuckles on both of his hands are thick with calluses, extending from his index finger to his ring finger. They must be at least a half-inch thick over his index and middle knuckles, less so over his ring finger. The sides of his hands are thickly callused, too. An uninformed person might think his hands were deformed. A martial artist would see them for what they are: highly destructive weapons.

"Thirty years of beating a metal plate," he says.

I look at him puzzled.

He lifts his hands. "You were wondering about them."

How did he know what I was thinking?

"In our tradition, we must strike the metal plate three hundred and thirty-five times a day, so that at the end of the month we have hit it ten thousand times, in honor of the system's name. We have to hit it more each day in February, of course." He smiles at his joke, then opens and closes his hands several times quickly. "It's warm in Vietnam; no arthritis." He drains his cup.

"So Temple of Ten Thousand Fists is about brute power?"

"It's about a lot of things. As to the physical, it's about speed." Samuel's face brightens, and with childlike enthusiasm, asks, "Hey, you want to see a cool trick?"

He perceives my hesitation as a yes. "Okay, put your right palm about three inches over your teacup and I'll put my hand over mine. Now, the instant you see my hand move, drop yours and cover your cup. Yours is almost full so don't spill it."

This is stupid, but I do it. I've been blessed with lots of fast-twitch muscle fibers, so bring it on.

"Ready?"

"Yes."

"Remember, when my hand flinches, you smack your hand down fast, but don't break the cup." He laughs at that.

"Gotcha."

Samuel looks at me for a few seconds; I return the gaze using my best cop instincts, but I'm getting nothing. He's at once childlike and not just a little scary. There's going to be a contraction of his upper arm and probably a slight whip motion of his wrist followed by—

He moves. I think.

I see a blur, a streak of sorts that is so minute that if I'd blinked I would have missed it. I slap my hand over my little cup just in case, though his palm still hovers over his.

"Pretty fast, huh?" he says giggling. "Want to see it again?"

I just look at him.

"Did you have that joke when you were a kid playing cowboys? You pretend like you are Wyatt Earp making a quick draw from your imaginary holster, but you do not really move your hand at all. Then you ask, 'You want to see it again?'"

I shake my head. "Funny. I'm laughing real hard inside. I laughed even harder at that when I was eight years old." I lean back and fold my arms. Samuel reaches for the teapot.

"More tea?" he asks.

I'm good," I say, picking up my cup. "So is your style pre-dominately hands or—"

My mouth drops open. "My cup! It's… empty." I look at the one in front of him. It's almost full.

"You switched the cups?!" I ask, my voice about ten octaves higher than normal.

He laughs uproariously. "Yes yes yes, Grasshopper." He shows me his wet palm. "But I sloshed a little of yours. I'm getting sloppy in my old age."

I am beyond stunned. In twenty-eight years of training, I have never seen speed like that. I feel like a white belt. Worse, I feel like I haven't even signed up for my first lesson yet. Only my ego prevents me from asking how he did it.

"Practice, son. Practice."

"How do you know what I'm thinking all the time?" I blurt. The hell with ego.

"I don't know *all* of the time, but I'm working on it." This time he doesn't chuckle. "For some reason, I can read you better than other people."

I look at him, I look at the teacups, I look at my refrigerator, and I look back at him again. Since I have no words, I get up to heat more tea water. I can feel Samuel watching me as I fill the pot and punch the numbers on the microwave.

"May I say something about your martial arts, Sam?" he asks. I turn toward him. He's sitting comfortably with his forearms on the table, hands clasped. "I can see that you're confused about mine and, judging by what I've seen on the Internet and on television, I can understand why."

"What do you mean?"

"Too many people, here in the United States and in Europe, focus on the external: flash, fancy uniforms, tattoos, acting tough, and acting negatively toward each other. Mixed martial arts are the worse with its bravado and posturing and bragging. These guys make horrible faces at the camera and bellow like water buffalo. Their grappling is good but their kicking and punching is no better than a beginner's.

"Then there is the breaking competition on the sports channels; it's so pointless, so unimportant. And the kata competition misses the whole point. Some of the kids are good, but again, their approach is all physical, all showmanship. Their energy is misspent."

I place the hot teapot back on the table and drop in new bags. "I agree about mixed martial arts, but remember, it's still new. I think it will get better in time. And the kata is supposed to be about showmanship. That's how you win."

"So unfortunate," Samuel says.

"I don't know if I agree. Some of the things you point out are superficial, but I believe they're part of a person's evolution in the martial arts."

He nods. "I do not think so." He nods and disagrees? "Too much wasting of time."

The doorbell sounds.

Normally someone buzzing the doorbell wouldn't jack-up my heart rate, but my hyper-vigilance is on overtime.

"Stay here and watch the kitchen door. It leads out into the garage and there is a smaller door that opens to the back patio."

"Check," he says. I pity anyone who tries to come in through the garage. At least they won't see what hits them.

I move quickly across the kitchen, through the living room and over to the window. I lift one of the closed mini blinds just enough to see out. All but one media rig has left; a police cruiser is parked where the other news vans had been. I lean the side of my head against the glass and detect part of a uniformed shoulder on the front porch.

"It's okay," I call to Samuel. "It's an officer."

"Hey Sam, how you doin'?" Officer King says when I open the door.

"Hi, Amy. How are you?"

The short-haired blond officer hooks her thumbs in her belt and nods. "I'm doin' fine. More importantly is how you're doin'. I'm working this district this evening and I just wanted you to know I'm in the area. I'll make a pass-by every hour at least."

I know Mark has requested extra patrol for Tommy and me but I appreciate the extra step Amy is taking by stopping by. I open the door wider. "Thanks, Amy. Much appreciated. You want to come in. I'll buy you a cup."

"Thanks for the offer but I'm on my way to a husband and wife fight a couple blocks over." She shakes her head and smiles. "Domestic bliss! Can't you straight people just get along?" She laughs, shoots me a salute, and heads off to her car.

I shut the door, turn, and jump nearly out of my skin. "Damn! I didn't hear you come up behind me."

"Sorry," Samuel says. "Everything okay?"

"Yes, fine. Let's chat out here for a while."

Samuel sits on the sofa and I sit across from him in my old brown recliner. "You ready to tell me about your life in Vietnam? During the war, I mean."

Samuel looks at me for a long moment, then nods.

*

Samuel and I talked to nearly seven o'clock. We would have gone longer but he had to pick up his daughter at Portland State University. He asked me to come along and meet her but I declined, saying that I was exhausted, which I was. What I didn't tell him was that I didn't want to add meeting my half sister to a day that has already been an emotional rollercoaster.

I'm tired, on top of which are the effects of the PEP pill. My stomach fluctuates between feeling as if I've been spinning on a tire swing while eating rotten sushi, to my intestines gurgling noisily in surround sound. I didn't tell Samuel about the PEP because... it's too personal, I guess. Besides, the less I think about it the better; the possibility of getting AIDs is just too much for me to deal with right now.

I walked him out to his car where we shook hands and agreed to meet tomorrow. Since I haven't a clue what tomorrow is about, I told him I'd call him at his daughter's place—my sister's place?—or he can call me. We swapped numbers.

That was an hour ago. Since he left, I've been lying here on the sofa watching the outside light through the cracks in the blinds fade to gray, and at last give it up to the darkness. I'm liking the dark a whole lot right now so I don't turn on the table lamp.

The more Samuel and I talked tonight the more of a connection I felt. My police instincts and all my other gut feelings that have served me well thus far are telling me that this man is indeed my father. Calling him that aloud, though, or just calling him that in my mind, is ... Well, it just isn't going to happen. I've suddenly got a sister, too! A half sister, anyway. After thirty-four years of being fatherless and an only child, it's all a bit surreal.

Talking with Samuel this evening was an amazing experience. Hearing a little about his life was certainly fascinating, as is the whole vibe thing that he's my father, a part of me that's been missing all these years. Then there is his sheer magnetism, how his presence filled the room. That was this afternoon.

Other times, when I saw him from a distance in the park, and when I looked at him as he stood behind the yellow police tape at Mitchell's, he seemed small and so unassuming. It's all very strange and dreamlike.

Samuel gave me what he called "the *Reader's Digest* condensed version" of his last forty years. "After all," he explained, "It's been said 'to not dwell in the past, to not dream of the future, but concentrate the mind on the present moment.'" When I asked him if that was from *Star Wars*, he just shook his head and said he'd tell me later. Then he said something like, "But sometimes you have to look at the past to understand the present moment." When I asked if those two quotations, or whatever they were, canceled each other out, he just laughed.

He began by telling me that in the third year of his imprisonment at K-Forty-nine, he physically stopped four Australian prisoners from trying to kill the camp commander. He said the poorly-designed plan would have not only failed, but the four Aussies would have been shot dead on the spot, and all the other prisoners tortured for not reporting their peers.

The commander was most grateful to Samuel for saving his life and impressed as to how Samuel triumphed over all four Australians. He was so grateful that he pretended to believe that the brawl had been just a fight between prisoners so he wouldn't have to punish the camp for an assassination attempt and further, he gave Samuel a choice, a bizarre one. He could go to a work camp near the commander's village, where he would spend half a day toiling in rice paddies, vegetable gardens, and fruit orchards, and the other half teaching his martial arts to the commander. Or, he could remain where he was and watch the four Australians' execution. It wasn't a tough decision for Samuel.

So by fighting the Aussies he saved the commander's life and by teaching the commander martial arts he saved the Australians' lives. I guess I'm not the only one who has days in which you wonder what's real and what isn't.

Samuel said that initially there were two other American POWs working on the farm, but later in the year they were both sent back to K-Forty-nine, leaving Samuel and about fifteen South Vietnamese prisoners. The number of guards watching them dwindled from eight to two, and eventually things got so lax that most of the time the guards slept and he and the Vietnamese prisoners played cards or napped. Escaping was not an option. Although Samuel knew he could live off the land using his Green Beret survival skills, he would have to do so for many months as he worked his way back to the South through North Vietnamese infested jungles. Even if they didn't catch him, and the odds were high that they would, the K-Forty-nine guards would take his escape out on those who remained behind.

As the long, sweaty months passed, Samuel and the camp commander, a middle-aged, painfully thin man named Nguyen Thi, began to—"and this sounds strange, I know" Samuel emphasized—become friends. He even looked forward to their afternoon training and their bull sessions afterward. It was obvious that Thi enjoyed it, too.

Samuel said he had learned to speak Vietnamese as part of his Green Beret training before he went overseas. He became fluent after teaching medicine and sanitation methods to villagers for several months prior to his capture, and then spending nearly four years incarcerated with no one to talk to except the Vietnamese guards and the camp commander.

Nguyen Thi's English was nearly flawless, a result of spending his college senior year at the University of Boston. Before the war, he had been a professor of literature at Hanoi University, a classical pianist, and a collector of Chinese string instruments. In 1964, at the age of forty-three, the government forced him into the army as the country prepared for the inevitable war against the Americans.

Because Nguyen Thi turned out to be a lousy soldier, his superiors sent him to be second in command of a small POW camp called Noi Coc. Two years after that, he was transferred to K-Forty-nine to assume the position of camp commander. He told Samuel he was reprimanded often for being too soft on the prisoners, but at the same time, he was praised for having a camp with few problems, no deaths, and no cases of malnutrition.

Samuel said that he came to realize that Nguyen Thi's threat to kill the Australians if he didn't agree to work in the fields and teach him martial arts had been an idle one. Of course, the guards might have killed the Aussies if they had attacked the commander, but Thi's threat was just that, a threat. The man was a scholar, a reluctant officer in the North Vietnamese army, and a kind friend. He wasn't a killer.

Nguyen Thi said he had always wanted to learn the martial arts but his upper-class family looked down on it and forbid him. He had learned a little in the army and had seen some expert instructors in action, but he had never seen anyone move like Samuel. Thi proved to be a good student, in spite of being nearly fifty years old, and the workouts kept Samuel in good shape.

The two men spent many evenings after their training discussing and listening to classical music on Thi's small phonograph, and talking about film and American literature. Samuel could hold his own when talking about the movies and Thi got a kick out of his amazing ability to remember quotes from them. He could also talk on American literature, but ironically, not to the same extent as Thi. Samuel knew very little about classical music but learned quickly under his new friend's tutelage.

As if things couldn't get any more bizarre, it was about this time that Nguyen Thi introduced him to his daughter, sort of. One noon during monsoon season, Samuel came in from the field for the afternoon training session and decided, because he was soaking wet and muddy, to clean up first. He stripped off his filthy clothes and was about to step under the outside shower when the most beautiful woman he had ever seen walked around a truck and nearly bumped into his nakedness. Two seconds later, Nguyen Thi came around the same corner and froze in step at the sight of his daughter, her hands covering her mouth and giggling madly, as Samuel tried desperately to cover his not so private privates.

At any other prison camp and with any other camp commander, Samuel would have been shot on the spot. Thi simply laughed along with his daughter as the American scrambled to pick up his dirty trousers, saying, "Samuel, may I introduce my daughter, Kim."

"Nice to *see* you," she said in Vietnamese, and both she and her father laughed uproariously.

Samuel paused in his story at this point. I couldn't be sure in the dim light, but I think his eyes had misted over. He looked down at his lap for a long moment where he had folded his hands as if in meditation.

When I asked if he'd like a sandwich and more tea before he continued his story, he looked at his watch, and said, "Oh my goodness. It's seven already. I'm supposed to pick up Mai at the university in fifteen minutes."

"Nooo," I protested. "You *can't* leave. I want to know what happened."

"I'm sorry. Mai will worry if I don't pick her up, plus she does not like to ride your MAX commuter train this time of night. We can meet tomorrow and I will tell you more." He looked at me for a second and probably read my disappointment. "Okay," he said with a smile. "Here is a tease as to what follows in my tale: Kim has been my wife for over thirty wonderful years." He smiled even wider when he saw my jaw drop. "Gotta go now."

"There's so much more I want to know," I said, following him to the door. Then, for just an instant, I wondered if his story was even true.

He stepped out onto the porch and turned back to me. "Maybe it is, maybe not. Buddha said to 'Believe nothing, no matter where you read it, or who said it, no matter if I have said it, unless it agrees with your own reason and your own common sense.'"

Again he had somehow read my thoughts.

"But in this case," he said, stepping off the porch and onto the walkway, "it is all true." He waved over his shoulder as he walked quickly toward his car.

He's been gone an hour now and I still feel a little overwhelmed by the whole experience. I get up from the couch thinking that some light stretches might be in order, but I'm hit with a wave of nausea and dizziness, a not so pleasant reminder that I'm due another pill before I go to bed. I ignore the ick and swing my arms about to loosen my shoulders. I'm half way through a set of ten side bends when the nausea increases to more than I can tolerate. Forget it. I'm going to bed.

My cell rings. It's Tiff.

"Sam? Are you okay."

"Hi. Yes, pretty much." I'm not sure how my voice sounds. Flat, maybe, emotionless.

"I'm in Seattle. Had my cell off all day running from meeting to meeting. Just got back to my hotel room and turned it on to find your message about Mitchell. My God, Sam. What happened?"

"We think it was someone from the boy's family. No named suspects right now."

"The boy who… was shot?" I don't have a problem reading *Tiff's* tone. Disapproval. No, that's not quite it. Distaste? Yeah, that's the word.

"Yes."

"My God. Are you in danger?" She's still playing the concerned partner. Old habits are hard to break, I guess.

"Who knows? I'm being cautious and the PD's given the house some extra patrol. I just wanted to tell you to watch your back. Hard to say if the perps associate you with me. You should probably stay away, too. You know, until we figure it all out." I take a deep breath and massage my forehead. "I don't know if I'm making any sense. I don't feel well." For a second, just to be mean, I think about saying *I don't feel well. You know, with me having AIDs,* but I restrain myself.

"You going to bed?"

"Yes, I'm beat."

"Okay."

"Thanks."

"Sam I…"

She wants to talk again. Enough! "Sleep well, Tiff."

"… okay."

Twenty minutes later I'm lying on top of the covers watching a—what the hell?—a chorus line dancing across my ceiling.

Is this real or am I asleep? Not sure. And what a line it is. The tweaker, Jimmie, Mark, Tiff, Dr. Kari Stevens, Dr. Hegrenes, Samuel, Tammy, and even The Fat Dicks, arms linked, and rhythmically throwing high kicks like the friggin' Rockettes. There's no music and they aren't singing, but their kicks are in unison and their enthusiasm is unbridled. The Fat Dicks are a little sluggish, of course, but the rest of them are actually pretty darn good.

I would enjoy the show a heck of a lot more if I didn't know that they were dancing to my *dukkha*.

CHAPTER EIGHT

An explosion rips me from sweaty sleep.

I had been sitting in my pickup and Tammy Dee, my over-sexed sixteen-year-old neighbor, had been leaning her ample breasts through the window, saying, "I'd kiss yuh, but your AIDs is making for some hardcore zits on your face."

I was about to protest and say that it wasn't *my* AIDs, when a small explosion or something yanks me out of the pickup and onto my feet next to my bed. I'm as startled by the noise as I am confused to find myself standing in my semi-dark bedroom. What little I can see around me appears to be okay. But the sound was so real.

I shake the fuzzies from my head, grab my Glock out of my nightstand drawer and move toward the door where I can see down the dark hallway and into part of my living room. Slits of streetlight coming through the closed mini blinds form a series of long, narrow lines on the carpet, a pattern I've seen there for years. This time, though, it's wrong: some of the lines are broken and angled. There's something sparkling on the carpet, too. Diamonds? Am I dreaming about diamonds? No, I'm not dreaming now.

Sounds like someone's trying to start a car outside. The grinding is louder than it should be. Is the front door open? I lean out from the door facing. It looks closed.

I would call dispatch but my cell phone is in my jacket pocket in the dining room, my regular phone is in the living room, my kitchen phone is lying in pieces next to my cookie jar, and I don't have one in my bedroom. Great.

The car engine grinds again. *Why can I hear it so clearly?*

I move down the hallway, hugging the wall, my gun clutched in both hands and angled downward, same thing I did two days ago in Jimmy's house. I peek one eye around the corner. The living room is empty. Okay, the sparkly stuff on the carpet isn't diamonds but shards of glass. I can see the mini blinds better, too. They're askew and a few are bent. I begin to take another step when I stub my toe on something: a gray brick. Weird that it didn't hurt my toes, but even more weird is that a brick is lying on my carpet.

Wait. A brick lying on my floor, shattered window glass on my floor, broken mini blinds, someone outside trying to start a car. *Voila!* A vandal!

I ought to be a detective.

I jump up on the sofa to avoid the broken glass on my bare feet, run its length, and jump down by the front door. Peering through its window, I can see an old gray beater in front of Bill's house next door and it looks like someone is behind the wheel. I open the door and slip out onto the porch. The sensible thing is to go back inside and call for a patrol car, but my jackhammering heart is pumping too much adrenaline through my muscles to just sit on the porch and wait.

I cut across my night-wet lawn and, with no other choice, approach the car from the front, my Glock gripped in both hands. It's an unsound tactic but here I am anyway.

I mentally note the license plate and can see the driver's bent head through the fogged windshield as he desperately grinds away at the weakening starter. He looks up, the streetlight catching his face just enough to reveal his eyes widen as he spots the tank top and baggy pants-wearing lug stomping toward him, the serious end of a gun barrel leading the way. I'm probably scowling, too.

"You throw that brick, prick?" I call to him through his closed side window. Not my best line of questioning but I'm pissed. This is personal. "I asked you a question. Did you throw that brick?"

A gray brick lay on the grass next to the beater.

"Dropped one, buttwipe!" I say, then front kick his door with the ball of my bare foot.

It flies open. "You going to shoot me cop?" Brick Man is about twenty-five, stringy, chopped hair that looks as if his last barber worked at Oregon State Prison, a scraggly goatee, black jacket, and he's coming out fast. "Aren't I a little old for you to shoot?" he says, moving toward me. His hands are empty.

My gun doesn't intimidate him and I got no place to put it. The waistband of my baggies won't support it and I'm not about to lay it on the ground. Why did I bring it, anyway? I don't intend to shoot the guy. Now it's a third wheel on my late-night date with this guy.

"Hold it right there," I say, although my gut's telling me he isn't going to hold it right anywhere.

Brick Man looks at me, my Glock, and then moves his eyes up slowly to meet mine. He shakes his head and snorts his disgust. I can't say that I disagree with his opinion.

"Look, pal," I say, lowering my weapon off to the side.

He steps in with a right fist that started way back.

I snap up my left arm to shield the side of my face and his knuckles slam into my upper forearm muscle hard, sending a piercing shock of pain all the way to my fingertips. If it had hit my skull, he would have made a dent big enough for a birdbath. Brick Man comes right back with a left hook to my other ear, which I duck.

I shuffle back a step or two, still holding my Glock off to the right and pointed at the ground. He lunges forward with a couple of fast jabs that I swat aside. I counter the second one with a crescent kick into his inner thigh, careful not to lose my footing on the dewy grass. Brick Man registers surprise and his leg wobbles a little, but that's all.

"That it, baby shooter?" He snaps out a couple more jabs, but they're too far away to bother blocking. He's no martial artist but he looks like he knows what he's doing. Probably learned a little boxing in the joint where he got that haircut. He's got good speed and, judging by the one that landed on my arm shield, good power. If Brick Man does get one in, I might end up kissing worms on the neighbor's lawn, as he scoops up my gun. My first street coach used to say, "Remember, in every scuffle you get into as a cop, there's always at least one gun present: yours." Well, Brick Boy isn't getting mine.

We're both on the sidewalk now, a dry, hard surface that's easier to move on. He changes stances to his right side forward and jabs. Ambidextrous son-of-a-gun. I swat it aside and step to his outside. I shuffle-step my lead left leg to the rear and then whip my shinbone across the outside of his upper thigh, specifically into his peroneal nerve.

His leg doesn't wobble this time; it simply crumbles under him, dropping him straight to the concrete. He frantically thrashes his arms and legs about in an attempt to get up, but that kicked thigh couldn't support a cotton ball right now.

"I just poked the 'delete' button on that leg, pal. Now I want you to—"

He lunges off his good leg and grabs my left ankle with both hands as he balances on one knee. I try to pull my leg away but he's gripping it hard and pulling himself toward me.

I drive my fist down twice into the biceps of his top arm, squishing that tender muscle against the big humerus bone under it. Brick Man yelps in pain and moves his struck arm out of the way. Thank you. I punch his other biceps twice. Because his top arm was braced by his other arm and that one was braced by the sidewalk, his tender muscles absorbed all the energy from my blows, no doubt numbing them both out of commission.

That frees my ankle. I grab a fist full of his hair all the way down to the roots and twist it hard to force him over onto his belly. Then I twist it even harder to jam his face into the sidewalk, jam, not smash. I could scoot his ugly mug back and forth on the cement a few times, too, but I don't.

"Okay, fun time's over. You try to fight even a little bit, and I'm going to jerk your empty skull up by your hair and slam your face down into the sidewalk not once, not twice, but seventeen times. Why seventeen? Don't know. I just like how it sounds."

I hear sirens and see a couple of units racing toward me, their lights flashing in the morning dawn. I wonder who called nine-one-one Oh, okay. There's Bill standing on his porch in his bathrobe, holding a phone.

"Morning, Bill," I say, watching Brick Man's kicked leg twitch involuntarily. "Thanks for calling nine-one-one." He grunts and slams his door. I bet he really does like me but his wife would prefer a quieter neighbor.

Forty-five minutes later, I'm sitting at my kitchen table icing my sore forearm and trying to ignore the intense nausea in my gut and head. It's been threatening me since I popped a PEP pill as soon as I came in the house. I'm trying to force down an English muffin with peanut butter in the hopes that a little food and coffee will help. So far they haven't. Apparently, I get to look forward to this unpleasantness everyday for a while, maybe several weeks.

The uniform officers took Brick Man down to Detectives to see if he's related to Jimmy's family. My hunch is that he isn't. Before they left, they ran him through their squad's computer and he came back with a dozen arrests, including two cases of Assault on a Police Officer and three cases of Eluding the Police. That means he likes to punch cops and flee from them in his car. He did fifteen months at OSP for the last one, got out just two months ago in late March. I'm guessing that the guy's hatred of authority peaked when he saw my shooting on the news. It's not impossible to find out where a cop lives but it does take effort. Maybe he's the guy who left the newspaper on my steps.

I handled him okay, even with one hand, and that's right after I kicked him that first time and my nausea came-a-callin'. I studied a little muay Thai once with an old retired Navy guy who had trained in Thailand for a couple years. The poor guy had smoked, drank and fought in every port in the world, and he showed it. He was about sixty-five but looked eighty-five. Incredibly, he could kick and punch as if he were a teenager, though he'd poop out in thirty seconds, coughing and hacking afterwards for five minutes.

He used to tell me, "Sam my boy, if we ever fought for real and it went on for sixty seconds, you'd clean my clock. But I gotta warn you. Those first thirty seconds are gonna be a mutha fucker for you."

That's where I am now right now, though I'm wondering if I could last even thirty seconds.

I call a window repair place called We'll Fix Your Pane and schedule someone to come out and look at my front window.

I hit the shower, get dressed, and am about to pour another cup when my cell rings. I don't recognize the number.

"Yes?"

"Is this Mr. Sam Reeves?" Female, Asian accent.

"Yes. Who's this?"

"My name Mai. I am Samuel's daughter."

*

"Mai? Oh, hi. How are you? Is every thing okay?" I didn't expect to get this call.

"I am fine. I am sorry I am calling you at seven thirty in the morning. I found your number on my father's nightstand."

At least she didn't say "our" dad's nightstand. So why is she calling me? "Is he okay?"

"Three men were waiting outside of my apartment building when my father and I got home last night. They were violent men. They attacked us."

What the hell? How did they find out about Samuel? Did they follow me to the park yesterday? To Mitchell's? Maybe they followed me to my house and then followed him when he left? But why? They wouldn't have a clue about our relationship.

"What happened? Are you okay? Is Samuel okay?"

"Yes, thank you. We are okay. But I am worried and I wanted to tell you."

"I don't understand. What happened to the men last night?"

"My father and I fight them very good. Two of them are hurt bad. I think one might have… uh… I do not know the word. Like a crack in the head?"

"A concussion?"

"Yes, yes, that is the word. Concussion." Mai speaks the same way as Samuel: stilted, no contractions. Actually, he's the

American so maybe it's more accurate to say that he speaks the way Mai speaks. Or is he American, anymore?

"What happened to the men?"

"A car came with another man driving and he helped the hurt men get in. They drive away very fast."

"Did you call the police?"

"My father said not to."

"I guess I'm not understanding. Why not call the police? Where is Samuel, anyway? Did he get hurt? Why didn't he call me?"

Long pause. Maybe too many questions given the language barrier.

"Is Samuel hurt?"

"No, he is fine. But he is hungry."

"Where is he?"

"He went to get Cinnabon."

"Cinnabon?"

"Yes, Cinnamon rolls with lots of frosting. My father likes them very much. He went down to the corner to get us some for breakfast."

Good lord! The daughter is as frustrating as the father. "Okay. So you waited until he left to call me?"

"Yes. I know he has been meeting with you. He has been very excited about that. But I do not think you know about these men."

"Yes, I know about them. They are related to my... *incident* that happened a couple of days ago."

"Yes, my father told me about your problems. I am very sorry. But my father's problems are not from your problems. His problems are *his* problems."

"His problems?"

"I think father will come back soon. He might get angry if he knows I told you."

"These men are *his* problems?" I ask again.

"I just heard the elevator door ding. I must go."

"Wait. Do you know where Tenth and Jefferson is, a few blocks up from Portland State?"

"Yes."

"Meet me there at eleven at my martial arts school, Reeves' Bushido Academy. Can you do that?"

"Yes." Dial tone.

I close the lid and it rings instantly.

"How you doing, Mark?"

"More importantly how are you doing? You okay after your run-in this morning?"

"I'm fine. Well, actually, I'm not. I feel like I've been shit out of a duck's ass. Those little pills deliver quite a wallop."

"Not as bad as the alternative. Slim chance you can get AIDs like that but you got to take the precaution. Okay, about your buddy. Uniform interviewed him in their car on the way down here and the Fat Dicks are talking to him now. You Bruce Lee'd his ass pretty good. He's limping and his arms are in bad shape. The nurse said his leg will be fine but the biceps in both of his arms are pretty trashed."

"What did he say?"

"He said they hurt."

I laugh. "I bet they do. I mean what'd he say about his visit with me."

"He told uniform that… hey, by any chance are you going to be out and about today, near the office?"

"I'm heading to my school shortly. I can swing by."

"Good. I want you to see some photos of the boy's uncles."

Thirty minutes later, I'm in the Justice Center riding up to the thirteenth floor after being greeted by a few cops in the lobby, all of whom wished me good luck. The elevator doors ding open and I head down the hall toward Burglary. Half way down, Mark steps out of the copy machine room and we nearly bump into each other.

"Good timing," he says, shaking my hand. "I'm just heading over to The Fat Dicks' cubicle. Walk with me. Wow, you look a little green around the gills."

"I was fine before you introduced me to Doctor Hegrenes. So what's up with the brick thrower?"

"The Fat Dicks say he's not involved with the family at all, and they don't think he's lying. They say he acted independently both times."

"Both?"

Richard Daniels and Richard Cary wave a greeting as we round the corner into the Homicide area. Their cluttered desks face one another, on which there are paper plates stacked with giant Cinnabons and what appears to be frappachinos in the largest cups possible. What's up with people eating Cinnabons today? There must be two thousand calories in each of the detectives' servings and, judging by the crumbs on Daniels's chest, they've already downed at least one each.

"Having some breakfast, guys?" I ask as an opener.

"Hey, Sam," Daniels says, wiping his mouth with a napkin. "Nah, just a snack. We had breakfast a little while ago. Grab those chairs, gents."

I nod. What can I say? They're great guys who are probably going to blow their heart gaskets one of these days. I sit and turn to Mark. "You said something about the brick thrower acting out independently *both* times."

"Oh, sorry. Yes, he delivered the newspaper two days ago to your house and to Mitchell's place. He works for the phone company, Qwest, so he had easy access to your home addresses. Tommy uses a cell, a different company, so he couldn't get his info."

Cary sets his partially eaten Cinnabon down and talks around what's in his mouth, which is a lot. "The shithead's got a real hardon for the cops, but he's not connected to the boy's family. We booked him on Assault and his PO is coming down to put a hold on him. He'll probably be going back to prison. Man, you did a job on his arms. Nurse said that one, maybe both biceps might be ruptured."

"Whoops," I say.

"He's crying lawsuit," Daniels says, before draining his frap.

"Why not!" I blare. "Why the hell not sue me?"

"It sure is crap-on-Sam week, huh?" Mark says sympathetically.

"You feeling like a port-a-potty these days, buddy?" Cary asks, with mock sympathy.

I smile and shake my head. "Okay, okay. So where are we at on the family?"

Cary turns toward his computer, taps the mouse until a screen pops up. I think you know some of this already. Mom Clarkson's name is Sybil, forty-five, doesn't work, legally blind. Her shock has transitioned from deep sorrow to extreme anger. She won't talk to us or with anyone from the PD or the DA's office. Father is Warren, also forty-five, owns Crown Trucking. Loaded with money. He, too, is outraged but he's talked with us a couple times. He's very tight with his two brothers, Kane and Barry.

"Kane is thirty-three. He's been in the joint twice, for a total of twelve years."

"Wait," I interrupt. "I alerted on that name earlier. I used to train with a guy named Kane Clarkson. Everyone called him 'K Man.' Got his black belt when he was twenty, same time I got my second black. We never hung out or anything. About the same time I was testing for the PD, he got into some trouble, drugs and robbery, if I remember right. Heard he went to prison. I got on the PD and never saw him again. Forgot about him, actually."

Daniels has been nodding as I spoke. "Same guy." He plunks down some mug shots in front of me. "Went by 'K Man' in the joint, too, even has it tattooed on his chest."

"Small friggin' world," I say, picking up the pics.

The first one was taken the year he went to Oregon State Prison, the same year I knew him. The cherub-looking face belies the fact that he was a darn good fighter then. His moniker, "K Man," was a joke, a gangster-type name for a kid who looked like his picture should be caroling on a Christmas card. The second mug, a release picture from OSP, is dated two years ago. Now the moniker fits him. Early thirties, chiseled face and—damn!—there's a chunk out of his left ear. Looks like a perfect bite mark.

"He did his time okay," Daniels says over the brim of his frap, "Except for one incident where he jammed a toothbrush down another con's throat. Did enough damage that he bought another year, some of it in solitary. He got out of OSP a couple years go. Apparently, he knew another con whose family owns Hot Videos, Inc, those porno stores you see all over town. Kane's brother, Barry, loaned him some money to buy a partnership into one at Hundred and Sixty-Second and Brookings Ave." Daniels looks over to his partner who's picking at the remaining Cinnabon crumbs on his paper plate. "You know that place, don't you, pard?"

Richard Cary doesn't bat an eye as he tosses the last crumb into his mouth. "Yes, I do indeed, Richard. I was just there last week with your misses."

"Anyway…" Mark says, bringing the two back on task.

"Barry Clarkson is the other brother," Cary says. "Thirty-eight, straight arrow. Divorced, no kids, makes good money as some kind of a repairman for Northwest Power. All we have is this company ID photo taken eight years ago."

I look at it. "Looks like a softer version of Kane," I say. I look at the recent mug of Kane again. "Hard-looking dude. Prison life: the ultimate makeover." I drop the pics back on the table. "If he's behind Mitchell's killing, he's going to go hard."

Mark nods. "Yup, cons in their thirties don't want to go back in."

Daniels retrieves a bag of Hershey's Kisses from his center drawer, shakes a few onto his blotter and nods toward the bag as he sets it near Mark and me. We shake our heads. "We got nothin' on them," he says around the chocolate. "All we know is that they're all plenty pissed. We don't have the manpower to tail them twenty-four seven but we can have someone on them intermittently."

Mark turns to me. "Before you even ask, Sam, no, you can't follow them or in anyway be involved. We clear?"

I nod and stand. "Thanks, guys. You're doing a good job. If I could trouble you to keep me posted, I'd appreciate it."

"Can do," Daniels says. "Hey, it's about lunch time. You want to go with us to the Bamboo Forest? Great Thai buffet up on Forth."

I smile, wondering where on Earth they're going to put it. "Thanks anyway. I got an appointment to meet someone."

*

I unlock the front door to my school and step in, kicking off my shoes. I haven't taught for a few days and I miss it. Thomas, one of my senior black belts, has been teaching my regular classes and all my private lessons. Normally, he's scheduled to teach four classes a week as part of his training for third-degree, but since times have been a little nutso for me, he's been teaching the others out of the goodness of his heart.

I look around and see that everything is in its place. I walk over to where the mats are stacked and push them this way and that way to align the pile.

I'm anxious to meet Mai. Three days ago, I didn't know I had a father let alone a half sister, one who is half Vietnamese. I wonder if we look alike in any way. I'm curious to see what she's like and I want to know what's going on with Samuel. Why would there be men after him? He hasn't even been here that long to make one person mad at him, let alone three people and a getaway driver. Maybe he's mixed up in something. Maybe there is another reason why he's in the states. Dope? Some kind of espionage? Gun runner?

Okay, I'm getting carried away.

I step over to the closest of three hanging heavy bags and smack it with a quick backfist. The sound is loud in the empty space. I smack it again. I shake out my shoulders, switch stances and backfist the bag with my left fist. A wave of nausea washes over me. So that's the way it's going to be? I exercise a little and I instantly get queasy. Damn! Could anything else happen to me?

Stop it! It's time to get control of my whimpering self and actually do what I preach. I always tell my students that when they have a limitation of some kind not to dwell on what they can't do, but emphasize what they can.

I got a new student about four months ago, a twenty-two-year-old man who told me that he had been born with a bad hip, a birth defect of some kind. He desperately wanted to train but his doctor made it clear that he shouldn't kick with his left leg at all because it was, in his doctor's words, "his Achilles' heel," his weak link and it would cause irreparable damage to his deteriorated joint.

First, I talked with him about never, ever using those negatives terms again when referring to his leg. Lots of people have had outstanding success while having physical limitations. Some have become world champions in the martial arts and other sports. Then I outlined a course for him that emphasized what he *could* do to bring out his best in those things. Afterwards, he nodded with steeled determination on his face and shook my hand with such enthusiasm that I worried for a moment that I might not get it back. The young man has been training hard, progressing quickly and has never once said a negative word about that hip.

So, unless I want to stop training for several weeks, I'm going to have to devise a program around my upchucking. Actually, I haven't vomited yet but I've come close a couple of times. Maybe I can make vomiting a technique. I can—

The street door opens.

Holy shit!

Okay, I've never liked that exclamation. It's not that I'm offended from a religious standpoint all that much, it's just that it seems like it belongs in a teenage slasher movie. The teens are camping, having sex, and giggling up a storm when suddenly a salivating creature springs out from the brush. One of the kids, usually the guy, shouts, "Holy shit!" just before his head goes rolling along the ground.

That said, the term is the first thing that rips through my mind when I see the woman enter through my door. Silhouetted against the outside daylight I know it's female. A slash of outside light illuminates her curves, shimmering black hair, and legs that go on forever. The fact that she must be six-feet tall throws me for a loop. She steps tentatively into my school and as Lord Byron wrote, "She walks in beauty…" Damn.

"Sam Reeves?" Same voice as on the phone. It's Mai. Holy shit!

"Yes, yes," I stammer as I move across the room toward her. The closer I get, the less she's in silhouette. Die-am! "Please come in. You must be Mai." I extend my hand.

I'm five feet eleven and she stands eye-to-eye with me. Early thirties, long legged in snug blue jeans, a well-filled out pale blue polo shirt, and blue/black hair that falls to her mid back. Her face is a wonderful blend of Asian and Caucasian with brown eyes that are at once shy, sensual, and intelligent.

"Yes," she says softly, gripping my hand confidently. "Thank you for seeing me." She looks into my eyes a few seconds longer than is customary for the situation, then blinks a couple of times as if to break it off. She looks about the room. "You have a nice school." Strained, like she's trying to make conversation.

"Thank you. I've been here a few years now. It serves my needs. Please, let's go back to my office where we can sit."

"Yes," she says with a nod. Her accent, which is incredibly charming, is thicker than Samuel's. She toes off her shoes.

"Have you trained in the martial arts?" I ask, as we walk toward the back of the room. I'm not just a little discomforted by the fact my half sister's presence is making my heart race.

"Yes," she says, again with that slight nod. "My father teaches me in Vietnam. I started when I was about five years old, I think. Father has told me about your training. He said that you are a champion."

I gesture for her to go through the office door. "I won some matches in my twenties, but now my job on the police department and my work here at the school keep me too busy to train for competition. Plus, I'm not a kid anymore. Please sit down." I scoot around behind my desk and pull up my chair.

She giggles as she sits. "Well, you are—how do you say it?—in good shape for not being a kid anymore."

I feel a blast of heat in my face. "Yes, that is exactly how you say it," I stammer. "I mean, thank you. If I may say, you are in good shape, too." Ahh, man. Did I really say that?

She covers her hand with her mouth, giggling. "Thank you." Her eyes penetrate mine.

I'm the first to break eye contact as I needlessly scoot a stack of papers to one side of my desk. I look back at her. "I'm anxious to know about what's going on with Samuel. I—"

My cell rings. "Excuse me," I say, retrieving it from my pocket. "Tiff," I say, wishing I hadn't said her name and then feeling weird because I wished that.

"Can I see you today," she says softly. It's her make-up voice. What is she doing? There's no way. I glance at Mai. She's looking at her hands, her brow furrowed. She looks up. Smiles that smile. Holy…

"Uh, I'm in a meeting. I'm not sure what's going on today."

"Are you downtown, at Detectives?"

"What? No. I'm… at the school."

"Can I come by there?"

"No." What does she want? "I mean, things are just weird right now." We've ended this twice. Why does she—

"Sam? You sound like… All right. Call when you have time for me."

"It's just that—" Dial tone.

I close my phone and look over at Mai. She raises her eyebrows slightly, communicating what? That she knows how bothersome phone calls can be? That she thinks it's rude that I took the call? That she knows it was a woman? Why did I feel a need to hide from Tiff that I'm talking with my half sister?

"Are you okay?" Mai asks. Is she smirking?

I wave my hand to indicate that it's nothing.

"Your hands," she says looking at my scabbed over knuckles. "From your training?"

"What? Oh, uh yes. I get too zealous sometimes. You were telling me about the attack last night. You said that Samuel had problems."

Her face sobers. "My father is a complicated man. He told me that he has explained to you his life in Vietnam."

"Just a little. A little about his prison experience and about teaching the prison commander."

Mai nods. "Yes, that happened when he met my mother."

"Is your mother named Kim?"

"Yes. They married and lived at first in a small village just outside of Lê Mât. It was a good place for him to hide for a while. Do you know it? It is very famous."

I shake my head. I'm listening but I'm absolutely captivated by this beautiful woman, the way she speaks, gestures, and how she gazes at me with those incredibly brown eyes. There might be some green in them, too.

"Lê Mât is known as Snake Village, a place where they breed and make very special snake dishes—to eat. Well, this was not a good home for my father because he hates the snakes. He is very afraid of them." She giggles a little at this.

"Me, too," I say, and she smiles, nodding.

"People in Lê Mật they are very religious. The religion is called Cao Đài. They believe very strong in peace and in harmony in each person. I think that is why they let my father and mother and me stay there. No problem, even though my father had been an enemy of the North. People of Lê Mật they were happy the war was over and want to forget all of that. They like my father and soon they thought of him as member of the village." Mai blinks a couple of times as if to bring herself back to my office. She looks at her watch. "I have class in thirty minutes. I think it best my father tell you about his early life in Vietnam. But I wanted to meet you now to tell you a little about the last year because his problems in Vietnam are now here. Tell me, have you noticed he is sometimes hard to talk to?"

This time it's my turn to laugh. "A little," I say, and laugh again.

"Yes, he can be difficult. He might seem like he is not serious, but he is very serious man. About a year ago, our family had big problems, money problems. Our family owns many jewelry shops in different cities in Vietnam, eighteen of them, but now not that many. I came here to finish my degree in business so I can help my family. About a year ago, a man we have been paying for protection tried to cheat us for more money."

"Protection? You mean like you pay him money so that nothing happens to your shops?"

"Yes. Many businesses in Vietnam have to pay protection money to the gangsters. You pay them so they will not destroy the businesses."

"I understand. The South East Asian gangs here sometimes get involved with selling protection, too. If the Vietnamese stores don't pay, they get arsoned or damaged."

Mai frowns. "Arsoned? Fired?"

"They set the place on fire, yes."

She nods. "Yes, same in Vietnam. We lose much money. We have to close three shops and perhaps more.

"Then my mother got sick. TB. It cost a lot of money for doctors but we did not have any because we spent too much money on protection. My father went to visit the big man, Lai Van Tan. He is boss of the gangsters. My father tried to talk to him and ask not to charge us so much, but Lai Van Tan got mad and he called my father names because he is Caucasian. When my father left, two men followed him. I do not know what happened because my father will not tell me. But I think he had a fight with the men and maybe hurt them. Maybe killed them, I don't know."

I lean forward on my elbows. "So, these men last night, they work for this Lai gangster? And they came all the way here to attack your father?"

She nods. "Yes. I think so. My father not talk about it, though."

"Did you recognize them last night? Did they speak English?"

"No, I do not know them. They spoke only Vietnamese. There was not much talking anyway; they just attacked. My father's fighting skill is mostly a secret in Vietnam. But now that they know he is good, they will probably use guns next time." Mai has been clasping her hands as she talked; now she is wringing them. "I'm very frightened for him."

"Did these men say anything to indicate what they wanted? How do you know they attacked you because of something your father did in Vietnam? Maybe it was just a robbery here. A coincidence."

Mai nods. "No, it was not a robbery."

"How do you know? It sounds like they attacked without talking. Maybe your father didn't give them time to get the robbery part."

"It was not a robbery."

"But—"

I jump, startled, as Samuel steps through the doorway.

How did he come in through the street door without it making noise? Mai looks at me questioningly, unaware that her father is behind her glaring at the back of her head.

Is that anger in his face? He rattles off something in Vietnamese.

Now it's her turn to jump. She twists in her seat and says something back, to which he utters one loud, commanding word. She turns back quickly and looks down passively at her hands.

"Samuel," I say standing. "Is everything all right?"

"I see you have met Mai," he says tightly. He's wearing a pale blue overshirt, black slacks, and his red converse shoes.

"Yes. We were just talking—"

"I heard what she was telling you. Mai is a wonderful daughter and very protective of her family. But sometimes her actions are too independent."

"I just thought it was important that Sam should know."

Again he barks that word and again she wilts. He must be telling her to be quiet or something.

"Mai was helping me understand some things about the family, the problems with the men. She just—"

"Enough," he says. Did he just tell me to shut-up? "Mai too often does what she wishes even when it is against what I say."

She twists toward him again. "I am worried about you, father. I thought it was important that Samuel know what is happening"

"Enough!" he snaps. That must have been what he said so harshly at her before.

"Samuel," I say, extending my palm to calm him. "Please sit down. Mai is just concerned that those men you encountered—"

"Enough!"

Now that pisses me off. "Stop with the 'enoughs'!"

Where did that come from? He looks at me with surprise, as does Mai. I'm guessing they're not used to people speaking to him this way. That's fine, but I'm not going to be pushed around by anyone, and certainly not in my school.

"You've basically told me to shut-up—twice. No more. I'm a grown man and you're standing on my turf. Maybe you can kick my ass, but you don't talk to me that way. And Mai is a grown woman. Maybe you talk to her that way where you come from, but I'd appreciate it if you didn't use that tone in my presence, and in my school."

Awkward moment as Samuel looks at me with… shock? Awe? Shock and awe? Mai seems frozen in place, except for her eyes that are looking at me with a combination of admiration and it-so-sucks-to-be-you-right-now.

Out of the corner of my eye, I note the distance to the samurai sword on the bookcase under the painting of Musashi. Should he lunge, the desk between us will give me an extra second and a half to dive for the weapon.

"I noticed a *phở* restaurant at the end of the block," Samuel says, his voice calm now, as it was yesterday in the park. "Have you had lunch?"

Since my bubbling fight-or-flight juices are about to boil over, I'm not tracking. I know that *phở* is Vietnamese soup. I'm just surprised to hear the subject mentioned at this particular moment, and so calmly and chatty-like.

"Vietnamese soup," he says, apparently perceiving my confusion. "It's very good. I'll buy." He turns and heads toward the doorway.

Mai looks at me as she stands and shrugs a what-are-you-going-to-do?' She hesitates for a moment as I come around the desk and move up even with her. "He is saying that he is 'sorry,'" she whispers. I think that's admiration I see in her eyes. I nod, and feel my face flush as I gesture for her to go ahead of me out the office door.

"It is a wonderful school," Samuel says looking around as he leads us toward the door. "If I may, I would like to look at it more at another time."

"Of course?" I say. Mai looks over at me and I shrug that I don't understand. She smiles. "I mean, I'd be happy to show it to you."

What a friggin' twenty minutes it's been. First I lust over my half sister, then she tells me that a gang is after Samuel, then he appears at my office door like a ticked-off dragon, then I'm standing up to him like I have no common sense at all, then just as I'm thinking about reaching for a sword, he asks me out for soup.

Samuel opens the door part way and then hesitates. "By the way," he says turning toward me. "You were making preparations. That is a good warrior trait. But for the record, you would have never made it to the sword."

*

Samuel and I are sitting here in the *phở* joint waiting for our soup. There are two things rattling around in my skull as I toy with a porcelain spoon. One is that I'm disappointed that Mai had to rush off to PSU.

Fifteen minutes earlier, she gave her father a terse goodbye, to which he only grunted something in Vietnamese, the tension between them still palatable. She turned and shot me a ten thousand-watt smile as she extended her hand. I took it, maybe a little too quickly, and we stood there for a moment, palm hugging, minus the usual up and down handshake motion, as the warmth from her touch shot up my arm like the onset of a heart attack. She pulled away first, reluctantly I think, saying something about how it had been nice to meet me. I said something similar back and then glanced at Samuel. I'm sure he hadn't missed a thing, though he was expressionless, as usual. She smiled again, turned, and walked toward the University. It would have been nice to have watched that walk a whole lot longer, but her father—my father—was standing right there.

Man, do I ever need a session with my shrink.

Two, I notice that Samuel is acting differently than he has in the days prior. Since we've been at the table, he hasn't uttered one bumper sticker quote and nothing at all from Yoda. There is a subtle tension in his body and the skin around his eyes and mouth looks too tight for his face.

When we first sat down, he looked at the pictures on the menu and commented that they were the same dishes he eats in Vietnam. He ordered beef noodle soup for both of us and something similar to egg rolls.

After the waitress left a few seconds ago, he leaned back in his chair and looked at me, his eyes searching my face, perhaps trying to decide how much to tell me. He is still doing that now.

"I enjoyed meeting Mai," I say, to break the awkward moment.

His eyes soften, those of a father who loves his daughter, unconditionally. "I had intended for you to meet her tonight, over dinner. But she has a strong will."

"She's worried about you," I say quickly.

He nods. "She is a good daughter. I am sorry that... I am angry that my problems have come here to the United States, to Portland, especially at a time when she is about to graduate. I am sorry that I took my anger out on you and Mai."

"It's understandable," I say, noting how he nods with genuine humility.

Our soup bowls arrive, giant tubs of rich broth, noodles, and chunks of beef. Another waitress sets down a plate of rolls and a second plate of sprouts, greens, and slices of lime.

Samuel says something to the waitress in Vietnamese and she looks surprised, probably because he's speaking the language. "This looks perfect," he says, after she leaves. He pinches a squirt or two of lime juice into the broth, then adds a few mint leaves and a handful of sprouts. I do the same, as if I'm an old hand at this. I've eaten here many times, but I always order dishes that are less complicated.

He lifts a few noodles out of the bowl with his chopsticks, drops them into his big spoon, and slurps them up. I try to do the same with mine, but they slide off my spoon and plop back into the bowl, splashing a little broth onto the table.

Samuel smiles faintly for the first time today. "Repetition is the mother of all skill."

"Buddha?" I ask.

"Anthony Robbins," he says, his smile widening a little.

I shake my head. This time I chopstick up the noodles and push them straight into my mouth. "You're always quoting movies, Buddha, and Tony Robbins."

He shrugs as he expertly picks up noodles, greens, and a hunk of meat, all in one pinch. He bends his head to receive the food. "I like movies," he says around the mouth full. "I try to follow Buddha's way, and Tony Robbins has some good things to offer. We can learn from everyone and everything. The closer you look, the more clearly you see that everything and everyone are interrelated, connected."

I nod, not finding anything to disagree with. "Well, I'd like to know about these men who attacked you."

He lays down his chopsticks and spoon and wipes his mouth on his napkin. "I thought it was over three months ago. Now my problems have followed me here and I am worried about my wife, Kim, Mai, and my other daughters. I called home this morning and Kim said everything is okay there. She has not seen or heard anything out of the ordinary. She is going to call her brother, Lu, to come stay at the house until we get home. She is ill with TB."

"I'm sorry."

Samuel nods and looks back at his soup. "*Cám ơn,*" he says, with the same tone one would say 'thank you,' his mind seemingly elsewhere. Does he know he spoke Vietnamese?

"Mai said it's about having to pay protection money."

He looks up at me and his eyes seem to refocus. "Yes. It is a very…" He frowns and shakes his head. "It is too complicated to explain right now. I will say, and you should know, that they are dangerous people. Vietnamese gangsters, with people in Hong Kong, Saigon, and the United States."

"Will they go after your family?"

"They will if they cannot get me. That includes you now. I am very sorry."

"Me?" What did I do?

"Many Vietnamese gangsters live a philosophy called 'One Thousand Year Revenge.' It means that they will get revenge even if it takes a thousand years. If it is you who wronged them and they cannot get you, then they will go after your family. Sometimes they will get you and still go after your family."

Samuel looks at me for a long moment. "I am sorry to have gotten you into this. I would have never looked for you, and exposed you, if I thought these men were after me here. It all started over—after I—after two of them died as a result of a fight with me three months ago."

"You killed two of them?" I whisper, realizing immediately that he didn't say it exactly that way, and for the first time feeling what it's like to be on the other side of killing news.

"It happened when…" His eyes drift over my shoulder and across the room. His body tenses ever so slightly. Is he reliving the experience? He looks back at me.

"How were you not arrested?" I ask. "I can't imagine that Vietnam justice is fair toward Americans, especially ex-servicemen."

"Do you have your gun?" Samuel asks, his voice flat.

"What?" His abrupt change of topic, as always, confuses me. I pat my hip out of habit. "What's going on?"

"Your gun. Do you have it?"

"No, I don't carry it off duty." I start to say that I'll probably never carry it again, but I stop myself. I'm not sure about anything right now. "Why do you—"

"Keep looking at me," Samuel says in a tight, low tone, stirring his spoon in his soup. "Do not look toward the door."

For a moment, I think he is toying with me again but the edginess I noticed earlier has increased. He's like an antelope that knows it's being watched. No, it's more like he's a lion watching its prey out of the corner of its eyes.

"What's at the door?"

"There are two men sitting at a table drinking tea. Both Vietnamese, one from last night, the other I have not seen before. The new one is muscular, like a short Arnold Schwarzenegger. He is probably slow and strong, but you never know. And they are probably armed this time."

I turn my head to the left and point to a painting on the far wall that depicts an old Vietnamese woman making baskets. I pretend to say something to Samuel about it, though I'm really checking out the men in my peripheral. Their image is fuzzy, but I can see that one is larger than the other, both appear to be looking our way.

A woman, who looks a little like the one making baskets in the painting, begins bussing a table next to us.

"Ma'am," I say, in a low voice.

She steps over to the table and nods. "*Phở* good, yes?" she asks.

"Listen," I look at her nametag, "Linh. I am a Portland police officer."

"*Phở* good?"

"Damn," I whisper, looking at Samuel. "Tell her that I'm a policeman and for her to call 911. If I use my cell they will hear me. "

"Please," he says to me. "We do not want to involve the police."

At the mention of the police, the women cries out, "Nonononono," nearly in a panic. So she does understand some English. "No *cảnh sát*, no *cảnh sát*." *Cảnh sát* must mean policeman, which she clearly doesn't want anything to do with.

She calls over to the woman working the cash register and says something. All I can make out is *cảnh sát*. So much for being quiet about this. I start to dig out my cell phone.

"This is not going well," Samuel understates. "The men are getting up... they are coming toward us now."

I twist around to see them winding their way through the tables, both wearing bad attitudes and dark suits; the big guy in fact does look like a mini Asian *Arnold*. He says something in rapid Vietnamese to the waitress of which I only understand *cảnh sát*. He probably told her not to call the cops. She nods, her face terrified.

"We got to get out of here," I say standing. "People might get hurt if these guys are armed. Come on. Through the kitchen."

Samuel follows me as I move quickly around the cashier's desk.

"Hey, you pay for *phở*!" the busswoman shouts.

"No go kitchen," the cashier shouts. "Kitchen off limits."

Samuel says something to them but it doesn't help. "You come back, pay for *phở*!"

The incredibly hot kitchen is a mini world of sweating cooks, sizzling grills, steaming woks, and chrome counters covered in vegetables and chicken parts, all of which instantly kick up my nausea about six notches. It's only by grabbing at greasy counters that I can stay upright on the grease-slick floor, though I probably look like a beginning skater. I slip and slide up to the backdoor, thumping against it with my shoulder. Samuel is a stride or two behind me and behind him are the two suits, both sliding side-by-side into a chrome counter. The one in the lead points at us and shouts something in Vietnamese. The cooks are yelling, too; one is waving a meat cleaver, at us or at the suits?

My greasy palm can't turn the doorknob. Something crashes behind me and I spin about to see a large trash can on its side and Samuel kicking it toward the suits. Like bad guys in a bad chase move, the lead one trips over it and goes down into the food scraps, then the buff guy trips over him and sprawls onto the greasy floor. I turn back to the door, cover the knob with my shirttail and twist it open.

I'm assaulted by a god-awful stench of rotting food in overflowing trashcans, and rat shit, lots and lots of rat shit everywhere. A wall closes off the alley to the right. A few feet away to the left, a small crate props open a bright-red door, and the end of the alley opens out into the street.

"We deal with them right here," Samuel says calmly, moving to one side of the door.

Good plan since we can't outrun their bullets. That is, I can't; Samuel probably can. I move over to the opposite wall, remembering for a moment how many times when I've introduced a new technique to a class, I've said, "Say you're in a dark alley when an assailant jumps you." My seniors always tease me with, "Why would you ever be in a dark alley in the first place? They're notoriously unsafe." Well, this one isn't dark, but now I can say I was in an alley because I was being chased by a couple of gangsters from Ho Chi Minh City.

Apparently, not everyone knows that when chasing someone you should never bolt through a door without knowing what's on the other side. I trip the first guy and Samuel trips *Arnold*. My guy only stumbles and does a nice job of stopping himself on the far brick wall, but the big guy falls into the slime uttering, I'm assuming, a Vietnamese curse. So much for his expensive suit.

I expect the smaller man to charge back into me, but instead it's *Arnold* who lunges out of the slime and tackles my calves.

This is the second time in two days someone has grabbed my lower legs and it's starting to get annoying.

He grabs at me as if my body parts are rungs on a ladder and begins climbing, or at least tries to. Mostly his feet just run in-place on the grease-slimed asphalt. All his pulling and yanking on me forces me back against a garbage can, which startles a family of rats into scurrying every which way, making *Arnold* squeal like a little girl and climb up me faster than I would have thought possible. He looks into my eyes and his suddenly widen. I guess the rats made him forget that he was climbing up a person. He's younger than I thought initially, maybe twenty-five, but close-up or far away, he's built like the proverbial brick outhouse.

I let him know that he's violating my personal space by slamming my forehead into his nose, missing by dumb luck and an inch that part of my forehead already sore from the coffee shop guy's punch. *Arnold* screams, cups his spurting *schnoz* and staggers back a few steps, this time managing to stay on his feet as he bends over and clutches his face.

To my right, Samuel has taken the other guy down onto his butt, moved behind him and pinned the man's arms between his legs. He twists a handful of the man's hair to force him to look up at him. Samuel says something in Vietnamese. When the man doesn't say anything, Samuel lightly slaps his exposed Adam's apple then repeats the same words—"Who sent you?"—maybe? No response. Again he slaps the hapless man's throat, hard enough to bug his eyes nearly out of his skull. If Samuel hits him any harder the man won't be eating *phở* for a while. Just as I start to wonder if this is some sort of prison interrogation method, my ignored guy kicks me in the stomach.

The blow launches me on a backward stumble along the greasy wall until I bang into the open red door, bounce off, and stumble toward the doorway. Without looking away from my pursuing kicker, I thrust my hand out to stop my fall. It purchases on something that lends enough support that I can launch a hard sidekick into *Arnold's* breadbasket.

"Doesn't feel real good, does it?" I say, as he stumbles back, coughing out another curse. I turn to push myself away from whatever it is I'm holding onto. What the…

A naked woman!

Wait. It's not a real naked woman but a very provocative and life-like and life-size love doll wearing only a black leather thong and matching bra. Someone has propped it against a stack of pink boxes that—

I'm slammed from behind, knocking me chest-to-busty-chest with Ms. Leather Thong. The pink boxes tilt, tilt some more, then topple the rest of the way over with me riding the big doll all the way down. The crash isn't that bad because the gal is made of some kind of soft rubber, but the landing splits open two of the cardboard boxes, spilling and scattering a bunch of… penises?

Glancing back over my shoulder, I see *Arnold* dive through the air, his big body descending toward me. I try to twist away, but he lands on my back like a rodeo cowboy riding a guy who's riding a love doll.

I start to buck him off but he's too quick with a massive arm that encircles my neck and begins squeezing like a steroid-fed python. I twist a little to one side, just enough to free my right hand and quickly pull down on his biceps so I can get some air. Then I twist my body a little to the other side to free my left arm.

Figuring he'll slow down if I gouge his eyes out, I jab my fingers over my shoulder, but I get nothing but air.

The harder he tries to squeeze my neck, the harder I pull on his arm, but my nausea has become a second opponent and is quickly becoming a most formidable one. He punches behind my ear, a jarring blow that lands with a sonic boom and has me seeing the birth of all the stars in space. The pain is excruciating. I roll a little to that side so he can't hit me in the same spot again.

He's thrashing around on my back, probably seeking a better position to secure his choke hold. I reach out with my free arm to brace myself on the floor, as his weight presses my face into an ample rubber breast, and my hand lands on something cylindrical.

He's extraordinarily powerful and I'm so weak now that I'm barely able to keep his massive arm from constricting my neck. It doesn't help that Ms. Leather Thong's boob is inhibiting my ability to breathe.

Whatever it is I'm gripping, I swing over my shoulder and hear it make a solid thump-on-flesh sound. The guy bellows in pain, a most pleasurable sound to my ears, so I blindly swing the thing back at him again. This time the impact weakens his constriction on my neck enough that I can shrug him off.

I struggle up onto my hands and knees, still ridiculously straddling Ms. Leather Thong, as a wave of dizziness and nausea stops me from climbing all the way off. As the nausea begins to subside, the weapon that I'm still gripping comes into focus. A two-foot long rubber penis.

Who in the hell would want such a long…

Arnold is trying to get up. I shift my weight to my far knee and lash out with the hardest right-leg roundhouse I can muster given my nausea and awkward love pose on Ms. Leather Thong. Nonetheless, my lower shin slams solidly across his eyes, dropping him heavily onto the spilled penises, sending them spinning off in every direction like pink rolling pins with veins.

Then, without the usual "uh-oh" tickle in the back of the throat, I spew my *phở* all over Ms. Leather Thong's face.

"Who the hell are you assholes?"

I struggle to look up toward the voice. My eyes are watering so it takes a moment to make out that the speaker is dressed like an outlaw biker, complete with oil-stained blue jeans, leather vest, no shirt, and a face tortured out of granite. Got enough ink on his arms and chest to print the next million copies of *Twilight*. Oh, and he's got a baseball bat cocked over his shoulder. Please, Lord, do you mind spreading the *dukkha* around a little?

"You puked on Lolita Luscious! She cost me six thousand dollars, pal."

He's moving toward me fast.

I let go of another eruption of broth, noodles, and sprouts, and watch with nauseous fascination as they arc through the air and splatter near his feet. A single noodle flies a couple inches farther and drapes its limp self over the toe of his left boot.

Biker Boy stops on a dime, his bat still cocked back and ready to knock my skull over the left field wall. He looks down at the mess and makes that scrunched-up face that people do when they see puke. "What the hell?" he says.

"Drop the bat," Samuel says calmly from behind me, maybe a little too calmly, given the situation and all. "You okay, son?"

I lower the side of my head slowly to Lolita Luscious's breasts and ponder for a moment Samuel's red shoes, this being the second time I've seen them while lying on concrete. I must say that they're a brave fashion choice for a guy who would be over ten years into AARP if he lived in the states.

"Son, are you okay?"

"No, I'm not. Do I look okay?"

"Did he hit you with the bat?" he asks in a tone that indicates he's about to unleash on the guy if I say yes.

"No. The unconscious guy punched my ear, plus I don't feel so good."

"Someone want to explain?" Biker Boy asks.

"Sorry about your, uh, stuff," Samuel says, probably looking around. "We were attacked out in the alley and it continued into... what is this place, anyway?"

"Hard Times Adult Video. The storeroom."

"Oh," Samuel says, sounding embarrassed. "Please tell me the damages."

I can't see him but I assume Biker Boy's looking around, accessing. "Okay man," he says with a sigh. "Shit happens." I hear something that I'm guessing and hoping is the bat being placed on top of a box. "Doesn't look like anything got busted and Lolita Luscious's fine. Just need to wash off her face. It's designed to be washable. Make it a hundred bucks for the clean up."

As I work my way to my feet, Samuel extracts a wallet from the unconscious *Arnold* and peels out a few twenties. "Let's make it a hundred twenty," he says, extending the bills to the biker. He stuffs the wallet back into the big guy's pants.

Biker boy nods and pushes the money into his jeans pocket. "Hey, your man is coming around."

"Where's the other one?" I ask Samuel, as he lifts *Arnold* by his sideburns into a seated position. The man's too dazed to notice the pain or the insult.

"He took off. No loyalty to his buddy here."

"You need an ambulance?" I ask the guy. Samuel says something to him that I'm guessing is the same question. The man grimaces and shakes his head.

"You're that cop in the news, ain't yuh?" the biker asks, looking at me.

My nausea has passed, but the side of my head feels like the Oregon Symphony's kettledrum player is banging on it. Plus, I'm getting real sick of that question. "Yes, I am. Your point?"

"Easy, man," he says, leaning against a barrel of who-knows what. "Don't mean nothin' by the question. Recognized you because I've been followin' the story. My bro's a cop on the LAPD. I tried to get on a few years ago, but didn't make it. But I support you guys a thousand percent, you know. I'm sorry somethin' like that happened to you. To anyone." He looks over at *Arnold,* then at Samuel. "You guys on the job?"

I tell him no as Samuel grabs *Arnold's* little finger, twists it and says something in Vietnamese. The groggy man winces again, nods, and the two walk out the door, more or less hand-in-hand. Normally, I would follow my partner out but I figure Samuel has it well under control. I wonder about the other thug's condition.

I turn to the biker. "Who you ride with?"

"Hey, I know what you're getting at. But I ain't no outlaw rider. I've been with Bikers Ridin' with Jesus for about twelve years now."

I know them. They helped my first partner nail a Red Satans biker for a homicide. As I recall, they attend a huge brick church up on Southwest Twenty-Four.

"You're a religious man working in a porno store?"

214

He shrugs, turns the boxes upright that I had knocked over and begins tossing loose dildos into them. I help him.

"Hard for me to get a job," he says, frowning at blood on the big penis that I used on *Arnold* during our intercourse. He rolls it over next to the doll. One more thing to be cleaned. "Especially since most people don't believe I'm a good guy, a good rider. But it's not so bad here, you know. It's a quiet job. Most of the people who come into the store are single guys, giggling couples, and even solo women. The store serves a purpose the way I look at it."

"Okay," I say, thinking he might know something about Kane Clarkson, the boy's uncle who's in the adult business, too. "Do you know anyone at Hot Videos, Inc?"

He nods. "Know the owners. Two guys: a Lawrence something and an ex-con named Kane... somethin'. Can't remember last names. He's only been there a couple years. Bought into the chain, I understand. I've talked to both of 'em at the convention this year in Vegas a couple times. Nice enough, dudes."

"You guys have a convention?"

"Sure, buyer's convention. Some real characters there."

"I bet," I say, eyeing the tat on his neck of Moses parting the Red Sea. "What else you know about Kane?"

"That's 'bout it. Nice enough guy. You can still see a little of the gray bars in him but he seems really driven to expand their business. I know they're doin' far better than we are, for sure. They offered me a job when we were in Vegas. I been thinkin' about takin' 'em up on it."

I pull my card from my wallet. "Listen, Mr..."

"Alex Brinkley but my buds all call me Big Peter." He extends his hand.

I shake it. "Big Peter after the disciple?"

He winks. "That too."

"If you hear of anything interesting about Kane, please give me a call."

"Like what?"

"Anything you think I would be interested in as it relates to the shooting."

He reads the card and nods. "Sure."

"Sorry again about your place. The hundred and twenty enough?"

"Plenty. Hey, that buff guy goin' to jail?"

"Damn straight," I say, touching my ear. "Thanks Alex." I walk out the door into an empty alley.

My heart skips a beat. They got Samuel! I'm three strides into a sprint toward the street, when from behind me: "Where you going, son?"

I spin around as Samuel steps out the back door of the *phở* restaurant, closing his wallet and stuffing it into his back pocket.

"What are you doing? Where's *Arnold* and the other guy?"

"I had to pay for our lunch. Nice people. One of the cooks has only been here for two months. Used to live pretty close to Kim and me. But I don't remember seeing him around. He remembers seeing me though. Of course I stand out over there."

Samuel must be okay because he's frustrating me again. "Where's the big guy?" I ask again, enunciating the words as he walks up.

"He left. Probably to hook up with his buddy."

"You let *Arnold* go? You let both of them *go*?"

"Yes."

"I was going to arrest them! They attacked us! The big one assaulted me! And you let them go?"

"Can we leave this alley," Samuel asks, nodding toward the street. "It smells."

I look at him for a moment, shaking my head in disbelief and anger. "I don't get it," I say moving toward the street. "You're concerned about your family and me, and then when we have them right in the palm of our hands, you let them go. Damn!"

"Son..."

I wave him off and start hiking toward the street. I might even be stomping a little. Samuel's quirkiness is becoming dangerous. I can't believe he—

"You saw Spielberg's *Close Encounters of a Third Kind*, right?" he asks from behind me.

"What the hell?" I pick up the pace.

He calls after me. "Remember all the UFOs, those little spaceships that came before the big mother ship's arrival?"

"No."

"You never saw that one?"

"Okay, yes." I stop to let him catch up. "I'll bite. What about it?" Damn.

"These young men are the UFOs. They were sent to test us to see how we resist, if we will at all. To the mother ship, these men are expendable. If we fight back and hurt them, that is information for the mother ship. If they hurt us but we keep fighting, that is important to know, too."

"Do they want to kill you... us?"

"Killing us would take care of the problem but I'm guessing the mother ship wants us to suffer, especially me. As for these guys who attacked us, they are not that important to us. Arresting them would be a waste of time and time is something we do not have enough of."

"That's the nuttiest thing I've ever heard," I say as we reach the sidewalk.

"I would have to agree. Can we go to your school for a while?"

I point to the right as we come out of the alley.

"You need to clean-up a little," he says, looking me up and down.

My shirt and trousers are slimed, one pant leg is stuffed inside my sock, and my shirttail is hanging out in front. Samuel, on the other hand, is clean and pressed.

I dig for my keys as we near the school. "So what is, or who is, the mother ship?"

*

"Are you hurt?" Samuel asks without the usual smirk as we step inside my school.

We remove our shoes.

"He landed a good shot just above my ear. Rang my bell for a moment but I've been hit worse. And my stomach is a little tender where he kicked me." I touch my gut. "Okay, make that a lot tender. Let's head back to my office."

"Did it make you sick or something?" he asks, following me.

"What? Oh, no. I'm taking some medicine that makes me nauseous and weak." I'm not telling him what for.

"Wait a moment," Samuel says, just before we reach the office. "I would like to sit here on the mat. May we do that?"

"Of course," I say. "But it's more comfortable in the office."

"Please," he says, gesturing for us to sit. "The training area is where I am most comfortable." He lowers himself straight down onto his rear and maneuvers into lotus posture, placing each socked foot on the opposite thigh. I'd have to have surgery if I tried that. He pats the mat. "Sit comfortably, Sam."

I sit cross-legged like I'm in third grade. I'm still angry at him but now that I'm in my school, my refuge, my anger eases up a little. It's just that Samuel is so frustrating, so—

"Sit straight, Sam, and lengthen your neck as if you're trying to touch the top of the back of your head to the ceiling. Good. Now place the back of your left hand into your right palm and rest it in your lap. Touch your thumb tips together. Good. Comfortable?"

"Not really."

"Do you meditate at the beginning and end of your training?"

I shake my head. "We just jump right into the kicking and punching."

"It's so important to connect with your inner self. Do it before class to transition your mind from the hectic outside world into the training hall and to help you be more receptive to learning. Then do it after the session to seal in the training and to calm your warrior spirit before you go back outside. It is also good for times like this when you need to restore quiet to your being."

I want to tell him that I'm hurting too much, and that I'm too sweaty and slimed to do this right now, but I'm guessing that my protests would fall on deaf ears. Besides, meditation isn't of interest to me at this time in my life. I don't practice Zen or tai chi or yoga. Mostly I stress the physical aspects of the martial arts, and the mental discipline of hard punching and kicking. The softer stuff I'll do when I get older.

"Okay, son. Close your eyes part way and look at a spot on the mat about three feet in front of you." He's pacing his words, slowly and evenly, just above a whisper. "Lower your eyelids and make that spot a little fuzzy. Now we do a body scan."

Ten minutes ago I was fighting and puking in a porno store and now I'm about to make *oms* like a monk. Do I get a begging bowl?

"In your mind, feel your head and face. Acknowledge the pain in your ear, on your forehead, and in the back of your head. Do not dwell on any discomfort in these places... just acknowledge it. Then move on to feel the contours of your forehead, cheekbones, nose, and your chin. Using your mind, feel your neck... then your chest, your back... now your pelvic area. Acknowledge the pain in your stomach... and move on. Feel your rear... your upper legs... your lower legs... your feet. If anything hurts or is uncomfortable, acknowledge it, accept it... and move on."

It's uncomfortable sitting like this, but his calm, soothing voice is, well, calming and soothing. I've never been hypnotized but I can imagine a hypnotist's tone sounding the same.

"Breathe naturally in through your nose and out through your nose. Feeeeel the air pass through your nostrils and flow down into your lower belly. Feeeeel your lower belly riiii-ise... and then drop as you allow the air to floooow back up through your chest. Now feeeeel the air pass out through your nostrils. Put all your awareness on your breath... in... out. Feel it on your nostrils, feel it swirling about in your abdomen, feel it reverse its way back up, and feel it pass out through your nostrils. Feel it. Be in the moment. Right now. Right here."

I've got to admit, this is pretty darn calming. I'm barely noticing my head and stomach now. Each exchange of air sinks me a little deeper into calmness, into relaxation, into the mat.

"Don't think about the process, Sam. Just do." Did he just read my thoughts again? "Just experience it. Ride your breath on its journey... in... out... in... out. If a thought comes into your mind, just acknowledge it and let it float away... then return to your breath. Don't force anything. Beeee with your breath."

We sit silently for I don't know how long, just breathing. My head seems light and a little buzzy. I like this. For the first time since the shooting, my face relaxes, and it feels wonderful. The tightness in my shoulders and back dissolve, too. The street noise outside is barely audible now; all I hear is the gentle exchange of air in my nostrils. Time dissolves as I float, float, float on my breaths.

Samuel's voice is a gentle command. "Take this wonderful sense of relaxation with you now as you open your eyes."

For a moment, I feel like I do when I first awaken from an afternoon nap and get that where-am-I moment. I widen my eyes and blink a few times.

"How do you feel?"

I smile and nod. "Good. I feel really good. Thank you." I turn my neck to the left to pop it and then to the right. "I will definitely start including—Holy shit!"

"Hi Sam," Mai says from where she is sitting slightly behind me, her legs in lotus, her hands folded together in her lap. "Oh, I'm so sorry," she says, putting a hand to her mouth. "I did not mean to frighten you."

I scoot around to face her. "I didn't hear you come in. I guess I was so focused."

"Good, good," Samuel says, enthusiastically. "Mai has been sitting here for about five minutes. You experienced the beauty of meditation much faster than most. Promise me you will do it once a day, more when you can. You get better at it each time. Some days you might not feel that it is going so well, but always remember that the benefits are accumulative. So keep at it. Promise me, please."

I nod at him and look back to Mai.

"I do it everyday," she says enthusiastically. "It helps me to center myself and it helps me to stay focused on my studies." She looks at her father. "My two o'clock class lasted only a few minutes. We talked about the final we took last week and said our goodbyes." She smiles broadly. "That means I am finished with school." She shoots me that smile. "I graduate Saturday. Yippee!" She pumps her fist in the air.

I laugh. Dang! She has a smile that could make a judge slap his mother.

Samuel beams at his daughter and says something to her in Vietnamese, this time without the anger that he had an hour or so ago. She nods quickly, says something back and then looks down. I guess they just made up.

"Congratulations," I say. "A bachelor's degree?"

"Yes," she says looking up. She frowns, leans toward me, and touches my shoulder. "What happened to your head, Sam? Your clothes? What did I miss?" She looks toward Samuel.

"Two men attacked us a while ago," he says to her. "One was the same as last night." He looks at me. "Again, I am sorry you got into the middle of my problems."

I shrug. "Well, you're kind of involved in mine, too."

He smiles a little. "That is what family is about, eh?"

"What no quotation about family?"

"Give me a moment… Okay here: 'A man that doesn't spend time with his family can never be a real man.' Brando from *The Godfather*."

"You're amazing."

"True."

"Humble, too?"

"Not really."

"What happened?" Mai asks again.

"And I'd like to know what's going on, too," I say, "now that I've got a knot on the side of my head the size of an apricot. What did you mean about mother ship?"

"Mai and I will catch you up as to what is going on. You need to know because now you are in danger, especially after today."

"Are you hurt, Sam?" Mai asks, looking at me intensely.

"I'm fine, thank you. The whole thing caught me a little by surprise, that's all." My male pride kicking in.

"Sam knocked the biggest one out," Samuel says.

Mai laughs heartily as she applauds. "You did? Very good!"

I feel a dumb smile spread across my face as my chest swells a tad. "Thanks."

My cell rings a text message. "Excuse me," I say, getting up and heading toward my office. "Normally I'd ignore it but with all that's been going on, I'd better get it. I left it on my desk."

I retrieve my cell and walk back out into the training area reading the text. "Where are you?" It's from Tiff. Damn! She must have radar. I slap the lid closed.

Mai has scooted closer to her father as he speaks in Vietnamese, probably telling her what happened. They look up as I approach.

"Wrong number," I say, sitting back down.

"I am afraid that the attacks last night and today are just the tip of the iceberg," Samuel says.

"Mai told me a little about your chain of jewelry stores, the protection money you have to pay, and the problems you had with men who work for... I forgot his name."

"Lai Van Tan," Mai says.

Samuel nods. "Every time we have expanded our business and added a new store, the more money he wants. Two months ago our sales slowed, just part of the ebb and flow of business. But Lai Van Tan still wanted his money. When we were slow to pay, one of our shops in Cholon burned to the ground."

"So my father went to visit Lai Van Tan, to talk to him, to tell him how difficult it was for our family," Mai says.

Her Caucasian side is obvious: the narrowness of her nose and its height, the length of her face, the largeness of her eyes, and her statuesque figure. The Asian side shows itself in the shape of her eyes, in her blacker than black hair, and her quiet, almost timid demeanor. But there's something about that timidity that... I'm wondering if it's just a cloak, something she puts on to present to the world? We all do that, I guess, but I'm wondering if what's underneath hers is... dangerous. I don't know why I'm thinking that, I just—

"It didn't go well," Samuel says, interrupting my thoughts. "There was a moment or two when I thought I might have to fight my way out of there. Tan is, as we used to say during the war, *điên cái đầu,* crazy. Plus, he has money, power, and a squad of people working for him. I have heard that he has the police on his payroll, too."

Mai touches Samuel's arm. "Two men followed my father after he finished talking to Lai Van Tan. But I do not know what happened." She looks at him expectantly. "You have never told mother or me."

Samuel looks down at the mat for a long moment, then takes a deep breath, puffs his cheeks, and blows it out. "It was late when I left Lai Van Tan's; there were few people out. It was raining hard, almost monsoon hard, though the season was still a month or two away. The only overhang for shelter was at the entrance of a very narrow side street. So I ducked under it thinking I'd stay there until the rain stopped or a taxi came by. I was not there but a few seconds when a car pulled up and two men got out pointing guns at me.

"I was not sure if they were Lai Van Tan's people or just a couple of cowboys out to rob me. But a gun is a gun no matter who is pointing it. They yelled over the roar of the rain for me to put my hands behind my head and walk backwards down the narrow street.

"As an old soldier I know that this position is often the precursor to an execution. But as a martial artist, it was not a bad position to be in. My hands were behind my head but ready to go, I was facing them and, since they were not saying anything or asking me questions, I had a moment to make a plan.

"I had backed up about twenty feet or so when I passed under another awning that ever so briefly blocked the light from a hanging bulb. As soon as the light was once again in their face, I lunged forward as fast as I could, and snatched his gun away, I think breaking his trigger finger. Then the second guy fired just as the disarmed guy tried to punch me with his good hand. The bullet struck him in the back of his head; it would have hit me square in the face.

"Shooting his own man startled the other one for a moment, which gave me a chance to knock his gun aside and hit him a few times."

Judging by Samuel's speed, I wonder what 'a few times' means. A dozen? Fifty?

"We were standing next to a low, heavy metal fence surrounding a set of stairs that led down to an outside basement door. The fence was topped with one-inch high metal triangles that had been welded into place. When the guy fell, the side of his head struck the top of the fence so that one of the solid triangles punched into his temple. My last blow was pretty hard, so he landed quite hard, too. His body twitched and then slid the rest of the way to the sidewalk."

"Father..." Mai says, tears streaming down her cheeks. She leans toward him and clutches his upper arm with both of her hands. "I'm so sorry that happened. Why did you never tell us?"

"I was going to, eventually. I wanted to handle it first, try to work with Lai Van Tan to make him see that both deaths were the result of cause and effect brought on by the attackers."

"So they were Tan's men?" I ask.

Samuel nods. "The one who was shot was Lai Van Tan's youngest son, Ly."

Mai twitches. "Oh!"

"Yes," Samuel nods. "Not good. I sent him a letter explaining what had happened. I did not dare go see him in person. I heard that he got the letter but I did not hear anything back. Then the next month no one came by to collect the protection money. So I assumed everything had just gone away. Obviously, this was naïve on my part, stupid."

"What about the police?" I ask.

Samuel shakes his head. "It would have been suicide to wait around for the *cảnh sát,* especially since some, like I said, are on Lai Van Tan's payroll. I feel bad about leaving the street where it happened but I had to think of my family. Fortunately, because of the downpour and the lateness of the hour, no one saw me, or if they did, no one reported it."

Mai sniffs and wipes a tear away.

"I am sorry I did not tell you and your mother. I did not want to worry the family. I thought it was handled and would go away. I was wrong. I am sorry."

Mai nods slightly but doesn't say anything. A tear rolls slowly down her cheek, over her chin and drops onto her wrist. She ignores it and nods slightly, which I take as her way of accepting her father's apology.

We sit silently in our circle, no longer meditating, though Samuel and Mai still sit with perfect posture, their hands folded together, their thumbs touching. I mimic them but I'm getting a painful knot in my lower back. I'm guessing they could sit like this all day. Samuel's eyes seem to focus on the mat, though I'm guessing his mind is somewhere else. Mai has closed her eyes, her breathing almost imperceptible.

I don't recall this room ever being this silent. It's as if that thing that emanates from Samuel, that cocoon of silence, has flowed out from him into this space. Okay, that's ridiculous but it's the only explanation I have right now. It's so calming, so peaceful. I close my eyes to better feel the quiet, feel the sereneness, and enjoy the dark behind my eyes. I'm looking there for only a moment before an image of Jimmy, slumped against the naked man, emerges from the blackness. I shiver a little and quickly open my eyes. SWAT guys like to say, "Darkness is my friend." Right now, I'd have to disagree.

Samuel's voice slices into my thoughts. "'The leaves of memory seemed to make a mournful rustling in the dark.' Longfellow."

I turn toward him. "What?"

He hasn't moved; he's still looking a few feet out on the mat. "The Chinese have one that I also like," he says, turning to look into my eyes. "'Better to light a candle than to curse the darkness.'" His eyes penetrate... into my thoughts?

A ripple of creepies shoots up my spine.

His eyes soften. Then in an off-the-cuff tone, as if he were wondering about the condition of my lawn mower, he asks, "Sam, may I ask you a question about your martial arts?"

"Uh, yes." I guess we're done talking about his involvement in the death of two men.

"You are a champion. But you got sucker punched at that coffee shop. Yes, you had been through a great ordeal, but still he hit you easily. And today the gangster tackled you, kicked your stomach, and punched your head."

"But I knocked him out," I say quickly, glancing at Mai. Her face is blank, unimpressed.

Samuel nods. "Yes, but had those blows you received been debilitating, the course of the fight would have been very different. Your defense has not shown itself in these incidents, probably because you are distracted by all the things going on in your life. But things are always going on in life, are they not?"

"Not like this," I whisper.

Samuel shakes his head. "Yes, understood. But believe me, meditation will help you to be calm and stay focused in the moment, which is important because a warrior must never be distracted."

Samuel says something to Mai in Vietnamese and she nods. She looks at me, again without expression. "Let us stand," Samuel says. "You saw *Enter the Dragon*, right? Remember when Bruce Lee tells that guy on the boat that he studies 'the art of fighting without fighting'?"

"Yes," I say, standing and shaking the stiffness from my legs after the long cross-legged sit. Mai and Samuel stand effortlessly, neither showing signs of stiffness.

"To my mind, the best block is no block," Samuel says, standing casually with his arms behind his back. "Call it the art of defending without blocking. The easiest way to do that is to sense when the attack is coming by being able to read the smallest signals. But that's not always easy. You think your opponent is going to be slow, but he is fast. You think he is weak, but he is strong. You think you can block his attack, but you find out too late that he is an expert at deception."

I nod. "I learned that early on in the ring."

"Yes, most good fighters do, but still they wait for the attack to launch *before* they defend." He says something to Mai and she nods. Her eyes, which suddenly make her look like a wolf about to attack a deer, look into mine. "Okay, Mai is going to throw a simple attack, a single blow. Please defend against it."

I've trained a lot of female fighters over the years, some good and some real good. One went on to win several local and regional titles in non-contact point fighting and first place in full-contact at the Northwest Grand Nationals. All of them would do well against an average guy in a self-defense situation. But against a trained man in an all-out fight? I'm not so sure. Women lack strength and speed compared to a trained man's strength and speed.

I look how Mai stands flat-footed, relaxed, her face calm, her eyes suggesting nothing. I'm guessing that she's good and I'm also guessing that she'll launch a lead jab, since it's close and probably her fastest technique.

"Shiiiit!" I blurt as her socked foot streaks to my ear, pauses for a moment, taps my lobe, then streaks back to the ground.

She stands passively and expressionless just as she was half a moment ago.

"What did you see?" Samuel asks, casually.

I quickly collect myself. I'm not going to say that I didn't see all that much. I look at Mai—is that a faint smile? At least the wolf eyes are gone—then over to Samuel. "I saw a beautifully executed roundhouse kick."

"Yes, yes, of course. But what did you see *before* she kicked? Just a second or two *before?*"

"I'm not sure," I say, looking at Mai. That's definitely a smile. But what kind?

Samuels rattles something off to her and the smile disappears. The wolf is back. Her right shoulder dips ever so slightly, a giveaway for a kick and—

Her fist touches the skin over my Adam's apple. I take a quick step back as I snap my hand up to protect my face, but her hand is gone.

"Your reactions are a little late," Samuel says in a teacher's voice, not the teasing one he had used in the park that first day. "What did you see that time, before her fist kindly stopped just short of destroying your talk box?"

I am beyond incredulous. Mai's speed and emotionless delivery… chilling. Too soon to tell if she's as fast as Samuel, but I'm guessing it's mighty close. Again she's doing that faint smile thing.

"I saw, well, I think I saw her shoulder move first. But I wasn't really ready. I didn't know she was going to—"

"You were not ready?" Samuel snaps. "*You were not ready?* What do you think we are doing here? We are all standing in your school and I am telling her things to do to you. Yes, it is in Vietnamese, but did you think I was giving her a recipe for spring rolls?"

Samuel's face isn't angry, but his words are jabs to my tender ego. I feel my face getting hot. I look back toward Mai, my eyes slightly watery with embarrassment. Her smile is gone. Uh-oh.

I slap at her shin, just as the side of her foot, a sidekick, stops at my Adam's apple. What does she got against my neck?

"Better," Samuel says, with that childlike enthusiasm. "You suspected something. What did you see?"

I look at Mai. There's that faint smile again. It's curls the edge of lips ever so slightly. This time the eyes are smiling, too.

"She stopped smiling before she kicked. That's what she did the other times, too. I anticipated that something was coming."

"Very good. That's a start. You saw that she attacks when her smile disappears. That must be her tell, eh?"

"Yes," I say, looking at Mai. Her smile broadens until her lips part, dazzling the room with her incredible teeth, her flashing eyes, her—

"Yowsa!" I cry out as her hand closes around my Adam's apple and then snaps back to simulate ripping it from my throat. I swear I barely saw her lunge forward and I just barely saw her arm thrust. She resumes standing casually in front of me, again with that—okay, it's getting annoying—smile. Her arm is still up, her fist clenched as if she were holding my Adam's apple. She opens her hand, one finger at a time, like a magician revealing that the hand is empty. Still, I have a phantom pain in my throat.

"What do you got against my neck?" I ask, with strained voice.

She bobs her eyebrows once.

"Tell me, son, did Mai stop smiling that time?"

I shake my head.

"So what you thought was her tell, was not? Did you notice her pretty smile?"

"What?" Can my face be any hotter?

He waits.

"Yes," I barely choke out. I look at her for an instant then back to Samuel.

He gestures toward the mat. "Let us sit back down for a moment. Tell me, have you ever faced an opponent in the ring whose appearance frightened you? Or at the least gave you pause, made you believe that he was going to be a tough opponent? Maybe he had a bunch of stripes on his tattered black belt or big muscles like our friend today?"

I settle into the sitting position again and try to pretend that it's not making my lower back throb. "Yes, many times. I once fought a guy in Chicago who had a large tattoo on his shaven head of two pit-bulls fighting, both bloody and shredded, one killing the other with a savage chomp to the neck. The guy even had a tattoo of blood dripping down over his forehead."

"How did you do against him?" Samuel is sitting in lotus position again and Mai is sitting comfortably on her knees, her palms resting on her thighs.

"Lost."

"Were you watching his tattoo as you fought? Did it intimidate you? Was he a superior fighter to you?"

"Don't know."

"But you said you lost."

"He broke a rib on my left side."

"Because you were looking at the tattoo?"

"I don't think I was looking at it then."

"But you had been. And it concerned you."

"To be honest, yes, it bothered me at first. But when the fight started—"

"The fight started before the bell and you began losing before the bell. You began losing the instant you were distracted by the silly ink on the man's scalp."

I'm thinking.

"And Mai's pretty smile distracted you from the exercise we were conducting."

Got me there.

"I watch *Cops* on TV a lot. When you pull a motorist over, when do you start paying attention to him?"

"The moment you alert on the car."

"Does it matter if it's a shiny red car or a brown pickup?"

"No."

Samuel looks at me silently. I nod that I understand.

Mai's eyes are closed and her breathing steady. I'm guessing she's listening, though she looks to be meditating. Her kicks and hand strike have loosened her pinned-back hair a little so that one shimmering black strand hangs over one eye.

"What tells do you look for when you actually stop the car?"

"Lots. Like how quickly or slowly he pulls over. Or if he turns onto a side street and keeps rolling until he finds an isolated spot. How often he looks at his rearview mirror. Or if his shoulder dips as if picking up something under his seat or in the door pouch."

"So lots of things before you make contact with him."

I nod.

"But you do not give any significance to the color of the car or the make, other than to note it for the record."

I nod.

"Because that information is not going to hurt you."

"Right."

He speaks to Mai in Vietnamese. Uh-oh.

Mai remains still, her eyes open now, but downcast. Make that a double uh-oh.

"So you watch only those things that might be a threat to your person."

"Yes." I'm looking at Samuel, but I'm aware of Mai in my peripheral, cautious of her. Her head moves ever so faintly. To see around the strand of hair? Gotcha!

I snap my forearm up to shield the side of my head so that her lower shin hits my arm in the same spot the brick thrower punched. At least she controlled the impact a little.

I hear Samuel say, "Very good, Sam!" just as my brain acknowledges the mild pain, a millisecond in which she retracts her kick to run rapidly on her knees toward me. Before I can fully register how weird that looks, she palm-pushes my fore-head hard enough to knock me off balance and over onto my back, my legs still folded monk-like in the air. Without missing a beat, she springs over them like a friggin' chimpanzee, a gor-geous one, and lands straddling my hips.

With her hands pressing my shoulders down, she scoots the rest of the way up to sit on my chest, her knees pinning my arms to the floor. She thrusts her thumbs into the corners of my mouth and stretches them into a smile that is on the verge of ripping my face. Her silky-black hair tickles my nose and her huge brownish-greenish eyes look into mine.

Samuel chuckles. "We call that technique the 'smiley face.'"

This could be an interesting moment if her father wasn't sitting four feet away and there wasn't that other little detail: she's my half sister.

Okay, missy, your speed and weird technique caught me off guard, but you erred because your butt is too high on my chest. Enjoy your flight.

I bring up my right leg and slam my thigh into her rear, catapulting her over my head and onto her back. For half a second, the tops of our heads are conjoined, then I kick my legs up into a backward roll, landing on top of her in the same position that she was on me a moment earlier. But my butt's in balance on her hips. I pin her arms, thrust my thumbs into the corners of her mouth, albeit more gently than she had done to me, and pull them downward.

"I call this move the 'frowny face,'" I say, looking down at her. Samuel chuckles.

I'm not pulling her mouth hard enough to hurt her, but it's still got to be uncomfortable. Yet I don't see that reflected in her eyes. Instead, I see…

I scoot off quickly. This is so wrong.

My cell rings. Mother of all that is holy! Does Tiff have this place bugged? I extract the phone from my pocket. Mai, her face flushed, scoots back over to sit by her father. Is it red from the tussle, or…?

"It's my boss. I best not ignore him. Hey, Mark?"

"Sam, where are you?" Mark asks with urgency. My heartbeat quickens; something has happened—again.

"I'm at my school. Why?"

"Tommy's been shot. Sniper."

*

I slowly lower my cell to the mat and try to digest what Mark just told me. Less than half an hour ago, Tommy had no sooner walked out of Big Dave's Muscle Shoppe on Grand Avenue when a bullet grazed the front of his pants. Apparently, the round ripped across his pubic area, slicing his jeans and splitting his pants zipper in half. A second shot struck about a foot away and blew out the gym's plate glass window, missing a bench presser by inches. Witnesses saw a large man with a rifle running on a rooftop across the street but he was gone when the cops searched there a few minutes later. There were no empty shells or any other evidence left behind.

"What's wrong, Sam?" Mai asks, looking at my face, which has probably blanched.

"Someone just shot my partner, the one who was with me at the hostage call."

Mai covers her mouth with her hand and says something in Vietnamese. Samuel scoots forward on his knees, stopping directly in front of me, his face hard as stone. It doesn't take much imagination to see what he was like on a Green Beret mission thirty-five years ago.

"Is…"

"He's fine," I say. "He's going to have to put up with a lot of teasing from cops and his gym buddies, but he's not seriously hurt."

"You are clearly in danger," Samuel says, sitting back on his heels.

I once read an old detective novel in which the writer described a man's eyes like "two black cigarette holes burned into a mattress." I thought that was funny at the time but right now that describes Samuel's eyes to a T: burn-black and scary.

"The PD is taking care of me, Samuel. Extra patrol in my neighborhood and I'll be checking out a radio today to keep with me at home, a shotgun, too."

"Did this policeman today and the one yesterday have these things?" Mai asks.

"I don't know," I say, getting her point. "I'm going to the hospital to see how he is. Maybe we can catch up later?"

"We will go with you," Samuel says, rising.

Mai nods. "Yes."

I shake my head. "Listen, I appreciate your concern but I think I'd like to go alone. I'm just going to check on Tommy and see if the dicks have learned anything else about the shooter. Then I'm going home. I need some time to myself to sort through all that's happening." Boy, do I.

"Understood," Samuel says.

"I would suggest we meet for dinner later but I'm guessing I'll be ordered to stay at home with around-the-clock police protection."

"Maybe we can come by," Mai says.

"Let me say yes for now, but I need to talk to my boss first. They might make it mandatory that I can't have visitors. They might even move me somewhere. So why don't I call you as soon as I find out?"

"Yes," Samuel says, as we walk toward the door.

"When do you leave to go back to Vietnam?"

"Today is Thursday, Mai graduates Saturday noon and we fly out Sunday at three in the afternoon."

"Not a lot of time," Mai says, slipping her shoes on and looking at me.

I return her look for a long moment. I glance at Samuel who is looking at me intently.

"Are you going to start carrying your gun?"

I don't say anything for a few seconds. Now isn't the time to try to explain the internal conflict raging inside of me. "I guess I need to start," I say weakly.

"Yes," he says emphatically, eyeing me, looking into me. When I don't say anything, he does. "You must do what needs to be done, son." Does he already know what's going on in my head?

I nod, figuring that's safer than saying anything.

He opens the door and peers out. "There are two police cars at the curb."

I step out onto the sidewalk and nod at the men in each car. I recognize Bob Thomas sitting behind the wheel in the rear one. He and Amy patrol my neighborhood regularly. I don't recognize the driver of the front one. I've been out of uniform for three years, so I don't always know the newer cops. They both wave before shifting their attention to Mai.

I gesture for Samuel and Mai to follow me over to the first car. The passenger window slides down. I lean in and smile at the driver. "Hey."

"Hi. I'm Kristos, Dan Kristos. I got you until midnight."

"Hi Dan. I'm Sam."

Bob walks up lighting a cigarette, nods. We shake hands. "Good to see you again, Bob. This is Samuel Le and Mai Le."

"Bob Thomas," he says. He shakes Samuel's hand and then Mai's, not even trying to be subtle as he gives her the up and down.

"It's Mai Nguyen," she says.

Nguyen?

"Where you going now?" Bob asks me. "We're sitting on you until midnight then you get a couple fresh guys for graveyard."

"You hear how Tommy is?" Dan asks me, leaning across the seat so he can be heard out the window.

"I'm on my way to ER now. Heard he just got a graze."

Bob emits a dirty chuckle. "Dang near got his Home Entertainment Center." Then quickly to Mai, "Sorry." He looks back to me. "I got a shotgun and radio for you in my trunk. Your lieutenant wants you to have them."

"Hold onto it until I get home, okay? I'm losing students already. I don't need to be moving guns out on the sidewalk."

I gesture to Samuel and Mai. "Listen guys, these folks are my family. They're heading out right now but you might see them at my place later today. They can come in."

"No problem," Bob says, again eyeing Mai."

"Jot down my cell." I give them my number and I type theirs into my phone. "How are you guys working the detail?" I ask, feeling not just a little strange being the focus of a police detail.

"Close to your elbow, Sam," Bob says. "Where you go we go. At your house, one of us will sit out front and the other will have your backyard. Can you supply a chair or something for us back there?"

"There's lawn chairs on the patio. I'll make up some coffee and sandwiches, too. Whatever you want just let me know. Right now, I want to get up to the hospital. Thanks guys." I turn to Samuel and Mai. "Talk to you in a couple hours?"

Samuel frowns as he shakes my hand. Is that worry I see in his eyes?

"What, no quotes?" I ask, with a faint smile.

Without hesitation and without changing his expression, he says, "If at first you don't succeed, skydiving is not for you."

I sputter out a laugh. "Very good. And quick."

Samuel's face remains serious. "Stay alert, my son. Be mindful of *now*. Stay in the moment. Always know what is going on around you, three hundred and sixty degrees."

I nod and shake his hand again. "Thank you." I turn to Mai. She extends her hand and I take it. That one loose strand of ink-black hair still partially covers one eye. Her eyes smile at me. Uncomfortable, I pull my hand away, turn, and nod at the officers, both of whom are eyeing Mai and me with that look cops get.

"I'm heading to the hospital now," I say, my face getting warm. I give Samuel and Mai a short wave and head toward my truck.

*

The population and traffic congestion in Portland has increased by half again over the last fifteen years. Rush hour used to begin at five PM back when I first got on the PD, but these days it starts to thicken at two thirty and by three thirty, which it is right now, we're all "going nowhere quick," as grandfather used to say. The two uniform cars are on my tail, and have been during the fifteen minutes I've been trying to get to Emmanuel. Now, we're all caught in a jam just five minutes away from the hospital.

Mitchell getting murdered and Tommy getting shot makes me realize how self-centered my anger is. Tommy, Mitch, and I entered hell together and things got worse from there. We had seconds to decide what to do and we each did what we thought was best to save the boy. Now Mitch is dead and Tommy was nearly killed. I need to talk to him and make it right.

My cell rings. It's Mark.

"Uniform guys with you?" he asks before I can say anything.

"Yes, right behind me. We're almost at Emmanuel but we're stuck in traffic at Vancouver and Failing. Okay, we're moving again."

"Listen, Sam. Everyone's left the hospital. Tommy's okay. He even wanted to come in to work tomorrow but I told him to take the rest of the week off. Once his adrenaline dies and he fully grasps how close he came to getting gut shot or at least his love tool blown off, he's going to be pretty shook up."

"Hold on for a sec," I pull onto a bank lot and park. "Okay. So there's no one at Emmanuel. I guess I'll just go on home then."

"Sounds good."

"But I do need to talk to him. I need to apologize, set things straight."

"I think that would be a very good thing to do." Mark's fatherly tone makes me feel even more guilty as to how I attacked Tommy.

"One of the uniforms has a shotgun for you and a radio," he says, to break the silence.

"We talked about it. I'll get them when we get to my place."

"Good. Okay, here's where we're at. The Fat Dicks sent a uniform car to Kane Clarkson place to have a chat, but no was home or they just didn't answer the door. The manager said he left in a cab a couple hours earlier and had a suitcase. We called one of his adult stores but the clerk said she was new and hadn't met him yet. The parents don't know where he is and they haven't talked to him since a day after the shooting."

"The other brother, Barry, is at a convention of some kind in Denver. His wife told us she had taken him to the airport. We're double checking that, but Barry's story looks legit. I'm putting my money on Kane as the doer. You remember what he looks like?"

"Pretty much," I say. "The release mug shows him with a bite mark out of an ear. Don't remember which."

"I got the mug right here. The right one. I'll have dupes of Kane and Barry to you and the uniform guys in thirty minutes."

"What about the boy's father and mother?"

"They're at the beach, Cannon Beach. They got a house there and want to be out of the limelight until the funeral. We had a Cannon officer swing by to see if they're there. They are. Like I said, they told us they don't know where Kane is, either. So right now we got an APB out for him. I got to tell you, Sam. It doesn't get heavier than this. You been carrying?"

Second time I've been asked that in twenty minutes. Mark always says I'm probably the only cop who doesn't carry a weapon off duty.

"I will from now on. Promise."

"Okay. Make sure you get the radio and shotgun and I'll get pics out to you within the hour. And if things get worse, the captain said we can put you up in a hotel for a while."

"Let's cross that bridge when and if we come to it. Right now I just want to get home. I'm beat. It's already been a long day."

"Something happen?"

Telling him about Samuel and his pursuers right now would only complicate matters. "I'll fill you in later, Mark. Thanks for all that you're doing for me."

"No charge. Well maybe some lunches on you."

"Deal. Later, boss."

Bob and Dan are parked at the side of the lot a few yards away. I poke in Bob's cell and tell him that everyone has left the hospital and that I'm heading to my house. He shoots me the okay sign out the window.

At my place, Bob parks across the street and one house down, and Dan parks behind him.

Dan drew first watch on my back patio. I set him up with magazines, a soda, and a promise of coffee and a sandwich in an hour. We shoot the bull for five minutes and then I tell him that I absolutely need to get out of these slimed clothes. When I turn to go in my backdoor, Bob steps through it, holding a shotgun and a portable radio, startling the hell out of Dan and me.

"Sorry gents, and sorry to walk through your house, Sam, but the side gate is locked and I guess you can't hear your doorbell out here. He retrieves two photos from his shirt pocket. "Five-Forty just dropped these off. Shots of the two brothers, Kane and Barry Clarkson. Your lou emphasized that he wants you to keep the big gun and the radio close to you. Oh, and he said 'tell him to carry his damn Glock.'" Bob probably wonders what that's about.

"Thanks," I say, cradling the shotgun in my arm and looking at the two headshots. Handwriting on the back notes that Kane is two eighty. Damn! Must have hit the weights and mashed potatoes hard in the joint. His head looks like a chunk of granite so I can't imagine that his weight is from overeating in the prison chow hall. He was about one seventy or so when I knew him way back. Barry's bio notes he's one eighty.

"FYI, gents," I say. "I knew Kane several years ago. He was a good fighter. I don't know if he's kept it up in the joint but he's obviously packed on some major mass, so be careful. The dude is seriously dangerous."

We discuss the situation for a few minutes, before I see Bob out the front door, put the radio on my bedroom nightstand closest to the window, and prop the shotgun against it. I double check that my Glock nine is in the middle drawer. It is, along with a copy of *Cat Fancy* magazine. I've been thinking for a while about getting one. Last week, I talked with one of my students who happens to breed Persians and he was pretty convincing that they're the one to get. He even brought me a copy of this magazine. Tiff teased me that I was a cat man if she ever saw one.

That was last week. About a hundred years ago.

I pull off my slimed jacket and put it in a bag for the cleaners, then strip out of the rest of my clothes and drop them in my bathroom hamper. The hot water feels wonderful as it scalds and melts my muscles, though I flinch when it hits the side of my head where I got punched. An ice pack should bring down the swelling some.

So far I haven't impressed Samuel with my martial arts prowess, but there are reasons for that. The first time at the coffee joint I was mentally deranged and on the mats today with Mai I was, well, distracted. Then at the *phở* place I was—

"Stop!" I say aloud. Dang! As my grandfather used to say, 'If I come up with anymore lame excuses I'll need a crutch.' I'm going to have to evaluate all this, just not now. I'm too trashed.

I towel off and pull on a black tank top and blue sweat pants. Tiff loved the top. "You look like a Greek statue," she's said on many occasions, as she would trace her fingers over my arm muscles. That was all the foreplay we needed.

I still haven't the slightest idea what's going on with Tiff. I can see that it's over and I thought she had no doubt that it was. Yet I'm getting these vibes from her that she isn't all the way there yet. What does she want? I mean, our issues are insurmountable. Can't she see that? I do. Don't I… Yes, I do. She said some ugly things to me and, okay, I guess I did, too.

I don't know if I'm coming or going anymore. And what the hell is the deal with Mai? I look at her and I think… Stop. *Stop!* She's my half sister!

So what is she thinking? Some of those looks she gave me. I mean, damn!

I need to work out. I haven't had a good session for about three days and I desperately need to blow some crud out of my muscles and my deteriorating, perverted brain. Ugh. Just the thought of it stirs up my nausea again.

I walk into my bedroom and sit on the edge of the bed. Maybe if I ate something it would kick up my blood sugar and help me think more clearly. But I'm so tired and I should ice my head. First, I got to lie down for a moment. Ahh, yes. My pillow feels great… My mattress feels great… My blankets feel…

I'm firing bullets into Jimmy as he sits alone and naked on the edge of his bed. One round jerks his body to the left and the next one to the right, the next one doubles him over, and the next one tears a ragged red chunk from his shoulder.

"That's some goooood shootin' there, Deeeetective, the naked hostage taker says in that slimy voice. He's standing at my right, pointing at Jimmy as each round whacks into his little body. "Oooooh! Another goooood one! Ssssmack in the heart? How about a face hit?"

I'm firing, firing, firing, firing… each shot ripping into my eardrums.

"Oooooh! Ssssmack in the nose!"

Riiiing.

Riiiing.

Riiiing. My eyes open.

I shake my head clear. *Riiiing.* It's my doorbell. I stumble out into the living room. Now my cell is ringing, too. I pick it up first.

"Yes?"

"Sam, it's Bob, out front. Hey, there's a hottie ringing your doorbell. She came out of a house down the street. Said her name is Tammy Dee and that you two are friends. She looks legit so I let her go up to your door."

"Yeah, she's okay. Thanks."

"Hey, she might be legit friendship-wise, but legal-wise? A word to the wise, my friend."

"I know, Bob. I know. I'll send her off in a minute or two."

"I'm just sayin'."

"Gotcha." I close my phone and open the door. "Hey Tammy, what's going on?"

"Hi Sam," she smiles, her open face bright and happy. She's pulled her dark hair back in a ponytail and laid the makeup on too heavy for a sixteen-year-old. But her voluptuous ready-to-do-it body, which she's barely covered in a pair of tan short-shorts and a bare-midriff red top, is all woman. She's carrying a cellophane-covered paper plate of cookies. "I know you been having a hard time lately, so I brought you some cookies. Warm, soft, yummy cookies always make me feel real goooood."

Lord, give me strength. I reluctantly reach for the plate but don't move from the doorway. "Thanks, Tammy. That's very thoughtful." Headlights from a passing car illuminate Bob sitting in his squad across the street. He's giving me a thumbs-up. I wave and shake my head. "Look, Tammy, I was about to get ready for bed—"

"At eight thirty?" she asks, her eyes devouring my arms and chest like I'm a burger and fries. She squeezes by me, one breast rubbing across my arm. "You're not that tired are you?" she asks, walking into the middle of the living room like a Tyra Banks protégé showing off the new spring collection. She turns back toward me, her eyes penetrating.

For a teenager she is incredibly self-aware, although there's something else about her that I've never before noticed, something that is now as obvious as the lumps on my head: her demeanor. The way she moves, speaks, turns her head. How she looks me up and down. Each by itself is no biggee; it gets missed. Put all the elements together and it's clear: The overall package is too old and far too mature for a sixteen-year-old. Of course she might have picked it up from watching movies, but my police instinct tells me there's a good possibility she's been groomed. She's practiced and she's got it down. But for whom? Her father? I don't remember if she has one. An uncle's request? A stepfather's?

"Who do you live with, Tammy?" I ask, remaining by the door. No way am I moving out of Bob's sight. He's my witness.

"My grandparents, silly. I told you before." She doesn't fidget as is the case with so many over-energized teens. Instead, she poses; she displays herself. I'm guessing she gets looked at a lot and it's obvious she wants me to do some looking right now. "Why are you standing by the door, Sam?"

"Tell me Tammy. How is your relationship with your grandparents? Your grandfather?"

Her composure falters, but only for a moment. "I don't understand your question." Her face turns white as a snow bank. Bingo! "It's fine. My grandmother's wonderful."

Her relationship with her grandfather isn't so wonderful, I bet.

"I want you to know that you can talk to me about anything that might be going on in your house." I pause to let that sink in. "I'm your friend and I'm a cop."

She drops her gaze to the floor. Guilt? Shame? "I don't know what you mean," she says unconvincingly. The adult demeanor, gone. Her poise, gone.

"You can talk to me about *anything* in your life that feels wrong to you." I let that sink in for a moment. "You understand what I'm saying, Tammy?"

She continues avoiding eye contact for another few seconds, then looks up at me with the face and comportment of a sixteen-year-old. An instant later, it disappears and is replaced by a twenty-five-year-old. She affects a pout, one hand on her hip. "You think I'm a dog, don't you?"

"No, Tammy, I don't think you're a dog. You're very attractive but I think you need to—"

"Really?" she asks seductively, moving toward me, again with that slow, one foot in front of the other supermodel walk. She's holding her arms down at her sides and slightly back, which pushes her ample breasts forward. "I've been attracted to you for a long time, and you know it. But you never do anything about it."

This isn't good. First thing tomorrow I'm calling our Sexual Abuse Unit and putting them onto grandpa. "Listen, Tammy. You've got to go back home. You can't be here."

She stops in front of me and looks up into my eyes with a practiced gaze that's all woman. "You *really* want me to leave, Sam?"

My cell rings. Thankful, I step toward the end table to get it when a familiar voice from the porch stops me.

"Sam?"

"Tiff!" I spin a one eighty.

She's standing stiffly, just below my step-up porch, her arms folded in that way women do when their ultra pissed.

"Am I interrupting something?" she asks tightly.

I put the still-ringing phone into my pocket and switch on the porch light, which deepens the anger lines in her face. "Hi," I say, dumbly and guiltily. "Uh, Tammy just came over for a sec."

We used to joke about how Tammy would always come over and flirt when I was working in the front yard or hitting the heavy bag with the garage door open. But she'd never been in the house.

"Is this why you kept putting me off?" She doesn't look at the sixteen-year old. "The real reason you didn't want me to come by the house?"

I remember when Jackson, a guy I worked with in a beat car a few years ago, got caught by his wife as he was doing a bartender in the family car. Actually, he was doing her *on* the family car. The misses, who had been out doing a midnight search of his haunts, found them behind a topless joint, the floozy draped over the hood of their station wagon as Jackson, his trousers and boxers bunched around his ankles, pumped away like a junkyard dog. With absolutely no possible alibi, Jackson looked at his wife, and said, "Who you gonna believe, me or your lyin' eyes?"

In my case, Tiff's eyes *are* lying to her. "It's not what it seems, Tiff. Nothing is going on."

Tammy leans against the door facing. "Don't get jealous. Me and Sam was only talking." She coats *me and Sam* with a ton of sweetener.

So that Tiff doesn't punch her out, I take Tammy's arm and escort her out onto the porch. "Go home. Now!"

"You don't have to push, Sam." She steps off the porch and stops before Tiff.

"Tammy!" I say, before she can say anything else. "*Go* home."

"Okay fine." She stomps off like the sixteen-year-old she is.

"Tiff, I know this looks bad but—"

"You mean you standing here in your sleeping clothes and that slut sticking her chest out and throwing herself at you? You think that looks bad?"

"Who you calling a slut, bitch?" Tammy shouts from half way down the walkway.

"Please!" I say angrily to her. "Go." I turn back to Tiff. "You know how she is? She just—"

"She what, Sam? Broke into your house wearing her sexy burglar clothes? Maybe she overpowered you and came in? Well, I can see how she overpowered you."

"Maybe he finds me more attractive than you."

"Tammy!" I take an angry step toward her. She doesn't budge.

Tiff's voice is low, her words barely able to squeeze through her clenched teeth. "I never thought you would—"

"Tiff," I say turning back to her and taking her by her upper arms. "There is nothing going on here. Don't be absurd. I was going to call you and make arrangements for us to talk."

She jerks her arms away, her eyes flashing angry. "You have to *make arrangements* with me to talk? For Christ sakes, how long have we been... were we together? Now I have to be *arranged* in your busy day. Well, I can see how you've been busy. Officer Thomas across the street sees it, too. What's statutory rape get you? Three years? Five if you're a cop, *Detective* Reeves?"

That jerk at the coffee shop said "Detective" like it's a dirty word, too, and so did that satanic hostage taker in my dream. I take Tiff's arm to walk her into the house. "You're being absurd, Tiff. My front door is open and Bob can tell you that I never left the doorway."

She smacks my arm away. "That's twice you've said that I'm absurd. I'm absurd and you're the one in your jammies with a teenage slut."

"Who you callin' a—"

I take a couple of angry steps toward Tammy. "I swear, Tammy..." I look over at Bob who is standing outside his car, uncomfortable and probably wondering if he should get involved. I've handled a couple of domestic beefs between officers and their wives; it's not a good place to be.

"Sam?" he says tentatively.

"Bob, would you escort the young lady to her house, please?"

"Okay, okay," Tammy says, spinning about and stomping down the sidewalk. I wave Bob off.

A car pulls to the curb.

"Has all this killing done this to you?" Tiff says softly, pulling my attention back to her. Her tone is low but her next words are ugly and hateful. "Am *I* expendable now? Has it become so easy for you to get rid of people?"

Any remaining feelings I have for her, any sense of confusion over the direction of our relationship, just died in the venom of those words. The look on her face shows that she realizes it, too.

"Sam, I—"

"Don't even try," I say, my hurt greater than my anger, but not by much. "I always knew that you were harboring those thoughts about me, but I kept denying it. Hoping that you couldn't be so naïve so... stupid."

"Stupid?" Her eyes do that flashing thing again. But before she explodes she takes a deep, controlling breath and lets it out slowly. It calms her, a little. "Look, I'm sorry I said that. What I meant—"

"You mean you're sorry you let it slip out. But it's how you feel, how you think, what you have never been honest enough to say to me. Until now."

Her anger rushes back. "Now you're making this about me."

This cannot be saved, nor do I want it to be saved. I hold up my palms. "Listen, let's go in and talk. Let's not let our emotions turn this into an ugly thing."

"What are we going to talk about, Sam? You see it and I see it. Don't get yourself into a tizzy. I was coming by to tell you that we needed to end what little we have left."

I nod. "I agree. I just thought it would be nice to sit down and talk about it. We did have something. I just don't want us to end this with anger and bitterness."

Movement behind her. Someone stepping up onto the sidewalk from the street. I look around Tiff's shoulder.

"Mai?"

Tiff spins. Mai stops in her tracks, no doubt feeling the tension. She's wearing snug blue jeans, a purple chemise under a short, black leather jacket. Her hair falls loose around her shoulders.

"Uh… Tiff, this is my… my half sister."

"Your *what*?" Tiff shrieks, spinning toward me. "Your what?! You bastard! You haven't been wasting any time, have you? How long has all this been going on?" I catch her wrist before her hard slap would have connected with my ear.

"Tiff, listen to me. I didn't know I had a half—"

She swings her other hand and I allow it to hit my chest with a hollow thump. "I don't know you, you bastard!" she screams. "It's all been a lie." She jerks her arm free, turns, and runs sobbing toward her car that's parked in front of Bob's.

I take a few steps across the grass, then stop. There's no point going after her. She won't believe anything I have to say.

Bob steps away from his car. "Tiff, it's none of my business but Sam wasn't—"

"Shut up, Thomas!" she blubbers, punching his shoulder. "All you goddamn cops are the same. You all stick up for…"

She takes a step toward her car, stops, turns, and punches Bob again, this time in the chest. She looks back toward me. "You're all… you're all fuckers!"

That's probably the second or third curse word I've ever heard her utter. She runs the last few steps to her car, slams the door behind her, starts the engine, and accelerates away in a squeal of rubber.

"Man-o-man," Bob chuckles, shaking his head and rubbing his chest. "Hell hath no fury… I called your cell but she got to your door too fast."

I exhale. This is going to be all over the department in two hours. "It's not how it looks," I say feebly. *Who you going to believe, me or your lying eyes.* "We've been having some—"

"Hey, man. I saw nothing, I heard nothing, I say nothing." He's rubbing his chest now.

"Thanks, Bob. You okay?"

He chuckles as he opens his car door to get back in. "No sweat. My ol' lady hits me harder."

I watch Tiff's tail lights grow smaller, brighten for a couple of seconds, then disappear around the corner.

"You want me to leave, Sam?" Mai asks gently from behind me.

I actually forgot about her for about fifteen seconds. She hasn't moved from where she stopped on the sidewalk.

"What? Oh, uh, no. Come in, please."

*

Okay, so that was a special fifteen minutes. Never in all my years have I seen such an example of bad timing. Tammy shows up and offers me her voluptuous goodies just as Tiff shows up to witness it. Then Mai shows up just as Tiff is trying to beat the crap out of me. All witnessed by the uniform officer who probably thinks I'm a real piece of work. Welcome to the trailer park, folks. What next? A tornado?

"I seemed to have come, as your expression goes, at a bad time." Mai says, standing awkwardly just inside the door.

"No, no. I'm glad you came. But I'm sorry for that uncomfortable scene a moment ago. Where's Samuel?"

"Father wasn't feeling well and wanted to sleep while I went to the university to return some books. I was going to go back to meet him and we were going to call you."

I gesture to the sofa. "Please, sit down." I sit across from her.

"Thank you. I called father on my way home and he said he still did not feel well. He told me to call you to see if you minded if I came by alone. But then he could not find your phone number. He had the address and gave that to me. I know this street because a friend from school lives down that way, maybe three blocks. I have been there several times. I even went past here before. But of course I did not know you lived here." She smiles. "Until not too long ago, I did not even know there was, uh, you."

"That's okay. Sometimes I don't know there's a me."

She shakes her head. "I do not..."

"I didn't understand that either."

We both laugh. "May I get you some tea?" I ask, starting to get up.

"I am fine, thank you. How is your friend, the police officer who was shot?"

"Amazingly, he is good. Thanks for asking. He even wanted to go back to work tomorrow but the bosses wouldn't let him. He needs time to process what happened. It will probably hit him tomorrow. He came very close to being seriously hurt, killed."

Mai nods. "It is so tragic what is happening. How are you doing with all that is going on?"

Her concern catches me a little off guard. I remember how she touched my arm in my school when she saw how tattered I was after the fight in the porno shop, and how she asked if I was okay with such genuine compassion. She doesn't seem to possess the typical self-awareness, self-centeredness, and all the other selfs that so many beautiful women do.

"I'm doing okay," I say. "Well, most of the time." Mai's eyes look into mine, as if reading the truth. "Okay, some of the time. What I have in my favor is that I know I'll be better."

"Do you know the word *dukkha*?"

I chuckle. "Yes, Samuel told me. He said I've got a lot of it going on. And he's right. You heard of the expression 'it never rains but it pours'?"

She frowns and starts to shake her head, then stops. "Oh, I think I understand it. You were not having many problems but now you are getting a lot of them."

"That's me all right."

She tilts her head and her mouth smiles ever so slightly. "For sure you have too many girlfriends," she says, nodding her head toward the door. She holds her palms in front of her chest. "That one who is big up here on top is too young for you."

I wave my hand. "No no no. The young one is a neighbor. We're friends, sort of. She's not a girlfriend."

Mai shakes her head a little. "She dresses like she wants to be your girlfriend. Very sexy. Who was the other one?"

I've had three Vietnamese students over the years and I remember how straight forward they were about asking personal questions. I guess it's a cultural thing but it's a little uncomfortable.

"That was Tiff."

"Very pretty. You love her?"

I laugh, embarrassed. "Well, she *was* my girlfriend. It's over now."

Mai shakes her head with mock sadness. "Yes, I think so. Bad ending. No more love. Very sad."

Again I chuckle. "How about you? You got a boyfriend? Ever been married?"

She shakes her head. "Yes."

I'm actually getting used to them shaking their heads and saying yes. I hope I don't start doing it. "Which?"

"No husband now." She hesitates for a moment and then her voice tightens. "I was married for four years one time, but no more. I did not like him. I..." She stops abruptly. What's that about?

"Well, liking him is important," I say, testing to see if she wants to say more about him.

She looks through me for a moment, her eyes in another place.

"Kids?" I ask, to change the subject a little.

She nods. "No. Someday."

"Boyfriend?"

A smile forces out from whatever was just going on in her head. "Too many boyfriends in Ho Chi Minh City." She lifts her hands in mock frustration. I laugh and she giggles. "I date a few times here in Portland, but no boyfriend. Mostly I wanted to concentrate on my studies so I can help my family business. My mother and my father pay lots of money for me to go to Ho Chi Minh City University to study business for two years, then one year at University of Paris, and one year here at Portland State University. It was difficult to get Paris and Portland to accept my credits from Vietnam, but they finally did. I am very happy because now I know business in two other major countries besides Vietnam."

"Sounds like a smart plan. Why Portland?"

"Thank you. Portland State has a very good business program. My father encouraged me to come here because he wanted to come when I graduate and bring my mother to show her where he grew up. But then she got TB and cannot make the trip. He was going to come by himself to see me graduate, anyway, but when he learned about you, that you are his son and living here, too, he was most excited."

"Why was he so strange to me when we first met? He teased me and kept quoting movies and different people. It pissed me off a little."

Mai smiles, nodding. "I have always liked that: 'pissed off.' Funny." She crosses her legs and leans forward as if to underscore her words. "I think my father was probably just nervous to meet you, but he always teases anyway. I think he does it a lot when he is uncomfortable. He always quotes things, which makes my mother very tired. Of course that makes him laugh and so he does it again. He loves my mother very much and enjoys teasing her. I think she enjoys all that but just pretends not to.

"He is a very smart man. He learns from everything, movies, TV shows, books. He is very, uh, what is the word? Oh, spiritual. He is very spiritual, too. He practice Buddhism in Vietnam but sometimes he goes to a big Catholic church near where we live."

"Was he a good father when you were growing up?"

"Yes," she answers quickly. "But it was hard many times because he is Caucasian and I am half Caucasian. Many Vietnamese people do not like that. It was a bigger problem right after the American war but now only sometimes. That is a very long story. Maybe better to tell another time."

"I really want to hear it, too. May I ask how you feel about him suddenly finding me." Maybe some insight from the daughter will help me understand the father. Our father.

"I am very happy for him. He have all daughters—me, Linh, and An—but I know he always wanted a son. He called me maybe two months ago and was very excited that you live right here where I am going to school. He said you were a policeman and a martial artist. I could tell he was very, very proud and very, very excited to come and find you."

"Why didn't you contact me?"

"I asked him that. He did not think it was a good idea. He thought that you would think it was a lie because you probably always thought he died in the war. He wanted to come here, watch you for a short while and if what he saw was okay to him, he would introduce himself to you. It is proper to have a letter of introduction but in this case, there was no one to write it." Mai smiles and shrugs. "He thinks and acts Vietnamese after all his years living as one." She unfolds her legs and leans forward, her elbows on her knees, hands folded. "Have you noticed that he act different today? Not so much teasing?"

"Yes."

"He is very worried about our problems with the gangsters. He is worried for all of his family, which is now you. Let me ask you a question. Is it strange to know that you have a new family?"

I nod. "It's been an insane week with all that's going on with my shooting and trying to grasp the idea that I have a father, three half sisters and... I haven't thought about this before, but technically I guess I have a stepmother, too."

Mai laughs heartily. The light in here brings out the green in her eyes. "Yes very hard for you, I can imagine."

I nod.

She sobers. "My mother is a beautiful woman, outside and inside. I am very scared and sad that she is sick."

"I'm sorry to hear about it. I know Samuel is concerned and worried, too."

Mai looks at the carpet for a long moment, lost in thought. When I move to cross my legs, her eyes flutter awake. She looks up at me, her eyes wet. "I am sorry."

"Are you okay?"

"Yes, thank you. I love my mother very much. She has had an incredible life."

"I cannot imagine" I say, watching her dab at her eyes with the back of her hand.

She frowns. "You say you are trying to understand that you have a father, stepmother and three half sisters."

I nod.

"But you have only two half sisters."

I shake my head. "Two? You, Linh, and An."

Mai leans forward and waves her palm. "No no no."

"What?"

"Linh and An your half sisters."

I shake my head, confused.

"I am not your half sister."

"You—"

"My father not explain?" She covers her mouth with her palm and laughs. "That is why you introduced me to your girl-friend outside as your half sister. I wondered about that." She laughs again.

I just look at her. Mai isn't my half sister?

"How did father call me when he talked about me?"

"He called you his daughter. 'I have to pick up my *daughter*.' 'My *daughter* is going to Portland State.'"

Mai nods and smiles. "I understand the confusion now. I am sorry. It is our fault. We confuse you. I call Samuel my father because he has been the only father I have known. My... what do you call it? Oh, my birth father was an American soldier. He and my mother had an affair when she worked for the Americans in an office. I was one year old when my mother met Samuel."

"Samuel never told me this."

Mai laughs again. "I just thought you knew, that my father had told you. He must have just thought that—what?—that you somehow just figured it out."

My mouth is probably hanging open. "No. He didn't." I look down and shake my head. "And I've been feeling so weird about..." I look up at her. "... you." Oh man. Did I say that out loud? Shitshitshit.

She cants her head to the side, her mouth smiling ever so slightly. "Weird? About me?" She twists her mouth a little. Fighting that smile?

"Never mind." Could my face feel any hotter?

"What, Sam? Tell me."

Outside, four gunshots in rapid succession.

*

I spring from my chair and pull Mai down onto the carpet with me. "Outside, from the back of the house," I whisper urgently. "Into the hallway." We've got to get some walls between us and the back of the house.

Mai moves across the floor even faster than she crawled over me a few hours earlier on the mat, and I'm right behind her. "The bathroom, to the left," I say. "Porcelain's good cover."

She scoots quickly in that direction, again without hesitation. She's a good soldier; Samuel has taught her well. We crowd in next to the sink cabinets. Mai's breathing is measured, in control. Mine's ragged.

Yelling from out back. It's Dan's voice, but unclear. "I'm hit!" That I understand.

"What the hell's going on?" I ask rhetorically. "Where's Bob?"

"What are we going to do?" Mai asks, cool as a cucumber.

"*You're* going to stay right here; *I'm* going to crawl into my bedroom and get my gun and radio."

"Are you coming back?"

I squeeze her arm. "Give me fifteen seconds." I low crawl on my stomach out of the bathroom, down the hall a few feet and turn into my bedroom. Again I hear Dan call out that he's been hit.

Is the gunman still back there with him? Is he down? Does Bob have him in custody? Maybe the suspect has fled and—

My bedroom window explodes as does the full-length closet mirror on the far wall, scattering glass and mirror shards everywhere. I flatten myself on the carpet and the shards, and yell out something but I don't know what. I quick scan myself. Incredibly, I'm not cut. Some luck for once.

"Sa… Sam?"

"I'm okay, Mai," I say in a loud whisper. "Stay where you are."

The shotgun is propped against the dresser right under the shattered window and my Glock is in the top drawer. No way am I'm going over there now.

Shouting outside. Bob's voice. Good, he's okay.

Running footsteps. A crash. Garbage cans, I think.

Another shot.

Damn!

A few seconds pass. Then Bob's voice coming from some-where by the side of the house, low, urgent. Is he talking into his radio? Then quiet. Five seconds pass… ten… fifteen.

"Sam?" Sounds like he's at the corner of the house.

"Bob!" I yell toward the broken window.

"You guys okay in there?" I'm crawling toward the bath-room, trying to avoid the glass and mirror shards. Sounds of the backdoor opening and then the kitchen door. My heart skips a beat. "Sam?" It's Bob.

"We're fine. What's going on out there?" Mai is sitting up and looking at me. "You okay?" I ask.

"Yes."

"I don't want to leave Dan," Bob shouts. "He's been hit in the thigh. I got an ambulance rolling and backup. The shooter fled around the other side of the house, but I twisted my ankle. I can't pursue."

"Hold it. I'm coming out." I look at Mai. "You should wait here."

"I am coming with you," she says, in a tone that isn't open for debating.

"Okay, but stay behind me until I see what's going on."

We head down the hall, though the kitchen, through the garage, and out the back door. Dan is sitting with his back braced against the wall of the house; Bob is kneeling at the corner, his gun trained toward the south side of the yard. I look out across the grass, straining to see into the shadows. "Where did the shooter—?"

"He split," Bob says over his shoulder. "Around the other side of your place. Dan caught a round in his leg. Asshole shot at me just as I twisted my ankle coming over your fence. Handgun. Missed me but got your window."

Damn. I forgot to unlock the fence for them.

Mai steps around me and scurries down the two steps. "Let me see," she says to Dan.

"Ma'am," Bob says, "an ambulance is on the—"

"*I said* let me see it," she says kneeling. "I was a nurse's assistant at the university in Saigon,"

"Yeah, partner," Dan says, his eyes full of Mai. "Let the lady check me out."

Sirens approaching.

"Any of you got a second weapon?" I ask.

"Ankle holster," Bob says.

I start to ask him for it so I can go check the side of the house, but I stop. "Did you see the guy's face?" I ask, stalling, hoping backup gets here quickly. I don't want Bob's gun. I don't want my gun. Bob has a good vantage point to see if anyone comes around that far corner. There's no need for me to go over there.

"Only his back when he was running toward that far fence over there on your north side. Big guy, two fifty, maybe two ninety. He couldn't get over the fence so he ran back across the yard to the south side of your house. I shot at him but missed."

The locked gates on both sides of the house are a foot and a half lower than those that surround the backyard. Even a big guy could climb over them. I'm sure he's gone. There's no need for me to take a gun and go over there.

My shaking hand isn't buying my rationalization.

"I was sitting on the steps there," Dan says, pausing for a moment as he struggles to slip his uniform pants down. Mai, kneeling beside him, carefully scoots his trousers down below the wound. Dan looks at her, then over to me. "Oh, anyway the guy shoots from under your weeping willow tree. I didn't hear him or see him until he's popping caps at me a bunch of times. They must have hit the side of your house about… there. Yes, see? There's the holes. I backed up—Ouch!"

"Sorry," Mai says, leaning over him a little to see the back of his leg.

"I backed up around the corner there looking for cover but he must have fanned out so that he still had me in view. His last shot hit my leg. Then I— Shit!"

"Sorry," Mai says, pulling her hand away from his thigh. "I do not think the bone is hit, and it did not hit the femoral artery. You will be fine in a few weeks."

At least two wailing sirens stop out front. Thank God.

"You got it, Bob? I'll have to let everyone in."

"I'm on it," he says, still crouched at the corner of the patio, his gun arm resting on his knee. Thankfully, he doesn't ask if I want his backup gun. I head inside, feeling lower than pond scum. I've got to deal with this. I need some time to analyze what's going on with me.

The front door's ajar. Guess I didn't shut it all the way after Mai came in. I open it wider so three medics can squeeze through with all their gear, followed by two police officers and the nightshift sergeant. I ask Sergeant Taylor if he got the info that the shooter was last seen on the south side of the house.

"Roger that. We got a couple guys checking it out. Asshole's probably long gone, though. Got a dozen marked cars cruising the neighborhood, too. You see him?"

"No, Dan did, a little." I might have if I hadn't wimped out. "He's out back."

I lead everyone through the house and out onto the patio. Within five minutes, two more uniformed officers, two sergeants, two lieutenants, and the precinct commander pass through the house. The medics quickly confirm that Mai was right about the bullet missing Dan's bone. They think Bob's ankle is only sprained, which I know from martial arts training can be slower to heal than a break.

The officers comb the backyard and find a Sig Sauer Forty-Five semi-auto out under the big tree in the back where the perp couldn't get over the fence. It's got to be Kane based on the description. So he's down a gun, but he's still got the rifle that nearly gut-shot Tommy, and maybe some other weaponry, too. The guys found dirt smudges on the wooden gate on the south side, typical of someone pushing with their feet as they scoot themselves up and over.

Mark phoned while everyone was here to see how I was doing. He said that David, his long-time boyfriend, had hurt his elbow playing racquetball and they were at ER getting it X-rayed. He said he'd come by in an hour or so, but I insisted that I was fine. I didn't tell him about my little episode of not acting like a policeman. I just wanted to clean up and try to collect myself. I didn't want to go to a hotel or stay at his place. The shooter was gone and all was peaceful, and I just wanted to get my head peaceful, too.

The night lieutenant made sure there were replacement uniforms outside, to include Amy, the officer who works the neighborhood in the evening. She's pulling a double shift and sitting in a car out front. A young guy who doesn't look old enough to be out of high school is sitting on the back patio. Simmons added a third officer to patrol the block on foot. I thanked Mark and told him I'd call in the morning.

By midnight, everyone except Mai has left, leaving the house strangely quiet after all the craziness. It's an understatement to say that it's disconcerting to think that there was a shooting out on my patio two hours ago, a place where I've trained, drank my morning coffee, and dozed on my chaise lounge on summer days.

A victim I once spoke with said that her home burglary was like psychological rape, a term I understand clearly now. I just want things to be normal in my life. The last two months have been loony tunes and they just keep getting worse. Did I piss off the cosmos or something? If so, I'm sorry. Can I have my life back now?

Mai seems to have ridden out the experience intact. We're sitting at my kitchen table drinking tea where Samuel had demonstrated his incredible speed trick with the cups.

"I drink green tea back home, too," she says, probably to break the silence.

"Mai, I'm so sorry that you were in danger tonight. You could have been hurt and I feel awful about that."

"You would feel awful? What about me? I would be the one hurt?"

I sputter a laugh. "True, true. I just meant—"

Now she laughs. "I understand what you said. But please do not feel bad about it. Like father say today, we are family now. We are all in this together."

"Do you think you should call Samuel and tell him what happened?"

She shakes her head. "He is sleeping. He should rest undisturbed so he will be fine in the morning. I will tell him then."

I start to argue but decide that maybe that's their way. I nod and sip.

"It is frightening that this man who shot three policemen has not been captured."

"He will. He's getting careless, brazen. I just hope we catch him before he hurts anyone else." I look at her for a moment. "You handled yourself very well. Calmly." Better than me, that's for damn sure.

Mai shakes her head. "Maybe I looked like it on the outside. But inside, not so calm." She looks down at her hands. "Too much violence," she says.

I shake my head. "Please don't judge my life by the last few days. Outside of the police job, I live a very quiet existence."

She smiles. "I meant in the world. Saigon can be violent. Lots of stealing, assaults, knife attacks. Sometimes it has been hard for me because I am *con lai*, uh, mixed race. I have to defend myself many times against people's ugly words and sometimes I have been physically attacked, too, because I am *mixed race*. Some in Vietnam call people like me 'Children of the dust.' It was considered an insult when I was growing up.

"Father has had problems, too, because he is Caucasian. It is strange, though, because there are many people who do not believe he is American or Caucasian, or one hundred percent Caucasian. He speaks Vietnamese so fluently, you see, and his… uh, demeanor? Yes, his demeanor is Vietnamese. Some think he might be *con lai,* too, but a mix of French and Vietnamese."

"Has he had to defend himself?" Man, would I like to see that.

"Yes. I have only seen him do it once, against some drunk soldiers, but my uncle has told me that my father has had to do it other times and those people were hurt very much. Father has never told me of these times. He doesn't tell my mother or me everything.

"Father is a respected martial arts teacher, at least among the few people who know about his ability. Beside teaching martial arts, he also help many people with problems. In our community they call him '*thị trưởng*,' which means 'mayor,' because he does so much for everyone and helps settle disputes. He is a very wise man. He truly loves Vietnam. People see that..." Mai shakes her head. Her ink-black hair caresses her shoulders. "I'm sorry. I got... sidetracked? Is that the right word?"

"What?" I mumble, sidetracked too, but by her hair. "I mean, yes. But it's okay. I'm learning a lot."

"Okay. Thank you. Uh, I think I was saying that Vietnam can be violent. Not like the American war, what you call the 'Vietnam War.' I've heard the stories, seen the photos, documentaries, and movies. Not that kind of violence but the kind that happens when many people, especially poor people, live too close together. I've seen people shot, stabbed, and beaten. What happened here tonight was awful but I've been around worse."

She sips from her cup and looks at me. "Thank you for protecting me. I can tell that you are a good policeman."

"Thank you," I say, a little embarrassed. I take a sip and lean back into the chair. "I've been having second thoughts lately about staying in police work."

"Really? Why?"

"I'm not sure. I'm like a teenager who's unclear about what he wants to be when he grows up."

She laughs, and my world brightens.

"Police work has lost its magic for me. And I've killed... three times..." My nose and throat suddenly burn and my eyes begin to tear. I smell gun smoke, the same that filled Jimmy's room.

Mai's warm hand covers mine. I look up at her.

"Are you?"

I look at her, confused. "What?"

"I asked you if you are okay."

"Oh, uh, yes." How embarrassing. "Sorry. I didn't hear you. I've been spacing a lot lately."

"Spacing?"

"Thinking of something else. Remembering, I guess." Reliving.

"Is there anything I can do?" Her hand is still on mine. Our eyes connect and I feel it all the way to my toes.

"Well, you're doing it."

Mai laughs shyly and blushes. She pulls her hand away. Reluctantly, I think.

"You want to help me clean up all the glass in my bedroom?"

"Is this a date?"

My face burns hot. "No… I mean—"

Mai giggles and touches my arm. "Where is your broom?"

A couple of minutes later we're sweeping up glass. I'd like to focus just on Mai right now but my mind is reeling. My ability to compartmentalize has been on and off lately. I'm feeling awful about what happened with Tiff and I'm shocked that a policeman was shot right here at my home while protecting me. Bob hurt his ankle because I forgot to unlock the gate and Mai could have been hurt or even killed. I shudder at that thought. What I need is sleep, but I want to spend more time with her. Sometimes I wish I drank.

"Missed a piece there," Mai says, pointing to a shard near the baseboard.

"This will be the second time this week that I've had to call the glass people to come out and replace a window," I say, sweeping pieces into a pile as Mai squats Asian-style holding a dustpan. "A cop hater threw a brick through my front window the other night. Maybe the glass people give discounts to frequent customers. Maybe I'll get the next one replaced for free. Or maybe they'll use me in a TV commercial. 'Sam Reeves is a real person,' they'll say. 'A real person who gets his windows broken every two or three days.'"

Mai smiles as she dumps glass from the dustpan into a paper bag. We clean up all the glass under the window and off the bed, and now we're on the other side where the mirror shattered. Mai places the dustpan next to another pile.

"I took a psychology class this year from a professor who had been a policeman in Los Angels, I think. He talked about policemen's dark humor."

I nod. "It helps to try to find the humor, even if it's sick humor." I sweep the pile into the pan. "But sometimes, no matter how hard you try, you can't find…" I'm holding a broom but I suddenly feel Jimmy's limp body in my arms.

She looks up at me.

"I… uh…" My stomach flips flops. Please don't let me throw up again. I stop sweeping and look down at the glass in the dustpan.

"Are you okay, Sam?" I'm barely aware that Mai has stood and is touching my arm. "Sam?" I look at her but I'm seeing the top of a little boy's head, his tousled brown hair.

"I held his little body in my arms… as he was dying." I look away. "It was my bullet… mine."

My eyes blur, burn. I can't breathe. My heart feels as if it was about to burst from my chest. "It wasn't supposed to happen that way. I was supposed to protect him, to… to save him. His mother called the police for help…"

arms from under Mai just as she begins to push herself up; her effort immobilizes my arms even more.

I'm too jammed to turn my head but I get a sense of a black mass, an overcoat maybe, moving toward us. Got to be Kane. I try to turn my head toward it but Mai's arm is in the way. Just as I start to push harder, she grunts loudly. I think she launches a back kick, and, judging by the loud exhalation of air from behind me, it lands hard.

When you're jammed in that small space between a bed and the wall, and you want to get up quickly, it helps to be the one on top. Mai is on her feet and stepping quickly over me. Unencumbered now, I reach for the shotgun.

She crashes into my back, knocking me against the weapon, sending it and the radio sliding down the two-inch space between the dresser and the wall.

I manage to twist just enough to see that Mai and I are back-to-back, and that she's being jammed by a big shoulder that's pushing against her chest. As she struggles to free herself, the back of her head strikes the side of mine a couple times, instantaneously setting off a wave of nausea.

Now I'm getting woozy and a whole lot pissed. I want this day to end and I want it to end *now*.

I wiggle myself free, which sends Mai thumping to the floor. I turn toward the hulk just as he turns his face away, probably in anticipation of getting hit in the head. He's right; I backfist his ear. Before he can fully react to that, I hit him again, trying for his brachial plexus on the side of his neck, a target that drops most guys in a quick hurry. Since my luck hasn't changed, I miss the target and hit a little farther back. Unfazed, he moves around the end of the mattress and heads toward the door.

Mai scrambles to her feet and leaps again onto my bed, using the bounce to spring over to the far end of the mattress, where she bounces again, this time drawing both knees into her chest. As slick a move as I've ever seen, she thrusts both of her boots, ala professional wrestling, smack into Kane's chest just as he turns back to face us.

Only it's not Kane. I think it's Barry, but it's hard to tell because he's stumbling and flailing his arms backwards. Kane I know from years ago; Barry I've only seen in a photo. It's Kane who's supposed to weigh nearly three hundred pounds, not his brother. This guy is for sure huge, made more so by his ankle-length black overcoat.

His back hits the partially open bedroom door, slamming it shut with a loud bang.

"Officer!" I shout toward the broken window. "Get in here now!"

The big man – I'm positive it's Barry now - shakes his head like a dog shedding rain. He pushes himself away from the door and kicks at me; it's sloppy, untrained. I swat it aside and drive right and left punches into his chest, a waste of time since he's so padded with muscle or maybe fat; I can't tell. His face isn't as hard as Kane's, but it's not terribly fleshy either.

Mai moves up behind him and slaps both of his ears simultaneously with cupped palms. It's a good technique that at best damages the eardrums; even a weak double hit rattles the brain. But Barry doesn't react. Maybe he doesn't have one. He throws a haymaker at Mai, which she slips like a boxer and answers with a groin kick up and under his overcoat. When she snaps her boot back, I slam in one of my own.

He groans and bends over, then straightens as if getting nailed in the cookies twice is no big deal. Damn! I snap my thumbs into both of his eyes, but he jerks his head back so quickly that I can't grind them in. Since it's the only accessible target at the moment, I follow with a pile-driving knee thrust into his twice-hit crotch.

Three is a charm because this time he stumbles back against the flimsy sliding closet doors, collapsing one in against my hanging clothes and loosening a thousand shards of already-broken mirror, sending them tinkling to the floor. He teeters precariously for a moment. Will he fall into my closet?

Nope. He gets his balance back.

"Officer!" I shout toward where the window glass used to be. "Get in here!"

Mai pulls open the bedroom door and shouts down the hall, "*Cảnh Sát! Cảnh Sát!*" returning to her native language in the excitement.

Barry pushes himself off the collapsed door, blows a glob of blood out of his nose onto my carpet, and rapid-blinks his vision back. He sniffs several times. Clearly, whoever wrote the height and weight on the brothers' photos mislabeled them. No matter, what's important now is that this giant is here and he's a whole lot pissed because I poked his eyes, we keep hitting his nuts, and Mai probably broke his nose.

Maybe I can talk him down. "Listen, Barry, there's a police officer out back, one in front, and another walking about the neighborhood. You don't have a chance of getting out of here. Even if you could, the police know you shot the officer today at the health club and the one out back a while ago. We're going to be on you like stink on a turd."

He looks at me, his face blank and eyes glassy like the fake ones taxidermists plug into stuffed deer heads. I'm guessing he doesn't care about getting caught; he just wants to take me out in the process. He sniffs, sniffs again, looking at me like he's minus the majority of his brain cells. If I didn't know he had a good job I'd think he was mentally deficient in some way. I assume he's sniffing because his nose is trashed, but given his glassy eyes…

"You do some coke tonight, Barry?"

His eyes seem to focus, as if seeing me in front of him for the first time. For a moment, I think he might smack his lips, and say, "Mmm, coke." Instead, his peepers return to that shiny glassed-over look.

Mai is inching her way off to his side, probably to divide his attention. Smart move.

"Listen to me. I can't tell you how sorry I am about Jimmy. It was a horrible accident, something that will haunt me all my life. I know I've hurt you and your family."

He's looking at the floor about five feet over to my right, his face so tight that I'm thinking his skin just might rip off his skull. His eyes fixate on one spot, like he's peering into another world. It's a look I've seen a few times before, and it's not a good thing.

I was about twelve the first time I saw that look.

I was playing in the yard when the biggest black Rottweiler I'd ever seen before or since came out of nowhere and backed me against the wall of our garage. It stood splay-legged about ten feet in front of me, its black lips pulled away from its fangs, its glassy eyes piercing the ground a few feet off to one side. When I heard that frightening rumble from somewhere deep within its massive chest, every cell in my body knew that this beast was about to rip everything from my young skeleton. That's when my grandfather stepped around the corner of the garage, casual as can be, and fired a bullet from his World War Two Forty-Five right into one of Fido's glassy eyes.

When I stopped crying an hour later, he told me that once a dog gets that look there isn't anything you can do to distract it. If you can't get away, then you got to fight him, and it's going to be tough because the dog's mind is in another world, a crazy place that's all about gnawing into soft flesh and gristle.

There have been three times on the job when I've faced people who had mad eyes like that Rottweiler. Two were flying on bad dope and one was over-the-top pissed and completely insane. There wasn't a thing anyone could do or say to keep these people from exploding. Two I put out with sleeper holds and I broke the knee of the third guy with a side thrust kick.

Well, Barry's big, like two guys combined, and he seems to eat pain like it's a snack. If I could get to my gun… No! I will not shoot the loving, bereaved uncle of a child I killed a few days ago.

I lunge across the space between us and smack his broken nose with another backfist. He stumbles back, shakes his head like he's trying to get rid of a bad thought, and then lunges at me faster than I would have thought possible for a guy his size. He comes in low with a sloppy wrestling shoot, but I manage to pop him with a weak knee strike to the face, his forehead, I think. Again he staggers back a step, shakes his head, apparently recovering just that fast, and in one smooth movement grabs the lamp off my other nightstand and hurtles it at me. I lean away from its trajectory so that it whizzes by me and thumps into Mai's upraised forearms before it crashes to the floor.

The moment provides Barry a second to dash out the door and down the hall. Mai follows and I'm on her heels.

"Officer!" I shout, as we pass through the kitchen and out the little door into the garage. Without slowing, Barry scoops a forty-five pound dumbbell off the floor and flips it behind him as if it were a ping pong ball. Mai deftly evades it, as do I, and it crashes into a stack of paint cans behind me. He jerks open the door. Hopefully, the cop in the backyard is ready to pounce.

I have just a second to see that the officer I've been calling to for the last several minutes is sitting with his back to us at the far end of the patio, cords dangling from each ear, his head bobbing.

"Hey!" I bellow.

This time he hears me and turns just in time to eat Barry's ham-sized fist. The impact, compounded by the two hundred eighty-pounds running at him full steam, launches the music-loving incompetent out of his chair, across at least six feet of air, and down onto the concrete where his face skids along the flesh-chewing surface.

"Help him, Mai," I shout, slowing for a moment. "And yell for Amy. She's out front."

"Yes," she says, dropping to her knees beside the moaning officer.

Barry is moving at full clip so he's gained a few yards on me. He runs out of the halo of my porch light and into the darkness toward the south side of my wooden fence that I had put up just last summer. It resisted a couple of serious January wind and snow storms, so it should support his big-ass body weight. Earlier, though, he tried to climb the fence on the other side of the yard, and failed, so maybe here is where he's going to give up or fight me again. I guessed wrong.

Barry runs into the fence like a charging bull, tearing loose one five-foot section and laying it flat. He stumbles over it, but manages to stay upright and keeps right on running into the neighbor's backyard. This guy is a friggin' bulldozer. You can't hurt him and nothing stops him.

I bound over the flattened fence, slip and slide awkwardly on the damp grass for one worrisome moment, recover nicely, and begin to gain on him. There is enough light leaking through the trees from surrounding houses and high streetlights out front that I can see him just ahead of me, maybe fifteen feet if that. Can he see the big koi pond?

I helped my neighbor dig and lay the pond so I know it's only about a foot drop to the water surface and about fifteen inches to the pond's bottom, enough to catch Barry by surprise in the semi-dark. It does. He yelps, the first thing I've heard out of his mouth, except for the hard exhalation when Mai gut kicked him. He sloshes to a stop, flails his arms about to keep from falling, and then lumbers about to face me.

Now, I haven't done jump kicks for years, believing they haven't a place in self-defense. As a teen, I practiced forms in which there were two of them, so maybe those many repetitions stayed in my brain all this time, waiting until this moment to resurface and launch me into the air over the six-foot stretch of water to ram my knee into the monster's chest.

The impact knocks Barry over into the water, landing with such an immense splash that it sends a little tsunami wave, carrying two hapless orange koi onto the lawn where they flop about in protest as the water runs back into the pond without them. I drop into the water, landing neatly on my feet, along with an incongruous thought that someone should have captured my jump on film.

I drop a knee with all my bodyweight into Barry's chest, forgetting for a second that I previously body punched him there and that he ignored it. He doesn't react this time either. So I stand quickly and drop another knee, this one solidly into the side of his neck. He grunts like a rhino, which turns to a gurgle as his head slips beneath the surface of the pond. I let him breathe some koi water for a moment and then grab a fist full of his hair and pull his bull-like skull above the surface. He sputters and coughs, then looks at me, his eyes big and attentive. I finally got his attention.

"Listen turds for brains," I growl. "It's over. Understand? It's—"

He grabs my entire face in his palm, pulls me down on top of him, then rolls me over onto my back. Without releasing my face and with more agility than I thought possible for a guy his size, he rolls up onto his knees, quickly straddles my hips, and pushes my face under the water.

The expression "swim with the fishes" pops into my mind as I sense, more than see, a koi's mouth kissing the side of my face. This would be a good time to take a deep breath to control my rising panic but given the fact that I'm under water... I look between his fingers and through the murky liquid at the distorted face above me. He's pushing hard on my chest to keep me down but not quite as hard on my face, probably because leaning into it would throw him off balance. I grab at the hand that's pressing on my head but his strength is incredible; there is no way I can pry it off.

A seasoned fighter would have trapped my arms. Fortunately, Barry's only seasoned at being a behemoth. I shoot both of my fists toward his throat only to discover that the water distorted the distance. My punches land at full extension, their impact no more serious than two bunny taps. He thinks the worse, though, and snaps both of his hands up to protect his throat. This is good.

Freed from his great weight, I thrust my head up and out of the water, raggedy inhaling precious air. Apparently realizing he's uninjured, he drops his big hands toward my face again.

I quickly draw my feet up in the slime and buck my hips as hard as I can. He doesn't fly off me as Mai did, but he leans to the right far enough that he has to reach out to catch himself. Fortunately, the pond bottom is slimy and his hand slips, causing him to topple part way off me. Good enough for government work; I twist and writhe my way out from under him, and get to my feet.

Barry stands, too, looking like he's ready to go again. This guy's a living nightmare, a huge, overcoat-wearing Energizer bunny. Eating my body shots I understand, but writing off the nose hit, the double ear slap, my earlier neck hit, and the triple groin slam? The most logical explanation is that the coke he's been snorting, and I'm guessing it was a lot, has elevated his pain tolerance to the stratosphere.

The big-ass Energizer bunny shuffles toward me as I take short mincing steps to the left so as not to slip in the slime. I'd like to get out of the pond but it will take some effort to do so without falling and I don't want to be off balance for even a second with this guy. If he takes one more step to his right, which will open a path to his groin, I'm firing in a special little kick that I've only done on the bag. In theory, the absolute intensity of pain that it delivers should penetrate his coked brain.

But he doesn't move; he just slips into that earlier glassy-eyed stare off to my right, like he's taking a head trip to outer bum-fuck Egypt. A porch light several houses over reflects in his eyes, making them luminous, satanic.

I think of what Samuel said this afternoon about the tell, the change. Does this guy have one given his nuttiness?

Right on cue, the glassy-eyed look dissolves. There it is! He's telling me that he's about to get serious, as if everything prior to this moment has been playtime.

I sidestep to the left to mess with his tracking a little. Then I snap part one of a front-legged shin kick up between his legs, creating a head-high spray of water, and forcing out of his gaping mouth a sound like a cow would make that's been shot in the eye with an arrow. Then he does some serious leg wobbling. I'm guessing his groin is a whole lot weary of all the attention it's been getting this evening. Well, it's not over yet, pal.

"Here's part two, asshole," I say, tilting my kicking foot straight up so that my hard shoe forms a hook on the back side of his privates. With all my remaining gas, I jerk my knee and foot back toward me as hard and fast as I can, ripping away everything he holds near and dear.

Of course his goodies don't really rip off, but judging by his scream, he thinks they did. For a moment he just stands there, bent at the waist and clutching himself, howling at the koi swirling and splattering about his legs. Then, in slow motion, and still holding his trashed goodies, he drops over onto his side, his big, bent body making a wave of water up onto the lawn again, washing the two beached koi back into the pond, their lives saved. Lucky for him his head landed on the bank because I'm not sure I would have pulled it out of the water if he'd gone under again. The son-of-a-bitch.

"What the hell did you do to him?"

I turn and see Amy a few feet behind me, legs spread like Clint Eastwood in *Dirty Harry*, her gun pointed at the moaning giant who has drawn his knees up to his chest and is rocking back and forth, sending waves in every direction. "I've seen kicks to the balls before, but that was like eerie, man." She chuckles. "You gotta teach me that one."

"You'll need to bring me a note from your mother first," I say, turning back to look at Barry. He's not getting up this time.

"Okay, you tub of shit," she says, coming around the pond, her gun trained on the whimpering hulk. "Unless you want Sam to do that Star Trek, Vulcan balls rip again, roll over onto your stomach and crawl all the way up on the grass. If I lose sight of your hands for even half a second, I'm capping a round into your spinal column. I won't kill you, you fuck, but I will make a paraplegic out of you so for the rest of your life you can sit in a wheelchair and think about this moment."

Damn! Got to remember to never piss off Amy.

CHAPTER NINE

It's almost four in the morning and once again the house is quiet. For the second time this evening, cops, medics and brass swarmed inside and outside my abode, taking notes, interviewing Amy, Mai, and me. The young officer bebopping to his iPod earned a broken jaw and some serious facial abrasions for his dereliction to duty. Before a uniform car whisked him away to the ER, I whispered in his ear that I was in a quandary whether to break the other side of his jaw when he heals up, or do what I can to get him fired. Maybe both. His stupidity jeopardized everyone.

It appears that after Barry shot Dan, he fled around the side of my house and then slipped in through the front door when Mai and I were out back. He failed to close it all the way, which I should not have ignored when I let in the cops and medics a short while later. He hid his big, bold self inside my guest room closet, waited there until everyone had left, and then jumped Mai and me when we were distracted. His ninja-like, cocaine-fueled attack completely caught us off guard, stunning us mentally and physically. Had he still been armed, the outcome would have been grim.

I saw the big guy without his overcoat on when they stuffed him into the backseat of a squad. He wasn't fat and he wasn't cut like a bodybuilder. He was just monstrously huge from a lot of years of pumping heavy iron and drinking beer. In a few hours, the drugs will wear off and he'll awaken to a broken nose, broken ears, ripped groin and whatever else was damaged.

Right now, Mai is asleep on my sofa. Once everyone had left, the events of the evening caught up with her and she began shaking. I've seen it happen to cops a few dozen times, and it's happened to me, too, most recently after both shootings. It's a normal reaction to an abnormal event, Kari says. Mental note: Call and make an appointment for some couch time with her. My head needs some shrinking right now.

Mai and I checked ourselves over for abrasions and lumps, of which we had many, but nothing we couldn't live with. However, the adrenaline rollercoaster ride we've had this evening has taken its toll on our energy. When her shaking began to diminish, I made some green tea for her and excused myself for a few minutes to go shower off the pond scum. The hot, calming drink combined with her waning adrenaline had its affect and when I came back into the living room, she had sunk into my recliner and was sleeping like an infant. I covered her with a throw from my sofa and then came into my bedroom, which is where I am now, assessing the destruction. I don't know if I can stick the city for the brick through my living room window a couple of nights ago, but I'm pretty sure they'll pay for the two broken lamps, the shattered bedroom window, the broken closet door, and my fence. Man, that guy was a bulldozer.

I'm suddenly trashed, more tired than I've been in I don't know how long, undoubtedly a combination of some major stressors going on in my life and the two long fights in the last eighteen hours. I've been in a lot of scuffles on the job and a few knock down drag outs; the one with Barry was one of the toughest.

If there is any good news, it's that in spite of all the action tonight the pills didn't make me terribly nauseous. I'm guessing that it's a fluctuating thing.

Back in the living room, Mai has turned onto her side a little and pulled the blanket up under her chin. I leave the hall light on, shut off the two end table lamps, and sit on the sofa. How beautiful she looks in the soft, tungsten hue that falls across part of her face. I don't know what I'm feeling here but whatever it is, it's intense and not just a little confusing.

I just got out of an unhealthy relationship with Tiff and then suddenly, out of nowhere, Mai enters the picture, hitting me over the head like an axe kick. There are several attractive women in my classes, in the DA's office, and at my coffee stops, but with Mai, there was, well, like what the writers are always talking about in Tiff's *Cosmo*: an instant connection. Yes, that's it, and unless my cop instincts are off, I think she feels it, too.

I stretch out on the sofa and look over at her again. There are only a few days left before she and Samuel have to leave. Samuel! Where was he? We could have used his skills a while ago?

I let my head sink deeply into the pillow. Has Samuel... noticed... the... connection? Has... he...

All is dark, except for a fuzzy glow around little Jimmy, the hostage taker, and the tweaker. They're pointing guns at me, their hollow eyes without emotion.

"Wanna know how it feels to have three bullets fired into your skull, detective? the tweaker says, in that gravelly voice. He's dressed in the same clothes he wore when I killed him. The other two are as naked as they were when I killed them. All three are bloated, their skin blotchy, black in places, their lips rotting away so that their teeth appear enlarged, grinning.

"It's like really painful," the tweaker prattles on. "You outta see for yourself so maybe you'll stop shooting everybody."

"*Oooh don't giiive us that saaad face, detectivvve,*" the hostage says, his voice dripping. "*Yooou shot us on puuuuurpose.*"

"*Help me,*" Jimmy whines, tears emanating from his hollow sockets.

"*Deeetectivvve?*" the hostage taker slithers.

"*Sam?*"

"*Sam?*"

"Sam?" Mai's voice. Hand patting my shoulder. "Sam?"

"Wha…"

"I am sorry to wake you." My eyes unfuzz to Mai's face just inches from my shoulder. "I think you were having a nightmare. You yelled out something but I did not understand it."

It takes me a moment to realize I'm stretched out on my sofa and she is sitting on the floor next to me, her shoulder braced against the cushion by my head. Across the room, morning light sneaks in through the bent mini blinds. I blink a few times, smile at her, and scoot up onto my side, resting on my forearm. "What time is it," I ask, squinting at the wall clock. "Six thirty!"

"Yes."

"Morning?"

"You are correct," she nods. "I can see why you are a police detective." Her eyes twinkle laughter and what's left of her perfume after the long night wafts into my brain.

I sputter a laugh. "You always wake up like a smart ass?"

She giggles. "I love that expression. 'Smart. Ass.'"

"You just wake up?"

"Yes. Thank you for the blanket. I did not wake up at all until maybe fifteen minutes ago. You did not sleep in your bed."

"Didn't seem hospitable. Plus I wasn't planning on sleeping. I just conked out, I guess."

She smiles that electric smile that would power up all of Vegas; I grin back, probably looking like a chimpanzee. Looking into her green-brown eyes makes me feel sort of fuzzy brained, which I haven't felt since I looked into Deedee McCormick's azures in the fourth grade.

Neither of us looks away, holding our gazes long past what one would consider uncomfortable. Yet I don't feel discomfort; I could do this all day. Apparently she can, too.

Her cell rings the Star Spangled Banner. Samuel? Mai extends her leg so she can pry her phone out of her jeans pocket. I sit up quickly and straighten my tank top as if he had just walked in on us. What is he going to think? Wait, Mai is thirty-two years old. She doesn't answer to him. Or does she? How do they do it in Vietnam?

Mai flips open her cell and says something in Vietnamese. She listens, nods, and listens some more. Samuel must be giving her an ear full for staying over. Oh man. I am sooo dead. I'd rather face Barry again than go up against the old man. She says something that sounds like "chao" and flips her phone shut.

"Is Samuel pissed big time?"

She frowns. "Why should he be pissed?" Pissed sounds funny when she says it.

"Because you didn't go back to your apartment last night. Did you tell him about what happened here? The shooting? Our fight? That you fell asleep? That we didn't sleep together?"

"But we did sleep together," she says, leaning against the sofa and looking at me with those teasing, twinkling eyes.

"What? Look, Mai. You're going to get me killed here. Daddy's little girl and all that."

"Are you scared of my father? *Our* father?" She smiles.

"No... Well, maybe a little. After all, we all just met and there was that whole confusion about you being my sister. And I'm still not use to having a father and—"

"Sam?"

"What?"

She holds up her cell. "That was Sau, a Vietnamese girl-friend who also goes to Portland State."

"What?"

"You say 'what' a lot. We were supposed to meet for break-fast this morning. We became good friends this year. We wanted to see each other before I go home. Plus, I am giving her my cat when I leave. Sau might come and see me in Vietnam this fall."

I inflate my cheeks and blow out a breath of relief.

She laughs. "I am a grown woman. Already been married before. You worried what our father will say about us sleeping together?"

I shake my head. "Please don't say 'what *our* father will say' when talking about *us* sleeping together. Besides, we really didn't sleep together. I mean, we did sleep together, but not... you know, *sleep* together."

"What is the difference?" she asks, tilting her head a little. "English is so confusing," She raises an eyebrow.

It's my turn to laugh. "You messin' with me?"

She sobers. "Yes, I am messin' with you." Her eyes smile first, then her mouth. "I talked to father before I wake you up. He is feeling better now after a night's sleep. I told him what had happened and he said he had just seen the story on the news. He said he saw a picture of this house and my car parked out front."

"Oh no," I say, getting up and walking over to the blinds. I lift one of them half an inch. They're back. Three news vans, one with a satellite dish and about half a dozen people with still cameras. "News crews out front again." I turn toward Mai as she crosses over toward the window. "Is Samuel coming over?"

She stops next to me, shakes her head and peeks through the blinds. "He wanted to, but I told him I was coming back to the apartment to clean up. I said you were still sleeping. He will call you later." She closes the blind and turns toward me. "You are very popular with the television news."

"Yeah, lucky me. Listen, I just want to say again that I'm very sorry about getting you involved last night."

"You could have been hurt, too," she says softly.

I nod, suddenly nervous. We're not touching, but I can feel her presence against me like a warm, comfortable, intoxicating, exhilarating, intoxicating, and just-plain-wonderful embrace. And intoxicating. Did I already say that?

She's looking up at me in that way women do when they want you to kiss them.

"I wish I could have seen you beat off that big ape," she says, her eyes moving from my eyes to my mouth and back to my eyes again. "That woman policeman—the one who is like a man?— she said that you, uh, you 'did a job on him.' What does that expression mean? Does it mean that you beat him off good?"

I sputter a laugh and feel my face heat up. "It's 'beat him *up*.' Beat him... well, what you said, means something else entirely."

"What?"

"Uh, ask your father."

"How should I say it?"

"How about 'you really thumped that jerk.'"

She places her hands on my chest; I feel their heat through my thin T-shirt. "You really..." she says, barely above a whisper, tilting her head up and looking so intensely into my eyes that I think I might... I don't know what. Her lips barely touch mine, her words tickling my mouth like the fluttering wings of a butterfly. "You really thumped that jerk."

My arms envelop her. We kiss, tentatively, then softly, then firmly, then hungrily.

We part, breathless as if we've just sparred.

Her eyes search mine for a moment. Hers suddenly confused? Pained? From a memory, maybe? She pushes against my chest and steps back.

Looking away, she whispers a single word. "No."

What does that mean? "Mai?" I reach for her. "What..."

"I have to go, Sam," she says searching the room. Spotting her purse, she moves hurriedly over to it, retrieves it from the end table, and heads for the door.

"Mai? Did I do something? I'm sorry if I came on too strong." Actually, I'm not. "I thought you wanted me to kiss you. I..."

"I am sorry, Sam," she says, turning toward me, her hand on the knob. "I should not have let it happen. I am... confused. I think you are a wonderful person and from the moment I saw you..."

She turns back to the door, opens it, and pauses. After a moment, she turns toward me a little, whispering her next words over her shoulder. "There is much you do not know about me."

I move toward her. "What do you mean? I don't care—"

"Just let me go back to my apartment, Sam. I need to think. I need to talk to my father."

I start to protest but she slips out the door quickly, shutting it behind her.

When I open it, I'm greeted by a horde of reporters out on the sidewalk shouting my name.

Mai pushes her way through them, swatting a couple of microphones out of her way, and gets into her car. A moment later she's accelerating down the street, in the same direction Tiff left last night.

I shut the door and lean my back against it. I can still feel the heat of her against me.

*

"Yo, Mark," I say in the doorway of his office.

"Sam!" He stands and steps around his desk to pump my hand and slap my shoulder. "Thanks for coming in this morning. That's quite a knot you got on your head. Just an inch over from the last one you got up there."

"It was one of those days."

"Good job nabbing Barry Clarkson last night. I'm so glad you're okay. How is... Mai, is it?"

"She's fine. She did an amazing job. Heck of a fighter. Put some serious hurt on Barry."

"So I read in the reports. She a martial artist or something?"

I nod. "Can we sit? I'm a bit tired."

Mark steps back and waves at the chair. "Of course," he says, shutting the office door. "I've read the reports but I'd like you to tell me what happened."

For the next twenty minutes I tell my boss everything that went down after I got home, excluding the last few minutes with Mai. When I finish, I sit back in the chair and close my eyes.

"I feel like I've been eaten by a coyote and crapped over a cliff," I say, repeating my bookkeeper's analysis.

Mark nods. "You've been through the mill, pal. On top of the shooting and last night's action, you got this whole thing going on with your new family."

I don't say anything.

"You're convinced they're on the up and up? That Samuel is your father and Mai... what is she, anyway? I'm getting confused."

"*You* are?" For a moment I can feel Mai looking into my eyes, leaning into me, her mouth so... I blink the image away. "Mai was raised by my father but her real father was another serviceman."

"So he *is* your father."

"Yes," I say, with absolute certainty. "No doubt about it."

My friend shakes his head. "A lot of stress."

"Speaking of, what's the story on Barry?"

Mark retrieves a stack of reports off a foot-high pile. "He was brought in both high on dope and high on hurtin'. You did a job on him. The guys ended up taking him to ER to have him looked over." He chuckles. "What the hell did you have against his dick, anyway? Now he's got nothing to offer the other fellas in the prison shower."

"If I could have reached my gun..." I let that die on the vine. I couldn't have shot him so why say it.

"Got a bunch of long doctor-word injuries down in his la-la land, as well as a broken nose, a minor concussion, and numerous lacerations all over his big-ass-ness. After ER patched him up and he came down a little from his coke high, The Fat Dicks jumped on him before they gave him pain meds. He copped to everything except Mitchell's murder. He admitted shooting Tommy at the gym, Dan behind your house, and of course, breaking into your place and assaulting you and Mai. The guys think he'll cop to Mitchell; they just need to lean on him longer."

I should be happy at nabbing Barry, and I am, I guess. He might have hurt a lot more people before he was stopped. But something's bothering me, something besides the shooting and Barry and all the rest that's involved in this case. Something else.

The phone rings.

"Yes?" Mark nods, nods again, then looks up at me. "You're shittin' me! What's his demeanor? I see. Sam's here. Yes, just got here, in fact. Yeah. Okay, I'll ask him. But it's his decision, got it? Hold on."

Mark looks at me. "You sittin' down?"

I gesture at my lap. "Why?"

"Kane Clarkson just walked into the front office."

"What?"

"Asked to talk to the detectives investigating the shooting of his nephew and the dicks investigating his brother, Barry. He also asked to talk to you."

"To me? But how'd he know I was here?"

"Maybe he didn't. Just assumed. You want to walk over there?"

My first thought is no, I don't want to see one of Jimmy's family members. I don't want to hear their accusation and threats. I don't want to see their tears and pain because of what I did. I don't want to add their faces to my dreams. That makes me a coward, but I'm reaching my limit of what I can take this week. I'm full. No more can come in. My cup runneth over.

"Sam?"

"Okay."

"You sure?" Not the boss asking, but a friend.

I look at him. "I am."

"We're on our way," Mark says into the phone. "Be there in one minute."

I stand. "You know that saying, 'God never gives you anymore than you can handle?'"

Mark moves over to the door and opens it. "Yes."

"It's a bunch of shit."

"I'd have to agree, big hoss." He slugs my shoulder. "But if anyone can handle it, it's you."

Half the desks in Homicide's section of the thirteenth floor are occupied, and every set of eyes look up from their keyboards as Mark and I round the corner. There's a scattering of "What's up, Sam?" I nod to them. Smile.

"They're in the conference room," Billy Chang says with a jerk of his thumb. "The Fat Dicks are in there along with Page and Rea for security. The Italian's got the outside."

"Thanks, Billy," Mark says.

The Italian nods a greeting from where he's standing by the conference room door and pushes it open for us. It's a sparse, deep, and narrow room with an oval twenty-foot long, shiny-black table. The Fat Dicks sit to the left, Page and Rea, jacketless and wearing shoulder rigs, sit on the right, the same side as Kane.

The ex-con looks like his release mug: hard faced, fit and lean, with eyes that could melt steel prison bars. His salt and pepper hair has been buzzed short, which makes the big bite out of his ear all the more apparent. He must have been mighty pissed at whoever made the grievous error of doing that to him.

Kane doesn't wait for introductions. "I recognize you from the newspaper," he says, tight lipped, his head bobbing slightly. "I also remember you from way back when you were doing martial arts. I trained too back then."

"I remember."

"They say you've been off duty since… what happened."

I nod.

"Guess I'm just lucky you was here today, huh?"

"Guess so," I say. He can feel me out all he wants but I'm giving him only what I want him to get.

He looks at me for a long, awkward moment, then, "How long you been a cop?"

"Fifteen years."

"Ever shot anybody before this time?"

"Yes."

"Did he die, too?" Kane keeps nodding his head faintly. Don't know if it's because he's nervous or because he's got a bad nerve or something.

"Yes."

"How did that make you feel?"

"Like hell." Maybe I gave him too much there.

"Do cops like to kill people?"

"I've never met one who does."

"Would you mind sitting down so I don't have to look up?"

Not a question I expected to get from an ex-con who spent years being told what to do. But it's a fair request. I sit at the end of the table, about six feet from him. Mark remains standing by the door.

"Thank you. Would you mind telling me how Jimmy's shooting happened?"

"He can't do that," Mark says. Kane's eyes stay on mine as the boss speaks. "It's an ongoing investigation and the court proceedings have yet to start. Check out the newspaper. It's fairly accurate."

Surprisingly, Kane's eyes aren't glaring or piercing with rage as I would expect, but they watch everything, mostly me. Cons and cops do a lot of watching.

"How did you feel when you realized you'd killed Jimmy?"

"He can't say that either, Kane," Richard Cary says.

I ignore Cary. "I died inside."

Kane's eyes look deeply into mine, as if searching for the color of my soul. "Good," he says softly, his head nodding slightly, up and down, up and down.

My eyes glisten, no matter how hard I try not to let it happen.

After another long moment of quiet, he says, "I was going to kill you, you know."

My heart flutters. The silence in the room hurts my head.

"The other night. You had your garage door open and you were hitting your punching bag. You were like going berserk on it."

"How did you know where I—"

"I know people who know people," he says, a little annoyed at the question's intrusion. "Anyway, I got an old Colt Forty-Five from a friend and parked across the street from your place. Your hands were bleeding but you just kept hitting. Then you had a fight with... was that your girlfriend?"

I don't answer. I think back to waking up on the garage floor and the feeling I had that someone was watching me from out in the dark. Guess I was right.

"You had a big fight and she left. Then you laid down on your garage floor and fell asleep. I watched you from my car. I watched for maybe an hour or more, thinking long and hard about walking across the street and emptying my clip into your brain."

I try to swallow but can't.

"But something told me not to."

"Who? God?" Richard Daniels asks.

Kane looks over at him. "Yeah, you heard of him? There's a popular book about him." He looks back to me. "No, not God. A gut feeling that you're a moral guy, an ethical guy, and that you were suffering for what you did, that you were in hell right there in your garage."

A shiver washes over me at the thought of this guy watching me and having an internal conversation about shooting me. I remember an old detective telling me about his divorce. He said that during the court proceedings his wife told the judge how every night she would point her husband's off-duty revolver at his head while he slept, how she would struggle for courage to pull the trigger. The old timer got the shakes just telling me about it, all the while I was laughing so hard I had tears in my eyes. It's not so funny now.

Kane never breaks eye contact with me. "My family is deeply traumatized. Jimmy was very special to all of us. He was smart, funny, and a tough little dude." His tone has changed from tight and restrained, to almost conversational. "He beat cancer, did you know that?"

I nod and squeeze my eyes closed against the tears. One escapes and rolls down my cheek. Without opening them, I whisper, "I don't have words for how sorry I am. I... uh..." I shake my head. "I don't know..."

"Barry had a special relationship with Jimmy. He was much closer to him than I was because I'd been in the joint during the boy's early years. My brother also beat cancer back in his teens, so the two of them shared that. Uncle Barry helped Jimmy through the painful cure. But now my brother's a coke head, been on the stuff for about a year and half. And he takes 'roids, too. Those things have changed him a lot. He's lots bigger and ten times more aggressive than he was just a couple of years ago." Kane pauses for a moment. "You had a heck of battle with him, I understand."

"He was not in his right mind."

Kane smiles. "He's really not a fighter, but he's very powerful."

"Did he kill the policeman?" Richard Cary asks.

The ex-con looks over at him, his face giving away nothing. "Don't know. Probably wouldn't tell you if I did; he's my brother, right? But the honest truth is I don't know."

He looks back at me. "You going to stay in police work?"

No! fills my head in big, bold font.

Wow. How long has that "no" been lurking in my mind? Do I have a look of surprise on my face? Is that what was bothering me a few minutes ago in Mark's office, the thing I couldn't put my finger on? I think so. I guess the ol' sub-brain knows something the conscious me hasn't realized yet: It doesn't want to be a cop any more.

"Are you?"

Softly, "I don't know."

Mark snaps his head toward me; in my peripheral I see The Fat Dicks look my way, too.

Kane stirs in his chair and turns a little more toward me. The head nodding isn't as frequent now. "I wanted to talk with you to confirm what kind of a man you are, to validate what I thought I was seeing that night in your garage." He looks at me for a long time as if taking one more reading. "I have a message from my older brother and his wife, Jimmy's parents."

Kane's face has softened a little from when I first came into the room. Then his face looked hard, though not as chiseled as his release mug showed. Now it looks softer and his body seems to have relaxed a little.

"They're in hell, and Barry's actions have made it even worse for them. I embarrassed Adam by being sent to prison years ago, and now Barry, always the good one, is doing a number on them." Kane focuses his eyes on the table top for a moment. "They want you to know that Barry is the only one who had the vendetta, not them and now, not me."

He leans toward me, his next words emphatic. "So this stops now. Pain upon pain only begets more pain. We all need to heal as much as possible."

I certainly didn't expect to hear that when I walked in here. My gut tells me it's not bull. The Fat Dicks, Rea, Page, and Mark look at me. Mark shakes his head, which I take to mean he isn't buying it.

"What are you doing now, Kane?" I ask, although I know he's working in the porno business.

"Barry helped me get a job with Hot Videos, Inc a couple years ago. I'm assistant to the VP now. I don't want to stay in this line of work for long but it's a great way to learn about business in general. Some day I'd like to work for Netflix or something like that. Regular movies, no adult stuff."

I nod, and we sit silently for several seconds, each looking at the other, as if no one else is in the room. Then he smiles faintly, and says, "Life has taken us on different journeys, huh? No one could have guessed our paths back when we were teenagers at the *dojo*."

I nod, though I'm not about to get into a philosophical conversation with him. "There's going to be a grand jury and maybe a public inquest," I say. "Will you and your brother and his wife be able to maintain this same wish that we all start the healing process?"

"Yes. They're good people, and me, I'm trying. Barry? He's got a ways to go."

Mark takes a step toward the door. He looks at Richard Cary. "You guys have a talk with Mister Clarkson yet?"

Richard nods. "Yes, but we got a few more questions when we're done here."

"I think we are," Mark says. "Kane?"

He stands. The head nodding has stopped. "Yes, I'm done." He extends his hand and looks me in the eyes. "Thanks for letting me talk with you."

I take it, and we shake.

*

Doctor Kari Stephens sips from her coffee mug calmly, in spite of my confrontational tone, and fixes those Marine drill sergeant eyes on me. "Yes, I did say that the chance of you getting into another shooting is no greater than it was the first time you got into one," she says. "And I stand by that. But as I'm sure you know, especially as a veteran cop, sometimes things can simply be summed up as 'shit happens.'"

I'm looking at a framed print on the wall behind Kari. It's a farm scene; rolling hills, hay fields, and a lone child, a nine- or ten-year-old little girl with curly blond hair, playing on a bale of hay by a barn door.

In my early years working uniform, I befriended a little blond-haired girl named Kate. She was nine and lived in a broken down house on Fifty-Seventh with an alcoholic mother named Alice and her crank-head boyfriend, Don. Kate's eighteen-year-old brother, Davis, was practically brain dead from all the glue he'd sniffed over two years. He was also an habitual burglar and car thief who had been popped at least two dozen times by all the neighborhood cops on all three shifts. I'd arrested him four times, myself.

Kate was a bundle of cute, charm, and brains, a real dynamo who appeared, at least on the surface, to be unaffected by her home life. I would pull to the curb whenever I saw her playing under the big oak in their yard, and she'd run over to me like it was Christmas morning. We talk about school and her studies and she'd tell me how much she wanted to be a nurse so she could help people who were "sick" like her family.

That August she told me she was going to spend three weeks at her uncle's farm in Turner. She was excited because they had lots of animals to feed, huge piles of hay to play on, and a creek to splash around in. She even got a "new" bathing suit, a pink one, from Goodwill. I wished her a good time and said I would see her the first week of September when school starts.

I missed our little visits while she was gone, though I went to her house a couple of times. One time on a loud drunken domestic fight between Alice and Don, and once to interview Davis, the glue sniffing burglar, as to his whereabouts the night the First Baptist church on Seventy-Seventh got hit.

The first week of September, I bought Kate a Pocahontas school backpack, but I didn't see her out front that Monday and I didn't see her the rest of the week. The following week, and two days after school had started, I saw her mother pull into her driveway and struggle on wobbly legs out of her old Ford wagon. She saw me, gave me a partial wave and then swayed slowly over to my car. She always looked bad, but today she looked even worse, and her eyes were half a jug of cheap wine into the late afternoon. She seemed oblivious that I could pop her for driving under the influence.

"Hear 'bout Kate?" she asked as a greeting. "I know you and her was friends. She always talked 'bout you." Mom's hands were shaking like it had been an hour or so since she'd last fortified herself.

"What do you mean 'hear about'?" My chest was beginning to cave in.

"Got kilt a couple weeks ago down on my brother Jack's farm."

"What?" I barely got out.

Tears erupted from the mother's eyes and rolled over the nooks and crannies of her rode-hard face. She took a moment to gather herself. Then, stammering, "My Kate... and her cousins went up on this hay silo... down the road from Jack's, and was jumpin' into it, climbin' out, and jumpin' into it again. One time Kate jumped and just... disappeared. The kids said it was like she got sucked down, like the hay just swallowed her up. And then all the other hay fell in on top of her. It took two days to get her out."

I couldn't move. Couldn't talk. I just looked at her.

"I know you two was friends and all. I... I ain't much, but I tried to be a good mom to her. I failed with my boy Davis, but I put all I had into Kate. She was smart. Was gonna... be somethin'."

I visited her grave on my next day off. My second day back to work I arrested her brother for armed robbery of a Seven Eleven.

Sometimes shit happens. Yes, indeed.

"I'm a little surprised you didn't come and see me sooner after this last shooting," Kari says.

"Doc, the last few days have been quite a ride." I give her the rundown about everything from my first rough nights after the shooting, Tiff's reaction, the attack at the coffee joint, meeting Samuel and Mai, Mitchell's killing, the shooting at my house, and the fight with Barry. I leave out Samuel's problems including our fight in the alley. I tell her of my feelings toward Mai, too.

Kari finishes off her coffee and glances at the wall clock. "You have had your share this week, Sam. But you look good and I think you are handling it well. We're almost out of time but let me throw a couple things out for you to think about until next Monday.

"As for Mai," she smiles, "'Love and a cough cannot be hid,' George Herbert said. You said you felt 'weird' because you were attracted to her when you still thought she was your half sister. Well, there is nothing strange about that, or wrong. Suddenly you meet this knock-down-dead gorgeous woman who you thought was your sister. But you have no history with her, no history at all with her as a sister. All you had was the immediate attraction to something pretty or whatever that thing that makes for, 'a connection,' to use your words, between two people. The fact that you felt uncomfortable with that feeling is a good thing. People who practice incest either don't have that discomfort or, if they do, it adds to their excitement.

"You're fine, Sam. You're not a 'perv,' as you suggested. You're a healthy male with feelings. Now that you know she's not your sister and you believe that there's a mutual connection, you can pursue it if you want. However, please factor in that although you and Tiff ended your relationship a couple of months ago, you continued it on a physical-only basis. Sometimes that's okay and other times it can cause all kinds of internal confusion in one or both of you. If you were experiencing this, starting a new relationship so soon might not be in your best interests or the new person's. What are your thoughts?"

"I didn't have any internal confusion over the physical part. I enjoyed it for what it was and I thought Tiff was enjoying it the same way. That is, until the last couple of times. Then there were all the phone calls from her and the scene when she came to my house. I think *she* has that internal confusion thing going on. I'd be happy to talk to her about it but she was over-the-top upset at my house and she didn't want to talk. Maybe down the road, but I don't think we can right now."

"Well, I believe there is power in ending things well but I also know that that can't always happen. I hope you two can find a way to do it, even if it might not happen for a while. As for Mai, I advise you to tread softly."

"I will," I say, leaving out Mai's strange departure this morning. "Thank you."

She smiles slightly. "Okay. Good. Now, regarding your shooting, this one will be with you for the rest of your life. You will have periods when you're just fine and you will have periods when you're not so fine. But no matter what you're feeling, always keep in mind that you acted as you thought best at the time. Teddy Roosevelt said 'Do what you can with what you have where you are.' And you did, Sam. All of you faced that situation with courage, caring, and your training. Someone bumped you at the precise moment you were trying to save that little boy from that beast. Shit happened. Why shit happens is one of the great mysteries of life. But you did your best. Think about that and we'll talk again next week. Now get out of here or I'll throw some more quotes at you."

Outside in the hall, I poke the elevator button and lean against the wall. What I wouldn't give for a normal, routine, boring day. Get up, read the paper, watch the *Today Show*, mow the grass, teach a couple private lessons at my school, and chow down at the Burger Barn.

I needed this visit with Kari today. "Shit happens," she said. Damn straight. Maybe if she'd popped that gem on me back when I first came in, I wouldn't have attacked my kitchen or been afraid to go out to buy coffee. Cops understand that shit happens because they see evidence of it all the time. My little friend jumps into a pile of hay in which there was a hidden air pocket; Tiff and I, great in so many ways, saw the world so differently that our love couldn't survive; Samuel's life took a hard right thirty-five years ago so that he and I missed out on a father and son relationship for over three decades. Tommy is blessed with a gift for calming volatile situations but the one time it didn't work... shit happened.

The elevator dings and the doors whoosh open.

"Sam!"

"Tommy!"

Talk about your awkward moments. Judging by the look on his face, I'd bet he's thinking the same thing I am: The last time we saw each other, I was going after him like a revenge-hungry pit bull on a feeding frenzy.

"How are you doing?" he asks, looking left and right. The elevator doors swoosh shut behind him, cutting off an avenue of escape and setting off a facial tick at the corner of his mouth.

I have no desire to prolong his agony. I extend my hand. "I am profoundly sorry for the scene in the office the other day."

His neck muscles relax a little as do his shoulders. He tentatively takes it and we shake, though I do all the work.

"I went a little crazy. Lately, it's all been..." No excuses, damnit. "I'm just sorry."

The elevator doors open again and a cluster of people spill out. We step over next to the wall.

"Hear you got Barry Clarkson last night and he's copped to killing Mitchell," Tommy says, more relaxed than a moment ago. "Good job."

"He admitted it?" I ask with surprise. "I haven't heard that. I was in the office an hour and a half ago but Barry wasn't talking."

Tommy nods. "You know The Fat Dicks. He didn't have a chance to deny it very long with those guys leaning on him."

"Oh yes, they're always motivated to get things done the closer it gets to chow time."

Our chuckles are forced. We're both thinking about Mitchell, a guy neither of us knew well, but who is now perpetually entwined with us.

"How are your wounds?" I ask, automatically looking at his casted hand and at the front of his pants.

He shakes his head as his eyes widen at the memory. "The bullet came within a hair—literally and figuratively—of hitting The Big Guy. But I'm fine. I have a small bandage over the groove but it's really nothing more than a long scratch. Doc's reattached my fingers, and he says that I might be looking at a couple surgeries before they are completely good. Mark's letting me do admin stuff around the office."

"Barry could have done a worse job on Dan Kristos, too," I say. "Hit Dan's leg, but mostly he shot up my house. Mitchell… he got it close range."

We're both silent for a while. I break it. "How you doing otherwise?" I know he understands the question.

"Not so good. Haven't slept more than a couple hours a night since. Work out a lot, but I'm so tired all the time that I'm probably not doing myself any good." There's something else that isn't doing him any good: booze. I can smell it on his breath and it's not even lunchtime.

He looks at me for a long moment, the pain in his face profound. He takes a deep breath. "Sam, I'm so sorry that I—"

"No need to say that, Tommy," I say quickly. "We did the best we could but shit still happened. If Mitch would have gone left and you and I had gone right, the outcome might have been different. If we'd positioned ourselves a foot or two more to the left or right, things might have been different. If that vermin wouldn't have taken Jimmy hostage, we wouldn't have been there in the first place. Same thing if the mental health people had done their job and better monitored his medication or kept him incarcerated, or whatever. We're all innocent and we're all guilty. Shit happens."

Tommy's been chewing his lip as I rattled on. I can't tell if he agrees; I'm not even sure if I believe it all. It just came out.

"I'll have to think about that," he says after a moment, his face tight. There's a small drop of blood on his lip. "And you? How are you?"

"I think I'm going to be okay," I say, believing it. "Been seeing Kari and there's been a lot happening in my life that's distracting me and helping at the same time."

Again, we sniff, cough, and look up and down the hall.

"Well," he says. "I got to visit with Kari, too. My first time. Not sure what to expect."

I give him a lopsided grin. "There's no way you can anticipate her. But be honest because she'll know when you're bullshitting. Plus it's the best way to get something out of the session."

"Thanks," Tommy says. We look at each other, both tight lipped, both nodding slightly, both understanding that this event has bonded us. He extends his hand. I take it and pull him into a tight hug. We slap each other's back. He turns without saying another word, and heads toward Kari's door.

*

The wind has kicked up since this morning, sending fall's remaining brown leaves skittering along the mile-long sidewalk that parallels downtown's Willamette River. I'm sitting on an uncomfortable cement bench facing the seawall, a four-foot high stone and cement barrier between the walk and the river. The water is gray and choppy, and only an old barge chugging upstream is brave enough to face the southerly wind.

I pull the hood of my black parka up over my head and take another bite of my apple. There are only a few noon-time joggers braving the cold weather, which isn't as bone numbing as it was three months ago when a heavy ice rain froze the city solid for seven days. In five or six more weeks, the heavy sweat pants, matching jackets, and stocking caps that brave joggers are wearing today will be replaced with shorts, tank tops, and sweatbands.

The mile-long, tree-dotted lawn that separates the walkway from the street is void of lunch-time picnickers, although a few yards away to my left, an elderly, long-haired Chinese man practices tai chi, while a few feet away to my right, a homeless couple moves around under a tattered sleeping bag. I'm guessing they're homeless based on their crap-filled grocery cart and the sad looking puppy tied to it.

The Chinese guy, his long black-gray hair blowing in a mad swirl about his head and shoulders, knows what he's doing. His movements are slow, rhythmical, and convey a sense that he's moving in liquid. I can't see his face in detail, but even from here I get a sense of peace about him, as if what he is doing, what he is feeling, and where he is in his mind, is most wonderful.

I practiced tai chi for a few months several years ago but I had to give it up when my shift changed. Its energizing "acupuncture without needles," as my teacher called it, is precisely what I need right now. What I wouldn't give to be in a wonderful place, if only in my mind. Especially in my mind.

The female giggle coming from the moving sleeping bag leaves no doubt as to what is going on within.

About six years ago, working uniform, I got a call to this very spot. Dispatch said that several people were holding down a violent man who was about to set fire to a sleeping bag with the sleeper still inside. After my partner and I saved the guy from the crowd and got him handcuffed, he told us that he had gone to sleep the night before with his girl friend next to him in her sleeping bag. When he awoke at daybreak, he saw her a few feet away on top of another bag and on top of another homeless guy, the two of them enjoying some early morning delight.

In a rage, the jilted lover ran a couple blocks to a service station and bought a five-gallon can of gasoline. When he came back, his girlfriend was gone but her new man was sound asleep deep inside his mummy bag. Still enraged, the jilted guy poured gasoline over it and was trying to flick his Bic when he was tackled to the ground by other homeless campers.

Incredibly, the new lover slept through the gasoline saturation and the scuffle that followed. It was only after some vigorous shaking that I got him to stick his head out. That's when the guy we had just cuffed, looked puzzled at the man, and asked, "Who's he? That's not the same dickhead who was porkin' my woman. In fact, now that I think about it, that's not even the same sleeping bag. Where they'd go?"

It turned out that after the two lovers had left, the new guy came along and plopped his bag down and went to sleep. When we told him why he reeked of gasoline, why his bag was sopped with it, and how he had almost been a crispy critter, he scratched his head, and mused, "Dang. That was close."

I smile at the memory as I watch a gray and white pigeon land on the seawall a few feet in front of me. A sudden wind gust nearly blows it off before the little dude hunkers down and braces against it, looking as happy as the tai chi guy. One with nature, they are.

I don't know how long the seawall has been here, though I've seen old black and white pics of it taken back in the forties, maybe the thirties. There have been a lot of jumpers off it during my years working the street. Most didn't drown, since it's only about a ten-foot drop, and the bone-chilling water has a way of slapping you out of your despair. Those who did drown were adamant folks who had to struggle down deep into the dark currents, and then take a big inhalation of the filthy water. One successful suicide who did exactly that carried a typed note in his wallet that read, "See, I told you I was depressed."

I had a partner once who said that if he ever committed suicide he'd come down to the wall late at night, sit on it with his back toward the river, and shoot himself in the forehead. His plan was that he'd topple backwards into the river and his gun would disappear into the depths. When they found his body miles down stream a couple days later, the headlines would scream, "Portland police officer gunned downed and thrown into the river." He thought it was funny to think how hard the homicide dicks would work trying to solve his murder. Cop humor, you got to love it.

The female cries out. I startle in their direction when a second cry makes it clear that she's having a good time. It's just the homeless having sex, making homeless babies for the state to pay for.

Man, what a bunch of happy thoughts I'm having. Maybe I'll just sit here and see how many other murders and suicides I can dredge up from my sick brain. When I'm done with those, I'll reminisce about the many accidental deaths I investigated and then I'll think about the animal abuse cases I've worked.

I look back to the seagull that's now checking for something under one of its wings. To be corny for a moment, all of us in this little patch of green are looking for something. The bird's looking for a flea, or whatever they get, the tai chi guy is looking for inner peace, the homeless couple is looking for temporary bliss in their otherwise miserable existence, and I'm looking for... Hell if I know.

I sure said "I don't know" quickly when Kane asked if I was going to stay in police work. The other coppers all looked surprised when I said it but they weren't half as surprised as I was when I heard the big "NO" inside my head. Apparently my subconscious is adamant. So what does that mean?

I've had my doubts about the job ever so often over the years but I've never taken them seriously. It's my career and what I've done most of my adult life. Besides, who would hire a used cop, especially one with my recent record?

"Tell me Mr. Reeves," my prospective employer would ask. "How did you handle difficult people on your last job."

"I killed them, sir."

I like to think that I could make a go of it just teaching. Even now there are some months when I make more at my school than I do on the job. I've done well saving and investing, and I've built a darn good nest egg. I could live on that for three or four years, even if I never had another dime coming in. If I resigned from the PD and just lived on what I made at the school, once I rebuilt the membership I wouldn't have to change anything lifestyle-wise. I couldn't bank as much at first, but then I'd be free to take on more students, especial big paying private ones. Within a few months I'd be netting as much as I do now from the PD and the school.

So financially, I could do it. But is my head ready for such a change? I'm not so sure…. Or am I? Yeah, I could do it. I could quit. Will I? Maybe. Yeah… I will.

"Hey, man. You got a buck?"

The homeless guy, who looks about twenty-five under all that grime, has pushed the sleeping bag down to his waist and is slipping on a tattered jacket over a battered sweatshirt. His short and fat-as-a-barrel girlfriend squints into the wind, her stringy brown hair blowing around like the Chinese guy's. She can't be more than sixteen, her bare breasts cow-like. She slips a dirty white T-shirt over her head.

"Do yuh, man?"

I feel like kicking this guy's ass. Don't know why, just do.

"Yes, I have a dollar," I answer, looking at him. He returns my look, waiting for me to say something else or at least reach for my wallet. I look at him some more, knowing that I'm not going to kick his ass, although the thought of it made me feel good for a moment.

"Well…?" he says.

"Well," I say back.

He looks at me like I'm the dumbest person he's seen all morning, besides the young girl he just nailed. "Can I have it?"

"No."

"You said you had a dollar."

"Yes, I did."

"So…"

"Sew buttons on your underwear." My mother used to say that.

Impatiently, "Can I have the dollar, man?"

"No."

He stands and pulls up his trousers. "You a smart ass? An asshole? What if I came over there—"

"What if I call the police, Einstein," I say holding up my cell, "and have a car come by and check your age and the girl's? I hope she was worth two years in the slammer." Now that's a good example of ol' Uncle Bruce's 'The art of fighting without fighting.'

"Fuck you, man! Just fuck you!" He gathers up the sleeping bag and slams it into the grocery cart. "Get the damn dog!" he snaps at the girl. He glares back at me, then yanks a jacket out of the cart and throws it at the girl. "You don't know me, man. You don't know me."

I shrug, wondering why people say that. What does it even mean? He yells at the girl again, this time to put her coat on, and they head out, pushing their cart before them—actually, it's a Food for Less cart—across the bumpy grass and onto the sidewalk.

I punch in nine-one-one on my phone and tell dispatch to send a car by the seawall to check on the runaway status of an underage girl with an adult male. I give a description and a direction of travel. I also tell them that I'm pretty sure they just had sex and to give me a call if they have any questions. Oh, and if the officers want to nit pick, he's pushing a stolen Food for Less cart.

Since I'm on a roll, I call the Child Abuse Division and talk to Alain Davidson, a copper who took martial arts classes from me a couple of years ago. I tell him about Tammy and my hunch about her grandfather. I give him their names and guess at their ages. He puts me on hold and does some searching through their files and on the computer. Five minutes later he comes back on.

"You nailed it, sensei," he says. "We've had two cases with grandpa back in the late nineties. The vic was a sibling of Tammy's, a fourteen-year-old name Millie. Must be an older sister. The case never went anywhere because Millie wouldn't talk and we didn't have anything solid. You think Tammy will talk to us?"

"Maybe," I say. "She floundered a bit when I hinted that she could get help. She might be ready. I have a relationship with her so if you can get a case going, I'd be happy to come in and help interview her."

"I'll make it happen. Thanks. You doing okay, sensei?"

There's genuine concern in his voice. I enjoyed him in class and I could tell he liked it, but then he got married and his wife put a kibosh on him training. That's happened more times than not. At least that's the excuse the men often give.

"Getting there, Alain. Thanks. Let me know if you need me."

"Will do."

Having done my cop thing, I stand up, hunch deeper into my hood, and head across the lawn to my car. I don't know which I feel better about, getting the underage girl some help or getting her shithead boyfriend jammed up a little. Both, I guess. Then there's Tammy. She'll probably be the next one to throw a brick through my window but at least her grandfather will be spending a couple years in the joint taking showers with tattooed guys.

I walk across the lawn, across Tom McCall Boulevard, and up Taylor Street to my truck. Just as I unlock the door, my cell rings.

"Sam? Mai. Can I meet you somewhere?"

*

"Hi," I say when she opens her apartment door. "Thanks for asking me over."

I'm thinking I should offer a hug, given all that we went through last night, but then there was that kiss. Actually, the kiss was most excellent. It was Mai's abrupt departure afterwards that's the issue. I opt to play it safe and restrain myself.

She opens the door wider and steps aside. "Come in, please," she says softly, avoiding my eyes.

"Thank you." I touch her arm as I step in. She's wearing a red polo shirt, blue jeans, and sandals without socks. I wonder for a second if this casual, yet chic, yet oh-so- hot look is something she wears in Vietnam?

"Thanks for coming here to see me," she says wearily, shutting the door and turning to face me. Is she tired from our long night? Or maybe the reason behind her departure is weighing her down. "This is easier for me than trying to find you downtown."

"I'm glad you called. I wasn't sure what to think about, uh, you know, what happened this morning." Time is too short to beat around the bush.

She nods, looking down.

"Where's Samuel?"

"He left before I got home from your house. I'm not sure where he is." She points toward a sofa. "Please, sit." She crosses her arms, hugging herself. "Excuse me a moment. I'll get us some tea. It's already made." She heads toward what I'm guessing is the kitchen.

The apartment is nicely furnished with stacks of school books here and there, a desk, a laptop on a corner desk, and a white cat eyeballing me on the windowsill. Its tail swishes about a little, friendly. I start to go to it when Mai's voice stops me.

"It is green tea," she says, walking into the room with a tray loaded with cups and a pot.

"I love green tea," I say. "I even served it to your father the other night."

She set the tray on the coffee table in front of the couch. "Did he show you his teacup trick? He always shows that to people."

"Yes! I couldn't believe his speed."

"He has another," she says, lowering herself to her knees on the far side of the table from me. She lifts the lid off the pot to peer inside, replaces it. She begins filling our cups. "He tells you to take out a coin. Maybe it's a quarter you have. He tells you to lightly toss it up in the air just a few inches from your hand, catch it, and quickly make a fist. He stands close and when you toss it up, you see him move a little, but not much. You catch your coin but when you open your hand, you are holding a nickel and he is holding up your quarter."

"Good lord," I say, "that's incredible." Most people would at least smile when telling such a story about a family member, but Mai's demeanor and her voice are without emotion.

She replaces the lid. "Green tea is very popular in Vietnam. Our coffee is very good, too. But we don't have Starbucks, springing up all over the place? Is that the right phrase?"

"Yes," I say, noticing that her words seem forced. "Springing up is right."

"People in Hà Giang Province like white tea," she says, placing a cup in front of me. "I like lotus tea, which we make by placing green tea leaves inside a lotus flower for half a day before we store it in a ceramic container. It is very special and it is very expensive." Her tone is that of a tour guide. "We mostly drink it during Tết. You know Tết? It's our New Year holiday. Mostly we just drink regular green tea all other days."

"Mai?"

"Vietnamese people like their tea much stronger than Americans do."

"Mai?"

She quickly clasps her hands to her chest and drops her eyes to my cup. Her mouth makes a quick, fake smile as she reaches across the table and pushes it a couple of inches closer to me. "You should take the first sip when it is hot so—" I intercept her hand before she can pull it back. She closes her eyes but doesn't resist.

"Sam… I wanted to see you… to tell you…"

"Mai?" She looks at me, her eyes miserable, full of… what? I let go of her hand.

"What is your cat's name?"

She frowns and shakes her head. "What? My cat?"

Old police trick. Catch the emotional person off guard with an unrelated question and it disrupts their emotion. At least for a moment. I used it a lot on family fight calls. Ask a screaming, frying pan-wielding wife about her salt and pepper shaker collection, and she'll stop to tell you where she got each one. Doesn't always work. but when it does it's quite helpful.

"I'm thinking about getting one," I say, keeping the momentum going. "One of my students has been trying to talk me into it."

Mai smiles and looks over at hers. "Her name is Chiến, c, h, i, e, n. It means warrior. One day she showed up on my balcony and she has stayed with me since. About two weeks after she came here, I invited some student friends here to study, a young man named Richard and an older woman named Mary. Mary left first and just a few minutes after, Richard became very... uh, insistent. Before I could even apply a hold on him to throw him out, Chiến attacked. Ran up his leg, clawed his privates, and when he bent over in pain, Chiến scratched his face. She clawed him real good before he knocked her away and ran out the door. That's when I named her Chiến."

I laugh and Mai giggles along with me, her hand over her mouth. When I stop, she studies me for a moment.

"Was that a police trick?" she asks. "The distraction, I mean?"

"Yes." Can't fool this one for long.

"Cute."

I laugh again, then sober. "Talk to me Mai. What's going on? What did you mean that 'I don't know you?' Of course I don't. You don't know me either. Actually, you've known about me longer than I've known about you. But... okay, I'm just going to say it. You have to admit that there is a something between us. Am I wrong? If I am, I just embarrassed myself. But I had to say it."

She's looking at her cup, turning it in her hands. "No..."

My heart stops.

"... you are not wrong."

My heart starts again, each beat so strong, I'm sure it's moving my shirt. My voice sounds strained even to me. "It's crazy. I'm not sure I even know what the *something* is." Her eyes lift to mine; the sadness has returned. She nods. "I mean, my breakup with Tiff has been complicated and ugly, and then all this crap has been happening and—"

"I was a prostitute." Her eyes lock on mine, drilling into me.

"What?" I'm guessing my lower jaw is resting on my knees.

Mai clasps her hands again and begins wringing them white. "I have... never told anyone. Only my father knows." She looks down at her hands. When she looks back at me her cheeks are wet with tears. "I only tell you this because when I meet you, I felt, uh, something, too. Something I have never experienced before. Something good."

My mind has screeched to a halt. I don't know what to think. I mean—a prostitute?

"So it is important that you know the real me. So you do not... waste your time."

"Waste my—"

"I should not have kissed you. You have a beautiful girlfriend."

"Mai, that's over. I told you. It's been over a long time."

"Three years ago..." she says, sitting motionless, looking at her hands as she continues to rub them so hard that it's a wonder she's not bleeding.

When it's apparent she's not going to finish, I cut in. "Mai, You don't owe me an explanation. Life shits on all of us. Sometimes all we can do is clean ourselves up and just keep on living. What little I know of you, I can't imagine—"

"I *want* to tell you," she half whispers, still looking down. "It is important." She takes a deep breath and eases it out slowly. "I was living in Hue when I got divorced. I did not have the courage to tell my parents; I did not want to see their shame.

I was working at a hospital and I was not making much money. My husband took all that we had saved when he left.

"One day my uncle called, my mother's brother, his name is Lu, and he said that my mother was sick again and it was hard for her to manage the jewelry stores. We were paying much money for protection and sometimes the government would take some, too. Some people in the government don't like my father and they say he does not have a right to the money. So my father went to Hong Kong to see a man he knew from when he was in the American army. He thought maybe the man could help him with money. But the man could not because he was having money trouble, too. Then my father had trouble getting back to Vietnam. Our government was giving him more problems and he was prevented from coming for two months. I…" Mai pauses and shakes her head, clearly distressed.

"There was a doctor at the hospital who liked me. He was from Germany, a neurologist and very rich. I did not like him because he was disgusting and he had too many women. Somehow he knew of my problems. I do not know how he knew, but he told me that if I was with him, he would help. He would pay for my apartment, pay for my mother's medical bills, and pay for someone to help with our stores. I told him no for a long time but then one day I was told that I would be—I forget the word—oh, evicted. So when I was about to be evicted and my mother was about to lose one of her stores in Ho Chi Minh City, I told him yes."

I lean forward, relieved. "Mai, if that is what you meant by prostituting, I hardly think that is the same thing."

She shakes her head vigorously. "It is! I should have gone to Saigon to be with my mother and to help, no matter if we lost everything. That is the Buddha way. Buddha said that 'A family is a place where a mind lives with other minds. If these minds love each other the home will be as beautiful as a flower garden.'

"But I stayed with the man. I thought the money would be better than going home. Then he brought others girls to his house and he paid them money, too. I just pushed it out of my mind that it was wrong. I took the money, sent some home to my uncle to help my mother and to save the store. I kept my apartment, too, and I sent money to my father in Hong Kong to bribe officials.

"I stayed with the man for three months and then he had to go back to Germany. I was glad that he was leaving but I was also sad that the money would stop."

Tears stream from Mai's eyes. She starts to pick up her tea cup but quickly sets it back down after her trembling hands sloshes the liquid onto the table.

"When he left, I left the hospital and returned to Ho Chi Minh City to be with my mother and father. My mother never found out, but when my father asked where I got the money, I told him. He was angry and ashamed. But not at me. He was angry at himself, blaming himself for not taking care of his family."

"Mai, what little I know of him I would have guessed that's how he would see it."

Mai sniffs.

"That's because he doesn't blame you for anything. He certainly doesn't see you as a prostitute. What I have learned from him these last few days is that he loves you deeply and he's so damn proud of you."

"No," she says, weakly.

"He does, Mai. It's so obvious. Just look at his face when he looks at you, when he talks about you."

"Sometimes he is too forgiving. He follows the Buddhist path like a monk. Sometimes he is more Asian than Asians. But his compassion does not make me feel better about what I have done. I think it makes me feel worse."

"You want him to be mad and disgusted with you so that you feel better?"

"Yes," she says, and looks at me. I lift my eyebrows.

"No?" she asks.

"Of course not. What's right and what's wrong isn't always clear. It's as the yin and yang symbol depicts, a little of the other in each half. You helped your family; you got them back on their feet. Your father doesn't judge you, I'm betting your mother wouldn't either, and I certainly don't."

Mai closes her eyes, as if to stop her tears. It doesn't work. They seep through her eyelids having been held back too long.

"And I'll tell you something else I've noticed."

She looks up at me and wipes her face with the back of her hand. No dainty tissue for this woman. I like that.

"Samuel saw how I was looking at you yesterday. I know because I kept looking at him when I was feeling so guilty because I though you were my sister."

Mai smiles, but quickly forces it away.

"And I saw him looking at you when you were looking at me a couple times. I didn't see disapproval in his face."

"Really?"

I nod and smile. I reach across the coffee table and take her hand. She looks at our hands and rubs her thumb on the back of mine. We sit like this for maybe five minutes. I break the silence. "Mai, you took care of your family. You sacrificed for them. Please stop judging yourself so harshly. Tell me, what does Buddha say about beating yourself up?"

"I don't understand."

"Does he say anything about judging yourself?"

She wipes her hand across her cheeks again. The tears have slowed. After a moment, she says, "He says not to judge others. Not to judge yourself."

"There you go."

She keeps rubbing my hand.

"Your mother is a Buddhist?" She nods. "And so is your father. I'd bet your left kidney that he has never judged you and would even be insulted if he thought you did."

"What do you mean my 'left kidney'?"

I laugh. "Dumb expression. Listen, I don't know what's going to happen. All I know is that the instant I saw you something hit me like a ton of bricks and I'd like to explore what that is. And it's not because you look, well, how you look. It's something more."

Mai smiles that trillion dollar smile and my toes wiggle. "I also got hit with… a lot of bricks?"

"Ton of bricks."

"Yes, thank you. I got hit with a ton of bricks, too."

I stand and move around the coffee table and pull her to her feet. Her arms slip tentatively around my waist. We look into each other's eyes for a long moment, then I bend to kiss her.

The front door opens. Mai twists toward it.

"Father!"

*

When I was about fifteen, my mother came out onto the back porch just as I slipped my hand under Carla Freedenberg's blouse. Embarrassing? Oh, yeah. But not as embarrassing as right now. Here I stand, embracing the beautiful Mai not fifteen feet from where her father, make that, *our* father, AKA the human typhoon, stands with a look of surprise on his otherwise blank face.

"Didn't you two just meet yesterday?" he says, shutting the door.

I'm thinking it's best not to say anything.

"Where have you been, father?" Mia asks, turning toward him. "How do you feel today?" She turns her head my way just enough to whisper, "See, I learned your police trick fast." She takes Samuel's coat and drapes it over a chair.

"I was never sick," he says, eyeing me as he moves to a comfortable looking chair that matches the sofa. He's wearing loose khaki pants, a pale blue overshirt, and his usual red running shoes. "I hear you had quite an adventure last night," he says to me, his face neutral as he sits.

"I'm so very sorry I got Mai involved," I say. "I would have never deliberately endangered her."

Mai moves over beside Samuel and places her hand on the back of his chair. "It is okay, Sam. I told father this morning that I had gone to your house unannounced and that everything started happening after I got there."

I nod, not just a little concerned as to where Samuel is in his head right now. I certainly understand if he's upset that Mai was thrust into a situation where she had to defend herself. Get this daddy's girl in trouble and daddy will peel off your skin.

Samuel crosses his legs and straightens a wrinkle in his shirt. He looks at me again. "Did Mai fight well?"

"Uh, yes." I didn't expect that to be his concern. "Quite frankly, it would have been an even tougher fight if she hadn't been there. The man was formidable, but together we brought him down."

"No, no," Mai says quickly. "I did not do much. It was you who had the real challenge in the koi pond."

The old man smiles. "So you are a team, eh?"

Is my face as red as Mai's?

"I looked into changing our flight," he says to Mai. "They cannot do it because the Saturday flight is full. We have to leave as scheduled on Sunday."

Mai and I look at each other. I didn't know it was possible to have a dozen emotions hitting me all at once: giddiness, exhilaration, pain, loss, and a crap load of confusion. A partner of mine once said that we're all high school kids when it comes to the opposite sex. Man, was he ever right.

"You two are not kids," Samuel says. "My only advice is to just keep in mind that you have very little time."

What does that mean? Is he saying for us to drop it or to speed it up?

"Father, how do you know—"

"I saw it the first time I saw you two together at Sam's school."

My face flashes hot; Mai covers an embarrassed smile with her hand. "Sam thought we were half brother and sister." She looks at me. "He knows the truth now."

I shrug and bob my eyebrows, not sure what I mean by doing that. I'm feeling most uncomfortable right now, while Mai seems quite comfortable, even exuberant.

"Sorry for the misunderstanding," Samuel says earnestly. Still, I wonder if the confusion was deliberate on his part. Since he seems to pick up my thoughts quite easily, how could he have missed my consternation over my attraction to Mai? If he didn't miss it, and I'm guessing that's the case, why didn't he say anything? Maybe he thinks our attraction to each other is a monstrous mistake. Or maybe he thinks it's a good thing and he wanted to see how I would work it out. Maybe I over think things too much.

"Well, it is very likely you were together in a past life," Samuel says after studying us for a moment.

I shake my head. "That reincarnation stuff is a little too much for this guy to swallow."

He chuckles. "It does not matter if you believe in it, and not believing in it does not mean it is not true. Excuse me." He stands and walks into the kitchen.

I look over at Mai and exhale a long stream of tension. "What does that mean?"

She shrugs. "With father, who knows? I know I want more time with…" her voice trails off in sadness.

"Me, too. Maybe we can—"

"Okay," Samuel says, walking back into the room, his demeanor suddenly all business. He sips from a glass of water. "We need to talk about our family problem now. Mai, I am sorry, I did not tell you the truth last night. The truth is that I was out investigating our situation." He looks at me. "Those men in the alley yesterday were just a tease. They were not from Saigon, but from right here in Portland. They were sent to test our capabilities. Unfortunately, by defeating them, we failed the test. Things are about to get a lot more hairy."

*

Samuel may be in his sixties but he's still got the Green Berets in his blood. For the last ten minutes he's been telling us that he has no intention of waiting around to see what the enemy is going to do; this old war dog plans to take the fight to them. He told us that he cruised the Vietnamese strip last night, a ten-block area the cops call "Little Saigon," to get a sense for the place. He said he drank tea and ate noodles at a couple of restaurants. No one suspected that he speaks the language so everyone spoke freely to each other. He said he saw several people who looked like some of the gangsters they have in Saigon, young people with lots of attitude, buzz cuts or pompadours, and over-stylish clothing.

I'm surprised to hear this. Black and Hispanic gangs are active, but I thought Asian gangs had pretty much died out a few years ago, literally and figuratively. As a burglary detective, though, I don't work around street gangs anymore nor have I been keeping up on them. Portland PD is a sprawling agency. Unless a crime makes big headlines or it crosses over into Burglary, I don't know about it.

It was a different situation fifteen years ago when the Bloods, Crips, Skinheads, Hispanic, and Asian gangsters were shooting up the city. Southeast Asian gangs, many of whom dressed in black and white to emulate the gangsters they saw in old movies, carried Uzi's and Mac-Tens, and would often shoot twenty or thirty rounds when one would have done nicely. The big constant was a thing called "dissin'," slang for a comment or a look that was deemed to be disrespectful by the enemy. All the ethnic gangs lived and died by the dissin' issue, which seemed pretty silly. But when you watched a seventeen-year-old kid bleed out on the sidewalk with a half dozen nine millimeter slugs in his gut, you knew how seriously they take it.

The shooting statistics are down these days, at least in contrast to a few years ago, but I've heard the homicide dicks say that the young thugs are still quick to snuff out a life if there's money in it or they feel they're not getting the respect they think they deserve.

Samuel leans forward. "Let me back up a little. Lai Van Tan, the mothership as I called him yesterday, decided that it would be best to use his contacts here in Portland, maybe some in Los Angeles, too. He has no shortage of people because of his, quote, 'business,' unquote, here in the US and in other countries. I know that his business is about drugs, but I have heard from people in Vietnam that he is also involved in hits for hire and sex trafficking. I have heard that he has associates in every major city and they all treat him like Don Corleone in *The Godfather*. I think you said you saw that one."

"Of course," I say. "So to be clear, these attackers are all from here? This Lai Van Tan guy paid local thugs to come after you?"

"Yes." He looks at Mai. "I called your mother last night."

"I talked to her yesterday, too. She's feeling about the same."

Samuel's face tightens. "I talked with Lu, too." He looks at me. "That is Kim's brother, Mai's uncle. He said that he has Kim well hidden but he is still worried. Lu has a few contacts in Saigon and probably contacts right in Tan's organization. Lu is a straight guy but he knows a lot of people, who in turn know a lot of people. He has given me much of this information about Lai Van Tan. He has heard that Tan wants me, wants me with extreme prejudice, as we used to say during the war. And he has expanded that to include Mai and you, son. I am sorry you two have gotten into this. Apparently he is in a rage and cannot be placated. It does not matter that he sent his son to kill me and that his son was inadvertently killed by his own people. He holds me responsible."

"What do you mean 'he wants us badly'?" I ask.

"He wants us dead."

Mai leans forward, her face void of emotion. "Father, what are we going to do?" There's no *Oh my goodness I'm so scared* in Mai's voice. It's more like: *Let's get these bastards?*

"Look," I say. "This is a police matter. We got gang officers who know all the players. We got SWAT teams who could wipe out this city if they wanted, and we got lots of undercover guys, even a Vietnamese cop and a Cambodian cop. I'll make a call and—"

"Normally, I would agree, yes," Samuel says. "But there are factors you must consider. Let us say the police get involved and they make an arrest. Who will have to testify about all this? It will be me and it will be Mai. Your superiors will make some calls to the US Department of State, Homeland Security or whatever, and Mai and I will be stuck here waiting for a trial."

My heart skips a beat. I look at Mai. "That doesn't seem so bad."

"It *is* bad if I cannot get home and protect my family." Samuel's right hand clenches, the ridge of calluses across his knuckles enlarge and whiten. "You see, if Lai Van Tan cannot get to me here, he will intensify his search for my wife and my other children. My other two daughters are grown and married, but they are nonetheless *my* responsibility, their husbands and their children, too. The husbands are not warriors. All were born after the war and have never had to defend themselves. If I am unable to leave here, Lai Van Tan will easily get them. The only reason he has not done it yet is because he thinks he can get me here in Portland. I would even bet that he knows where Kim is. My children's families, too."

Samuel looks down at his fist. "I would be there now, if I could."

Gone is Samuel's quiet persona, what Mark called his "David Carradine thing." There's no joking, no movie quoting, no driving me nuts. Now he is all business.

My role here is a little shaky. I'm not sure how much longer I'm going to be a cop, but I still am one and that fact can get me seriously jammed up for stepping outside the law. And that is exactly what I think Samuel has in mind.

On the flip side, I got to consider the issue of family. Suddenly I got one, and while it might be brand new, they are nonetheless my responsibility, my duty. That was engrained in me by my mother and especially by my grandfather. "You're walking around armed, son," he said to me after I earned my first black belt. "With those deadly feet and hands of yours, you got an edge. You owe a responsibility to your teachers, and you have a responsibility to your mother and me who have been driving your ass to lessons four times a week for the last four years. That responsibility is to use your skill to serve and protect others, especially your family. Your mother is tough, but you still need to protect her. I'm tough, too, but I'm an old fart and might need some back-up." I sure miss him. Mother, too.

"What do you want to do?" I ask.

"Lu gave me a name yesterday," Samuel says. "A guy named Do Trieu. He owns a restaurant called Trieu's Noodles out on One Hundred Eighty-First. I checked it out. It's a small, run-down place, which belies the fact he is making tons of money working as a middle man for Lai Van Tan. According to Lu, he has about seven guys, armed, who run dope down the I-Five Freeway to San Francisco, Orange County, and San Diego. Apparently they are heartless. They have wasted a few people, all Vietnamese, who crossed them, and they are not above using torture to get information. Some are martial arts trained and a couple have been well-schooled by old ARVNs, South Vietnamese troops who served along side the Green Berets. I am guessing those two people yesterday were his. Unfortunately, we cannot count on all of them being as inept as those two."

They might have been inept but the knot behind my ear still hurts.

"My plan, such as it is, is to go talk with Do Trieu. Take it to him instead of waiting for his people to spring out of the bushes. Approach him with preparation and take him when he is unprepared."

Mai nods, and says offhandedly, "Sun Tzu said, 'He will win who, prepared himself, waits to take the enemy.'"

"Very good," I say, nodding at her. She smiles faintly and shrugs her shoulders.

"Unfortunately, we do not have time to prepare as we should, or wait. We must act now. I want to go out to his restaurant. Would you go with me?"

"Of course, Samuel. Are you sure you don't want me to call the office and—"

"I am positive. Mai, I want you to stay here."

She drops her chin, looks up at Samuel and bats her lashes. "Riiiight. I can do some ironing while I wait for you men to return home from the front. Maybe bake some bread."

Samuel's mouth drops open.

I stifle a laugh. Daddy's little girl has learned some American sass.

She stands. "Tzu also said, 'Regard your soldiers as your children, and they will follow you into the deepest valleys; look upon them as your own beloved sons, and they will stand by you even unto death.' Well, I am your child and I'm going with you."

Samuel struggles against the pride that's spreading across his face, and fails. He turns to me and spreads his hands in a "what's-a-parent-to-do?" gesture. "I insisted that she read *The Art of War* several years ago. I had no idea she would memorize it and use it against me to get her own way."

*

I'm driving my pickup, Mai is sitting next to me and Samuel is riding shotgun. Now, I've had a crap-load of oddball experiences as a cop, but nothing has prepared me for guiding my Dodge to a fate unknown, with my martial arts genius of a father who I thought was long dead sitting by the door, and his daughter, but not really, my half sister, but not really, on whom I have a crush, but really, riding next to me, her warm thigh pressed against mine. Out of the corner of my eye, I see that there are about six inches of space between Mai and her father but apparently she's perfectly okay touching legs. Works for me!

It's "a light sweater day," as my mother used to say. The sky is spooky with layered clouds, each a different hue of gray, all moving rapidly north. It's not cold but it's become so windy that pedestrians are turtling their heads into their jacket collars and leaning into the gusts as they scurry to their destinations.

I just made a quick call to a buddy in the gang unit. I told him a student of mine was doing a paper for school on street gangs and I asked if he could catch me up in three minutes. He did and now I hope he forgets ever talking to me about it. I don't know what's going to happen in the next few hours but I don't want to leave a trail.

"I was just a rookie back when street gangs, including South East Asian gangs, were shooting up this stretch of Division

Street," I say, thinking that a little background might be helpful. "Young people were dying weekly, and cars, businesses, and homes were getting shot up nightly. It was insane for a while. The chief even asked the National Guard to help us for about six months. It's probably not strange for you to see in Vietnam, but here in Portland, it was definitely surreal to see Army vehicles with armed troops cruising the streets."

"What happened to all of them, the gangs?" Mai asks, as we cross one hundred sixty-second.

"Lots went to jail, lots went to the graveyard, some moved into white-collar crime and, I suppose, most grew out of it. But now there's a new generation of bangers. Like the first ones, they don't think anything will happen to them. I don't work gangs so I'm not up on all of it, but a cop friend just told me that they're still in the dope business, just more underground than before. Some are running prostitution rings via the internet because it's harder for the police to catch them. Fewer arrests means fewer dampers in their business routines. But according to what Samuel saw last night, it sounds like some are flaunting it again, at least dressing the part. Part of being young and stupid, I guess."

"I am guessing that your police do not know anything about these dope runners of Do Trieu's. If your thugs are like ours in Vietnam, they have regular straight jobs and conduct their criminal activity on the side. Their straight jobs give them alibis."

"What do you know about this Do Trieu?" I ask.

"Last night I went back to that *phở* restaurant where we had that run in. I asked the old woman if she knew of Do Trieu. She likes me because I came back and paid. Anyway, she said she knew him and that he was no good. Apparently he has owned his restaurant for about three years and owes other restaurant owners money for supplies. She said it is not that he cannot pay; it is that he *will* not. She said one restaurant supplier was beat up when he threatened to take Do Trieu to court. Beaten quite badly she said. When I asked who beat the man up she said it was cowboys. She's about my age so she still uses the word 'cowboys' for thugs, as we did in the war. I was about to ask some more questions when a man, her husband, I think, came out from the back and told her not to say anything more. He is probably afraid of Do Trieu and his boys."

"Okay," I say, pointing out the windshield. "We're coming up on One Eighty Second. Are we going right or left?"

"Left," Samuel says, as calm as if we're just looking for a restaurant, which we are, but a whole lot more. "It is on the right about a half block down. It is next door to a place called "Dancing Fingers Massage," which you cannot miss since it is painted a bright purple." He snorts. "It is indeed becoming a 'Little Saigon' here in Portland."

The small restaurant is fronted by about a dozen parking spaces of which only two are occupied. I park on the street in front of the massage joint so we can check out the eatery from afar before we make our approach. We got a clear view since Dancing Fingers Massage's parking slots are empty.

"Only two cars," I say. "But then it's two PM, a couple hours past the lunch hour."

"That BMW was parked out front last night," Samuel notes. "A regular customer or maybe it is Do Trieu's car."

"Easy enough to find out," I say, speed dialing Records. "Hey Sal, Reeves here. Give me a reg on an Oregon plate, Adam, Charlie, David, four, nine, zero. Yeah. Just a sec." I extract a pen and a scrap of paper off my dash. "Fire at will. Okay. Okay. Got it. Have a good rest of the day, Sal."

I close my phone. "It's Do Trieu's, a Seven Hundred series and this year's. Spendy car for the small profit he's likely making with this place. Registered to this address, too, but Sal found a second address out in Gresham, a real nice area. I'm betting that's where he lives."

"So he is inside, maybe?" Mai wonders.

I shake my head. "Don't know. I don't like going in on something potentially dangerous without having any intelligence or backup."

"Sometimes you have to seize the moment, son, and rely on your own intelligence and training."

"I would agree if we had just chased him into the place. Hot pursuit and all that. But the moment isn't that hot."

"Okay," Samuel says, his face not giving anything away. Is he acknowledging that we're playing on my home court? "How do you want to do it, son?" Ha. I guess so.

"Let's compromise and call them first." I tap in Information's number and ask for the restaurant's number. "Thank you," I say, jotting it down. "You want to call them, Samuel?"

"Let Mai. My Vietnamese is accent free but it might seem even more innocent if a female calls."

I raise my eyebrows to Mai. She extends her palm.

I tap in the number and hand the phone to her. She listens for a couple of seconds before saying something in Vietnamese, pauses, speaks again, and then utters two or three words before closing the lid. She hands the phone back.

"I told the man that I was looking for a job as a waitress and asked if Do Trieu was in." Mai turns to Samuel. "He said that he had stepped out for awhile but would be back in thirty minutes."

I frown. "Thirty minutes, huh? But his car is still here. Maybe he left with someone. Or maybe…"

"Maybe what?" Samuel asks. "What are you thinking?"

"I'm curious about the massage place. The only three businesses on this block are a Firestone tire store that takes up half of it, Do Trieu's restaurant, and the massage joint."

"Dancing Fingers." he says, looking at it through the side window.

"Notice that the big signage on the restaurant and the massage place are the same style, color, and design. Might not mean anything or it might mean he owns both and had them painted by the same company."

"Really?" Mai asks. "You think he might be in there? Now?"

"Let me try something." I speed dial Records again. "Sal. Reeves again. You the only one working today? Listen, would you do a quick scan of two, four, one, five Southeast One Hundred Eighty-Second. Dancing Fingers Massage." I look at Samuel. "Sometimes our records will show an owner, especially if there's been police calls to the place. And I'm betting that a massage joint will get lots of police attention and— Yes, I'm here, Sal. Yes. Yes, that's the same guy on the Beamer's reg. Thanks, sweety. Bye."

Mai's brow furrows slightly.

I smile. "Sal is sixty-three and retires in November."

"You like her?" she smirks.

"I like her peanut butter cookies," I say, bobbing my eyebrows. Mai giggles.

"May we return to the task at hand?" Samuel asks like a reprimanding parent.

My face heats up. "Sorry. Do Trieu owns the massage joint, too. The PD has been called here three times since last summer. Drunk customers twice and a disturbance of some kind."

"Okay," Samuel says. "I am making a wild guess that he is there. And if he is doing what I think he is doing, he will not have any of his troops with him. You both ready?"

A soda can, pushed by a wind current, rolls and bounces across the parking lot as we make our way toward the massage joint. Funny how these places are always painted purple or pink on the outside. Probably so there's no doubt in the customer's mind as to what's going on inside. If the color isn't a clue, the sign: *Beautiful Masseuses With Happy Fingers Inside. No One Under Eighteen Allowed* on the door should rid all doubt, and serve as a bit of foreplay, too.

I'm first through the door into what must be a greeting room; I take in everything in one quick look. Should the naïve miss the exterior indicators, they should have an ah-ha moment when they step inside and hear the low trance music, see the purple carpet, the soft, pink whorehouse lighting emanating from two red faux-fur lamps, and walls covered with red fuzzy wallpaper. Purple mini blinds cover a small window to my left, tilted so that no one can see in, though people inside can look out toward the front of the building and part way across the parking lot to Trieu's Noodles.

"Hell-oooo," a middle-aged and still attractive Asian woman sings from her desk in the far corner, sounding a little like the Queen of England. She scoots her chair back and stands, sing-songing, "Thank you so much for coming to Dancing Fingers Massaaaaage." Mai and Samuel enter behind me. "Oh! Oh my goodness," she cries, the *ku-ching* of a cash register ringing in her voice. "There are three of you. Will all of you be having a massage?" She gives me an appreciative up and down but frowns when she looks at Mai, no doubt making her for mixed race.

"Is Do Trieu in the backroom?" Samuel asks, not wasting time.

The hostess's demeanor changes from forced glee to somber as her hand slips beneath the edge of her desk top. "Who?" she asks, her eyebrows raised to feign innocence. Her hand returns to the surface to fiddle with some papers. I'm guessing Samuel saw the move.

To her right, a door opens a few inches and a set of eyes peer out, female, I think. The door closes quietly.

Samuel's eyes flick to the door and back to the woman. "Is Trieu in the back?"

"Who are you asking about?" she asks innocently. She shakes her head. "If you don't want a massage then I must ask you to leave."

Samuel snaps something in Vietnamese. The woman's eyes widen in surprise for a moment then she turns her head just enough to see the door out of the corner of her vision. "Are you talking about a customer?" she asks, lifting her chin toward Samuel. He returns her look without saying anything. If he's getting annoyed, he's not showing it. "There is no one here right now," she insists.

Again, the door behind the woman opens part way and those same eyes look out for a moment. Then the door opens all the way.

I don't know who I expected to come out. Maybe a fat masseuse in white pants and white t-shirt, or even Do Trieu himself. Or perhaps one or more of his goons. What I didn't expect is a gorgeous twenty-something Asian woman with long, straight blue-black hair, a muscular neck, and a swagger like a mixed martial artist stepping into the ring. She's dressed in gray cargo pants and a red T-shirt under a black pea coat, standing at least five feet eight. She's not as tall as Mai, but she looks proportionately larger. She's at once feminine, buff, sensual, and dangerous looking.

The woman pauses by the desk. Her eyes don't appear to be angry, but they nonetheless laser into me as if trying to burn a hole into my face. Without turning her head, her eyes move over to Samuel and then to Mai. They come back to me. This gal is one scary masseuse.

"These people are looking for Do Trieu," the hostess says. "I've assured them that he isn't here. *That one* speaks Vietnamese," she warns, pointing at Samuel.

"He isn't," the masseuse says in flawless English. "What do you want with him?"

"Business," Samuel says. "I want to talk to him about business."

Movement out of the corner of my eye, from the window. Between the slanted blinds I see a man's legs moving quickly from the side of this building toward the restaurant. It appears he's slipping on a coat.

The entrance door behind us opens and two more women enter, both a tad shorter than the first one, equally as attractive in a spooky sort of way, and about the same age. The one on the left is wearing black cargo pants and a gray double-breasted pea coat. The other's got on blue jeans and a brown leather jacket. They look fit, and move with a confidence that comes from self-knowledge.

I'm getting a funny-bad feeling about this. If these young women are masseuses, their clients must all come from the sadomasochist community. Their eyes are hostile, they're not carrying purses, they're not wearing jewelry, and they all stand with their arms hanging loose at their sides, hands unclenched. Could it be that Do Trieu's hired guys are really hired gals?

Samuel and Mai step aside from the door to the back room. It's appears to be a polite move, but I'm guessing it's more about positioning themselves for a clearer view of everyone. They stand calm but ready. I back toward the window and do the same.

"What kind of business?" the taller one by the desk asks. When did the hostess leave? The exotic one takes a couple of steps into the room but still blocks the pathway to the door. If I had to guess, I'd put this one as the leader.

"My business is with Do Trieu," Samuel says, more calmly than I would have. "Would you be so kind as to go get him from the back?"

The woman's face tightens. "I said he is not here."

Samuel steps toward the door, though the woman hasn't moved out of the pathway. He's forcing her hand, no surprise given what I've seen of his tendency to skimp on small talk.

She holds up her palm. "Stop. The back is off limits." Her voice is calm, collected. Am I the only one jittery here?

He keeps walking. Oh shit.

The woman retracts her hand and, in one smooth, trained move, yanks back the flap of her pea coat to unholster a black semi-auto. I reach under my jacket for my Glock as Samuel lunges toward the woman. A blur of motion... and he's holding the gun. He extracts the magazine, works the action to pop out a round, works the action again, removes the barrel and tosses all the pieces under the desk in a clatter. My God! The whole thing didn't take more than five or six seconds.

"No guns," he says, dusting off his hands.

I still have my hand on my holstered weapon when all three women, as if by some invisible cue, emit a sort of hissing sound as they simultaneously drop into low fighting stances, each with their lead foot barely touching the floor, their arms up at the ready like a boxer but with their hands formed into claws. It's pure Hollywood and a whole lot eerie.

They attack simultaneously.

The exotic one charges Samuel like a jungle cat, screaming and tearing at his face with her claws; Gray Pea Coat hisses and lunges at Mai with an onslaught of kicks and claws; and Brown Leather Jacket crosses the space with a great leap, her hands formed into feline shredders. Before I can complete my thought that this is some kind of kung fu tiger style, my gal clamps her legs around my waist in a crushing squeeze, and whips multiple elbow smashes toward my head with both arms. What, no claws? I snap up my forearms in time to shield the sides of my head against her boney elbows. Better to get my arms pummeled than my tender head. It's been hit enough this week. So have my arms, now that I think about it.

Her R-rated tackle knocks me back against the window, tearing down the mini blinds in a loud crash. From my double shield, I slap both my palms into her face, which is less than a foot from mine, and ram her back into the edge of the desk. Once, twice, going for three when she releases her powerful thighs and drops back to the floor.

Without hesitation, she whips a horizontal claw toward my face. I reflexively jerk my head back so that her nails, I don't know how many, groove burning trails across my throat. Instinctively, I reach for the front of my neck just as she strikes with another claw. I block it and use the same forearm to slam against the right side of her neck, right on the brachial plexus. I tried to hit Barry there last night, but missed. This time I nail the target nicely.

She emits a kicked-puppy yelp and her eyes roll like spinning reels on a slot machine. I've been struck there a couple of times, so I know that she saw a blinding flash of white light, and her right arm and right leg are no longer obeying her brain's commands. She sinks to the floor as if all of her bones have turned to dust. She's not unconscious, but she might as well be. I get no resistance as I roll her onto her stomach and apply an arm lock.

I look up to see Mai sweep Gray Pea Coat's legs out from under her. Amazingly, the hard landing doesn't knock the wind out of the young woman, or if it did, she's handling it. She rolls seamlessly over and up onto her all fours.

Because I was busy with my tigress, I don't know what all has happened in their fight, though I can see that Mai has caught a little of that clawing action on her forehead. What is definitely clear is that my former sister is as pissed off as a wet hornet. She looks at Gray Pea Coat's closest support arm…

Oh no. I start to call out for her not to do it, but I'm too late. Lightening quick, she slams a full-contact muay Thai roundhouse into the woman's elbow joint, her shin smashing the elbow in a direction it isn't supposed to bend, probably destroying the tendons, ligaments, nerves, and the woman's ability to ever again bend her elbow to scratch an itch.

For a hair of a second, the sickening sound of the breaking joint reminds me of a kickboxing smoker I saw in New York about five years ago. The taller guy launched a high roundhouse kick that would have knocked the shorter fighter's skull all the way to the Jersey Shore. The short guy leaned away, simultaneously delivering a powerful sidekick straight into the big one's support knee. The splintering sound, like that of a large breaking tree limb, has never left my memory.

Now I got another bone-breaking sound stuck in my head, this one louder because of the small room and my proximity to the blow. Couple that with the horrific scream emanating from the marrow of the woman's shattered bones as she thrashes from side to side clutching her warped arm. Mai uses the screamer's other arm to roll her onto her stomach, and then straddles her to lock her remaining good arm into a tight control hold.

Mai's face has remained blank throughout. She didn't grimace with the effort of the hard kick, and right now her eyes don't acknowledge in the slightest the pain and damage she just inflicted on the young woman. There is something in that blank face, though, something a little chilling. Could it be that the kick wasn't meant to knock out one of the attacker's supports but was delivered with cruel intention to destroy that limb? Note to self: Add Mai to my list of women I never want to make angry; put her name above Amy's, the cop. Then create a second list of possibles: Tiff, Tammy, and these three tiger-style women.

Samuel is still by the hostess's desk, but he's sitting now, his legs folded in lotus posture on the floor and the exotic gal's head resting in his lap.

"Tiger Woman unconscious?" I ask him.

"It is more of a nap."

As if she heard him, her eyes open and blink rapidly, seeking consciousness. Samuel reaches casually toward her neck and, with his thumb and index finger, pinches her right carotid artery, one of the pipelines that carry oxygenated blood from the heart to the brain. I've put out lots of people in training and on the street, but I did it by using the crook of my arm to vice grip both sides of the neck. Sometimes it only takes about four seconds for the artery's owner to go to sleep. I've never seen it done with a mere finger pinch.

The woman tenses a little, then relaxes as her eyelids flutter shut.

"How long you been doing that?" I ask.

"I've used this technique for years."

"I mean, how long right now?"

"Oh, sorry. Since you and Mai have been dinking around. Three or four times, I guess. I wanted all the ladies down and out so we can talk about our next move. Okay, bring your prisoner over here. You too, Mai, so you and Sam can watch them while I go check out the backroom."

"I saw a guy running outside the window from the side of this building toward the restaurant," I tell him.

"That was probably Do Trieu. Clearly a coward."

My gal, her faculties back, begins to squirm against my hold and curse like a fisherman's wife.

"Oh, my goodness," Samuel says, as I line her up next to Tiger Woman. "Such a potty mouth, young lady, and in English. And Mai, your prisoner isn't any better. Of course she is suffering. But yours, Sam. She's not hurt too badly, and still such language!"

"What's the plan?" I ask, not knowing if his indignation is real or an act.

Samuel gently places Tiger Woman's head on the floor and stands. "Watch the women for a moment." He pulls the door open a few inches, peers in and enters.

"You okay?" I ask Mai over the din of all the moaning and cursing. "You got a good scratch on your forehead."

The savage intensity that possessed her a moment ago is gone. "Really?" she frowns, pretending to be confused. "It feels more like a bad scratch." She looks down at her father's prisoner. "Oh, she is waking."

Tiger Woman stirs, turns her head toward us and lifts her head.

345

"Not yet dear," Mai says. Without letting go of the arm-lock on her prisoner, she reaches over with her other hand to pinch off the woman's artery. Again the exotic woman's eyes close in sleep. Actually, her look isn't all that exotic any-more. Now she has this pale-pissed-unconsciousness thing going on.

Mai points at my neck. "How about you? She scratched you."

"It burns."

"Oooh," Mai moans sympathetically, like a mother would to a child.

I smile at her. "I think I need to be held."

"I can do that. Remember, I used to be a nurse. My pre-scription is that you need a lot of... what is it... oh, TLC."

My prisoner stops cursing, twists her head up and looks at me, then to Mai, then back to me again. "You two have *got* to be shitting me!" she says in flawless English.

"Hey," Mai says. "You want to go to sleep, too?"

The woman puts her head down but continues her swear-ing rant, though not as loudly as before.

"Okay," Samuel says, from the doorway. "There's no one in the back. The hostess who greeted us and anyone else who might have been back there have slipped out a rear door." He steps over the women and moves quickly to the front door, locking it. "I found a perfect place to stash the ladies. We have to hurry before anyone else comes in."

He slips his hands under his slumbering prisoner's arms and drags her through the doorway. Shuffling backwards, he says, "Follow me, and bring your ladies."

Mai and I add a little pain to our respective armlocks and command our gals to stand. Mine is seriously pissed and Mai's is in serious pain. I've had my elbow hyperextended and it was agonizing. I can't begin to imagine what an elbow bent ninety degrees in the wrong direction must feel like.

The backroom looks more like a hospital with four curtained mini rooms on each side of a common walkway that extends to what looks like an outside door.

"Over here," Samuel says, setting Tiger Woman's head down on the floor before a heavy-looking cedarwood door with a smallish thick-glassed window. "It is a steam room. Just big enough for three."

My gal begins to scream and kick back at my legs. "Stop!" I say, cranking on the pain. "Kick at me again and I'm going to have the lady break your arm, too."

"Oh may I, please?" Mai winks at me.

She stops kicking, but lets me have it with another string of what I assume are Vietnamese curses.

Samuel opens the steam room door, releasing a wall of heat, and slides his gal in. "There's a control thing behind the door," he says. "I will turn it down so they do not turn into spring rolls."

My gal shouts something at Samuel as I push her into the room.

"Or maybe not," he quips.

I hold my gal's armlock in place as Mai forces her screaming prisoner into the room. Then as Samuel begins to push the heavy door closed, Mai and I release our holds at the same time and slip out a second before the door thumps closed. An instant later, the side of my gal's face flattens against the glass as she tries to push the door open. Her curses are muffled now, as are the cries of the one with the trashed arm.

"Push that hostess's desk in here," Samuel says, leaning his back against the door and twisting the heat knob to "off."

Out in the greeting room, Mai and I sweep papers and files off the desk and begin pushing it toward the doorway. Good idea; this thing is heavy. After we clear the doorway, I tell Mai to hold on for a second as I scoop up all the gun parts from where Samuel had tossed them under the desk; I drop them behind a file cabinet. One less gun is one less worry. Samuel continues to brace the door against my gal's onslaughts until Mai and I scoot the desk the rest of the way over. Within a second of it being in place, the enraged woman again slams her shoulder into the door. The desk holds the door fast, which sets her off on another barrage of muffled cursing. Even when Tiger Woman awakens to add her weight to the pushing, the door and desk won't budge.

"Look to see if that BMW is still parked out front," Samuel tells Mai. He shoots me a look of concern as she heads into the other room. "I know it is unwise to enter that restaurant, son, but we are here and it might be our only opportunity. What do you think?"

I agree with both points. For police officers, such questionable tactics would get them stripped of rank and exiled to the midnight shift to monitor an empty school crossing. Sometimes, though, you got to play the cards you're dealt.

"You're right," I say. "These three may be his only personal protection right now, but he's likely called for more. Did you notice the restaurant had lots of windows in the front?"

"Good to see in," Samuel says. "And good to see out."

"The car is still there," Mai says, coming back. "I did not see anyone outside and I could not see into the restaurant window past the empty window tables."

I gesture with my head toward the back door. "Let's look from here."

We're not the police so we don't have the luxury of man-power, firepower, time, negotiators, and super-duper tactics. Okay, technically I'm the police, and that cop imbedded in my psyche is shouting, "Call for back-up," but I can't operate in that capacity. Samuel and Mai need to leave Sunday to get back to Vietnam. If they got hung up here, their family's lives would be at stake. It's all crazy.

I open the back door a crack and quick-peak outside. "No one between the buildings. Let's call again. Tell him to come out the front door."

"Yes," Samuel says. "Give me your phone. Mai take the door." I speed redial the number and give it to him. They must be sitting on the phone because Samuel immediately begins talking in rapid-fire Vietnamese. He hands the phone back. "He's coming out the front door."

"Alone?"

"There will be a male cook and a male waiter with him. I asked if they doubled as his guards and he insisted that they are elderly and quite portly."

"Can we believe him?" Mai asks, peering out the door.

"I cannot get a read on him," Samuel says. "But my guess is that the two are not a threat."

"Someone stepped out the door and is looking around." Mai whispers. "Older man. Now there are two others. Heavy set and about the same age."

I peer around the door facing. "The tan slacks and the dark brown sports jacket are what I saw through the window a while ago." I look back at Samuel. "Let me go first." He nods and they follow me out the door.

I pull my jacket flap back so Do Trieu can see the butt of my Glock. "All of you keep your hands away from your body," I tell them. Samuel translates.

"We speak English," the man in the brown sports jacket says.

"Are you Do Trieu?" Samuel asks.

"Yes."

"All of you turn around and face the door," I say. "And put your hands behind your head." They comply.

"This is not necessary," Do Trieu says with annoyance as I pat down all three.

"Your guards made this necessary," Samuel says. "I came to talk and you turn your bitch dogs on us."

Do Trieu turns back around when I finish, as do his helpers. "I apologize for that," he says, his smirk contradicting his words. "My people are zealous. Where are the ladies?"

"Taking a sauna," I say. Do Trieu looks quizzical but doesn't pursue. "I'm going to check inside," I tell Samuel.

It's a small place with a dirty, greasy feel. Six tables out front, a small kitchen, and two bathrooms. All empty. I make sure the backdoor is locked then go back out the front. I nod to Samuel.

"We will go inside," he tells Do Trieu. He looks at one of the other men. "You, bring us all some tea." The man nods and scurries ahead of us through the door.

Inside, Samuel directs the other man to sit at a far table. "We will sit here at this one," he says to Mai and Do Trieu. In less than two minutes Samuel has established who is in charge.

I remain by the door where I can see out into the parking lot and the front door of the massage joint, as well as keep an eye on the waiter sitting in the back. Do Trieu says something in Vietnamese to Samuel. "Speak English," I tell him.

"Yes," Do Trieu says, looking at me like I'm a soggy piece of *bok choy*.

"Tell me about your boss, Lai Van Tan," Samuel says, amazingly calm considering that he's talking to a paid assassin. "Do not lie. If you choose to lie, I will ask my daughter to pluck out both your eyes and feed them to you. Any questions about my simple request?"

I glance over at Mai. She sits erect, her hands folded in her lap, her eyes watching Do Trieu like a dog looks at a chew treat. She's at once beautiful, extraordinarily focused and—a little scary. The way she broke that woman's elbow was so… cold. If she's even aware I'm in the room or aware that I'm looking at her, she gives no indication. She wants a piece of Do Trieu and there is no doubt in my mind that she would, indeed, obey daddy's request to remove the man's eyes and serve them to him as hors d'oeuvres.

"I understand," Do Trieu says, with just a hint of accent, his gaze darting to Mai, and then to the teapot and four cups the waiter is placing on the table.

"I have a business arrangement with Mister Tan. That is all."

"Running drugs," Samuel states. "You," he says to the waiter. "Sit with your friend over there."

Do Trieu looks up at him, then looks back to the teapot. He retrieves it and begins filling the four cups with a shaky hand. "I do not understand what you—"

"Did you think," Samuel's voice is as chilling as the wind in a winter graveyard, "it was an idle threat what I said about removing your eyes?"

The man looks up at Samuel, his right eye twitching. He looks at Mai, who remains motionless, save for an almost imperceptible body quiver. Anticipation?

"Yes," he says, the color leaving his face. "I mean, no." He coughs and rubs his chin. He looks over at me. "You are a policeman?"

"Yes," I say, taken back that he knows about me. "But I'm not here in that capacity. I'm only here to help my family." Whoops, too much info.

He looks intently at me, then nods. He bought my half lie but makes no indication that he understood what I meant by "my family." Since he knows I'm a cop, chances are he knows the relationship between Samuel and me.

He looks back to Samuel and clears his throat. "I help Mister Tan deliver certain types of drugs. We sell them to a third party in Los Angeles, who distributes them to a number of bars, dance clubs, that sort of place." He looks at me. "They are never sold to children."

Samuel nods, and sips from his cup. "I already know about the drugs."

The man's eye twitch accelerates. "You do?" He looks over at me with an expression that says: If *he* knows, then so do the police.

"Yes, the police know," Samuel says, looking over his teacup; Do Trieu's mouth drops open. Samuel smacks his lips. "Mmm, this is good green tea." It's starting to look like Mai won't have to pluck the man's eyes out because they're on the verge of popping out all on their own.

"How did—"

"Were the men who visited my apartment two nights ago and the two men I met at the *phở* restaurant yesterday, yours?"

Do Trieu's doesn't react to the question. "I do not know of these men you speak of."

Samuel glares at Do Trieu until the man looks down at his tea cup. Even an honest man would admit to crimes he hadn't done under the heat of those laser-beams.

"Tell me about the arrangement to kill me," Samuel says, a question that does nothing to reduce Do Trieu's bulging orbs.

"I do not know what you…"

Samuel leans back in his chair and looks across the table at his daughter.

Do Trieu looks worriedly at Mai then sighs in resignation. "Mister Van called me early this week and offered a large sum of money to… But," he adds quickly, "I turned him down."

Samuel's eyes burn into the man. Mai is as motionless as a coiled spring. I don't think she's moved so much as an eyelash in five minutes.

"Why did you turn him down?" Samuel asks.

"We all have that place where we will not go," he says, sounding a tad philosophical and a little believable.

"Go on." Samuel's tone doesn't give away anything he's thinking.

"I told him no. Because that is not what I do; it is not who I am."

"A dope runner with a conscience?" I ask.

Do Trieu looks over and nods at me eagerly, as if I'd just paid him a compliment.

"What was his reply?" Samuel asks, after shooting me a glare. Father reprimands son for speaking out of line, I guess.

"He asked if I knew Le Tan Nho."

Samuel blinks a couple three times. "Who is he?"

Does Samuel know this guy?

"He owns a store. Asian antiques on Eighty Second. I have heard that it is only a…"

He says a Vietnamese word to which Samuel says, "Front."

"Yes, a front for his criminal activity. I have heard he gets girls, very young girls for Hong Kong, Taiwan, and maybe other places. You know, prostitution."

"It's called sex trafficking," I say.

"Yes," Do Trieu says. "Sex trafficking."

"You think this man accepted Lai Van Tan's request?"

"Yes, I think so. He has people who work for him. Some are very violent."

Samuel looks at Do Trieu for a long moment; I can't tell if he believes him. I don't even know if I believe him. Mai looks over at me for the first time since she's sat down, that ready-to-pounce-and-remove-a-pair-of-eyeballs demeanor gone. Does that mean she believes him?

"How easy is it to find Le Tan Nho?" Samuel asks.

Do Trieu nods, his body noticeably relaxed now that Samuel's focus has turned from him. "I am told he is almost always in his store. He drives a black Lexus."

Again Samuel studies Do Trieu. "I hope for the sake of your eyes that you have been telling me the truth," he says.

Do Trieu blinks rapidly and forces a smile. "Yes, yes, I have been."

"Outside!" I warn, backing away from the window. "Two cars just pulled onto the lot—fast. A white Mazda and a black one. Asian drivers, I think. They're wearing sunglasses. The front passenger sides look empty. I can't see into the backseats."

"Those are my people," Do Trieu says, his tone suddenly confident. "I called them when I left my massage parlor. I did not know who you were. Maybe robbers." He stands. "I will go tell them it is a misunderstanding."

I extend my palm toward him. "Wait."

"We will all go out together," Samuel says, moving toward the door. Mai gets up, but stands fast, her eyes studying Do Trieu's every nuance.

"No one's getting out of the cars," I say, thinking that it's a dumb tactic to pull right up in front of the place.

"They are waiting for a sign from me," Do Trieu says.

"Then you go out first," Samuel says from the side of the door. "But if you communicate anything to them that causes me concern, I will kill you before you take another breath. Is that clear?"

Damn.

Do Trieu nods gravely. After his guys have failed twice to hurt Samuel, I'm guessing that Do Trieu is being extremely cautious.

"Take just one step out from the doorway," Samuels says. "Then tell them to get out of their cars."

"Wait," I cut in. Samuel looks at me, as does Do Trieu. "I don't want them to get out all at once. Order the driver of the black Mazda out first." He's closest to the restaurant door. The white car is about two car widths to the left, nearly centered on the front window. "Then I'll tell you what to do next."

"You heard him," Samuel says. Proudly?

I move toward the side of the plate-glass window, but far enough back for those outside not to see me. This is not good. Bad guys outside, good guys and bad guys inside. We got one gun, mine. At least I brought it this time. I could go out the backdoor and position myself at the front corner of the building, but I wouldn't be able to hear any of the communications. Plus, if the occupants of the car rushed into the restaurant, I'd be outside and Mai and Samuel would be trapped inside.

Do Trieu opens the door and takes one step out onto the sidewalk. Samuel moves right behind his shoulder, but stays just behind the door facing, unseen from outside. "The black car driver only," he whispers. He turns toward Mai. "Watch those two," he says, indicating the two older men at the back table. She nods.

Do Trieu says something in Vietnamese loud enough for the occupants to hear.

"It is okay," Samuel whispers out of the corner of his mouth, assuring me that the words were translated accurately.

The black car door opens and a twenty-something Asian male gets out, complete with a two-inch high buzz cut, wrap-around sunglasses, and a white sports jacket over a black shirt. I can't see his pants because he's still behind the car door, but I've seen enough to know that he needs to fire his 1970s fashion consultant.

"Tell him to step away from the door," I whisper to Samuel, "and to lift his *Miami Vice* jacket above his waist. Then tell him to turn around once. Let's see if he's carrying in the obvious places."

Samuel tells Do Trieu, who tells the driver. The guy steps away and does a slow twirl as the wind flaps his jacket about. I know I'm far enough back from the window that he can't see me, but his hard stare toward the glass still makes me feel uncomfortable.

"Same procedure with the White Mazda," I say to Samuel.

He tells the old man who calls out something to the driver in the white car. The door opens and another Vietnamese male gets out, same age as the other, same buzz cut and wrap around shades, and—you've got to be kidding me—he's wearing opposite colors from his buddy: black jacket and a white shirt. Who are these dorks?

Do Trieu says something and the kid steps away from the car, lifts his jacket to expose his waistline, turns and centers back on the restaurant window with that same glare into the glass as his buddy. As goofy as these guys look, I have to admit that they're a little spooky.

"From here," Samuel whispers, turning his head toward me a little, "the backseats look empty."

"Okay." I glance back at the cook and waiter, who still sit dutifully at their table. Samuel's pluck-out-and-force-feed-the-eyes threat must have made an impression, but I still don't trust them. I look over to Samuel. "I'm not comfortable with his people in here *and* out there. How about telling Do Trieu to tell these bozos to get back in their cars and leave."

"The white car!" Mai says loudly from just behind my right shoulder, making me jump. A third Asian, same age as the others, minus the sunglasses, and with a head topped with at least an eight-inch high bleached-white pompadour, is draping himself over the roof on the passenger side, pointing some kind of a weapon toward the window. He probably can't see us but he knows we're behind the glass. This is not good. These guys have a history of spray-and-pray: Fire on full auto and pray that at least one round hits someone.

Mai and I drop to our knees below the window sill, as Samuel and Do Trieu shout at the armed man. I quick-peek over the sill. Both drivers have placed their hands behind their heads but the one draped over the roof hasn't moved. The barrel of his gun, possibly an UZI, still points our way. He shouts something and Do Trieu barks something back.

Whatever the boss said, which he uttered with unmistakable anger, makes the gunman slide off the roof and begin moving around the front of the car, his weapon pointing downward.

I tell Mai to stay put, then I crawl quickly on all fours to the door, whispering to Samuel to move aside so I can get into position with my weapon. He does. Gripping my Glock in both hands, I stand up just behind the door frame, leaning out far enough so I can see the gunman with one eye. I whisper to Samuel to watch the drivers and for anyone else coming out of the two clown cars.

"Tell him I've got a nine millimeter pointing at his forehead," I say quietly to Do Trieu. "Then tell him to put his weapon down on the sidewalk."

Do Trieu says something to him. I'm guessing it's what I told him to say because the kid slowly squats down Asian style and sets the weapon on the sidewalk. He's not more than fifteen feet from me, about three healthy paces. He drops forward onto his hands and knees, his right hand still on the weapon, his eyes looking toward my one eye that's peering around the door frame. A strand of bleached hair blows loose from his heavy gel and whips across his forehead.

"He speak English?" I ask Do Trieu.

"Of course," he says, as if it's a dumb question.

I ease out a foot or so from the doorway so the kid can see more of me, especially how I'm holding my gun in both hands and looking down its barrel at him.

"Take your hand off the gun," I say. Damn! It's a TEC-Nine. A burst from that will make a lot of big holes.

He remains motionless on his hands and knees, his eyes boring into mine with absolute, make-no-bones-about-it, hate. His hand doesn't move from the weapon.

"Take your hand away from the TEC-Nine," I say, faking calm, while my guts twist and churn. Oh no, here comes the nausea. I haven't felt sick in a couple of days and I was hoping it had gone away.

"Come on, kid. Let go of the weapon."

Please take your hand away. *Please.* I can't kill again. I can't.

From behind me, Do Trieu shouts something in Vietnamese, as does Samuel, but the sounds are barely audible to me, as if the volume has been turned down. I'm guessing they're yelling at the kid not to be stupid. *Please* let him not be stupid.

He doesn't move a muscle, his eyes locked on mine, his palm still resting flat on the side of the TEC-Nine near the trigger guard. I don't think he's even blinked, all the while that strand of white hair continues to brush back and forth on his forehead like a windshield wiper.

The scary end of the barrel points a foot or two to my right. If his finger was *in* the trigger guard, I would have already sent him to see the Buddha. Still, it would take him only a half second to raise the gun and slip his pointy finger into position.

Why are this young man's eyes filled with hate We just met! Maybe he hates all white people.

They're brown eyes, like—Jimmy's.

Damn.

The little boy's were so afraid that day, terrified. Then for one brief moment they changed from terror to hopeful as I assured him that we were the police and we were there to save him. Then I fired a bullet into his chest.

Nausea wafts over me and settles into my head, my belly, my intestines.

The Vietnamese kid and I continue to look into each other's eyes. Minutes, hours, days, weeks pass. Seems like it, anyway. Then:

Realization.

It—the indisputable recognition of truth, my truth—hits me like a freight train, like the proverbial lightening bolt, like a headfirst sprint into a brick wall. It wasn't in my mind ten seconds ago but here it is now, and it fills me with its certainty.

There is no way in hell I can shoot this young man. I just can't do it.

What was that? A flicker of something just passed across the kid's face. Did he read the epiphany in my eyes? My tell? Yes, he must have and now he knows I can't shoot him. And he knows that that opens the door for him to…

Movement from my right; from behind me Samuel and Do Trieu shout something. I turn my head just enough to see in my peripheral that the driver of the black Mazda has lowered his arms. Samuel comes into my field of vision; he's rushing toward the driver.

Three paces to my front, the young man remains kneeling on his hands and knees, his eyes… deciding? Then something changes in his face, in those eyes; it's quick and nearly imperceptible. He doesn't blink; he doesn't look to the side; he doesn't look down at the gun. But that thing that passed across his eyes…

His tell… telling me… he's going to raise his gun.

He does.

He lifts it off the sidewalk and begins rocking back on his heels.

I move toward him about as fast as I've ever moved, crossing those three paces in two big steps to front kick his mouth.

His head snaps back so forcefully that for a second I think it's going to break off at his neck. When it springs back, his mouth is open and spilling bloody teeth down onto his white shirt and black jacket. I slap the side of his face with my Glock, probably warping my gun. Oh well, I wasn't going to shoot it anyway.

360

He drops heavily onto his side—

—and discharges a round, loud and ear piercing. I jump reflexively as glass shatters behind me. Do Trieu shouts something and so does Samuel.

A swift kick launches the TEC-Nine across the sidewalk and under the white Mazda. My weapon holstered, I grab the lethargic guy's arm and flip him over onto to his stomach. I jam his bent arm high up around his shoulder. I feel something give way—a shoulder ligament maybe—but he's too groggy to complain.

Sounds of grunting and flesh hitting flesh coming from the direction of the black Mazda. Through the shattered passenger window I can see distorted movement, fast movement.

I start to bend down to look under the car to maybe see Sam's red Converses doing a little quick step as they did at the coffee joint, but the driver of the white car leaps behind the wheel, pulling the door shut behind him. The engine roars to life and, for just a second, I think that he's going to jump the sidewalk and run me over. Instead, he accelerates backwards, laying a patch of smoking, squealing rubber. It completes an arc and then lays another patch as it gooses forward across the small lot, over the sidewalk, and out into traffic where it's greeted by an angry chorus of honking horns.

Like a lot of gangbangers, he's a good poser, but when the caca hits the fan, he's gone.

The TEC-Nine lies in an oil spot. Goose bumps shoot up my spine when I think how the last sixty seconds could have gone differently. At point blank range, TEC-Nine Boy could have done a spray-and-pray leaving me beyond the need for prayer.

Still kneeling on him, I peer around his shoulder to see how he's doing. His eyes are half closed, and blood still flows heavily from his mouth and nose. It's a milk shake diet for him for the next three months. I leave him on his stomach and move over to pick up his weapon. I pop out the clip and jack the round out of the chamber. Watching that bullet drop in slow motion onto the pavement sends another chill up my spine, making me want to hit him again.

I don't, but I do vomit all over the oil slick.

Feeling better but with bad breath, I glance toward the restaurant's big picture window. The waiter and cook look back at me, watching the show without expression. At least they aren't participating.

I step over to the corner of the building and, like a chopping woodsman, slam the gun over and over against the brick. By the third whack, pieces are breaking off and the barrel has warped into a shallow U. I chop it a couple more times and then toss what remains of it onto the sidewalk.

Do Trieu, standing by the black car's front left headlight, is glaring toward the ground near the driver's side and shouting vehemently in Vietnamese. I look over the roof to see Mai's and Samuel's head and shoulders as they stand side-by-side a few feet from the driver's door. Where's the driver? What's going on?

I double check that my guy is sleeping soundly then go over to join the others. Moving around to the far side of the black Mazda, I see Wrap-Around Sunglasses Dude crumpled on the pavement, chunks of glass all around him from the shattered door widow. I look over at Mai and Samuel standing side-by-side about six feet away, both looking as if they've been waiting for me.

"What happened?"

"He has been shot, Sam," Mai says, a quiver in her voice.

I step over to the driver and peer down at him. His eyes are open and his mouth is moving silently, like one of those beached koi. "Where'd he get hit?"

"That one has not been shot," she says. "Father kick the shit out of that guy because he was reaching under his car seat for something. It is father who has been shot."

"What?" Her words aren't computing in my nauseous brain. "I don't understand…" The Mazda driver lies crumpled on the pavement under the shot-out window as Do Trieu bends over him and rips him a new one. Mai is standing beside Samuel who… my God, he's so pale!

I take a couple of tentative steps closer… Mai's palm presses against Samuel's shoulder as blood streams between her fingers, down his arm and drips off his hand.

"We have got to get out of here, Sam," he says, his voice small. "Before the police come."

*

"Kaiser ER is about fifteen minutes from here," I say, flooring my truck. Mai is in the middle again, pressing a wad of fast food napkins she found on the dash against Samuel's bleeding shoulder. Other than his colorless face, he has yet to indicate that he's bothered by getting shot.

"No hospital, Sam," he says. "Just take us to our apartment. Get me inside and then maybe you can go get some medical supplies while Mai tends to me."

"Are you sure?" I ask incredulously. "I know you don't want the police involved but that wound is bleeding badly."

"I'm sure. Mai is a good nurse. We can get my injury fixed up enough for me to see her graduate tomorrow and for us to fly home Sunday."

"It looks like the bullet went all the way through," Mai says. "I cannot tell if it hit the bone. But we can fix it."

I don't agree that this is the best thing to do for a bullet in the shoulder but I understand his reasoning. "I've got a pretty complete stock of first aid stuff at my place. One of my students works for an ambulance company and stocked my school as well as my house."

"May we go there, instead?" Samuel asks.

"Of course. I can give him a call to come over."

"It will not be necessary," Mai says. "But thank you."

I look over at her, at the back of her head. *It will not be necessary.* How can she be so absolute?

I pull into my driveway, happy that nosey Bill isn't out in his yard or that lusty Tammy isn't hanging around. No media, either. I'm already yesterday's news. Good. I scurry around to the passenger's side, open the door and help Samuel out onto his wobbly legs.

Inside, Mai guides her father into my kitchen while I close the curtains and flip on some lamps. I grab a few first aid things in the bathroom, and a couple of clean washcloths and towels out of the hallway linen closet.

"Be right back," I say, dropping the things onto the kitchen table. "Oh, and there are water glasses in the larger cupboard over there." Out in my garage, I retrieve the first aid box. On the way back in, I notice the dried blood on my hanging bag and on the floor. Much has happened since I went nuts out here a few nights ago.

When I walk back into the kitchen, Samuel is sitting shirtless, his eyes closed. Mai has scooted her chair closer to his side, her knees touching his hip. The hole at the front of his shoulder oozes blood and, judging by the red rungs on the back of the white wooden chair and the small red pool forming on the floor behind him, the exit wound is bleeding heavily, too.

"Shouldn't you be applying direct pressure?" I ask. "Or is there a way to apply a tourniquet around his shoulder?"

"Please open the box and lay the contents out onto the table," she says, ignoring my questions. She picks up her father's hand and places it in her lap. She speaks softly to him in Vietnamese and he says something back.

I just begin to unload the gauzes, disinfectants, bandages, and other supplies, when I hear—whistling. What the hell? It's coming from Samuel. Mai looks at me and shakes her head.

"What the?"

She frowns, shaking her head harder. Satisfied that I'm going to be quiet, she places her index finger lightly against his upper arm, just below the bullet hole. In an instant, blood rolls over it and down onto the floor.

Samuel sits motionless, his eyes closed like a pale, sleeping man. He has placed his left hand palm-up on his knee, the thumb and index finger forming a circle. His right palm now rests flat against his lower belly as it rises and falls with a faint whistle through his puckered lips on each exhalation.

Mai's eyes are closed now and she appears to be breathing in sync with him, inhaling, holding it in for a few seconds and exhaling with a whistle. It's a strange sight, indeed: A beautiful woman and a sixty-plus-year-old man with the physique of a ripped thirty-year-old, sitting together, breathing deeply in harmony, and whistling a happy tune.

A first for my kitchen.

Five minutes pass on the microwave clock, then ten. It's at the ten-minute mark that I notice Samuel's coloring. It's no longer death-white. It's... normal: pinkish, healthy. The red river that had been rolling over Mai's finger has stopped. Still, her finger touches his arm, near the point of entry.

They remain like that for another twenty minutes. Just as I think I can't remain motionless another moment, Mai retracts her hand and Samuel opens his eyes. They appear to be finished with whatever it was they were doing.

I move stiffly over to the remaining kitchen chair and sit, as Mai washes blood off her hands in the sink. She looks tired, drained.

"What on Earth were you doing?" I ask whoever wants to answer.

"I feel better now," Samuel says, as if what I had just witnessed was normal. "But I feel like I must sleep. Getting shot takes it out of me. It always has." He slumps back against the chair, and for the first time I notice multiple scars on his chest and side. The two on his side and two above his right pectoral are old bullet wounds. A couple of short, pinkish lines on his right biceps look like old knife slashes.

He stands, picks up a washcloth and towel from the table and moves over to the sink without any of the wobble he had earlier. Oh man! What does he have on his back? There are one, two... eight... no... eleven grooves across his spine. Those are—my God! Whip scars? Tiff and I watched that old made-for-TV miniseries, *Roots,* about six months ago. In the movie, the whip slashes on the slaves looked just like the crisscross slashes on Samuel's back.

They must have whipped him in that North Vietnamese prison.

Mai takes the washcloth, wets it with steaming tap water and begins wiping the drying blood off his arm. "Sam," she says. "Do you have a clean sweatshirt father can borrow? Something warm."

"Of course." I head off to my bedroom and return with a burgundy hoody that displays an image of a white unicorn standing under a sunbeam in a forest. One of my students gave it to me as a joke. "Sorry, it's all I have that's clean." Mai giggles.

"Cool," he says, enthusiastically. "I like unicorns."

I lay it across the back of the chair and watch Mai gently towel him off, her love for this man abundantly clear. For the next ten minutes she bandages the entrance and exit wounds, where a half hour earlier the leaking blood had appeared unstoppable. "Thank you," he says quietly, as we help him slip his wounded arm into the sweatshirt. "If I may, I would enjoy sleeping now."

"I have a guest room. Where the intruder hid."

"He gone now?"

"Yes," I say with a short laugh.

"Good, I do not want him bothering me."

I lead them down the hall and open the guestroom door. "There's extra blankets and pillows in the closet."

"I am good, thank you," he says, moving into the room. "I just want to lie down for a while." He looks at Mai. "Wake me in an hour please."

"Yes father," she says, pulling the door closed.

"Is he going to be okay?" I ask when we're back in the kitchen.

"Yes." She rips several paper towels off the counter spool, kneels, and begins wiping up. "He lost a lot of blood and it tired him. I hope you understand that anyone else would have required hospitalization."

"I do," I say, shaking my head in amazement as I retrieve the trashcan from under the sink. I hold it as she drops the paper towels in. "I can't believe how quickly he came out of that."

"He was in shock but he hid it well. We will have his shoulder checked out by a doctor when we are back in Saigon on Monday. But I think it is fine now and will heal quickly."

I spray Four-O-Nine on the chair and floor and we commence wiping everything clean.

"What were you two doing? The breathing and whistling, I mean?"

She stands, drops the towels in the trash and washes her hands in the sink. "I understand that it was probably strange to you."

"Oooh yeah. His color came back so fast, and the bleeding…"

"It stopped." She leans her hip against the sink and folds her arms. "It is a Tibetan breathing technique for healing. It helped him lower his blood pressure, and it diminished his shock and sealed his wounds."

"How do you know his blood pressure was high?"

"Because he had been shot," she says, with a shrug. Okay, dumb question. "It reduces pain, too. I have seen him do it two times before. It is hard for me to understand how it works; I just know it does. I think it will cut his healing time in half, as long as there are no other problems that the doctor finds." She shakes her head. "I do not think there will be any."

"What were you doing when you touched his arm?"

"Just touching it. It helped him focus on the problem spot. If he was not in so much pain, I would not have needed to do that. But because of his blood pressure and the numbing all around the wound, my touch helped him see the spot with his eyes closed. So he could focus on it. I breathed with him to help with his energy flow and so he could use some of mine. Together, we reduced his pain and helped begin his rapid healing."

"It's all so incredible." I touch her arm. "You look exhausted."

"I am. It took much from me. But it took more from him."

"Can he heal others?"

"Not yet. He says he is working on it. Like he is working on reading minds better. He is always working on something. By the way, he told me that when he first met you he discovered he could, uh, perceive? Yes, perceive your thoughts better than he can perceive what other people think. He does not really read minds but he, uh, picks up, I think he calls it, what people have in their heads. He thinks it might be because you share the same blood."

I shake my head in wonder. "He knew what I was thinking several times. He's so incredible. You must be so used to him, but do you understand just how incredible he is to me?"

"Of course," she says, looking at me as if trying to peer deeply inside my being.

"All of this… him, you, me. It's just so overwhelming."

"So are you, to me."

"I'm sorry?"

"For what?"

"I mean, I didn't hear what you said. I heard you, I just—"

"Overwhelming," she whispers, her eyes drawing me, enveloping me. "I think you are overwhelming, too."

Now I know what the poets mean when they speak of the eyes as pools. I splash about in them like a happy dolphin.

"Sam?" Her whisper heats my face.

"Yes."

"If you don't kiss me, I'm going to kick your ass. And I can do it."

I sputter a laugh, then stop. When I was a kid I jumped from a forty-foot cliff into a lake and I remember how the wind rushed past my ears as I dropped and dropped. I'm hearing that again now.

Having had all the violence I can handle for one day, I do what she says.

*

"Are you awake, Sam?"

"What?"

"Are you awake?"

"I'm not asleep if that's what you mean."

"Yes, you are. I mean, yes, you were."

"Okay, I'm awake, but I can't see anything. Am I in a cave?" It's a wonderfully perfumed cave. I can't see anything and I don't want to see anything. I just want to stay wherever I am, so warm, so right, so at ease, forever.

There's wind outside the cave. Howling. No, not howling. Moaning. Sad.

Something is tickling my nose, my cheek. I don't know where my hands are. I rub my face on whatever it's leaning on.

"Are you wiping your nose on my shoulder?"

"What?" I lift my head and the darkness falls away to reveal Mai's smiling eyes, not more than three inches away. How did I get here? I can't remember what I was doing.

"You always fall asleep in the middle of a… what do you call it here? Oh yes, a make-out session?"

We're on my sofa and I'm leaning against her, and together we're slumped against a stack of pillows at one end. My fog dissipates. We'd been embracing and kissing up a storm and I. Fell. The. Hell. Asleep?

"I'm so sorry!" I say, quickly sitting all the way up. I'm mortified. "Oh, man, I can't believe I—"

Mai interrupts me with a gentle kiss, giving me a shot of that jump-from-the-high-barn-rafters roar in my head again. She pulls back, smiling at me. "I liked that you fell asleep."

"What? No, no. I'm so sorry. I don't remember falling—"

She touches the side of my face with her fingers and looks at me with eyes so bright, happy. "We were kissing and holding each other. It was wonderful. You whispered that you 'had not felt this relaxed in months.' Then you pushed your face into my neck and went fast asleep."

"Mai, I'm sorry, I don't know what…"

She touches my face again, her fingers on my cheek, her thumb tracing my lower lip. "Stop apologizing. It was the best first make-out session I ever had." She leans in and we kiss again.

"How long was I out?" I ask a couple minutes later.

"Two hours or so. I dozed, too."

"Well, I feel pretty good right now." We're chest-to-chest, our arms entwined and looking into each other's faces. Outside, the wind rushes intermittently through the big fir tree. She begins slowly tracing a finger over my forehead, around my eyes, over my nose, across my lips, and over my chin. It's wonderfully intimate and heart-thumping sensual. When I do it back to her, she closes her eyes and lifts her chin slightly. When my traveling finger reaches her full lips, she kisses its tip.

Her eyes open again and I can see in them that she is thinking the same thing that just ripped across my heart.

"I leave Sunday," she whispers.

"Nooo."

"I am sorry." She embraces me so tightly that I can't breathe for a moment, but I'm okay with it. She rests her head on my shoulder, her lips touching my ear. "I must. In the Vietnamese family, there is a… collective? Yes, a collective responsibility and mutual obligation to take care of one another. For me, it is even greater because I have been trained in the warrior ways by my father."

She lifts her head and meets my eyes. "Father says that he thinks I have the blood of Trieu Thi Trinh, a female Vietnamese warrior who lived in the third century. She was born in northern Vietnam when it was divided into three kingdoms in an area of China called the Eastern Wu Kingdom. After she was… what is the word? Oh, orphaned, she was raised by her brother and his wife, working for them as a slave. When she was twenty, she escaped into the jungle and built an army of over a thousand men and women soldiers. She lib… liberated part of Vietnam and claimed it as her own. After three years of fighting, she had defeated over thirty advances by the Wu. It is told that she rode into battle on the back of an elephant, wearing golden armor and wielding two swords."

"I can see you doing that," I say teasingly, but meaning it. Mai nods seriously.

"Father also says that I have the spirit of Ani Pachen, a Tibetan nun who died at the beginning of this century. When her parents tried to marry her at seventeen, she escaped to a monastery and became a Buddhist nun. After her father died, she became a warrior nun. She even took up arms and led her people in guerilla warfare to keep the communists Chinese out of Tibet.

"When she was caught, she refused to destroy… no, not destroy, uh… denounce, to denounce the Dalai Lama. So they hung her by her wrists for three weeks, then put her in leg irons for a year, then threw her into a cell without lights for nine months. Then they made her serve eleven more years in Drapchi prison."

I suddenly feel like a girly man for calling in sick when I had a cold.

"But right after she was released," Mai continues, "after living all that *dukkha*, she led many protests and demonstrations. When it looked like she was going to be arrested again, she walked over three weeks in deep snow to escape to Nepal.

"Father says I have the spirit of these two women. And with it comes a responsibility to do what warriors do. To protect. To go toward what others run from. So, you see, it is my duty to help my family. It is my duty, and because I love them."

I nod. "I do understand and I do agree with you one hundred percent."

"But it hurts you inside because I have to go?"

Like father, like daughter; she doesn't mince words. "Yes."

"Me, too. Very much."

"Can you come back?" I ask, hopefully. "Do what you got to do in Vietnam and then come back to, I don't know, maybe work on a master's degree?"

She shakes her head. "My parents paid for my school so I can help them with the business. That is what I must do now. It is my family obligation."

We sit looking at each other for a long moment. "Talk about your LDR, that means long distance relationship," I say dumbly.

Mai's eyes tear, incredibly making them even more beautiful. "Can you come over to Vietnam? Visit me. Visit father and meet my family."

"Yes," I answer without hesitation. "Yes, I can. I have a lot to do in the next few weeks, but—Yes."

She smiles and so do I. We sit in silence for a few moments, shoulders touching, both of us looking down at our clasped hands, thinking, wondering. A pain gnaws in my chest. Outside the wind moans loudly and then slams the side of the house hard, jarring the windows.

"What time did we get here?" I ask, looking at the clock over the TV.

"Six thirty, I think," she says, rubbing her thumb thoughtfully over the back of my hand. "Why?"

"It's almost nine thirty."

She looks up at me and follows my eyes over to the clock. "Oh my! Father wanted us to wake him in an hour. That was over two hours ago." She scoots to the edge of the sofa. "He might be angry. But he needed to rest."

"We could just let him sleep as long as he wants, all night even."

"And I stay, too, right?" She gives me a look, one that says she's heard a lot of come-on lines in her day.

I touch her arm. "No, no. It's not about what you're thinking. Maybe we shouldn't complicate things even more. You're leaving, we're being hunted, I've got a crapload of problems, as do you, and Samuel is lying in there wounded. And it's not over, yet. Oh, I want to—it's just that the timing is…" If the guys in Detectives heard me say these things to such a gorgeous creature they'd turn their backs on me and say that I'm an embarrassment to males everywhere.

She gazes into my eyes for a long moment, a look that makes my toes wiggle. She turns her head away a little without losing eye contact, and arches an eyebrow. "Are there many men like you in America?"

I shake my head. "Nope. I'm it."

She laughs and kisses me. "I must wake father. It is what he wanted."

Part way down the hall she stops and turns toward me. We move into each other and embrace without uttering a word. A few seconds later, maybe it's minutes, she whispers into my chest, "I do not want this to end."

I squeeze her harder. "It won't. I can feel it."

She looks up at me. Nods, and we kiss once more. When we part, she smiles, and says, "We must go wake up our pop." She leads the way holding my hand.

"I thought we shut the door," I say. "It's open."

We peer in. "Father?" Mai calls. The covers are mussed but the bed is empty.

The hall bathroom door behind us is open. "Samuel?" I say, looking in. Empty.

"Father!" Mai calls out loudly down the hall.

"Where could he have gone?" We move toward the kitchen. Mai splits off into the living room toward the window as I cross over to the door that leads into the garage. He's not in there.

"Sam?" Mai calls. "Your pickup is gone."

*

We're standing at the front window looking out at my empty driveway. "At least he left my house keys," I say, not just a little perturbed. "He must have left when we were sleeping on the sofa. You think he's gone back to your apartment for some reason?"

She shakes her head, frustrated. "No. Oh, I do not know. Maybe. But why not awaken us? It was not even nine o'clock when he left, maybe eight."

After a minute, I ask, "What was that guy's name Do Trieu talked about? The guy he claimed was the real hitman?"

"Le Tan Nho. I remember because father used to have a friend with the same name. The one Do Trieu told us about owns an antique shop on... was it Eighty-Second?"

I head for the kitchen. "Let me get the Yellow Pages."

"Try Le's Antiques first," Mai suggests, following. "Or Le's Asian Antiques. Something like that."

"Nothing," I say, running my finger down the names. "Wait. How about 'Nho's Number One Asian Antiques?' Forty-five, forty-nine, Eighty-Second Avenue."

"Yes, that must be it. But how do we get there?"

"Normally, I'd have a squad car give us a lift but we want to keep the police out of all this." Oh man, I'm so deep in the doo-doo I don't know if I'm looking up or looking sideways. I've been in two scuffles today and a shooting. A shooting! If I don't get fried for Jimmy's shooting, they'll put me on a slow boil for not reporting today's activities.

"A taxi?" Mai asks, cutting into my doomsday thinking.

"That's what I'm thinking," I say, already fanning the Yellow Pages to "Taxi."

I tell her we got ten minutes before the cab comes. "We won't go straight to the store on Eighty-Second. I told them forty-five, fifty on Eighty-Third. That way there's no record of us going directly to Eighty-Second should something go down."

"Go down?"

"Happen. Should something happen. Who knows what we'll find? Hopefully, Samuel won't have beaten everyone to a pulp."

Mai smiles and then quickly sobers, studying me.

"What?"

"Do you think you will ever call him 'father'?"

I gesture at the sofa and we sit. "I hope so, but I want it to feel natural. Right now I'm just getting adjusted to the idea that he is alive." Mai is caressing my hand, nodding.

"My situation is just the opposite. Father and I are not related but I do not remember when he was not in my life. So it is just natural for me to call him father. But for you, he has been in your life for only a week. So I understand."

"Thank you. I just want all this crap to be over. If only we could have met with less drama."

"You mean like sharing a soda at the Dairy Queen?"

I laugh. "Hey, you've caught on to American culture very well. So what's the situation with your graduation? You still going to go through with it?"

"Yes, well, I think so. My graduation is a huge wish for father and my mother. I told him that I can pick up my diploma in the school office or have it mailed to me, but he did not like that at all. It even made him mad a little. Of course, he wanted to meet you, but he also came to *see* me graduate, *see* me get the diploma. He wants to see that for himself and to represent my mother since she is so sick; to be her eyes. They are very proud of me. I do not think he will let anything stop that."

"I understand. It's an amazing education you've gotten. Hanoi, Paris, America."

"Yes. I owe my parents a great deal."

A car honks.

"It's the cab," I say getting up. "Grab your coat."

Twenty minutes later we're on Eighty-Third. Mai and I mostly rode in silence in the dark cab, sitting close, and holding hands. Half of me is loving this closeness and the other is anxious about all the unknown factors of where we're going.

"Right there, driver," I say, pointing at the upcoming intersection. I hand him a twenty and struggle for a moment to push the car door open against the force of the wind. Mai takes my arm and tucks her head into my side as we lean into the gale and stagger toward Eighty-Second.

"There's my truck," I shout into Mai's ear as we near the corner. "Good tactic parking on the side of the street." All looks normal inside the cab. "Over here," I say leading her to the side of the building. I peek around the corner. Based on the address, the antique store is probably about three doors down. There. A sandwich board that looks to have been blown against the side of a parked van, reads: Nho's Number One Asian Antiques.

"No bodies lying out on the sidewalk," I say, only half joking into Mai's ear. "I have an extra truck key in my wallet. Why don't you wait in it while I check out the store and..." She leans away, shooting me a look that makes it clear what I can do with my suggestion. "Okay, never mind. You ready?"

"Let's go." She leads the way.

"Slow down, Mai." Thankfully, the roar of the wind is considerably less on this side of the building. "Stop right there at the edge of the front window. Don't expose yourself." I move up beside her. We lean out enough to see a window display of antique bedroom furniture, bookcases and old chairs. Craning our necks a tad more, we're able to see into the store proper where Samuel, a middle-aged Asian man, and a woman are sitting around an ornate wooden table... laughing and drinking tea?

Mai's eyes widen. "Oh, my gosh!" she says, giggling. "It's okay. Come on."

"What is..." No brawling, no shooting, but tea?

"Mai!" Samuel calls out as we enter. "Sam! Come on in." He's pretty chipper for a gunshot-wounded truck thief.

The other man, sixtyish, slacks, shirt, and haircut all suggesting money, stands quickly and says something excitedly in Vietnamese to Mai. He's barely five-feet tall and at first blush appears to be a bundle of barely restrained energy. They embrace, laughing. It's a short hug and a little awkward given their size difference.

"This is my uncle Nho," Mai says, turning to me, her face happy. Then to Nho, she says, "This is Sam, father's son."

The man pumps my hand with both of his. "Very wonderful to meet my friend's son," he says excitedly, in thickly accented English. "Samuel tell me he is very happy to find you, which make me very happy for him, my friend."

"Thank you," I manage, not having a clue what the hell is going on.

Nho turns to the seated diminutive, middle-aged woman and says, "This is my wife, Tu."

"Nice to meet you," Mai and I say at the same time.

Samuel stands and extends his hand. "Sorry about the truck. You two were sleeping so I thought I would do a little scouting. When Do Trieu told us that the real hired shooter was Le Tan Nho, I thought of my friend here, but I thought the name was just a coincidence because my friend left Saigon many years ago, and the last I heard, he was living in San Diego. It is a long, story but I have known him since my second year of freedom in Vietnam. He has been a good friend and has helped me countless times over the years. He is like an uncle to Mai."

"No, no," Nho says with a vigorous shake of his head. He grips Samuel's uninjured arm. "Your father has helped *me* many times in Vietnam. He is a very, very good man." He says something kindly to the woman and she heads toward a back room. He looks at Mai. "You are as beautiful as ever," he says. "Many boyfriends at Portland State University?"

"Hundreds," Mai answers with a wink.

"Ooo-weee! I do not think you lie."

Everyone laughs, me not quite as hard as the others.

"Please sit," Nho says, pulling chairs out for us. Tu returns with two extra cups and another pot. He beams as he watches her, his love obvious. "We meet here in America and married four years ago. She is very good for me. Tu is a good woman, a good wife."

She slaps Nho's arm and struggles not to smile. "He is a good catch, too," she says shyly.

"When I drove by this store," Samuel says, "I could see Nho washing the door window. I knew immediately that it was him because of how he combs his hair and, although he is a rich man, he is too cheap to hire someone to clean the windows for him."

"Ooo-wee!" Nho laughs, slapping his knee and shaking his head. "All these years pass and still your father breaks my balls. That is the correct term, right? 'Breaks my balls'?"

"Yes," Samuel says innocently. "It is perfect. You can use it anywhere: church, city council meetings."

"Father!" Mai reprimands with a barely restrained smile, which sets Samuel off in a gale of laughter. It's strange seeing him like this, so loose and informal.

"How is your shoulder, father?" Mai asks, touching his hand.

"I've been working my magic," he says. "It will be okay by morning. One hundred percent."

I can't believe this. "What? How?"

Samuel winks at Nho conspiratorially and jerks his thumb a couple of times at me. "Next, I will sell him Eighty-Second Avenue. For fifty dollars."

His friend cracks up again, which is so infectious that I laugh a little, too, though I don't get the joke.

"I'm sorry for teasing," Samuel says to me after a moment. "I'm good at healing, but not that good—yet." He looks at Mai. "My arm hurts. But it will be okay in time. At the moment, I can't move it. The bullet must have damaged the muscle."

"You should be resting," Mai scolds.

"You are right, and I will in a short while."

"What's going on with everything?" I ask.

"Nho tells me that he and Do Trieu are enemies, which is why he accused my friend and made up all that stuff about drugs and prostitutes. He owes Nho money, about five thousand dollars for remodeling of his restaurant, although the remodeling never happened. Do Trieu's refuses to pay my friend. As I learned last night, the man borrows money from people, needlessly, since he is wealthy, but he never pays anyone back."

"A good way to stay wealthy," I interject.

Samuel nods. "Yes, but it is perhaps more about him being a bully. I think he wants to be the big boss here. Also, Nho has another business that is interfering with Do Trieu."

"I own two city blocks here in Southeast Portland," Nho says, topping off everyone's tea cup. "I have bid on a third block, one that Do Trieu wants. I think he wants to hide money because the purchase includes seven businesses that will all pay leases to the owner. You call it… I forget the word."

"Money laundering?" I suggest.

"Yes, that is it. Money laundering. Hiding dirty money with clean money. He sells drugs, you know? I understand you are a policeman."

"Yes. I will be letting the right people know about him." I sip a little tea, then ask Samuel, "So we are back to Do Trieu as the hired gun?"

"I don't know."

"You didn't pick up anything in his mind?"

"A little, but nothing important. My ability is inconsistent." Samuel sighs, shrugs. "I don't know what to think now. I'm hoping that if it is him, our run-in today with his people will have changed his mind."

We sit around the table and talk for a while. Mostly Samuel and Nho reminisce about their times together in Vietnam while the rest of us laugh at their tales. At one point Tu slips on a coat and leaves, returning twenty minutes later with take-out boxes of pad Thai noodles with peanuts and sprouts, chicken and broccoli in peanut sauce, and sweet and sour chicken. She is so slight I'm surprised the wind didn't blow her away.

"I cook it up real good over small fire in the parking lot," she tells me with a wink. We all laugh and dig into the food, chatting and teasing one another. I instantly feel a part of their camaraderie and friendship and, for the first time in weeks, I feel happy, relaxed and, well, just darn happy. Actually, I'd have to rank sleeping with Mai on my couch as the most happy, and then eating and laughing with these fine people as the second most happy. For just a moment or two, Samuel, Mai and I don't think about Do Trieu, Lai Van Tan and their thugs. We pretend not to, anyway.

As we stand and set about putting on our coats, Samuel tells Nho he will try to see him before he leaves. "Things are a bit crazy right now," Samuel says. "I might try once more to get us an earlier flight out tomorrow night. So I don't know anything for sure. Here is my cell phone number" He hands Nho a piece of paper. "We can at least talk before I go."

My heart sinks at the thought of Mai leaving even earlier.

"If I don't see you this time," Nho says, "I will contact you in July when Tu and I visit Saigon."

"Yes, yes," Samuel says, smiling broadly and shaking his friend's hand vigorously.

Nho turns to me. "I hope to see you again, young man."

"You will. Maybe in Saigon, also in July."

"You are coming over?" Samuel says, looking at me.

I glance at Mai. Her face flushes; I can feel mine heating up, too. We're suddenly teenagers.

"Ooo-eee," Nho and Tu exclaim in unison.

"I thought I see something heeeeere," Nho laughs, wagging his finger at Mai and me. Then he frowns good naturedly at me. "She is my number one niece. You treat her good or I will bust your balls for real."

"He is very handsome," Tu says to Mai behind her hand, then laughs.

"Not so much," Mai says, looking at me stone-faced, then smiling.

"I have not been told about what is going on," Samuel says, slightly annoyed.

"Sam and I just talked about it earlier," Mai tells him.

"So the father is in the dark!" Nho teases.

This is getting a little out of hand. "Look," I say. "Mai and I don't really know what's going—"

"We will talk about this later," he says flatly. Uh, okay. Wasn't he okay with it back at the apartment?

383

We say our goodbyes and head out to the truck. The wind has grown stronger even on this side of the building where it's relatively sheltered. When we step around the corner, its wail is deafening.

In the truck, Samuel reaches across Mai and hands me the key. "Again, I am sorry for taking your truck without permission," he says, as I start it and adjust the heater. "I did not want to wake you, but mostly I did not want to jeopardize both of your safety. I have exposed you both to too much already. By the way, do you still have the address to Do Trieu's home that your police people gave you today?"

"Right here," I say, pulling the scrap of paper off the dash.

"I would like to go by his restaurant first and then by his home to see if there is any unusual activity there. Intelligence gathering only. No stopping. We only get into trouble when we stop."

"Can do," I say, turning in the right direction. "About your concern as to our safety, understand that I have been a police officer for fifteen years and I have been in a ton of crap. I appreciate you not wanting to get other people mixed up in this…"

"You are not just *other* people, Sam. You are *my* son and Mai is my daughter. I do not want to place my son and daughter in danger. I know you have been a policeman for fifteen years, but you have only been my son…" Incredibly, the old man's voice cracks. Mai pats his leg. "… I have only known that I have a son for three weeks."

"I understand," is all I manage. We ride in silence until we get to Do Trieu's block. Because his people might have seen my truck today, I pull into the inside lane and slow until two cars come up on our right. Then I match their speed to hide us as we pass the restaurant and massage joint. It turns out not to be an issue anyway since both appear to be closed, their parking lots empty.

"I can understand the restaurant being closed at ten o'clock," I wonder aloud. "But I assumed the massage parlor was a twenty-four-hour operation."

"It was torn up pretty good," Mai reminds me.

"Oh that's right." We both laugh, but not Samuel, who sits emotionless as he looks out the window. I try again to get a chuckle out of him. "I wonder if the Tiger-Style girls are still in the sauna room?" Nada.

I catch the freeway east to Gresham where Records indicated Do Trieu lives.

"Okay," Samuel says, "we must talk about you two. What is going on?" Straight to the point as always.

"What do you mean?" I ask, innocently.

"Sam," Mai touches my arm. "I have always been completely truthful with father. It is what he taught me when I was growing up and what I honor still."

"Uh, okay. I think." This is a whole lot uncomfortable.

She turns toward Samuel. "As you already noticed, Sam and I like each other very much. He would like me to stay here but I explained to him that I would not. We have talked briefly about him coming to visit us and to meet mother and the others."

"You had a girlfriend," he says.

"We ended it over two months ago, but we continued to see each other occasionally as… friends. We realized after a few weeks that for a number of reasons that was not a good thing to do. So we ended it completely a couple of days ago."

"You move fast, son."

"It's not like that. The relationship was long over. We won't reconcile."

385

"Tell father about all the bricks," Mai says.

"Bricks," Samuel says.

Okay, this is embarrassing. "I told Mai earlier that when I first saw her that it was like I'd been hit over the head with a ton of bricks."

"I see."

I glance over at him, unsure what's going on in his mind. The light bouncing off his face reveals nothing. What did he think when he saw us curled up on the sofa sleeping?

"That you two are related—in a way," he says.

Shouldn't it tickle or something when he goes into my head like that?

"In my heart," Mai says, "I am related to you, father. But on paper, I am not. I am not related to Sam on paper, nor am I in my heart."

"What else does your heart tell you, Mai? What does it tell you about this man?"

Is Samuel playing the Devil's advocate or is he being protective of Mai? Traffic is suddenly heavy making it impossible to look over at him.

"I am not sure," she says softly. I can sense her studying me. "I just know when I first saw him in his school this week, my heart went…" Out of the corner of my eye, I see her lower her head. "I do not know."

"But you want to find out?" Samuel says.

"Yes, I do."

"Sam?"

"That is what I want, too."

"Okay," Samuel says. We ride in silence for several minutes. Then, "Tomorrow you graduate."

"Yes?" Mai says without turning to look at him. I know what he's getting at and I'm sure she does, too.

"We leave Sunday. Maybe tomorrow night."

"I remember," Mai says.

"Not much time."

"A day and a half," she says.

"It is hard for two people to—"

"Father," Mai says, exasperated. "I am thirty-two years old. Thank you for your concern. But I can take it from here."

Silence.

I struggle not to smile. Mai's year in Portland has Americanized her. I'm staying out of this.

"I just think that—"

"Father! Sam and I have talked about this already. I have it under control. *We* have it under control."

Long, loud silence. Aaaawkward silence.

"About another mile," I say into the thick quiet, turning left at a stop sign.

Another minute of silence. Then.

"Father?"

"Yes?"

"I love you."

"Yes. Me, too."

Whew!

I'm leaning over the wheel straining to see house numbers. "I'm guessing it's that two-story house there, the one with two pine trees out front and the unlit porch. Look, there's Do Trieu's Beamer in the driveway."

"It looks like there is no activity," Mai whispers conspiratorially. "No other cars in the driveway, not even parked in the street." She looks out the side windows and twists around to look out the back. She's loving this detective work. "Think we ought to sneak up and look in the windows of his house?"

"No," Samuel says. "After yesterday's action in his massage parlor and at his restaurant, I think he is no longer a concern. He knows we have reversed the tables and we are watching him. I think we can leave."

"I agree," I say. "But since we have a good spot here in the shadows, I suggest we watch the place for half an hour or so and then take off if there's no activity."

"Good plan," Samuel agrees, as a gust rocks the truck.

I've been on a lot of stakeouts, which are never enjoyable since most are tedious, painful on the bladder and butt, and only rarely get results. But what's not to like about this one? Mai's side pressed against me, and on the other side of her, my long-lost father, a guy who continues to be beyond amazing.

Now that we've slowed down for the first time today, we're all feeling our fatigue and owies. Well, I am, anyway; they don't seem to notice theirs. I got hurt in the most places: a rib, the front and back of my head, a deep burning scratch on my neck, and perhaps most of all, my ego's been bruised. Samuel received the most serious owie, if you can call a gunshot wound an owie. The only indication that a bullet ripped through his flesh is that he favors that arm a little. Mai got tossed through the air in my bedroom and hit her head on the wall. She just shook it off and hasn't said a word about it. Today she took a nasty claw hand just below her hairline, which she's covered with her bangs. Not a peep out of her that it hurts.

Mai talks about her year at PSU and Samuel talks about how important it is for him to see her get her diploma and to photograph the moment so her mother can see it. I ask about their life in Vietnam. All I know of the country is what I've seen in old news clips, documentaries, and movies. What they describe is a life not a lot different than mine—working, training in the martial arts, and spending time with family and friends—but they experience these things in a culture and environment that's miles apart from mine.

Five days ago I didn't have any interest in Vietnam but now that these special people have entered my life, I want to know everything about it, about them, and especially the sudden and overwhelming feelings that Mai and I share. Then there is Samuel, my *father*, for crying out loud. Here's a sixty-something man who has lived over half his life in Southeast Asia. He's more Vietnamese now than Caucasian/American. He's a Buddhist, a Christian, he loves movies, he moves like lightening, he knows what I'm thinking, and he's "working on" self-healing bullet wounds.

"Whoa! Big one," I say when a strong wind gust slams the side of my truck. "We ought to roll."

"I agree," Samuel says. "Like I said, I think Do Trieu is no longer an issue."

"What about the big guy in Vietnam?" I ask, guiding the truck toward I-Eighty-Four to catch the freeway back toward Portland. "Will he hire one of his other contacts here to come after us?"

"Maybe," Samuel says. "But I am thinking that Lai Van Tan might not have enough time. By the time he gets someone new on us, we will be home and setting up a defense there. That means you will have to watch your back here, stay vigilant."

"Always do," I say. "Especially of late."

"I am so sorry about all this, son," Samuel says softly and for the umpteenth time.

"Please don't say that. We're family."

"I am sure that once he knows we are back in Saigon, and he will within a couple of hours, he will put all his efforts there. Still, you must be on your guard."

I nod. "Okay, what now? Am I dropping you two off at your apartment or are we going back to my place?" I'm hoping the latter.

"I will need to be at my apartment so I can get ready in the morning for the ceremony," Mai says.

"Son, I know you are a police officer and all that, but I would feel most comfortable if we are all together tonight. I suggest we go to our apartment and stay there. It will give us a little more time together and Mai can prepare for her graduation. Mai has to be at the school tomorrow two hours before the ceremony. So you and I can drop her off there and we can go back to your house so you can change clothes if you want. Then we can go back to the university early to get a good seat."

I thought I was good at compartmentalizing, but Samuel is a master. He can fight, do a one-man reconnaissance, talk about Lai Van Tan's revenge, and then plan for Mai's graduation, all without breaking a stress sweat. Don't know how he does it, but I would think it's a good way to keep one's blood pressure in check. Mine, I'm sure, is blipping past red and into the near-stroke zone.

"The ceremony is going to be outside," Mai says, excitedly. "Under the trees in the Park Blocks. It should be very beautiful."

"I hope this wind dies down by then," I say, after a gust pushes my truck partially into the next lane. Fortunately there's no vehicle next to us. "Maybe after we drop Mai off tomorrow, there will be time for me to show you how I have things set up at my school."

"Yes, yes," Samuel says enthusiastically. "I would enjoy that. What I saw, I thought was wonderful. In Vietnam, we train outside most of the time. If I am not too rude, may I ask how much a school like that costs?"

"About a half million dollars, not counting the contents. Of course, I don't own it. The bank does. I did some complicated loans to get it several years ago. It's been successful so I've paid off all but one of them. I'm hoping I can pay the last one off in about eighteen months. I'm really awful at bookkeeping so I have a woman who takes care of some of it, billing students, advertising, scheduling private lessons, and such." I nudge Mai with my elbow. "Hey, now that you've got a business degree, I could hire you to be in charge of promoting and looking into setting up a branch school." She smiles.

"I got her first, laddy," Samuel says, affecting an Irish accent that sounds strange with his Vietnamese one. "She is going to be working in the family business."

"That's what I mean. Remember, I'm family now," I tease.

"*Xin lỗi*, GI," Samuel says, which I assume is an expression left over from the Vietnam War.

"That's old slang for 'sorry about that, soldier,'" Mai confirms. "My dad's a funny guy." We ride in quiet for a moment as I negotiate past a large semi that's getting knocked about by the wind.

"I'm having so many doubts about my future in police work," I say. "Of late, the idea of resigning and just running my school sounds most appealing. Maybe opening one or two more. The martial arts is very much part of me. Police work... well, I just don't know any more. If I had to... kill again, I don't think I would come out of it emotionally." Mai touches my arm.

"I understand," Samuel says quickly, as if to help me from floundering further. I'm sure he understands what I'm going through. "I think it would be a good life for you," he says. "You can do much good for people teaching the martial arts."

"Yes." I take the off-ramp that will take us to Mai's apartment.

"And by the way," Samuel says, "You are sleeping on the couch tonight."

"Father!" Mai blurts.

*

It's nearly eleven o'clock by the time we get to Mai's apartment building. We're quite the bedraggled sight as we walk through the lobby. Fortunately, no one is checking their mail boxes or sitting on one of the couches this time of night.

In the apartment, Mai changes Samuel bandages and applies fresh Neosporin to my scratch and hers. Samuel retrieves a plastic bag of Cinnabons from a cupboard, apparently his food of choice when he isn't eating Vietnamese *phở* and sets them on the kitchen table. He gestures for me to sit. I can't even remember when I last ate, so I hungrily devour the sweet treats that any other day I wouldn't touch.

Although we have much to talk about, Mai goes about quietly making a bed for me on the couch, as Samuel and I eat in silence at the table. It feels most pleasant and natural to be simply enjoying each others' presence in silence. Must be a Vietnamese thing; I like it.

After what must be ten minutes, Samuel ends the quiet with, "Have I showed you my teacup trick, Sam?"

I sputter a laugh, and then laugh even harder when Mai says, "Yes, you have father. Now give it a rest." Samuel chuckles mischievously.

"I think you will like Saigon," Samuel says around his Cinnabon.

"So is it Saigon or Ho Chi Minh City?"

"It is both. Many people in the city still call it Saigon from the old days. But it was officially renamed Ho Chi Minh City when the war ended. Many people use the names interchangeably."

"I am anxious to see it," I say, shooting Mai a look. She fires back a smile as she heads toward the kitchen.

"It's very hot and quite noisy with all the motorcycles, trucks, and blaring horns," Samuel goes on. "But all that eventually becomes background music, like a movie soundtrack. Food is always being cooked somewhere—in houses, apartments, restaurants and on the sidewalks—delicious smells permeate the air twenty-four hours a day. The tension that was so thick during the war years is gone from the streets as well as from the people. Now there is a sort of frantic urgency, at least in Saigon, to catch up with the rest of the world. As a Caucasian, I only occasionally have problems; I am even accepted by most of the old soldiers who fought with the North Vietnamese Army."

"But father, many strangers don't even know you are not Vietnamese," Mai says, pulling out a chair at the table. She looks at me as she sits. "He speaks Vietnamese without an accent and he acts like a native; he almost looks like one."

"I do not have problems where we live. I have been there so many years that most do not remember when I was not part of the community. I am fortunate to have many dear friends."

"What do they think of your martial arts?" I ask.

"I do not show the totality of my ability. I have a few students I teach, but I never show them all that I have learned either."

"Like your mind reading and your speed?" I ask, sounding like a white belt, and feeling like one, too. I've never before felt so humbled and awed just sitting in someone's presence. I don't feel intimidated, though I know he could clean my clock before I could finish asking the time. The word aura is so new-age-hippy, but there really is something that radiates from him. Not all the time, but much of it.

"My teacher knows, of course, and so does my family. But I keep it secret from others. In some ways Saigon is like the Old West. There is always some gunslinger out to test you."

"Gunslinger?" Mai frowns.

"Other martial artists who want to see how good you are," he explains to her. He looks back to me. "Since I am Caucasian, they would be most anxious to test me. So I try to... what is the phrase? I try to fly under the radar. I teach a few students and I study with my Chinese teacher, Shen Lang Rui, whenever his health allows. He makes me feel like a beginner, a very slow beginner."

"Slow?" I chuckle. "I've never seen anyone move as fast as you."

"Yes, I am fast. But Shen Lang Rui has surpassed fast."

"Surpassed?"

"I can show you a few things now—"

My cell rings.

I look at the wall clock: Eleven thirty. "Who would be calling so late?" I dig my phone out of my jeans. Don't recognize the number. Maybe I won't answer it... Something tells me I need to.

"Yes?" Sirens and the unmistakable sound of a police radio.

"Detective Reeves?" Female voice, authoritative.

"Yes. Who is this?"

"Officer Lisa Ann, Unit Eight Forty-Two." So many new officers now; I've never heard this name before. "Reeves Bushido Academy is yours, correct?"

"Yes, it's my school." My heart rate doubles. "What's wrong?"

"Just a moment," she says. She yells something. "I'm back. Sorry. Detective, the building, the Reeves Bushido Academy, you own it, right?"

"Yes, I told you. What's going on, Lisa?"

"Sorry. Kinda crazy here. It's in flames. Totally. The north and west walls have both collapsed. I'm sure it can't be saved."

*

"You the owner?" the fireman shouts over the sound of police radios, idling fire truck engines, shouting firefighters, wind. The fire.

Amazing! The sound of a building completely consumed by fire really does roar. Who would have thunk? *Who would have thunk?* That has always annoyed me when people say that about something. Why say thunk? What does it add or subtract to the question? It just sounds stupid. And why does the fire department need all their flashing lights and spotlights shining on the fire? Don't they realize that the fire itself puts out a lot of light? They're just wasting power. They need to think green. Who would have thunk it?

I shake my head to chase away the monkey bouncing around in my brain. Mai is holding onto my left arm and Samuel is sort of leaning into me on my right. Have they been here the whole time? Of course. We all came together. Who would have—

"Sam?" Mai's voice.

"I own the martial arts school." Was that my voice? I think it was.

"What was that?" The fireman shouts, lifting his sooty helmet up a little to expose an ear. I look away from him and look intently at the fire.

Every time my grandfather and I went camping, he'd say the same thing as we built a campfire. "Indian say, 'White man foolish. Build big fire and stand far away.'" Then grandfather would rub his hands together and scoot up to our small campfire "But Indian man smart. Build little fire and sit up close." He'd laugh at that every time. I was too young to get it. I do now.

Mai tugs lightly on my arm; I know she's looking at me; why doesn't she look at the fire? It's more entertaining. "Yes, it is his building," she shouts. "He is a policeman, too."

"You Portland PD?"

"Yes," Mai shouts when nothing comes out of my mouth. "He is."

"Okay. Listen, you folks can't be inside the lines. There's a lot of flying debris, some of it quite large. A couple of parked cars have already been lit up."

On cue, a loud pop from inside the carnage. We all jump except for the fireman, who hunches his shoulders a little and twists around to look. After a moment, he turns back to us. "We think we got it contained enough not to spread to the attached businesses. *Think,* is the operative word right now. I'm sorry, but in this wind your place took off fast. We can't save it."

"Too soon to know what started it?" I hear myself ask, amazed at how calm I am. I should be feeling something, but so far, nothing. *Nada.* It's like my mind can't focus on it, can't accept it. Maybe this is the proverbial straw that broke the ol' camel's back. I can't absorb any more *dukkha*. I've had my fill. *Dukkha* schmukka. So I'll think of other things.

Like how gorgeous Mai looks in the firelight.

"The cops didn't tell you?" the fireman yells over a particularly loud surge that hurtles flames an easy one hundred feet into the air.

When I don't answer, Mai asks, "Tell us what?" shielding her eyes with her palm.

"Witnesses saw two people throw something burning through the front window. I'm guessing Molotov cocktails. Somebody mad at you?" He alerts on his handheld radio, listens, and says into it, "Will do." To us: "Excuse me, I got to go talk to the chief. You people should move on back behind the lines."

Mai and Samuel take my arms and guide me toward the yellow tape. At first, my slug-of-a-brain thinks I'm walking through hip-high mud but as we duck under the yellow tape, my head clears so abruptly that it's almost as if I just woke up. In front of us is the fire, its heat intense even at fifty yards away. All around us, rubberneckers, twenty or thirty of them, their orange-lit faces alive with the thrill that is my loss. Assholes.

"Hey," a short, sweatshirt hooded street person barks with indignation as he peers around Mai's shoulder. "I was standing here first. I can't see now. You think I'm nothin', don't juh? Who do you think you are? Big shots, huh? Is that who you are?"

Without releasing my arm, Mai glances at the man. "Let me introduce myself. I'm the person who is going to knock you on your ass if you say another word."

"Hey, I like that," the shaggy man says, smiling with a mouthful of bad teeth. I do, too. "You got spice. Lots of spice."

He looks her up and down. "You wanna buy me a drink or sumtin'?" Mai turns all the way toward him, as do I. "We could…" His smile disappears as he alerts on something behind us.

"Detective Reeves," a female officer greets, walking up.

The street person slinks back, disappearing behind the crowd.

The officer stands silhouetted against the dancing flames that are busily consuming a chunk of my life, my future plans. When I don't say anything, she says, "I'm Officer Lisa Ann, the one who called you. I'm sorry about this; it must be awful for you. It's a hell of a blaze. We've never met, but I've heard of you, especially all the shit you been in over the last few days. That capture of Barry Clarkson was really something. Heard you really put the hurt on him. Heard he was a really big one and—"

"What's up," I say just to shut her up. She's obviously a rookie and uncomfortable talking to me. I've gotten a lot of that over the years from officers, especially new ones. Usually, I joke with them to put them at ease but right now I don't care about making her comfortable. I watch the fire as she prattles on in her affected police voice.

"I got a street cleaning crew," she begins, "who at eleven fifteen saw two people throw something through your window, something burning. The crew guys said they heard a fairly loud whoosh, then saw flames. They were too far away to get a good description of the perps but their sense was that they were males. Said they fled around the corner after."

I just watch the flames, which are starting to subside now from the crisscrossing spray of water hoses and the hard, cold fact that there isn't anything left to burn. The wind is at our backs, blowing the smoke away from us. The occasional gust is strong enough that we have to brace ourselves.

"Detective Reeves?"

I lift my eyebrows at her.

"You think this might be related to your shooting?" When I don't say anything, she asks, "Any suspects in mind?"

I watch the fire for a moment. *Any suspects in mind?* Good one.

"Yeah," I say. "Half of Portland."

After the officer leaves, the three of us stand silently and watch the fire dwindle. The north, west, and east walls are gone, leaving the south wall standing alone as water runs down its charred remains and dirty smoke whisks away in the wind. The inside of my school is now nothing more than black, smoldering sludge. An inner wall, I think it's the one that separated my office from the training area, is only partially intact, but also charred and smoking, my observation window shattered.

Minutes pass, I don't know how many. "You have this joke in Vietnam?" I ask. "You want to make God laugh? Tell him your plans." Mai and Samuel nod without saying anything. "A couple hours ago I was telling you how much I love my school." I shake my head. "Now there's some irony for you."

Mai squeezes my arm and rests her head on my shoulder. Samuel has moved a step or two away, standing solidly against a strong gust, his arms behind his back, his graying hair blowing about. A strobing red light from a fire truck flashes across his face, illuminating his slightly lifted jaw, tight lips, and tear glistened eyes.

*

Jimmy's in my school and he's on fire.

His naked body drapes awkwardly over a stack of blue mats, fire all around, its burning tongues lapping at his blackening legs.

I don't remember shooting him but somehow I know I did. It's just the two of us here.

I'm standing helpless as the fire creeps up his thighs toward his bullet-riddled chest.

His mouth begins to move. "Sam? Sam?

"Sam!"

I feel myself sit up straight. Blinking, confused. Where's Jimmy? Where are the flames?

"Sam? Are you okay? Do you know where you are? You are here with us, father and me."

Mai's hand is on my chest and she's looking into my face. On the other side of her, Samuel. We're in my truck. I don't remember getting in.

"You slept for about an hour. We did not want to awaken you but then you started crying so hard." Her hand slips into mine, immediately comforting me. "I am so sorry about this, Sam," she says, looking out the windshield.

I follow her gaze. There are only two fire trucks now, their red lights still flashing, every strobe revealing the charred remains of my school. A blast of wind rocks the pickup. Although it's blowing the dying smoke away from us, the stench of wet and burnt dreams is gut wrenching.

"Everything in my life has changed this week," I mutter, mostly to myself.

We sit silently for a moment and then Samuel speaks. "Sam, Buddha said, 'Neither fire nor wind, birth nor death can erase our good deeds.' You are a good man and you have done much good in your life. You have done much good with your school. I am proud to call you my son. I know it is way too soon to see much of anything clearly, but you will. I know you will."

I nod and we sit in silence. After five minutes or so, I ask, "So I fell asleep again?"

"Second time tonight you have fallen asleep on me," Mai says, feigning concern. Then like a rapper, "What up wit' dat?"

That actually makes me smile. What else can I do? Run screaming into the night and jump off the Fremont Bridge? I've covered enough suicides off that tall one to know that it's a guaranteed skull popper. But I don't need to drive to the top to do it. Considering the way it's been going lately, I'll probably sleep walk to the top some night and fall off by accident.

"I want you guys to know," I say, leaning forward so I can see Samuel as well as Mai, "that I am most grateful for your support these last few days. You haven't exactly seen me at my best."

"Nor you us," Samuel says. "Understand that we do not always have people attacking us and shooting us."

"Well not everyday, anyway," Mai says. "Sometimes two whole days pass without... gun, what do you call it?"

"Gunplay," Samuel says.

"Yes, gunplay. Or kung fu fighting."

"Or arson?" I ask.

"Hardly any arson," Mai says.

"Attacks by tiger kung fu women in a massage parlor?" I ask.

"Occasionally," Mai says.

"Brawls in a porno store?"

"Yes," Samuel says, then says nothing more as he looks out the window. Mai and I snicker.

"Giant guys in overcoats in your bedroom?" I continue.

Mai chokes off her laugh and acts as if she is thinking. "Well, there was one time..."

"Okay, okay. Enough," Samuel says looking back at us, shaking his head, and fighting back a smile.

For a moment I feel a little better. "Let's go back to my place," I say, pulling away from the fire trucks.

"You okay to drive?" Mai asks.

I nod. Two blocks away the extraordinary loss hits me as if my school were a loved one. Which it is. *Was.* I struggle to hold back the tears, but they have a mind of their own.

I'm aware of Mai looking at my face, but she doesn't say anything. After a moment she looks back out the windshield, squeezing my hand a little tighter.

The only other sign of life on the street at three thirty AM is a lone cab pulling onto the lot of my favorite Seven Eleven, no doubt stopping for a coffee hit. I've stopped at that same store many times for a caffeine and sugar blast when I was exhausted from work and needed a jump start to teach a couple of classes. How many times over the years have I driven this route between my school and my house? How many classes have I taught? How many students?

I've put so much sweat and blood into my school, working hard to make it a good place where people can come and learn, and change for the better. I tried to create a place for students to gain knowledge of the human condition, theirs and others, a place where all of us can strive to find the best within ourselves. Most of my students recognize this and understand that the school is so much more than just punching and kicking.

Like many schools, we bow to the room when we enter and leave as a show of respect to the place where we change physically, mentally, and spiritually. I believe that even if it wasn't a rule to do so, most students would bow anyway. I even do it when no one else is around.

I'm a good teacher and I know I've helped my students in all kinds of ways. Likewise, they've helped me, taught me. We've all changed together in the school. Now it's gone.

"Sam, I know I can be annoying with my quotations…"

"Father, I don't think this is the time."

"Please, let me be annoying once more because time is short. We leave soon and you will mourn your loss for a while. These simple quotes are probably meaningless to you now, but please think about them in a week or so."

I'm too numb to care. If he wanted to shove a thumbtack in my forehead, I'd just shrug and tell him to push.

"These aren't Buddhist or Christian, but they could be. The first is by Robert Frost, who wrote, 'In three words I can sum up everything I've learned about life: it goes on.' I like simple thoughts like that. I read it in college before I went into the army, before I went to 'Nam. Then one day I thought about those words after my buddy's brains had been splattered all over my face during a firefight near Cambodia. And I thought about it while in prison over there. Frost got it right. Life either ends or it goes on. It is your choice.

"A great writer from early last century named Willa Cather, wrote a little ditty. I don't like poetry, but I like this one. It goes, 'Oh, this is the joy of the rose: That it blows, and goes.' That describes impermanence, you see, a big part of Buddhism. Right now, you are sad because your school and all that it meant just died. Granted, it died suddenly but it was always going to die someday. You know that, right? You would get a permanent injury and would no longer be able to teach. Or you would get too old to teach. It is safe to say that you would not be sad when a rose blew away because you knew all along that it would. But you believed that your school was permanent, although it never was. And now it is sad for you to accept that it was impermanent all along."

Samuel's right. I'm not ready to hear this right now. But I understand what he's saying.

"Good," he says. I turn to look at him, startled again that he knew what I was thinking, though I shouldn't be anymore. "Thich Nat Hanh," he says, "is a wonderful Vietnamese Buddhist. He says, 'Impermanence is good news. Without impermanence, nothing would be possible. With impermanence, every door is open for change. Impermanence is an instrument for our liberation.'"

We ride silently for a moment. "I understand, Samuel. And I promise I'll reflect on it later. But like you said, it's too soon right now, especially when we all still reek of smoke."

"Understood," he says. "Normally I would not be saying these things so soon, but the clock is ticking. On that note, here is one more thing, and it is also too soon but given the circumstances…"

"Shoot." I turn left onto my street.

"You like Mai, right?"

"Father, for crying out loud!"

I laugh that she knows that expression. "Okay, yes. I like Mai."

"You do understand that she will die, right?"

I sober. "I don't understand."

"And Mai, you do understand that Sam will die, too?"

Long pause, then almost imperceptibly, "No."

"You see? You understand that a rose will die, but it is hard to accept that another living thing, a loved one, is also impermanent. Because you cannot accept it, you suffer when it happens. But when both of you accept the impermanence of yourselves and the other, you do your best to make that person happy. Thich Nat Hanh says, 'Aware of impermanence, you become positive, loving, and wise.'"

I pull into my driveway, shut off the engine and look over at Samuel. "Thank you." And I mean it. I look at Mai, at her smile. She must be thinking the same thing I am. Samuel just recognized and okayed our relationship.

"What will happen now?" Samuel asks. "With the school, I mean."

"I'll talk with the arson guys in the morning and they'll take it from there. They'll look for witnesses, check if there are any closed-circuit video surveillance cameras mounted on rooftops, and so on. It was no doubt done by cop haters, someone upset about the shooting. So the detectives will likely take that angle."

"I see."

"What time is your graduation?" I ask. Mai is still holding my hand.

"Eleven, but I have to be at the school by nine. We are all going to be so tired today."

"We'll be just fine," I say, rubbing the back of her hand with my thumb. "It will be an honor to be there. But I have to go to the station first to talk with the investigators."

"I want to try one more time this morning to get an earlier flight," Samuel says. "I am afraid that Lai Van Tan will step up his efforts to get Kim and the others. I need to be there." He looks pointedly at Mai. "*We* need to be there."

She nods at him and looks back at me. Our eyes lock for a moment, each of us weighing the reality of obligation, separation, and hurt. "I understand," I whisper. She squeezes my hand.

CHAPTER TEN

"Keep your eyes closed as you become aware of your body... your head... your chest... your rear... your legs... your hands." Samuel's gentle, melodic voice has me floating in the room's darkness, drifting a little that way on one cluster of words, and a little this way on the next. "Feel... how the back of your left hand rests comfortably in the palm of your right one. For a moment... put your mind in that place where they touch... and feel the skin on skin... how the tips of your thumbs touch one another... feel where the edges of your hands... touch your belly.

"Now... become aware of the softness of the carpet we are sitting upon... the temperature in the room... the sound of the wind outdoors... the creaks of this house. Feel these things... hear these things... pull them into your senses."

His words stop and all is silent. A minute passes, an hour, I don't know. Don't care. Then Samuel's voice floats through the darkness to my ears.

"Breathe in... breathe out. Feel the sense of peace that has bathed your body and filled every inch of your being. Breathe in... breathe out. Take this wonderful sense of peace and well-being into your day.

"Now... open your eyes and welcome the day."

I don't want to open them; I don't want to welcome the day. I just want to remain floating in the wonderful quiet, not thinking, not doing, just riding in on my in breath and riding out on my out breath. I just want to—

"Open your eyes, Sam." Samuel's voice is a gentle prod.

I do, blinking several times. I roll my shoulders and pop my neck to the left and right. Outside the wind is still howling although I didn't hear it at all during our meditation. Samuel and Mai sit on each side of me, their bodies motionless, backs and necks straight, hands resting one upon the other in their laps, their eyes open and looking at the floor a few feet in front of them. There is something almost eerie about how they sit so incredibly still.

I must admit that I peeked a few times over the last... whoa! No wonder I'm hurting. We've been sitting nearly three hours in the lotus position! That is, they've been sitting in lotus, crossed legged with each foot resting on the thigh of the opposite leg. I've just been sitting with my legs crossed like a school kid.

Mai moves first, then Samuel, both using their hands to gently untangle their legs before stretching them out on the carpet. "Good morning," Mai says sweetly, as if we had just awakened side-by-side in bed. I wish.

"Feel better, Sam?" Samuel asks, pushing himself into a standing position.

I struggle to get up, my muscles complaining stiffly all the way. I turn to help up Mai, but she's already standing, looking chipper.

"In fact, I do," I say. "I'm a whole lot stiff but I feel pretty good. Thank you."

When we walked into the house at four thirty, I commented groggily that sleeping for just a couple of hours would probably make us feel worse. I believed it, but mostly I wanted to be awake for what little time we have left together. That's when Samuel suggested that we all meditate.

"It is quite powerful," he said. "Most often you come out of it feeling refreshed as if you had slept. I once replaced sleeping with meditation for five nights in a row. Let me take that back. On the third night I slept three hours but that was the only time during the hundred and twenty hours. I worked during the day per my usual and trained in the evenings. It was a wondrous week of clarity of mind and focus. My energy level was the same as always, even greater at times. I do not know if I could have gone on longer but I plan to find out sometime."

When Mai said she wanted to meditate, too, I nodded, figuring I couldn't possibly feel any worse. So we plopped three sofa pillows on the floor and Samuel helped me get into the best position that my novice body could achieve. He turned off the lights and then, as he did in my school three days earlier, he began talking us through the meditation.

My mind wouldn't allow it, though. I couldn't stop thinking about my school: the flames, the smell, how the water from the hoses poured down the charred wall. My heart was racing and my muscles felt like I needed to stand and run, just run like a madman down the street. Samuel must have picked up on this because he very gently said, "Breathe, son. Just breathe and follow your breath."

In the beginning, the sounds of our inhalation and exhalation were out of sync, but soon we were in unison, as if the three of us shared one set of lungs. A thin bar of streetlight snuck through a couple of my warped blinds and fell across our laps, faintly illuminating our legs and folded hands, leaving our upper torsos mostly in darkness. Thirty minutes into the session, my back throbbed, my butt ached, my neck felt as if the bones were splintering, one leg fell fast asleep, and the other began cramping excruciatingly.

I started to get up, but a sudden thought held me fast. All week my life has been careening out of my control. Like in a bad car chase movie it smashed into fruit carts, garbage cans, knocked over cages of squawking chickens, love dolls, and ran over pedestrians. There have been times when I've wondered what's real and what isn't. Well, that's over. Right here, right now, sitting in this peaceful place, I'm going to retake my head. Yes, everything hurts, but as my first instructor used to say, "It's only pain." He'd shout this at the other white belts and me as we struggled to hold deep stances. "Pain is weakness leaving your body," he'd say. "Your mind is stronger than the discomfort and the hurt. Make those negatives unimportant. That cramp isn't going to break your thigh bone, it's not going to make you cough up blood, and it's not going to make your balls fall off and roll across the floor."

We all cracked up the first time he mentioned our balls, though we held fast in our wobbly stances. "See?" he said. "You forgot the pain for a moment and laughed. But nothing has changed, you're still in your stances. Could it have been your dirty minds that distracted you? I think so. So put that pain in perspective. It's not going to harm you. It just hurts. It's just pain. Wrap your brains around that concept."

It took a lot of classes, a lot of stance holding, and a lot of brain wrapping until I eventually did understand. It was then that I began to grow as a martial artist.

So as I sat on the carpet in my living room, in the dark, with my new family, I was able to put the physical pain in perspective. The loss of my school… well, it's too soon to put that into perspective; right now it hurts even more than all my body aches. Samuel's hypnotic voice and the controlled breathing helped a lot, though. It sort of sedated me and made me feel like I have some control. Of course when the full impact of losing my school hits, it might be a different story.

Okay, don't start thinking negatively again. When it hits, I *will* be in control. I will eat the pain, I will grow stronger from it, and I will carry on.

I hunch my shoulders and make big circles with my arms to splash in some fresh blood.

"Perhaps Mai can make something in your kitchen and I can show you a couple of ideas from my style," Samuel suggests.

"Really? Sure. Mai, do you mind? I've got eggs and English muffins."

"Not at all," she says, and immediately heads to the kitchen.

I look at Samuel and shake my head. "A few hours ago I watched my school burn and now I'm getting a lesson in my living room. Things just keep getting weirder and weirder."

"Through it all," he says, "your martial arts remain the constant."

So true, I think. Through thick and thin, and shootings and breakups, and public outcries, and my school burning to the ground, through all that, my martial arts are still here, still part of me. Is that Samuel's reason for wanting to show me something from his training? The timing is a tad incongruous for this, especially with Mai needing to be at PSU in an hour, but then everything lately has been friggin' incongruous.

"It's in your mind," Samuel says. "Your knowledge remains in your mind. Your real dojo, you see," he taps his head, "is right up here. It's your most valuable weapon."

"Better than Bruce Lee's nunchucks," Mai calls from the kitchen, with what sounds like forced levity. It's nice of her to try to make me feel better. A plus in her column. One of many, actually.

"I would not go that far, Mai," Samuel says, with a faint smile. "He was really good with those." Turning back to me. "Did you ever wonder where Bruce carried them? He would fight a couple dozen people, the last dozen with his shirt off, of course, and then suddenly he would reach behind himself—behind himself—and extract a pair of nunchucks. One could only imagine where he had been hiding them and how hard it must have been to kick with them there."

"Eeeeww!" Mai calls out.

Samuel rotates his shoulders a couple times, not indicating any discomfort in his freshly-shot arm. "Let me show you something that can help you move as fast as Bruce, maybe faster. It is from my style, Temple of Ten Thousand Fists."

For one monkey-brain instant, I imagine this a Norman Rockwell painting depicting a dad and son playing catch with a football out in the back yard while mom, seen through the kitchen window, prepares the Sunday dinner. Dad imparts some simple wisdom and the son is better for it. I like it.

"I'm going to throw a medium-fast jab at you. You block it and counter with a punch."

"Okay," I say, thinking that his medium punch is probably the same as my fast one.

Surprise! It really is medium-fast. I sweep it aside with my left palm and counter with a right cross, stopping it on his shirt.

"Good!" he says encouragingly, as if this were my first lesson. "Now, how can you make your counter a little faster? I know we were just moving medium speed, but how, besides simply moving faster, can you increase your speed?"

"I'd do it all with the same hand. I would block the same way I just did, and from whatever place I moved your punch, I'd counter with a backfist to your face."

"Yes, yes. Please show me. I will throw another jab, a little bit faster and you block and counter as you describe. Please do it fast."

He raises his fists into on-guard, and then without one iota of telegraph, snaps his jab toward my face, about as fast as Mike Tyson in his prime. What's scary is that I know he can move much, much faster.

I swat it aside and flow my sweep hand into a backfist to his face, stopping it an inch away from contact.

"Very good!" he says. "Good economy of motion. You did not use as much of your body as you did when you threw your rear hand. You did it all with a simple hinge action of your elbow and lots of fast-twitch muscle fibers, which you got from me. Now do it again, but this time engage your mind. Let me show you what I mean. Throw a jab at my face as fast as you can."

"Yeah, okay," I say sarcastically, since I know that my *fast as you can* jab is probably as fast as his *a little bit faster* one. I swallow my pride and thrust.

About five years ago, everyone on the PD had to attend a three-day class put on by our Explosive Ordinance Division. On the last day, the instructors blew up a few things to give us a sense of the power of different forms of explosives. While everyone loved the noise and the destruction, I was mostly impressed with the shock wave that slammed my body like a giant's open-hand slap and knocked me back a step or two.

I barely saw Samuel move just now, but I know he did because I felt an incredible wall of energy against my face, a little like that explosive shock wave during my police training. I also know because my fist is now six inches off to the side of his head, though I didn't feel him swat it, and because his index finger is barely touching the tip of my nose, sending feather-like tickles into my snot box.

The first time I saw Mai that day in my school, I at least had enough class to think *Holy shit!* instead of shouting it out loud like a construction worker. This time I blare "Holy shit!" in lieu of screaming like a little girl.

Mai laughs as she sets plates and utensils on the dining room table. "Well said, Sam. But you should know that that was not father's fastest."

I realize my mouth is hanging open. I shut it.

Samuel retracts his fist. "First, let me explain what I just did. And yes, Mai is correct. That was relatively slow."

"Somehow the word 'slow' doesn't fit anywhere in this conversation," I manage.

"I told you a few days ago that Temple of Ten Thousand Fists is based on speed. There are four levels, you see. First Level is what the student brings to his first class, his natural ability. Second Level is what he develops through hard training after a few years. Most people do not progress past that. The Third Level is what I just demonstrated, what I call 'igniting speed.'"

"You're telling me that there's a speed faster than what you just demonstrated?" He just said that but it's all a little hard to accept.

"There are two more," Mai says.

"Technically, one more," Samuel says, confusing me. "The Fourth Level. I have achieved it, but only a little. My teacher, Shen Lang Rui, has achieved it totally. He keeps telling me I move like a slug."

"Good Lord!"

"Yes, the Lord is good. Okay, let me explain what I just demonstrated to you, which was The Third Level, part one.

When you performed your block and counter, you used only the physical. When I did it, I used a little bit physical and a whole lot mental. Mostly I used what I call 'igniting.' Since you say you have had training in explosives, you might want to think of it as the blasting cap, the small explosive device that detonates a more powerful explosive, like dynamite."

"Actually," I say, "I wasn't *talking* about my explosives class. I was just *thinking* about it for a second."

"Oh," he says surprised. He looks at me for a moment, studying my face. "Interesting that I can sense your thoughts more clearly and more often than anyone else's." He shrugs, and adds offhandedly, "It is that bloodline thing."

I shake my head in a feeble attempt to make things less *Twilight Zone*. It doesn't help.

"Okay, son. Extend your fist out toward my good looks. Good. Now, instead of just swatting your hand aside and then backfisting you, I am going to think of the contact my swatting hand makes as a blasting cap. The instant, and this is critical, the absolute instant my flesh touches yours,"—his palm lightly swats my wrist—"the blasting cap explodes, which ignites the bigger bomb, me." He taps his head. "I explode, meaning my mind explodes and my body explodes. That is what I want you to do.

"Be careful that you don't first feel the contact, then think explode in your mind, and then hit. That is too slow. You must practice until you can do it all at once: touchexplodehit. Understand?"

"I think so."

"Okay, try it. I will jab, you swat it away and use the same hand to backfist counter. But remember, the instant your hand touches my wrist—the *instant* it touches me—that is the blasting cap, and you, grasshopper, are the bomb. *Feel* it explode in your chest and in your stomach. Ready?"

"Yes."

He jabs and I respond as directed.

"Very good!" Samuel says. "Very smooth. Not very fast, but nice and smooth and that is good. Okay, I will jab again, just a little faster."

He's been doing all this with just his good arm, while holding his wounded one behind his back, probably so he won't use it by mistake. He hasn't indicated that it's bothering him, but I can only imagine that it hurts. Scratch that. Considering that it's *his* shoulder, it's probably healed by now and he's just giving it a little rest.

He jabs more quickly and I sweep and backfist faster. But I get no encouraging comment this time. He jabs again, faster still, and I respond a little faster, too.

"Better, but you are matching my speed too much. That is because you are responding only physically. You must counter faster than my offense, and you will if your contact with me— *sets off*—your internal bomb." He has been progressively talking faster and faster. It's obvious he loves this and is still psyched by it after all these years.

"Use your mind to *feel* my arm when your sweep touches it. Yes, it is your hand that is doing the touching, but I want your mind to feeeel it. Feeeel it in your mind. Feeeelexplode. Feeeelexplode. EXPLODE!"

His jab moves like the flick of a snake's tongue. An instant later, my backfist stops a hair width from his nose.

"Yes, yes!" he laughs. "And look at you. You are smiling now. Why? Why the big smile, son?"

"Well," I stammer like a second grader basking in his teacher pleasure. "It felt pretty good." Geeze. Make that a first grader.

"It looked fast, too," Mai says, arms folded and leaning against the kitchen door facing. Her admiring eyes make my stomach feel all funny. Yup, a first grader.

"Yes, it did," Samuel says. "Very fast. The concept is at once easy and complicated, but you have the hang of it. Now you have to build on it. And you do that by practicing. You ever tell your students that? 'You must practice?'"

"A couple times."

"Good. Now, Mai said there were two other phases. She is correct, although one of them is the second part of The Third Level. In that one, you ignite off your offensive blows rather than your blocks. You hit the target, and that hit ignites you into another hit. Understand that it's much more than simply throwing multiple blows. When you engage your mind correctly, you ignite a chain reaction of explosions that leaves your opponent filling his trousers."

"Ha ha ha."

"May I demonstrate?"

"Uh, what?"

"Father, I think that might be enough for today, and remember your shoulder." Mai's tone is that of a warning. But for whom?

"It's okay, Mai," I say, with false bravado. "That is, if it's okay with Samuel's shoulder. I would like to see what I need to learn."

"I am fine." Samuel gestures for me to come forward.

I center myself on him. "What do I do?"

The old man doesn't assume any kind of position of readiness but just stands casually as if waiting for Mai to call us to breakfast. "As Bruce Lee says in *Enter the Dragon*, 'Hit me.'"

"With?"

"Whatever you want. Oh, I forgot to mention one thing. You might feel a sting."

Feel a sting. What does that mean? Oh man. If Mai wasn't standing there I'd tell him to forget it; but she is, and she's pretty.

I snap a fast roundhouse kick at his midsection.

Just as I expect my foot to land with a controlled tap, an invisible wave presses me backwards, staggering me I don't know how many steps. My vision, all of my perception, is suddenly distorted into swirling colors, sounds of torrential rain, and a sense of something sucking my strength. Most frighteningly, I'm inexplicably overwhelmed by a sense of absolute, total helplessness. Then it's over. The wave, or whatever it was, is gone. But now I'm falling backwards...

"You okay, son?" It's Samuel's voice. He asks twice, I think.

"I..." It's as if I'm emerging from a dream. I feel someone gripping my arm. Samuel's hand comes into focus. Holding me so I don't fall?

"Father! I told you that you had shown him enough." It's Mai's voice. I think that's her gripping my other arm. "Sam? Sam, are you okay?"

There's got to be at least a hundred Alka-Seltzer tablets fizzing in my brain, and my body feels limp, drained. They lower me onto a dining room chair.

"I... I think I'm okay." I look up at Samuel. "I couldn't see what you did." I run my hands over my chest and legs. "I sting all over. I... I feel so tired."

"You will be okay in a minute or two," Mai says, glaring at Samuel and patting my shoulder. "Father's energy drew your strength from your body so that it would be hard for you to hit him back. He hit you many times, maybe thirty, but of course he controlled the blows so they did not penetrate your body; they just touched it lightly."

I'm looking at her, listening, thinking that she could be describing how the flowers grow in the spring. How can she be so unemotional about this. I mean—shit!

"Each one fed the next one," she continues. "And the one after that. They all took from your energy. Because he ignited without penetrating his blows into your body, you feel just a sting, instead of feeling damaged bones and tissue. Also, because he did not make hard contact, he did not demonstrate it as fast as he can when actually hitting hard. You understand?"

The fizzing in my head is subsiding. I look at Samuel and wonder, for a second, maybe five seconds, if he might be an alien. "Not as fast as you can? But I couldn't see what you... I only saw a blur."

"Oh yes," Samuel says, sitting down on the other side of table. "Like rain that falls so fast that you can't see individual drops but yet you get soaked? Did you hear the rain?"

"Yeah, something like that," I say. My energy seems to be returning.

"Someone said that to me once," he says. "I thought it was pretty cool." He lifts a bowl. "Ready for some eggs?"

I take the bowl and set it on the table. "I don't feel like eating right now." I look at him for a moment, wondering where to begin asking questions. I settle for an easy one. "To have hit me so many times, you must have used your bad arm."

"Oh no, it is not ready yet. I do not want to hurt it more. I used my right arm and my feet."

I'm shaking my head in disbelief. "But if that's the Third Level..."

"Yes, yes. The second part of the Third Level." Samuel is as bubbly as a cheerleader.

"Then what in the name of all that's holy is the Fourth?"

Mai laughs as she sits down holding the coffee pot. She begins filling our cups. "Want father to show you?"

I hold up both palms and shake my head in wonder. "I'd rather have an acid enema."

Samuel throws his head back and roars with laugher.

"What is an enema?" Mai asks.

"Samuel? Care to explain it to your daughter?"

His laughter sputters to a stop. Then he looks at Mai's puzzled face and cracks up again. He eventually manages a choked, "No."

"So what is The Fourth Level?" I persist, after he recovers.

Samuel sips from his cup. "I cannot demonstrate it because I am not always successful with my ability to control it as can my teacher. I am still a beginner, you see."

"Sam," Mai says. "The uncomfortable feeling you just experienced," she shoots Samuel a glare, "is what you feel when you are the victim of The Fourth Level. Except you feel it ten fold. That is the right word? Ten fold?"

"You mean ten times what I just felt?" I ask incredulously. "That buzzing in my head and the intense weakness? Ten times *that*?"

She nods. "Do not forget to include the effect from the penetrating blows. It is a most strange and painful effect."

I shake my head that I'm not understanding.

"It is still hard for me to comprehend all of it," Samuel says. "Maybe Shen Lang Rui is being deliberately vague right now because he feels I am not ready, that I am still too much of a white belt to grasp it. What I do understand is that there might not be any actual hitting going on at all."

I look at him for a moment. "I don't get it. The person feels ten times what I just felt, and I felt like crap warmed over for a few moments, but he may not be getting hit at all?"

"Yes, that is, in the normal sense of how we think of hitting." He bites into an English muffin, as if to stall for a moment to decide how he wants to continue. "I can tell you that when I have done it, and I've done it only twice with a training partner under Shen Lang Rui's guidance, that I'm not positive if I..." He looks at Mai as if wondering if he should continue. She nods. He looks back at me, takes a deep breath, and says, "I'm not positive if I actually moved, you see. If I actually punched and kicked at all, physically that is."

I'm shaking my head, looking, I'm sure, as dumb as a horse.

Samuel leans forward. "It is all in the power of the mind, you see. Using a part that is rarely tapped."

"So the hits are... what?"

He looks at me for a moment, then in a whisper, he says, "*Willed.* The ignition and explosion and the hits... happen through thought."

Mai nods, looking at me as if we were talking about a ghost sighting. "It is really weird."

I look first at Samuel, then at Mai, then at Samuel again.

Samuel meets my eyes for a long moment, he's wide-eyed, as if he too is in awe of what he just said. A few seconds pass before he blinks a few times and straightens his posture. He looks at his daughter. "Mai," he says. "We need to get you to the apartment so you can get ready."

*

I dread each passing minute that ticks me closer to when Samuel and Mai have to leave. My Timex has become my enemy, and with my grip on my truck's steering wheel at ten o'clock and two o'clock, my watch is right under my nose, ticking and taunting me, ticking and taunting... . Adding to my misery is that just before Samuel and I left Detectives, he called his airlines and managed to get an earlier flight, one leaving at five PM this afternoon. This afternoon! Now every sweep of the secondhand brings me pain.

"How is it permissible for those two detectives to be so overweight?" Samuel asks. "And doesn't the name "The Fat Dicks" bother them?"

I chuckle. "Yes, they are overweight, about double what they should be. But they are two of the best we have. They're well-liked by every cop and most citizens. I'm grateful they're handling my shooting and Officer Mitchell's homicide."

"Will they get the arsonists?"

A wall of wind hits the side of the truck, nearly jerking the wheel out of my hands. "Man, this wind is getting worse," I say, looking out the side window at the whipping trees. "Yes, I think the arsonists will be caught. The Fat Dicks aren't handling the case personally. Two other detectives caught it and are working in conjunction with the fire bureau's investigators. But since it's all part of the same deal, The Fat Dicks will get all the reports when the investigation is completed."

"I see."

"Did you hear them say they've collected four rooftop video cameras? I'd bet they find even more of them. Hopefully, at least one will show the perps."

"You do not seem angry about the fire."

"I'm not sure what I'm feeling. Maybe my anger just hasn't surfaced yet or maybe I've reached an emotional saturation point."

"Or maybe it will come later. If it does, it is okay to be angry. But do not let it control you or eat you up. Be angry and then move forward. Too many people carry hate and anger their every waking moment. Those who did this to you probably do not know you, but they hate everyone and everything so much that they wanted to destroy part of you."

"Oh yeah, the police always have their haters. It's part of the job. Partly it's because we have the authority and partly because of whatever they have going on inside of them."

He nods. "You remember in the park when I told you about *dukkha*? Suffering? These haters are suffering, too. And because they do not understand it, because they do not know how to fix themselves, how to stop the suffering, they hurt others. Sometimes they internalize their hate so much and so intently that it drives their behavior. Hurting others is their comfort food. But it only gives them comfort for a moment, and then their hate begins to build again. Buddha said, 'There is no evil like hatred.'"

"Never thought of it that way," I say. "But I think you're right."

"Yes. Anyway, I enjoyed seeing where you work."

After we left my house, Samuel and I dropped Mai off at her apartment and then raced to the Detectives Office.

"I just wish there had been time to show you all the floors, like the firing range, the self-defense area, weight room, and a bunch of other things." I chuckle. "Man, I would have loved for our defensive tactics instructors to have seen you do something."

Samuel smiles shyly.

"But at least you saw a little of the floor that I work on."

"You have done very well with your life, son. I am proud of you."

"Thank you." It feels good to know he is okay with my choices. "I'm not sure what I'm going to do now, but I have an idea."

"You might come to visit in July?"

"I'm thinking about taking a leave of absence for a few months, in part to think about what I want to do, and to go to Vietnam to see you. But first I have all kinds of court proceedings to go through. If they all conclude by July, I'll take a leave. If not, I'll take a vacation and come over for ten days or so."

"That would be very good. You said, 'To see *you*.' Me?"

"Of course."

"You want to see anyone else?"

"I want to meet your wife, your other daughters."

"Uh huh."

"Okay, okay. I know what you're getting at." I clear my throat, which doesn't need to be cleared. "Time is short…" I take a deep breath, which I really do need. "I'm not getting a clear read on what you think of Mai and me? Our feelings, I mean."

Samuel turns from me and looks out the side window. Ten seconds pass. Twenty seconds. Thirty. He turns back. "I'm okay with it."

That sounded pretty darn positive. It didn't sound like an I'm-not-sure kind of an 'I'm okay with it.' It sounded more like an "I'm-fine-with-my-son-and-daughter-liking-each-other kind of 'I'm okay with it.' I hope.

"You are?" I ask. That was lame.

"Yes, I am," Samuel says.

That sounded really positive.

"It was."

"Then why—" Wait, he just responded to something I thought.

"You're right."

I shake my head. "Uh, okay. Anyway, why did you take so long to answer?"

"Just screwing with you."

I laugh.

"It is the father's right, especially since I'm the father to both of you."

I laugh again and so does he.

I'm a little more relaxed, but not much. "Listen, this is a little awkward, to say the least, but again, time's running out. When Mai came into my school, I was awed by her looks. I'm sure most guys are. But five minutes into our conversation, she... I don't know what it was, what to call it. She just overwhelmed my head. I felt this incredible, overpowering draw to her."

"You 'got hit with a lot of bricks,' as Mai said."

I chuckle. "Yes."

"Like in *Jerry McGuire,* when Rene Zellweger says, 'You had me at hello.'"

"Something like that. My heart hasn't stopped hammering since I met her. Now it's hurting more and more every time I look my watch." I slow to let a car into my lane. "*Cosmo* says that—"

"The magazine?" he asks, with surprise.

"Long story... *Cosmo*... uh, I forgot what I was going to say. Man, I sound like a dumb teenager."

"Not at all," he says smiling. "Well, maybe a little. But love, especially love at first sight is not rational. Some say it is not valid, either. Benjamin Disraeli, a writer back in the eighteen hundreds, wrote: 'The magic of first love is our ignorance that it can never end.'"

"Gee, thanks. That's pretty negative."

"I am trying to help you keep an open and realistic mind, which is hard when that same mind is enamored."

Another blast of wind pushes my truck, this time toward a minivan parked at a meter. It's starting to mist now too making the day feel like early January instead of late May. We're almost to the University. "I hope the rain holds until after the graduation."

"You did not hear this from me," Samuel says. "But I told Mai the same thing."

"What do you mean?"

"You did not hear it from me, right?"

"Right. You told Mai what?"

"She told me you affected her the same way, except she did not say anything about *Cosmo*. I have never seen her read that one. I have seen her read *Black Belt* magazine, though. And one out of the Philippines called *Knife Fighter*."

I laugh at that.

"Anyway, I told her the same thing I just told you."

My heart does a triple beat. "No shit! I mean, really? What did she say?"

"What is this, high school? This is for you two to work out. I just hope you both tread softly."

"I promise. I certainly don't want to hurt Mai, and I don't want to be hurt either."

"Yes, a good goal."

"We're here," I say, as we near the first of many campus buildings. "I'm not even going to try to find a meter on the street." I pull into the structure, pay the attendant, and begin circling to find a slot.

"There's so much I want to talk to you about," I say, repeating what I've said to him before. "Your war experience, what you did, what you saw, how you were captured. How you survived."

"We will talk much, son. When you come over. And don't forget there's email. Look, there's my rental, the Toyota. Mai used it to get here so we could spend some time together."

I make one more upward loop. "There's a spot," I say, guiding my truck into the space. I turn off the key. "I'm anxious to meet your family."

"They will like you. You have a stepmother and two half sisters. Have you thought of that?"

"Only a little. There's been so much going on, so much to absorb. But I really want to know everything about my new family."

"You will. And you will be fascinated with my teacher. He is quirky."

I laugh, as I open my door.

"What?" Samuel says, as he climbs out. He looks at me over the roof. "You think I'm quirky, too?"

"You are who you are." I try hard not to *think* the word 'yes.'

"Well said!" he says, as we begin walking toward the stairs. "Very Zen-like."

The howl of the wind grows louder as we descend the cement stairwell to the sidewalk exit. "I wish Mai's mother could be here for this," Samuel says, more to himself than to me. "She worked very hard so Mai could go to this school. She is beyond proud." He extracts his cell phone and holds it up. "But at least I can take photos and email them to her as the ceremony is happening. I am a techie, you see."

I laugh. "We left in such a hurry this morning that I didn't even think of grabbing my camera. I'm sorry."

"No sweat. This one takes good photos. I will call her as soon as the ceremony begins and give her a running commentary."

I can just barely hear his words over the wind wailing through the stairwell's sidewalk entrance as we go down the last set of stairs to the ground level. "Damn! Do we really want to go out there?" I ask rhetorically.

We stand in the cement doorway for a moment, watching what must be at least a forty mile-per-hour wind gust push an assortment of papers, leaves, and a trash can lid along the sidewalk. Another wind rush, smaller than the last, sends an orange traffic barrier sliding along the closest lane until it slams into a gray Volvo parked at a meter, jamming itself under its axel. It doesn't help that Broadway, a four-lane street bordered by five-story campus buildings, accelerates the wind even more. Overhead, a skywalk that stretches over the street seems to act as a giant musical reed producing an eerie, almost constant banshee-like moan. To our right, two students dressed for graduation, hug a lamp post, laughing hysterically as their black robes flap out behind them like Batman's cape.

Abruptly, the wind and the mist stop, except on the roof of the beige Science Building across the street where a maverick wind current whips and cracks the American flag. High above it, ugly black clouds agitate, darkening the noon day into ominous twilight.

*

Two hundred or so ready-to-party graduates, wearing black gowns and caps, perch anxiously on chairs before a portable stage that has been erected on the grass of the tree-lined Park Blocks that borders the campus on its west side. On the stage are the usual array of university dignitaries, a podium and a twenty-foot high red-curtained backdrop with "Portland State University" occasionally readable in its wind-churned folds. Hundreds of excited families and friends have gathered on both sides and to the rear of the graduates, their mass extending over to the campus buildings on one side and along the sidewalk and under a grove of tall fir trees next to the street.

The wind dominates the party-like atmosphere, forcing people to shout to one another above the din. Most of the graduates hold their tasseled caps firmly on their heads, while others have given up and removed them. In the few minutes we've been standing under the trees, I've seen several loose ones take flight on wind currents, possibly never to be seen again. The last loose cap flew from the back row, cleared the heads of all those in front, shot over the open grassy space between the front row and the stage, looped up and over the podium, and nailed a gray-bearded man smack in the chest. This startled the elder, who had been introduced earlier as University President, Professor Charles Akins, and likely the hard and pointy corner of the cap hurt. Like a trooper, he laughed it off, rubbed his chest, and continued with his boring speech.

One of the large black box speakers sets just a few feet away from us, its volume so loud that Samuel and I can feel the sound from where we're wedged between a giant-trunked fir tree on one side and a pride of massive young men, who must be football players, on the other. Twice, female graduates—I assume they're females since the gowns and caps make it difficult to know for sure—have waved to one of the big boys. Whenever a player returned the gesture, his buddies teased him mercilessly.

I'm guessing the graduates will file up the steps at the right of the stage, walk across to Professor Akins, who will likely stand at its center, and receive their diplomas from him. Since we're to his left, we're in a perfect place to get some good photos of Mai crossing to get hers.

Because everyone looks the same and there are so many, we have yet to spot her. With the last name Nguyen, we're guessing that she is seated somewhere in the middle. Earlier, Samuel snapped several shots of the graduates filing in and sitting, and sent them via cyberspace to his wife. He has been on his cell constantly since we worked our way over under these trees talking excitedly with Kim in Vietnamese, which has drawn a couple of curious looks from people around us. It's fun to see him having such a good time; he and Kim have looked forward to this for several years.

His happy face disappears into tension. He listens intently for a moment to whatever Kim is saying, he says something to her, and listens again. His face jerks toward me as if startled, then looks away quickly and he says something else into the phone.

"Samuel? What's going..."

He listens a moment longer, utters a single word, then lowers the phone.

"What? What is it?"

He takes a deep breath—for courage?—and leans in close to my ear. "Do you remember when I mentioned Lu, Kim's brother?"

I think that's what he said. Between the wind and the professor's drone of a speech blaring from the big speaker next to us, hearing is nearly impossible. I don't know how he can hear his wife on the phone.

"Lu?" I say into his ear. He nods. "The one who is getting some inside information about Lai Van Tan's organization?"

A simultaneous break in the professor's speech and a quieting of the wind allows me to hear. "I have been talking with him and Kim everyday keeping them abreast on everything that is happening here. Lu has been very busy talking with his contacts in and out of the organization. He just called Kim on her other cell and told her..." Samuel pulls away from my ear and looks across the sea of graduates. He swallows hard.

"What is it? What did he say?"

"It is my fault," he says. "I am so sorry I brought this to you."

"I don't understand."

He looks at me and takes another deep breath. "Lai Van Tan ordered Do Trieu to burn your school." His eyes drop. "I am so foolish to have thought we had intimidated him into stopping."

I'm stunned. "It was Do Trieu's people?"

"Yes. I am so ashamed."

A wave of anger washes over me, fueling my muscles. I look toward the stage, though I can only see my school in flames. My fists clench on their own. The arsonists weren't cop haters after all, but organized thugs sent on a mission initiated half way around the world. I don't know why but that bothers me more. I want to hit something, somebody.

"Sam, it was my responsibility and I will take care of your loss."

"Do Trieu," I wheeze. "But why burn my school. What does that have to do with—"

"Revenge. It shows how far Lai Van Tan is willing to go to get it. You are not safe and neither is my family at home. You must take great care until I can get all this under control. The only way I can do that is by getting home and doing what needs to be done. When it is settled there, the situation will end here."

Just as I start to ask him what he means by *"doing what needs to be done,"* a wind gust rushes through the Park Blocks, staggering all who are standing, launching a dozen or so graduation caps into the air, and nearly toppling the stage backdrop before scrambling stagehands manage to secure it.

"Ladies and gentlemen, and esteemed graduates," the professor says into the mic after conferring briefly with another bearded man. "Because of the harsh wind and the rather portentous-looking rain clouds heading this way, we're going to dispense with the speeches and get right to the awarding of the diplomas." The graduates burst into raucous cheers and applause.

I take a deep breath and release it slowly. Me going ballistic right now won't solve or help anything. Besides, I've gone nutso enough this week to last three lifetimes. I need to show Samuel that his son is a grownup and has a handle on things.

"Samuel," I say, motioning for him to lean his ear in close. "Let's not worry about my school right now. There's plenty of time for that later. Let's just enjoy Mai getting her diploma." That wasn't bad. Now if I can just get my hands to unclench.

"Very good, son," he says with a faint smile. "Again, very Zen. Let us then be in the moment." His face sobers, no doubt struggling with the news about the arson. A shadow passes across his face. Whatever it is, it's brief because he again looks happy and as excited as he was earlier about being at the graduation. He snaps a photo of me, pokes the commands to send it to his wife, and then resumes talking with her.

I force my hands to relax. They do. I'm getting there, though I'm no match to Samuel who is a true master of compartmentalizing.

I again try to find Mai, but most of the grads in the center of the mass are still wearing their caps. A graduate waves from the far side. Could it be… The student removes his cap and waves frantically with it. No.

Up on the stage, the podium has been removed and a helper, struggling against the wind to hold a stack of diplomas, has joined the professor to assist with the distribution. As I suspected, the students form up on the right side of the stage and when called by the professor stroll across to receive their diploma. It's just beginning, but already friends and family in the large gathering are cheering, whistling, and applauding their loved ones.

Maybe it's the wind or the abrupt change in the program, but twice there has been confusion and corresponding laughter from the crowd when the wrong name was read so that the graduates had to do some awkward shuffling on the narrow steps. They're only up to the Bs.

Again I think I spot Mai among those still seated, but then one of the football players steps in front of me and blocks my view. When I can see again, I'm no longer sure where I thought I saw her.

Samuel is poking at his phone and looking perplexed. "Can you believe the luck?" he says close to my ear. "I lost my connection. I have called back twice, only to lose her again. The phones in Vietnam are poor to awful."

"Just keep taking pics and send them when you can get through."

"Yes, but I am concerned because the last thing she said was that Lu was calling again on her other cell. Maybe he has new information."

I'd guess the sustained wind has slowed to about twenty miles-per-hour now, although the occasional gusts are still hitting at least forty. Fortunately, the mist hasn't returned, but the clouds are looming near and darkening the setting with a twilight glow.

Those who have received their diplomas mingle near the stage to hug and shake hands with one another.

"Julie Anne Kingsley," the professor calls. "Stanly James Knight."

"We're getting close," I shout. "Look at the bottom of the stairs. Is that her? The tall one looking up at the stage?"

"Might be," Samuel says excitedly, snapping a picture. "If she would only look this way."

"Phillip R. Lake. Kathy Sue Losendale."

"I see her!" Samuel yells. "There, at the top of the step. Two or three people back."

"I think you're right. Mai!" I shout, but the wind drowns it out.

"David B. Miller."

Just to let us know she's still in charge, Mother Nature sends a strong wind gust to whip tree branches, billow gowns, and send more caps flying. The stagehands struggle to keep the backdrop upright. Just as quickly as the wind blast hits, it fades to a strong, steady blow. An even stronger current agitates the high tree tops. The students continue up the stairs and across the stage, all of them trying to control their flapping gowns and goofy square caps.

"Mary Lynn Murray. Matthew B. Nathaniel. Richard Evans Neil. Mai Li Nguyen. A'lyse Nace."

"There!" Samuel shouts and laughs, peering into the cell phone screen.

Mai ducks her head against the wind, with one hand holding her cap and the other pressed against the front of her gown, and moves laboriously across the stage toward Professor Akins. Several of the graduates applaud. She must be popular.

"Had her in my psyche class," One of the football players near me muses to his buddy. "Whew!" He fans himself with his hand.

"You wish, man," his buddy ribs. "You wish. I know her and she is way outta your sorry-ass league, dude."

I chuckle, feeling a little smug. Dream on boys. Dream on. Mai lets go of her gown and reaches for the diploma.

Her head snaps to the side. Red mist envelops the professor's distinguished face and white beard an instant before Mai slams into him, bounces back, and topples over the edge of the stage.

*

People running in every direction, screaming, shouting, falling. Those who have the presence of mind to prone themselves on the lawn are trampled, tripped over, cursed. Some stare transfixed at the Science Building rooftop. The wind surges hard, followed by a loud crash when the curtained backdrop, no longer supported by the stagehands, blows over. It must have struck the sound equipment because now loud feedback screeches from the giant speakers.

Samuel and I move as one, knocking the big football players aside as if they were hollow bowling pins. He's at least two strides ahead of me, screaming. Or maybe it's me screaming. Or maybe it's speaker feedback coming from the one closest to us, which has been knocked off the stage and down onto the grass. Samuel leaps over it like a gazelle.

About a dozen graduates surround Mai where she lay on the ground, all of them crying, holding onto each other.

One of them keeps shouting, "Whatthefuck, whatthefuck, whatthefuck…"

"Run!" I shout at them. "Get behind cover! Go!"

"Mai! Mai!" Samuel cries desperately over the roar of the wind and the god-awful sound emanating from the speakers.

The students don't move. "Go!" I shout again, pushing two of them.

Samuel, as if he doesn't have the strength to push through the students, drops to his knees in slow motion behind them. "Nooo! Nooo!"

All I can see through the black gowns are her legs, one splayed, the other folded awkwardly underneath her. "Get the hell out of here!" I shout. "He might shoot again!"

That snaps the students out of their collective trance, launching them in every direction. One clips my shoulder and nearly spins me around. Another, apparently blind with panic, runs smack into the edge of the stage, slamming it with her chest. She falls back into the grass, nearly landing on Mai, then jumps up, screaming. She dashes madly toward the trees.

I drop onto my knees next to Samuel. Through my tearing eyes I see Mai's legs, her twisted torso, her—my God! Her face. Gone. Maiiiiii…

Samuel leans forward onto his hands, his entire body wracked with heavy sobs. He punches the ground again and again. I should pull him away from this but I know he won't budge. Nausea hits me like a tsunami. I turn away to vomit, but I don't.

The screeching speakers are suddenly silenced and the gushing wind carries on it the sounds of wailing sirens and people shouting and crying. The mass of chairs where moments earlier hundreds of graduates sat waiting their turn to receive their diplomas, are now empty and askew, as people flee in ever direction. Some between campus buildings, and others along the street and sidewalk. A few crawl under parked cars. Farther down the lawn, a crowd of faces look in our direction. Are they crazy? Do they think they're safe? I need to tell them to—

"Father? Sam?"

What...?

"Father?" From behind me.

I twist around.

Mai walks slowly toward us from where Samuel and I had been standing under the trees, her movements measured, confused. Blood droplets cover her face and neck.

"Mai!" I cry, grabbing at Samuel. "It's Mai!" I pull him to his feet. "Look!"

"Mai?" Samuel says, turning. "How..."

I rush to her, engulfing her in my arms. "My God, Mai. We thought that person on the..."

Samuel's arms embrace us so hard that we all stumble and knock over a metal chair.

"They called my name by mistake," she says, her eyes wide, dazed. "They were supposed to call A'lyse Nace's first but they called mine... her head... her face..." She begins talking faster. "Just before I got to the stage, I saw you over by those trees. When A'lyse... I ran to be with you but everyone was panicking and running. You were not there."

Her arms are trembling so hard that it takes me two tries to capture her hand into mine. "A'lyse—her face, it..."

"We need to get under the trees." I say, looking up at the surrounding rooftops. "I think the shot came from atop one of those buildings."

"Young lady..." The university president walks toward us, legs wobbly, his black gown billowing out behind him. "Young lady, are you hurt?" His beard is more red than white and he is so pale I think he might faint at any moment.

Samuel, miraculously in control of himself again, touches the man's arm. "She is in shock, professor. We will take care of her. But you need to be seen by someone, to be checked over."

The old man seems oblivious to everyone but Mai, his dazed eyes struggling to focus on her.

"We need to get out of the field of fire," I say, looking back at rooftops. "Let's move over behind the trees."

The professor touches Mai's arm, as if confirming that she's actually there. "You were right behind the young woman who was… I thought you had been hurt, too."

"It was a mistake," Mai manages to get out. "They should have called her name first, Nace, then Nguyen. But they called mine when A'lyse was walking across the stage… and she got hit… instead of me."

"It's a school shooting, you see," the professor mumbles. "Columbine, Virginia Tech, now here." I don't believe that and I know Mai and Samuel don't either. "It was a loner. It's always a loner, isn't it." He looks at the stage and frowns. "I must reprimand the person responsible for doing such a poor job of organizing the diplomas and…" His voice fades as if he's lost his train of thought. He gestures with both hands at the chaos all around, "I'm not sure what I should do. I—"

Gunshot!

The professor spins about, arms still in mid gesture. When he comes back around his mouth is agape, and his neck looks as if it has been chewed by a pit bull.

He falls straight back, his head clunking the seat of a metal chair, the sound of a dull bell.

"Professor Akins!" Mai shouts.

I grab Mai and pull her to the ground. I think Samuel is down, too, but he's behind us so I can't see him.

Fresh screaming, fresh shouting. All those who had bunched up are now running into the trees and between the buildings.

"Go to the trees!" Samuel shouts, duck walking up along side us.

The professor's foot... tapping the ground, tapping so rapidly. *Taptaptaptaptap*.

"But father," Mai says, confused. "We have to help the professor."

"Go!" Samuel shouts. "Run!" He pushes Mai ahead of him. "To the trees. Hurry!"

The professor's foot stops.

Another gunshot. Dirt and grass geysers into the air besides me. Or did the sound follow the geyser? I'm not sure. Either way, I'm running to the trees.

Another shot; a chunk of sod rips up from the ground.

"Cut to the right," Samuel shouts. The three of us turn as one, just as another chunk explodes from where we would have stepped. We make it into the trees and bunch together behind a massive one, the trunk of which must be five feet in diameter. Fir cones crunch under our feet as we jockey to compress ourselves.

"It is coming from that direction," Samuel says, careful not to extend his pointing finger beyond the tree. "The shooter is high, maybe on the roof or on one of the upper floors of that beige building."

"I think you're right," I say. "And it's obvious he's shooting at us."

"Do you have your gun?" Samuel asks.

I shake my head. "At my house." When Samuel doesn't react, I say something that is neither the time nor the place, but it comes out nonetheless. "I wouldn't shoot it, anyway."

I don't know how to take his silence, but there's no time to worry about it now. Or to consider what I just said.

Mai pulls off her gown and drops it to the ground. She's wearing jeans and a blue hooded sweatshirt. Blood droplets dot the lower part of her pants and her black Nikes. Amazingly, her dazed demeanor seems gone. I grip her shoulders and look into her eyes, silently asking if she's okay.

She returns my look with icy determination. "We must stop them—now!" she growls. Yup, her spirit's back.

"Is everyone okay?" Samuel asks.

"Yes," Mai says.

I nod. Happily, my nausea faded when I saw Mai alive.

"Good. We must put all of our emotions on hold and focus on the task. Can we do that?"

"Yes," Mai and I say in unison.

The first officers to arrive take cover behind their police cars out in the street, behind trees, and stone trash containers. An officer near us shouts at three students who are lying prone a few feet away from Professor Akin's body, telling them to crawl behind one of the large trees. The professor's gown has blown over his face and flaps in the wind.

"You got any tissue?" Samuel asks Mai. "Try to clean off your face and neck so no one asks questions."

Mai digs into her jeans.

Samuel scans the roof of the beige Science Building, being careful not to lean out too far. "The shooter has got to be one of Do Trieu's people, maybe someone we have met. The man himself would not dirty his hands here. Mai put one of the females out of commission and I sent the black Mazda driver to sick call. That leaves four others, the white Mazda driver, the passenger Sam hurt, and the two women Sam and I fought at the massage parlor. There could be more, but that gives us four faces to look for."

"There's more police rolling this way," I say, watching two cars stop on a side street.

"We cannot get involved with them. Mai and I must get on that plane."

"Understood," I say. "Okay, let's think weapons. The sniper has one, a long-range rifle and maybe a side arm. People are likely to stay with the same type of gun so your woman at the massage parlor who had a Glock, probably has another. The guy in the Mazda had a Tec nine, until I smashed it. The driver of the white car might have had one but hopefully he's a coward and still running."

"Yes," Samuel says. "Lu says all have been trained in firearms."

I exhale some tension. "You're not supposed to take kung fu to a gunfight but that's exactly what we're doing."

Samuel looks at the roofs. "I think now that the police are here there will not be more sniping. We act now. You two go to… what street is that on the other side of that beige building?"

"Broadway." Mai and I say.

"Go to Broadway and watch for a black or white Mazda. Watch for any of Do Trieu's people in the crowd. I have my cell; you both have yours, correct?"

We acknowledge and I ask, "Where are you going?"

He quick peeks around the tree. "I want to go to that beige building." He looks back at Mai and, for a moment, seems to sag within himself. He grips her arms with both hands. "When I thought that was you," he whispers, his eyes tearing, "I…"

"I know, father," Mai whispers. She kisses his cheek. "Let us end this here. For Sam."

He smiles at her with his eyes, looks at me, nods, and then walks away along the tree line. When he is straight across from the Science Building, he steps out of the trees and walks casually through the scattered chairs, like a matador turning his back on the bull.

Except this matador is walking toward the beast.

*

Samuel keeps walking, acting as if he is heeding the police officers shouting at him to take cover. When he gets to the other side, he doesn't go into the building as I thought he would, but turns right and disappears around its far side into the breezeway between it and the next building over.

"He must have changed his mind about going in," I say.

"Who knows when it comes to father?" Mai says. "He can still enter the building from that side or he can walk between the buildings out onto Broadway."

"There are police all over here now," I say, looking around. "I'm thinking that Do Trieu's people wouldn't be in the crowd; they'd want to get out of the area quickly."

"Are we going to walk the same way as father?" There's no fear in her question. She just wants to know which way we're going.

"We could go north or south around the park but that would take way too long. Too many police on the other side of the stage; I don't want them to see me. The fastest way is your father's way: walk out in the open and through the chairs."

"Okay," she says.

"He went to the right so let's go to the left of the building and on out to Broadway. See if anyone is waiting to pick up the shooter, or maybe parked in one of the parking structures, or maybe... Hell, who knows? Let's just head that way."

Mai nods. "First, would you be so kind as to wipe the blood off me?"

"Of course." I back up until I'm against the tree, out of the sightline of the cops. Mai steps in close, placing her hands on my chest as I wipe her cheeks and forehead. "Some of it's starting to dry," I say.

She takes a fresh tissue, places it into my hand and moistens it with her tongue. She guides my hand up to her head.

"That's better," I say, removing the last smear from above her eyebrow. I grip her shoulders and look into her eyes. The terror that was there a few minutes ago is gone. In it's place, determination. "You good to go?" I ask rhetorically.

"I am fine. I can function. I will not let this hit me until later when I am on the plane. Then I will cry."

"Damn," I whisper, shaking my head. "I've never met anyone like you." She nods and places the side of her head against my chest.

I've seen at least three ambulances arrive, but the police are holding the crews back until the area has been declared clear. There's no hurry to get to the young woman and the professor, anyway. Thankfully, the officers are so busy with the crowd that they haven't paid us any attention or recognized me.

"Ready to go?" she asks.

I turn my jacket collar up to hide as much of my face as I can and tell Mai to cover her head with her sweatshirt hood.

We hug, then step out from behind the tree and take off in a sprint through the chairs. I try to watch the rooftops but it's hard because I'm trying not to trip over the chairs. I'm guessing the shooter is long gone. *Guessing* being the thing that makes being out in the open a whole lot crazy.

We're running as fast as we can, ignoring the chorus of shouts for us to get back behind the trees. We want to look like we're in a panic run. We stop just inside the breezeway out of sight from all rooftops, and take a couple of calming breaths. There's nothing like exposing yourself to sniper fire to get a good cardio workout.

"Damn!" Mai says.

"I agree."

"That wasn't smart." I jerk my head toward the voice, a young uniform officer crouching behind a large stone trash receptacle, his eyes wide with fear. I don't recognize him and hopefully he doesn't know me.

"Keep moving toward the street," he says, peering over the receptacle in the direction from which we came. "We got a situation here."

I want to say "No shit, Sherlock" but I bite my tongue.

Mai points to a set of double doors on our right as we walk quickly toward Broadway. "That one leads into the Science Building. Father could have used the side door on the other side to enter or he could have kept walking to Broadway and gone into an entrance there."

"So there are entrances on all four sides of all these buildings," I say, thinking out loud.

"Yes, and there is an entrance on the street side from the skywalk that connects this one to the parking garage across the street."

I look up, noting that it's basically a cement pedestrian bridge with cement beams for railings and no roof. The shooter could have moved up there to catch any of us who might come this way. Or maybe he wasn't shooting from this building roof at all. Too many possibilities.

We stop at the edge of the building and I lean out a little to look south. Across the street and about half way up the block, two uniform officers, probably assigned to watch the east side of the perimeter, brace themselves behind their marked unit. Even from this far away, their tension is palpable as they scan the many rooftops. A roadblock of police cars about two blocks north explains why there's no traffic on the usually congested Broadway.

It's deadly quiet: no jackhammers, no cars, no busses, no horns. Only the wind, moaning. Besides the two coppers standing by their unit, the only other people I see are three students with backpacks running across the street a block down.

"Something's going on," I whisper, when both officers tilt their heads toward their shoulder mics.

Mai leans out and looks where I'm pointing. The two officers turn as one, looking toward the breezeway at the other end of the building where Samuel would have come out if he had walked all the way through. They listen for a moment longer. Then, without saying a word to each other, they extract their Glocks and begin running toward the passageway. They disappear around the corner a moment later.

Before I have to chance to tell Mai that I would bet that Samuel is somehow behind whatever alerted those officers, we both look up at what sounds like running footsteps on the skywalk. There's enough space between the cement rails for anyone down below to see the lower legs of people walking across the bridge. Because someone is running across it right now, one of their shoes appear between the rails each time their foot lifts.

Red shoes.

The double doors at the side of Science Building burst open, followed by a man and woman charging out into the breezeway.

Last time I saw the exotic one, she was sleeping like a baby in the sauna at Happy Fingers Massage after Samuel and Mai had taken turns pinching off her carotid arteries. Her buddy is the same young man with the bleached-blond Elvis pompadour I kicked in the teeth as he was about to blast me with his Tec Nine. Tiger Woman is still wearing her black pea coat and Toothless Man has added a large white chin bandage to his fashion statement.

Toothless Man looks at us dumbly, but Tiger Woman recognizes us with a flash of unbridled rage. She pushes her buddy toward the door and they charge back into the building.

"Come on," Mai shouts, leading the way.

"Wait," I say running behind her. "Could be an ambush. Remember, they both had guns before."

We position ourselves on each side of the double doors. I quick-peek through the window at what appears to be an empty hallway and then look over to see if the young cop we encountered has seen any of what's going on. Good, he's looking the other way toward an ambulance crew that's moving toward the dead professor.

"Let's go in," I whisper. "Slowly."

There are rooms on both sides of the long hallway, probably classrooms. I'm guessing that it must intersect with another hallway at the other end because we can hear voices and police radios around its corner. A sign above the door to the immediate right reads: Skywalk.

Mai asks, "Maybe into one of the classrooms?"

"Maybe. Be tough to check, though. Plus I don't want us to be seen by the coppers down there." I look at the door to the skywalk. "Fleeing bad guys almost always turn right, and the skywalk door leads out. Let's check it first."

Mai peeks through the door's window, nods to me, then creeps it open. Steps lead up to the first landing, eight of them, with a wall to the left. That means the stairwell continues to the right. We listen for sounds of anyone in the stairwell. Nothing. We move upward, side-by-side, Mai on my right. I gesture for her to stop on the next to last step. I cautiously lean out far enough around the wall to see where the next set of steps begins. I can see the first two steps, both empty.

We move up onto the landing but stop short of moving around the corner. The little hairs on the back of my neck are telling me that I need to see the rest of the steps. I start to lean out, but Mai, who thus far has been going along with my cop moves, slips by to peer around the wall.

"No, no," I whisper, reaching toward her shoulder.

Mai grunts a loud "Uhh!" and her body crashes into me, sending us stumbling over each other into the far wall.

Sound of feet running up the stairs. A door opens. Shuts.

"You okay?" I ask, as we untangle ourselves. There's a dusty foot print on her sweatshirt.

"That was not smart. Sorry. All I saw was a blur. I think it was supposed to be a kick but it turned into a hard push. We must go."

We inch along the back wall of the landing until we can see that all of the stairway is empty. Then we move quickly up to the next landing, hugging the left wall just in case the sounds of the door opening and closing were a ruse to make us think they left. Again we do some slow sidestepping until we can see that the next set of steps are empty.

"That leads out onto the skywalk," Mai says, indicating the door at the top of the next landing. "They are probably across it by now."

We scoot up the stairs and position ourselves on each side of the door.

"There they are," I say, looking out the little window with one eye. "Across the bridge at the door to the parking structure. They're trying to get it open."

"But father had to go through it."

"Don't know. Maybe someone locked it right after him, a security precaution so that no one can go from the garage to this building."

"Look, they are coming back."

"Scoot back from the window. Okay, the instant they open it, we slam the door and rush them." Even a poor plan is better than no plan, some chess player once said. We'll see.

Mai nods, bracing her hands on her knees like a sprinter waiting for the sound of the starter pistol. Her beautiful face steeled, determined. I remain upright, on guard.

Where was Samuel running to? The Toyota? Where would he go? I'd guess he was running from whatever those two police officers were running to and maybe what these two knuckleheads were running from. I haven't heard sirens for the last several minutes. Okay, there's one. An ambulance, I think. Sounds like it's on Broadway but still a ways off. Maybe it's heading to whatever is happening on the other side of the building.

"Look," Mai mouths, pointing toward the far wall where light from the door window has formed a warped rectangle. Within it, two shadows—head shapes—bob up and down several times, then stay up. Soft voices speaking Vietnamese. I don't know what they're saying but Mai straightens a little higher, her hands fisted. I'm coiled, too, ready to launch.

The door opens outward a few inches. Mai rams her shoulder into it at about waist height near the handle as I slap my palms on each side of the window. It's a heavy door, but our combined weight slams it into someone who emits a startled yelp.

Through the window, I see Toothless Man stumble backwards a step or two before he sprawls hard onto his back. I hope the door smashed into his chin. Tiger Woman, I assume, either fell beneath the window or avoided the door with a fast sidestep to one side or the other.

The door slams back into us, hitting my foot and Mai's shoulder, knocking her off balance. As quick as a blink, Tiger Woman snakes around the small opening and lunges into Mai with a double-palm push that sends her back against the wall. She follows with a series of furious claws that Mai avoids with some incredibly fast bobbing and weaving.

I start to grab the wild woman from behind, but movement out of the corner of my eye draws my attention toward the door window. Out on the skywalk, Toothless Man is up and charging toward the now-closed door. I turn the handle... wait... wait, and then push it hard into him again. He's smarter than he looks because he sidesteps to the right, bracing himself against the skywalk railing.

He grabs the edge of the door, probably to whip it back into me, but having had enough door-fu fighting I lunge through the opening and whip-slap his bandaged chin, bringing forth another yelp and a look of disbelief that I would hit him there again. He tries to back away, but I'm quick with a penetrating cross punch into his chest plate that sends him against the cement railing. He makes a quick, worried glance toward the pavement three stories down. He looks back at me, then at his chest as he brushes madly at what I know is a deep, penetrating pain.

Sounds of a struggle behind me. Mai and Tiger Woman are thrashing about in the entry, the automatic door bumping against them over and over.

I sense more than hear Toothless Man. I turn toward him, instinctively lifting both of my forearms to shield my face. Good thing because a fist slams my left arm, sending a stab of pain all the way into my shoulder. He follows with a front kick to my chest, a highly-trained one that I barely manage to avoid with a back shuffle. His next front kick is aimed at my groin; I check it with a raised shin. That hurt, but not the same as catching his shoe in my happy place. Avoiding these trained blows without the protective equipment we wear in class is no picnic.

The ambulance is closer now, its screaming siren deafening as it reverberates off the cavernous buildings.

He kicks again. At least he's not scratching me like a big cat. This one comes in fast but a tad sloppy. I block it with my forearm and simultaneously slam my shin into his groin. He bends over quickly, uttering something in Vietnamese, probably "mama." I grab a two-fisted wad of his big, white pompadour and swing him in a half circle, releasing him to stumble and flail his arms for balance. He doesn't find it and falls hard onto his stomach. Maybe that will take the fight out of him.

The ambulance passes below us and finally cuts that damn ear-bleeding siren. It hangs a right at the end of the Science Building, then disappears.

Toothless Man rolls over onto his back and kips up into a standing fighting stance. What the hell? Why doesn't this bozo stay down? He smiles, all lips and one tooth, like he's showing me why he's going to dispense some *dukkha* on me. Been a lot of that going on lately. Time for Lesson Thirteen, the one I showed that big bully who came into my school a week ago— has it only been a week ago? No pulling the punches this time, though.

I hit him twice in the chest, the same spot I hit earlier, then smack two palms into his chin, a straight punch to his throat, another shin kick to his cookies, an instep kick to femoral artery, one to his knee, an elbow into his snotbox, a bitch slap to the ear, a knee-ram to his inner thigh, followed by another to his already crumbling cookies. I stomp the top of his foot and when he bends forward I meet his chin with my elbow. A hard whip-slap across his mouth finishes the set. That might have been fifteen hits; I lost count. He would have gone down sooner but my last few blows kept him from falling.

He does now. First onto his butt, as if he were resting on the skywalk on a windy day, and then over onto his side, moaning and writhing. He curls into a tight fetal position, probably because he doesn't know which hurt to hold. His remaining tooth drops out onto the cement.

"Look out, Sam!"

Something hits the back of my head, sending me stumbling forward to trip over Toothless Man and land on my all fours on his other side, facing away from what hit me. Over my shoulder, a glaring Tiger Woman bounds over her fallen comrade.

I throw a back kick, but she stops on a dime inches short of getting hit. Behind her, Mai leans against the skywalk wall, holding the side of her head. She looks stunned.

Tiger Woman stands motionless, eyeing me as I get to my feet. Is she allowing me to get up? A trickle of blood curls out of her nose and that large, red abrasion on her forehead looks painful. She favors her left leg.

"Did you shoot those people?" I ask, not expecting an answer.

Her eyes penetrate mine with hatred. Anger I understand, but such intense hatred?

"The old *Caucasian* man got her," she says, spitting out "Caucasian." Okay, she doesn't like white people. Wait. Samuel found the shooter? She said, "her." The one I fought at the massage parlor?

"The old *Caucasian* fuck blinded her. He did not have the decency to take her life, to give her a warrior's death."

Man, this nut job's been watching too many samurai movies.

"But he did not end her life," Tiger Woman spits. "He wanted her to live. And suffer."

"How did he blindside her? How—"

"*Blinded* her," she spits, her body shimmying with rage. "He ripped her eyes from her face."

My God.

"She is my… friend," she says, her lips trembling.

Friend, I bet. That's lover's pain she's got going on there.

She takes a single step toward me. "After I kill you and your whore, I will personally see that he dies with great pain. I will tell Do Trieu—"

"Where is your boss?"

She smiles. "How do you like your school now?"

"You!"

"Who, me?" she says mockingly, touching her chest with her fingers.

The wind has been quiet for a few minutes or maybe I was too busy to notice. Either way, a strong gust forces both of us to brace ourselves. Then Tiger Woman flows smoothly into the same cat stance she and her cohorts assumed just before they attacked us in the massage parlor: feet staggered, the ball of her front foot lightly touching the ground, hands formed into claws. I'm betting Tiger Woman is their teacher.

Behind her, Mai still leans against the wall, her hand cupping her ear.

Incongruously, my mind flashes to something I saw on the *Animal Planet* about great cats. Tigers like to attack their prey by latching onto its neck, allowing them to bring down much larger animals, even water buffalo that weigh six times more than they do. The scratch across the front of my neck suddenly stings, giving authority to that bit of trivia.

Tiger Woman's eyes, narrowed to mere slits, watch me. Another strong gust fans out her hair, but her eyes never waver. I step toward her, stopping just outside of her kicking range. To reach me, she has to cross the space between us, and to do that she must shift her weight off her back leg, which she can't do without telegraphing.

A tiger attacks a weaker prey faster than one it respects. With the latter, it watches and waits until the right moment. Thank you, *Animal Planet*. Well, I'm not going to let her choose that moment.

I scoot forward and launch a deliberately weak, lead-leg roundhouse kick. She ignores it, apparently recognizing that it was an inch or two too short. Smart gal. I set my kick down and throw a cross punch to her body. As I'd hoped, she drops her lead hand to block it, which opens a path to her face. She evades my palm-heel strike with a slight movement of her head and sends a counter claw to my ear. I quick step out of the way so that her fingers rake harmlessly through my hair. She's good and that was close. When I step back again, my hip hits the cement railing hard enough that I teeter over it a little. It's a long way down to the still-empty street. The police have the shooter—*He ripped her eyes from her face*—but they're still keeping traffic out of the area in the event there are more suspects. Uh, yes there are and they're right up here.

Tiger Woman scoots toward me low and fast, her claws leading the way. My sidekick nails her in the gut, drawing from her a short cry of pain as she stumbles backwards until her lower back hits the top cement railing on the other side of the skywalk. She doesn't grimace but she sucks for air as her eyes glare at me, though they no longer have that narrowed, burning intensity she had a moment ago. Now she's looking at me with... lover's eyes?

No, not lover's. *Love* eyes.

Maybe it's because we're on a college campus and because I got an animal theme going on here, but I suddenly remember something from my lit' class, from George Bernard Shaw: "Oh the tiger will love you. There is no sincerer love than the love of food."

I circle her, putting the still-moaning Toothless Man between us. I'd like to move in quickly to take advantage of her oxygen depravation, but I need to do so strategically since this tiger is nobody's fool.

She steps up on Toothless Man's hip and launches herself into the air, feet and claw hands extended like a friggin' cat leaping from a fence. Impressive, but it's a foolish move to go airborne. I sidestep and thrust out a pile-driving sidekick, timed to greet her as she lands. She's a sharp one, though, and quickly twists her body cat-like so that she straddles my horizontally-moving thigh, riding it all the way down until her feet are once again on the cement.

The sudden and almost vertical drop on my extended leg wrenches my hip and jerks my upper body straight up, where she meets me with a five-fingered shred from my forehead to my chin. The burning pain in my face is intense as I half shuffle, half stumble back. Fortunately, her claws missed my eyes.

She could come in for the kill but like a cat playing with a mouse, she doesn't.

I clench my fists on each side of my face and move toward her before she changes her mind. I toss out a jab to see what she does. She swats at it and leans back a little. Perfect. I launch another and she reacts the same way. Now to break the pattern.

I jab a third time and, as she swats it and leans away, I lunge in and sweep her front foot out from under her. I do it with enough force from my hips and legs that it lifts her body almost horizontal and level with my belt. If someone snapped a photo right now, it would look like I'm a magician levitating my beautiful sleeping assistant. Unfortunately, Tiger Woman isn't sleeping. Just as she did before, she twists herself cat-like in midair, grabs the front of my jacket and takes me down with her.

She hits the cement a hair of a second before I do, so that my ribs land on her extended thigh. We both emit a loud "Oomph!"

That hurts, a lot. I manage to wiggle my upper body off her leg and onto the cement, but the stabbing pain in my ribs stops me from sitting up. I'm guessing the hard fall has knocked the wind out of her for a moment because she's not getting up either. At least I've created enough distance so I can sidekick her closest leg a couple of times, the left one she was favoring earlier. She grunts as I land each thrust, though I'm not in the best position to drive them home with maximum authority. I'll switch to my roundhouse.

Still lying on her side, Tiger Woman shields her chest and face with her arms as I slam two round kicks against them using my shinbone with all the power I can muster under these less than desirable conditions. Each time my leg lands, I hear a pronounced *crack!* followed by a cry from her grimacing mouth. I used to give demonstrations of breaking baseball bats with my shin kicks, and the breaking sounds those Louisville Sluggers made are the same I just heard emanating from Tiger Woman's arms.

One of her limbs drops limply to the cement and the other drapes over her chest, unmoving. I'm guessing both are broken. I scoot onto my left side and chamber my right leg again to break her arms in a couple more places, but the pain in my ribs snuffs that idea.

Tiger Woman's face is purple with pain and rage. She rolls onto her stomach, wincing from the agony in her arms, which now lay dead on the cement along her sides. She uses her feet to push herself up onto my thighs, holding her head up as she slithers over my shins like a snake. I try to buck her off but she's pinned me on my side with my left arm under me; my effort to worm out from under her sends stabbing pains into my ribs. I punch her head a couple times with my right, but my blows are weak and only draw blood from her mouth. When she shakes her head, red droplets fly right and left. She commences slithering up me.

My shirt and jacket have pulled away from my waist, exposing a patch of my belly. She alerts on it. I push against her face for a second but I have to jerk my hand away when she tries to bite it like a toothy serpent from Hell. From tiger to serpent, this one.

She cobra-strikes her face into to my belly, chomping hungrily into my flesh. I scream and lash out at her head but hit only her shoulder. Her head lifts and she smiles at me, blood running from the corners of her mouth. Her blood, my blood. The shearing pain in my abdomen makes me forget my ribs long enough to sit part way up and punch at her again. My feeble blow clips her cheek, not fazing her, and I drop back down onto my back, the pain in my ribs so intense that I have to fight to keep it from curling me into a ball. At least my left arm is free.

She's slithering up my body again, propelling herself by wiggling from side-to-side, her dead arms dragging on each side of me. When I grab her face with both my hands and dig my thumbs into her eyes, she quickly drops her face onto my chest. I slap at one of her ears, knocking her upper body off me, but she slithers right back on. Before I can slap her again, she makes one last push with her legs so that her face is just above my chin, her hot, panting breath—the smell of rotten garlic. Her hyperdilated pupils shine like luminous black onyx, her bloody mouth smiling with promise as she lowers her head as if to nuzzle my throat.

I reflexively pull my chin in and start to smash her skull with my fists when her head unexpectedly snaps up, her eyes wide with surprise and disappointment.

Suddenly she's off me.

Now she's standing. What the hell?

The pain in my ribs and stomach slows my understanding for a moment. Then I realize that Mai is holding up Tiger

Woman by her hair and saying something to her in Vietnamese. Mai speaks calmly, chatty-like, as if the two of them were shopping and talking about the cuteness of a blouse. Then Mai punches her in the face. Tiger Woman can't fall because Mai is still holding her up by her hair, and she can't defend herself because her arms are hanging dead. She does manage to kick Mai in the thigh, though the two of them are too close for the kick to do any damage. Mai's only reaction is to yank the woman's hair downward, then stop the descending face with a fast-lifting knee.

Tiger Woman opens her mouth to releases a gush of blood and teeth. Now her mouth matches Toothless Man's, who remains curled into a tight fetal position a few feet away. Mai's face is cold and tight, just as it was when she was ready to remove Do Trieu's eyeballs and just as it was when she destroyed the tiger fighter's elbow in the massage parlor. The fierceness in her eyes and the deadly determination of her mouth are far more chilling than if she were to snarl or grimace. She releases the woman's hair and punches her chest hard enough to drive Tiger Woman back against the railing.

Incredibly, the woman finds the strength to launch another kick, one that Mai catches easily in the crook of her arm.

I struggle to my feet, the pain in my ribs and the bite's burning sting intense. I wad the bottom of my shirt and jacket, pressing them against my bleeding stomach. For an instant, I think of helping Mai, but I stand fast.

This woman, or at least her partner, just tried to shoot Mai, killing two innocents instead and causing major panic. Half way around the world, Tiger Woman's boss is trying to kill her family. So I think the least I can do is let Mai give the woman some dukkha payback.

Tiger Woman doesn't try to free her caught leg but instead just watches her captor. *Animal Planet* would say that the injured tiger waits for the right moment, knowing it's her last. If her arms weren't hanging uselessly at her sides, her injured support leg hadn't been weakened, and her head hadn't been struck so many times, I have no doubt she could jump up with her free leg and kick Mai.

Tiger Woman says something in Vietnamese and then spits a glob of blood at Mai. Some of that might be mine, blood that's being treated for the HIV virus. A wind gust catches it, though, and carries it back into the woman's own face. She shakes the blood from her eyes and repeats the same words.

"No," Mai whispers, then shouts something in her native language before she rams the caught leg so high that Tiger Woman drapes partially over the top railing.

Again the woman spits and again the wind blows it off course. Mai flinches reflexively, a brief distraction that weakens her grip on the leg. Unable to use her arms for support or spring off her other leg, Tiger Woman leans farther back over the wall for leverage. Then, in an implausible show of raw power, she lifts her leg straight up out of the crook of Mai's arm until its nearly vertical, the bottom of her black boot pointing skyward.

"Axe kick!" I shout.

Mai shields her head and lunges forward to stop the descending leg at the calf.

Though her leg is jammed at about a forty-five-degree angle, Tiger Woman again uses her awesome strength and flexibility to lift it quickly off Mai's forearms until it's almost vertical. Then, probably realizing that this is her last chance to give her all to the technique, she rocks her upper body back a little to gather force, but the weight of her leg and her inability to support herself with her arms, tips her upper body back too far.

She rolls over the top of the wall and drops from sight…

… screams.

A strong wind gust muffles the thump.

*

My right arm is draped around Mai's trembling shoulders as I guide my truck one-handed through the streets to her apartment. Man, does my stomach ever hurt. Mai says that the bite didn't go that deeply, in spite of how the front of my jeans is saturated with blood. At least the bleeding seems to have stopped. My ribs aren't broken, Mai says, but they're killing me, anyway. I'm sure in a lot of pain for a guy whose bite isn't that bad and whose ribs aren't broken.

Mai is crying into my chest and compressing her bleeding right ear with the bottom of her blue sweatshirt. She said she took a hard punch to the back of her head that stunned her for several minutes and had her seeing double. She apologized for not helping me with my scuffle with Toothless Man and helping me sooner with Tiger Woman.

Twice she's called her father but there's been no answer. Her cell works fine, although the outer case was broken in her fight. Samuel just isn't answering.

"He's probably shut it off," I say, not really believing it myself. "He might even be at the apartment waiting for us. He'll ask us if we stopped for lunch or went to the zoo to sight-see. You know how he is."

That didn't get the chuckle I hoped for but she does stop crying. I hang a right onto her street. The Toyota isn't where it's usually parked. Mai notices and grips my arm.

I look at my dash clock: two thirty. "Your flight's at five, right?" I say, to distract her.

She nods against my chest.

"You got just enough time to pack whatever you need for the trip, then we got to get you out to the airport."

"Not without father."

"He'll make it," I say, hoping I'm right. "I can pack up the rest of your stuff and send it to you."

"Thank you," she whispers.

"What about your car?"

"I used a girlfriend's. She will come get it, so that is not a problem."

"And your kitty?"

"Another friend at school, a professor, talked about taking Chiến, but it was never confirmed and now there is not time to contact her."

I pull to the curb and shut off the engine. "Well, I've been thinking about getting one."

"Would you take her? Please?"

"Yes," I say, touching one of the tiger-style scratches on my face. "Is she declawed?"

That didn't get a laugh either. Instead, Mai looks up at me, her eyes full of pain. "That woman…"

"She fell, Mai. *Fell.* It was her own doing. Actually, I broke her arms. If I hadn't done that,, she could have stopped herself from going over. Bottom line is that she fell trying to hurt you. Maybe even kill you."

"After I jammed her kick, I thought about pushing her over the railing. I actually thought about it for maybe two seconds."

"But you didn't. Her actions did it. *Her* actions ended her life. Not yours."

She doesn't say anything for a long moment. Then, almost to herself, "She wasn't moving…"

We peered over the railing after Tiger Woman had fallen; she was as motionless as only the dead can be, lying about twenty feet from the empty police car. She must have landed on her head, judging by the blood that was quickly haloing it. Fortunately, the street was empty. I don't think, I'm hoping, no one saw it happen.

We limped and hobbled down the stairs and exited out the same side door we had entered earlier. Luckily, the uniform officer was no longer at his post. We walked as nonchalantly as possible out to Broadway and headed north for a block. One more down is where the police were still blocking the intersection. Once they found out there was a dead woman lying in the street just up from them, all hell would break loose on Broadway.

We crossed the lanes quickly, headed east to Sixth Avenue and then south for another block and a half. We entered the parking structure on that side and rode the elevator up to the third floor where Samuel and I had parked. In the truck, Mai examined my injuries and I checked hers. Then we just held each other. Afterward, I backed out of the slot and spiraled down to the first floor, noting that the Toyota was gone.

"What did she say to you before she tried to kick you that last time?" I ask.

She shivers then inhales deeply. "She said that they failed today but Lai Van Tan will still get his revenge on my family."

"Damn."

"He will not give up, Sam. It is called *Ba'o th'u,* revenge. For some, it is like a religion, a passion; *Ba'o th'u* must be carried out."

"I feel better knowing your father is on it."

"Oh yes. If my family did not have him, we would all die. I have no doubt about that. But it will still be a struggle for him and for me because I will be at his side."

"Man, I wish I was going over there with you. But there is no way I could leave this soon. I have a passport but not a travel visa. And I got court coming up. Skip that and they'll issue a warrant for me." I look out the side window. "I feel so helpless."

"I feel better knowing I can talk to you on the phone and by email. I am just glad... I am just happy that I... have you."

I pull her into me more tightly and rest my chin on the top of her head. "Me, too," I say. "You have no idea." We remain like this for a moment. Then, "I'm glad we didn't pass anyone when we took the long way to the truck," I say, looking down at the front of my bloody pants. "Now we got to get through your lobby."

"Yes. Sometimes people sit in there for something to do."

"There's a newspaper box next to the front door. How about you get one so I can hold it in front of me?"

"You will have to hold your head down, too," Mai says, studying my face.

I look at my face in the rearview mirror, at the five vertical scratches. The center one that crosses over my nose is the deepest. None of them have bled to any extent but the outer layer of skin has been ripped away, exposing the blood-red layer underneath. They burn every time I make any kind of facial expression.

"I got a baseball hat in the back and a change of clothes in a workout bag," I say, reaching over the back seat to retrieve both. I dig out some change from my console cup holder. "You should put up your hood."

Her ear has been clawed quite nastily. Fortunately, the blood has seeped down inside her sweatshirt and has yet to soak through.

She puts up the hood and walks over to get a paper. She extracts one from the yellow box and heads back toward the truck, paper in one hand, her cell in the other. Considering she's been kicked, punched, thrown into a wall, and who knows what else when she and Tiger Woman were fighting, she's walking like it's just another day.

She's almost to the truck when she looks down at her cell. She pokes a button, says something into it, then looks toward me and smiles. "He's okay," she mouths, her relief obvious. I put on the baseball cap and step out of the truck as Mai walks up to me. "He's on the way."

"Where's he been?"

"He wouldn't say, and I asked him twice. I started to tell him about what happened to us and he interrupted to ask if we were okay. When I said yes, he said he would get the details when he got here. He sounded very strange, very subdued. He said we need to pack and get to the airport."

*

"You are lucky today," Mai says, pressing the bandage firmly against my stomach. "The bite is above your belt line so your belt won't rub it. It is not deep but it bled much."

I'm lying on the sofa with my sweatshirt pulled up to my chest; Mai is on her knees next to me tending to my wound. I've popped four Excedrin but I still feel my pulse throbbing within the bite.

"Can you really say that I'm lucky *and* I got bit on my stomach by an insane person in the same sentence?" She smiles a little. Finally.

I'm feeling so many emotions right now, and judging by how subdued Mai is, I know she too is finding it difficult to think clearly. We're both doing a so-so job of pretending but it's tough to ignore the fact that she's going away in less than three hours and it's tough to not talk about how the fight with Tiger Woman ended. I think she understands intellectually that the death wasn't her fault, but she has yet to accept that in her heart. Of course it's only been an hour.

When we first came into her apartment, I went into the bathroom and washed the blood from my abdomen and rinsed my face as well as I could around the five tiger stripes. Fortunately, my workout bag contained clean sweatpants, a sweatshirt, and skivvies.

By the time I came out, Mai had cleaned and bandaged her ear, changed her top to a black polo shirt and put on clean jeans. She said that about half an inch of her ear had been torn away from her head, a result of not blocking Tiger Woman's first claw attack. If she hadn't blocked the second one, she said, her ear would likely have been torn completely off. The bandage would suffice until she got back to Vietnam and could have the wound checked by a doctor. Her long hair covers it well. I commented that she has yet to complain about the pain, though I've whined about my stomach and bruised ribs at least three times. "That just makes you a typical man," she said, surprising me that she's capable of humor right now.

When the tape is on to her satisfaction she pulls my sweatshirt down over the bandage and looks into my face, her eyes filled with pain. Before I can say anything she turns away, knee-walks a couple of steps to the coffee table and begins repackaging her medical supplies.

"Mai?" I start to sit up, but piercing pains in my abdomen and ribs forces me back down onto the sofa. When she doesn't answer or turn around, I put my hand on the floor and half scoot, half roll off the edge of the cushions down onto my knees. I hobble over next to her and gently pull her shoulder. She resists for a moment, but then turns, her eyes downcast. I lift her chin and look into her face.

"Will you really come to Vietnam to see me?" she asks softly, her eyes teary.

I pull her into me so hard that we both nearly topple over with a mutual grunt, a painful reminder of our respective injuries.

"Oh! I'm sorry," I say, cupping the sides of her head. "Are you—"

"My ear!" she cries, twisting away from my hand, her hip striking my lower abdomen where I had been bitten.

"Ow!" I knee-shuffle back a step.

"Sam! Are you okay?"

"No," I say, grimacing a little more than necessary. "That moment just before you hip-rammed my bite wound? That's when I was okay. Now, not so much."

"Oh my gosh, I am sor…" She sees the smirk on my face and folds her arms in a pretend pout. "And my ripped-off ear was just fine before you… what do you call it? Oh yes, before you bitch slapped it."

We sputter into laughter, lacing our fingers together and cautiously moving toward one another. This time our embrace is gentle.

I nuzzle into her good ear. "*Yes,* I will come to see you." When she tightens her embrace, I add, "The only thing that I know for sure right now is how I feel about you."

She nods. "I feel the same. And we haven't even been out on a date yet."

I chuckle. "A dinner and a movie would be a little anti-climactic, don't you think?"

She shakes her head and whispers into my ear, "I think it would be wonderful."

We remain like this for a long moment, on our knees, pressed together, floating. We kiss, sealing an unspoken promise to each other.

Then our father walks in.

*

"Father!" Mai says excitedly, as the two of us struggle to our feet. I'm sure my face is as red as it feels. She rushes over to greet him but stops short. "Father?"

Samuel looks dazed. Fresh blood dots the front of his pale-blue shirt, his bare forearms and the backs of his hands. My guess is that none of it is his.

"Are you hurt?" Mai asks, tentatively touching his shoulder.

"I am fine." He looks at me. "Mai said you found Do Trieu's people."

"The woman who had the Glock at the massage parlor and the young man I hurt at the restaurant. We never saw the driver of the white Mazda, the one who fled." Samuel's face is blank, like stone. When he doesn't say anything, I continue. "The woman fell from the skywalk. She's dead. And the young man won't fight again for a long while."

He turns to Mai. "Are you packed?"

"It will only take ten minutes," she says, her face confused. She strokes his upper arm. "We can just pack what we need for the trip. Sam will send our other things… Father are you—"

"Could you return the Toyota to the car rental people?" he asks me. "The paperwork is on the kitchen table."

"Of course," I say. "Samuel, you seem to be... Are you okay?"

"Do Trieu will no longer be a problem for you," he says in monotone, his eyes those of a dead fish.

"I don't under..."

"*Ever.*"

My God! My heart rate leaps into the red zone.

"Father, was it you who found the person who shot the student and the professor?" Mai is holding herself stiffly, as if moving would cause her to break.

"Yes," he says. "But I could not... terminate her. That was my intention when looking for the sniper, but when I found her... a woman..." he shakes his head, "I could not. She was just a soldier with a rifle carrying out orders. Immoral orders, but ones she thought were right because she had been convinced they were, maybe brainwashed that they were."

His face flushes red and his eyes seem to focus on something... on someplace that Mai and I aren't privy to. "I... many years ago... I was young, naïve, and filled with passion for my leader, for the mission. In the Green Berets, it was always about the mission. I carried out an immoral order... then I carried out two more after that." He looks away for a moment and then back to me. "If only someone had stopped me..."

"You *blinded* the woman?" I ask, maybe with more accusation than I intended. I haven't had time to process any of this, but a thought passes through my mind that blinding the enemy is... what? Malicious? Killing them, though, seems more... I don't know. I'm not sure what anything seems right now.

"She shot at me in the stairwell," Samuel says, probably reading my thoughts. "Missed. Now she will never shoot anyone again, never carry out such an order."

I don't know what to say to this but I do know for sure that I'm about to have a panic attack. By killing Do Trieu, he's implicated Mai and me. The Fat Dicks and the rest of the crew are going to put all the pieces together, and I'll be going to prison—forever. I have knowledge of the suspect who shot two people dead at the graduation. I have knowledge of the person who tried, convicted, and punished her on the spot. I beat a guy senseless on the skywalk and I fled the scene after Tiger Woman was killed.

"Sam, you will just have to trust me that there were no witnesses, not on those stairs and no one saw me with Do Trieu. I know you have CSI, but it will not be an issue."

I'm barely holding it together. I take a calming breath. "I'm sure you think you're right. But you're not law enforcement and you don't know about evidence and how an investigation unfolds, how things fall into place."

"You're getting angry, Sam, and maybe I would, too. But I did it for my family, for you here. And now I have to go and make sure the rest of my family is safe. I guarantee that my problems in Vietnam will escalate as soon as Lai Van Tan learns of what happened today. If I do not end the situation there, and do so quickly, you will be in danger again here. I do not know much about American law enforcement, but I do believe I am right in thinking that it moves slowly. Mai, you, me, and my family in Vietnam cannot afford for us to have to wait here."

Samuel walks over to me and looks hard into my eyes. "I am sorry I am leaving you with this mess, but it was the lesser of two evils." He turns to Mai. "Please pack, and do it quickly;

it's almost three o'clock." Then to me: "Sam, I'm leaving you to do clean-up here. As I told you a few days ago, some of these criminals live by the Thousand-Year Code of Revenge. If they do not obtain it in their lifetime, then their children will have to get it for them. If they cannot get to me, they will get to my family. This must be stopped. And that is what I am going to do."

I nod that I understand and, heaven help me, I agree. Not an easy task for a guy who has followed the law his entire life, and who has been in the business of enforcing it for fifteen years.

"You can take us to the airport?" Samuel asks.

"Of course," I say, my heart rate still hammering at about two hundred beats per minute, which is where it's likely to stay for a long while.

*

This is the last time all of us will ride together in my truck, Mai in the middle, Samuel riding shotgun. My Dodge has taken· us to and from several life changing, emotion-heavy experiences this week, and this time is no different. The airport is about twenty minutes from Mai's apartment but to my chagrin the trip feels more like two. I don't want them to go. I want to be with Mai, to explore a normal relationship. I want to learn more about my father, and I want him to know about me when my life isn't so upside down.

"Me too," Samuel says.

"Okay," I say, "five days ago that would have startled the hell out of me, but I've almost gotten used to it. Almost. Yes, I want those things, but now, after today, I don't know what's going to happen."

"There has been much *dukkha* this week," he says. "The events caused us suffering and our wishing things were different caused us suffering. Buddha said: 'Chaos is inherent in all compounded things. Strive on with diligence.' That is what we all must do now."

Samuel's quotations are actually becoming less annoying to me. But to quote Buddha right after you have brutalized one person and killed another has a loud ring of hypocrisy to it.

"Wasn't Buddha a man of peace?" I ask. "As was Christ? Yet today at the college and wherever you met Do Trieu and whatever you did to him…" I stop, wishing I had kept my mouth shut. This is neither the time nor the place.

"I understand your question, son, and it is a good one. What you really want to know is how I can quote these great words of peace, yet seemingly not follow them myself. Well, consider this. Ecclesiastes Three says: 'A time to love and a time to hate; a time for war and a time for peace.' The Byrds sang those words in a song back in the sixties.

"Psalm one: forty-four says: 'Blessed be the Lord my strength which teacheth my hands to war, and my fingers to fight.' In Buddhism as well as in Christianity, fighting in self-defense is about intent. My intent, the intent of all of us in this truck, is to protect ourselves and our family. None of us fought for evil purposes today; we fought against it."

I nod but don't say anything. Samuel's words are short, sweet, meaty, and simplistic. Maybe too simplistic. Too much for my tired and bruised brain to absorb right now. I turn onto Airport Way.

"One other thing," Samuel says. "Remember how I lost contact with Kim just before the shooting? She finally got through to me when I was heading out to find Do Trieu. She said that Lu learned that Do Trieu's people were going to make a hit on Mai today. To shoot her in front of a crowd on a day of celebration so as to maximize the emotional impact on me and my family. I was not to be harmed. I was to be kept alive so that I could suffer. Son, they were to take you out if they had the opportunity. That might have been the shot that hit the professor. We may never know."

"Those bastards," Mai says under her breath.

I don't say anything because I'm having trouble swallowing.

"That is why I did what I did. I terminated Do Trieu to preserve peace. At least for you here."

We ride in silence the last mile, each of us thinking our thoughts. Samuel has made his case but it's just too overwhelming to know what to say. I have to think about all this and try to make sense of it. I still haven't come to terms with Jimmy.

I turn into a short-term parking garage and take a ticket from the machine. "I'll walk in with you. Walk you up to security."

Mai's been holding my hand, squeezing it as if she'll never let it go. We have so much to say to each other but there's no time. There's never been enough time. Yet somehow we have come together as if words are unnecessary.

I find a parking slot and pull in. "Well, the police didn't pull us over at gunpoint," I say, only half joking. "So far so good. It's three fifteen. You're supposed to be here two or three hours early for an international flight, so let's hope there's no problems for you."

Samuel gets out and moves to the pickup bed to get their luggage as Mai and I kiss the kiss of lovers parting.

"Hurry," Samuel calls, rapping on my window.

We ignore him and kiss a moment longer. "Don't go," I whisper against her lips.

She presses her cheek against mine and hugs me even tighter. "I'll talk to you in a few hours." When I nod, she kisses my cheek and scoots across the seat. I climb out my side and smile at Samuel; this time I'm not embarrassed. He keeps a somber face and picks up his suitcase. Before he turns away to head for the glass doors, I detect a faint smile.

I check my reflection in the truck window to see if the brim of my baseball hat covers my scratches. I need to be careful in case a witness somewhere saw a man with several scratch marks on his face leave the Science Building this afternoon. If that description got into the paper and someone saw me out here, they might put two and two together. Or a security person might ID me on an airport video camera. I tilt the brim a little lower.

"That looks good like that," Mai says. I smile at her, we link arms and follow Samuel into the terminal.

There are only about twenty ahead of us at China Airlines. To our right, a couple hundred shorts- and T-shirt-wearing happy people jam the Hawaiian Airlines' zigzagging cattle lanes. What I wouldn't give for Mai and me to be in that line.

As we work our way up to the ticket agent, Samuel says that with two layovers, it's about a twenty-three hour flight to Ho Chi Minh City. The good news, he says, is that they show lots of movies. Same old Samuel. We all exchange emails, and Mai and I discuss getting cams so we can see each other when we talk.

Just as we're leaving the check-in counter, I spot a chin-bandaged man limping our way. I whisper a warning to Mai and Samuel, who quickly drop their carry-ons and turn to face him. A moment later, it's obvious that he's not Toothless Man nor is he even Asian. Mai wishes a middle-aged couple in the Hawaii line, who are frowning at our strange antics, a lovely trip and we scurry away.

Since we've got a few extra minutes, we stop at a Coffee People. "This is for the one you brought me in the park that first day," I say to Samuel. His eyes smile a little at me, then darken before they look back at his green tea. Maybe even the master is having trouble compartmentalizing this day.

The two of them didn't want to sit, since they were going to be doing a lot of that for the next full day, so we're standing around one of those stand-up tables on the concourse. We're half way through our muffins when I notice a young airport cop looking our way from where he's leaning against the wall next to the men's room. I drop my head even more and nonchalantly move next to Mai.

"We're being watched by a police officer," I mumble.

"Yes," Samuel says, sipping his tea. "I have been watching him. And now he is headed this way."

"What are we going to do?" Mai asks into her cup.

"Stay calm," I tell her, looking down. "It might not mean anything."

"Twenty feet away," Samuel says, picking at his muffin. "Fifteen."

A moment later, I see him out of the corner of my eye as he swaggers by, his thumbs hooked into his pistol belt.

"He smiled at me," Mai whispers, exhaling. "I looked up just as he passed and he gave me a big, flirty smile."

"Can't blame him for that," I say, watching the officer nod to every attractive woman he passes as he saunters up the concourse.

I stand in line with them at the security checkpoint as long as I can, but too soon, we come to the place where I can no longer go with them. We all exchange quick hugs and I send them off through the zigzagging lines toward the X-ray machines. Mai and I keep in constant teary eye contact as they shuffle along in the line of people. As she rounds the last turn, a heavyset woman in front of them stops to adjust her carry-on and Mai bumps into her, knocking the woman's glasses askew. I laugh out loud as Mai apologizes profusely and struggles not to smile.

At the X-ray machine, they strip off their shoes, belts, and jackets and, with a final wave and a smile from each of them, step through the metal detectors and are gone.

EPILOGUE

Although the park crew is noisily grinding limbs that broke off trees during the windstorm four days ago, it's still a wonderfully pleasant day here. I saw a couple of clouds earlier when I left my house but all I see now is blue through the tall trees that populate this beautiful park, this best-kept secret in Portland.

I managed to get a coffee across the street without anyone slugging my forehead and without an eccentric, red-shoes-wearing sixty-some-year-old man half carrying me to this park bench. Just a little more than a week ago, Samuel was sitting here busting my chops about me getting busted in the chops. Eleven days ago to be exact! How time flies when your father returns from the dead, folks are punching and kicking you, burning down part of your life, shooting at your family, changing most of what you thought you knew about the martial arts, and turning your dead heart into a swooning, cooing love bird.

Mai called me a few minutes after they landed in Saigon, which was three AM my time, and we talked until five AM. We've talked a bunch more times in the four days since they left and swapped a hundred emails, give or take. Our long-distance relationship is working out great. We're able to chat like people do when they're first learning about each other without being shot, punched, clawed, or kicked.

Mai emailed a list of what she wanted out of her apartment, a surprisingly short one considering she's female and females love their stuff. She wants only a few of her clothes, about ten specific school books, and a few knick knacks she bought as keepsakes from Portland.

She really misses Chién and I told her that her cat really misses her, too, which is not quite true. The truth is that the kitty really likes my house. So much so that I bought a cat box and now he never wants to go out.

Samuel moved his family to another location in Vietnam for two days and then moved them to another one where they are now. He thought it best not to tell me where they are in the event Lai Van Tan's crew can somehow intercept emails and phone calls. He said that he plans to move again in a few days to a place where he hopes they will be able to stay for a while. He said they will be hiding in plain sight. When I asked what that means, he said he couldn't tell me but would show me when I came over. Ever the mysterious man.

If you can accurately judge another person by the tone of their emails, Samuel seems more relaxed since he got back and is able to take care of his people. He even ended one email exchange, asking, "Did I ever show you my teacup trick?"

Mark and I had coffee a couple days ago and he filled me in on the case, all the while I pretended to only know what I'd read in the newspaper. No where in our conversation did Samuel's, Mai's, or my name come up, so I'm assuming the investigating team hasn't connected any of us to the events of four days ago. Mark told me about four Vietnamese people involved in several incidents that occurred around the same time as the double shooting. The only name I recognized was Do Trieu, the others I guessed were the real names belonging to Tiger Woman, Toothless Man, and the female sniper with the rifle.

The dicks are working hard to find whatever it is that links them all together. Should my name get implicated in covering up the serious assault on the sniper, not reporting Tiger Woman's death, and hiding my knowledge of Do Trieu's demise, well, I'll be spending the rest of my days in the joint being some biker dude's sex toy.

Mark said the wind had jostled four rooftop surveillance cameras and broke a fifth, which means there's no footage of any of us near the stage or on the skywalk. They did get a few frames of someone's legs running on the walk about fifteen minutes after the professor had been shot. I wanted to ask if the runner was wearing red shoes, but of course I didn't. Mark said they don't know if the legs belonged to the shooter or just someone frightened and running into the parking garage seeking safety. Apparently, a few seconds later a wind gust spun the camera toward a brick wall where it remained, so it didn't capture our subsequent fight.

Of course with everyone and their brother having cameras these days, I'm sure there is a lot of footage of the stage area before and after the shooting. There is probably video in cameras and cell phones of the professor getting shot with Samuel, Mai, and me standing next to him. The only thing I can do at this point is to hope that no one recognizes me. I'm sure there will be clips all over Youtube, but unless they are really high def and shot with a quality zoom, the cops and anyone else who knows me won't make the connection. I hope.

Nietzsche said something like 'hope is the worst of all evils because it prolongs man's torments.' Got that right.

Mark said there were no cameras in the stairwell where someone confronted the shooter. "It's like an animal had torn her eyes out," he said. He also said that judging by the phone calls coming into the office, whoever did it is being held up as sort of a hero.

I asked if the shooter had said anything. He said that she had refused to talk about it other than to say she hated Caucasians. Same thing Tiger Woman implied a few minutes before she took a header off the skywalk. Mark said the shooter, whose name is Nguyen Phuong Nga, declined to say if she knew two other Vietnamese who were found in the same area: Ai Nhu, who was found dead under the skywalk and Nguyen Van Ly, a young man found beaten on top of the skywalk. She also didn't say anything when they asked her if she knew Do Trieu, although she did react when The Fat Dicks told her that both Ai Nhu and Do Trieu were dead. They're pursuing that reaction.

He said that Ai Nhu appears to have been beaten before she went over the rail of the skywalk. The male, Nguyen Van Ly, who was found semi-conscious on the skywalk, isn't talking either. "It could be a lovers' quarrel gone real bad," Mark said. "But I don't think so. It's too much of a coincidence that the shooter was maimed and not saying anything, that the young man was beaten nearly to death and not saying anything, that the young woman went over the side of the skywalk, and that the elderly restaurant owner was beaten to death. All Vietnamese. I don't believe in coincidences. We'll find out eventually."

Samuel told me via a phone call that the police won't connect them because the sniper and the young man on the skywalk will never talk for fear of Lai Van Tan's people ordering a hit on them as well as on their families. He said that would keep the three of us out of the picture. I have a gut feeling that Samuel might have told the shooter that he would kill her family, too. That's just a wild assumption on my part, but given the nature of everyone involved, I'd bet twenty bucks on it.

Tiger Woman and Toothless Man must have found her right after Samuel had fled and just before Mai and I saw them charge out the side door. They probably left her there when they heard the police coming.

Do Trieu was found in his Beamer behind his restaurant. Mark said that the man had been beaten to death and, judging by the number of blunt trauma wounds, they think that there were several assailants, maybe four or five. He said one medical examiner believes he was beaten with some sort of object, though he hasn't a clue what it could be since the markings don't fit the usual pattern of a baseball bat, tire iron, and so on. A second medical examiner said that some of the marks on Do Trieu's body are consistent with those made by a human hand, though he doesn't think that's possible given the extreme internal damage inflicted.

Mark says that both MEs are stymied over how Do Trieu's heart was so severely damaged since there is no indication that he was struck there by the assailants. Apparently, there was no external damage: No bruising over the heart, no abrasions, no marks of any kind.

"The ignition and explosion and the hits are willed." Samuel said about The Fourth Level.

Samuel would say it's about protecting what you hold near and dear. Others might say it's cold revenge; *báo thù,* Mai called it. Maybe sometimes they're the same thing.

Even if Mark had noticed Samuel's hands that day at Mitchell's condo—the enlarged, thick knuckles and the rough calluses on the edges of them—I really doubt he would ever link them with "some sort of object." Besides, I never mentioned anything about Samuel's prowess.

When Mark saw the scrapes on my face, he asked if one of my students had gotten the best of me, I told him yes and feigned embarrassment.

I asked about witnesses. Mark said there were none. If it had been a weekday, there would have likely been people in the buildings and someone would have been looking out the window. But it was a Saturday. No one was around except for the panicky crowd on the other side of the building in the Park Blocks.

As we sat there having coffee, I was straining to remember if I had said anything to Mark about Mai's graduation. I don't think I did and he hasn't asked me anything about it. There is the issue of her name being called just before the shooter took out the wrong person, but I'm thinking that that will never be linked back to me. I doubt if Mark even remembers her name. Did I even tell him? I don't remember that either. If he asks, I'll tell him it's Le, same as Samuel's.

So right now I'm feeling fairly safe, safe for me and safe for my new family. I have to wait for the grand juries to convene to consider the accidental shooting of Jimmy and the intentional shooting of the creep who took him hostage. Now that I think about it, I've never heard his name. I've never read a police report about it, watched any of the accounts on TV, or read a single newspaper article. Well, I did read the headline when I found a newspaper on my porch that morning.

Since the media's been all over the shootings at Portland State University, mine hasn't appeared anywhere that I know of in the last four days. It will when the Grand Jury returns with their finding, but it will likely fade out of the public's mind quickly. I hope, anyway.

I still haven't decided what I'm going to do about my job, though I'm leaning hard toward resigning. I've given the PD fifteen years but it has taken twice that much out of me, and I got nothing left to give. Besides, there is no way in hell I could ever shoot another person, and once I reveal that to Doc Kari,

480

I'll be declared unfit to go back to work. She'd be right to do exactly that.

I have to think about opening another martial arts school. I'll have the money from my insurance company in a few weeks, a handsome sum, too. I would open a new one for sure if I knew I was going to stay in this country, but going to Vietnam has pretty much dominated my thoughts these last few days. Of course, I could go there first and then open a school when I came back. What if I didn't want to come back? What if... I don't know anything other than right now I'm just going continue to teach my students in the basement of a church that one of my brown belts, a Baptist minister, is kindly allowing us to use.

I haven't experienced nausea for a while, though I'm still taking the PEP cocktail. I'm so glad that didn't hit me in the middle of the Battle of Skywalk. Tiger Woman was formidable enough without me having to pause to upchuck, although as a technique that came in handy against the Christian biker dude in the back of that porno shop.

My gut tells me I didn't contract HIV but I know that's just a feeling and feelings sometimes lie. So I'll just keep on popping the pills until Dr. Hegrenes says I can stop.

Lots to think about and lots to worry about.

Finished with their clean-up, the park crew rigs are heading out of the park. Now I can enjoy the sounds of the birds, the hum of distant traffic, and the warm spring sun that's beaming down on my still-sore body.

I think I'll do a few minutes of that meditation Samuel taught me and then stretch out on this park bench, close my eyes, and maybe take a little nap.

It's been quite a week.

ACKNOWLEDGEMENTS

Many thanks to my family, friends and helpers who made this book possible: David Ripianzi for taking a chance, Leslie Takao for her sharp editing and insight into the characters, Lawrence Kane and Marcus Wynne who read the first draft and made right-on suggestions, Dr. Matt Hing for sharing his knowledge of HIV and post-exposure prophylaxis, Carrie Christensen-LCSW-R, Dr Mike Asken and Dr. Timothy Storlie for their help with the psychologist scenes, A'lyse Place for her help with Tammy's voice, and to Dr. Dan Christensen, Amy and Jace Widmer for their encouragement.

And as always to Lisa Place, my love and best friend for her encouragement and willingness to hear me read my day's writing even when she was exhausted from her job.

About the Author

Loren W. Christensen is a Vietnam veteran and retired police officer with 29 years of law enforcement experience. As a martial arts student and teacher since 1965, he has earned a total of 11 black belts in three arts and was inducted into the Masters Hall of Fame in 2011. As a writer, Loren has penned 45 nonfiction books, including over two dozen books on the martial arts, and dozens of magazine articles on a variety of subjects. He has starred in seven instructional martial arts DVDs. Dukkha is his first fiction. He can be contacted through his website at www.lwcbooks.com.